W9-CCD-002

Girls From da Hood 9

Cabarrus County Public Library
www.cabarruscounty.us/library

Girls From da Hood 9

Amaleka McCall, Chunichi,

Meisha Camm and Ni'chelle Genovese

URBAN BOOKS

www.urbanbooks.net

Urban Books, LLC
97 N18th Street
Wyandanch, NY 11798

Friend or Foe Copyright © 2013 Amaleka McCall
Torch Copyright © 2013 Chunichi and Meisha Camm
Church Girl Copyright © 2013 Ni'chelle Genovese

All rights reserved. No part of this book may be reproduced
in any form or by any means without prior consent of the
Publisher, except brief quotes used in reviews.

ISBN 13: 978-1-60162-572-4
ISBN 10: 1-60162-572-3

First Printing December 2013
Printed in the United States of America

10 9 8 7 6 5 4 3 2 1

*This is a work of fiction. Any references or similarities to
actual events, real people, living or dead, or to real locales
are intended to give the novel a sense of reality. Any
similarity in other names, characters, places, and incidents
is entirely coincidental.*

Distributed by Kensington Publishing Corp.
Submit Wholesale Orders to:
Kensington Publishing Corp.
C/O Penguin Group (USA) Inc.
Attention: Order Processing
405 Murray Hill Parkway
East Rutherford, NJ 07073-2316
Phone: 1-800-526-0275
Fax: 1-800-227-9604

Friend or Foe

Amaleka McCall

Chapter 1

Kelsi Jones

August 2010

Whir, whir, whir . . . The incessant drone of two tall metal fans situated at the back corners of the stuffy, hot courtroom felt like small flies buzzing in my ears. The annoying kind of flies that buzz around shit and then come land on your skin. The ones you keep swatting away but can never seem to get rid of. The hottest day of the year and I was on the literal hot seat. My legs swung in and out. It felt good to move them apart and then back together without the restraint of the leg irons I had worn to court from Rikers Island. I ignored the hum of the crowd in the courtroom. It wasn't lost on me that everyone there was talking about me. Some probably came because they wanted a piece of me, too—hood vigilantes who wanted justice for the wrong. Yeah, right. They wanted to be nosey.

My lawyer kept telling me, "Not since the Long Island Lolita has New York seen a case like this. The difference is Mary Jo Buttafuoco lived." I was probably the most hated twenty-three-year-old in all of New York City. That was all good with me. Shit, I had hated myself since I was about eight or nine. My mother hated me. My father must've hated me because he never tried to find me. Girls in school hated me.

Teachers hated me. Adults I met hated me. Right now, my best friend in the whole world definitely hated me, so what the fuck did I care if all these strangers hated me? I knew the one person who had ever really loved me was in the back of that courtroom talking about me, too. I kept seeing Cheyenne's face behind my eyelids like I was watching still photos on a projector screen. I could picture her in all of the stages of our lives: little kids playing double Dutch; preteens taking up for each other on the battlefield we called a neighborhood; teenagers sneaking out to parties; and, now, as women both in pain and distress. Cheyenne wasn't ever going to forgive me for what I'd done. Never. I didn't deserve to be forgiven either.

The court officer's booming baritone interrupted my thoughts. "All rise! The Honorable Rowena Graves presiding."

The rustle of suits and dresses as the crowd inside the packed courtroom rose to their feet was so pronounced it was like someone was scratching sandpaper next to my ears. It sent an uneasy feeling through my empty stomach. Trying to eat breakfast had been a wrap. Who could eat when the fate of their life was in the hands of some white bitch judge with the last name Graves? Grave as in a place where people are buried. Grave as in something that signaled danger or harm. Those were the definitions of grave I had read in the jail library. Yeah, shit was grave for me all right. Grave as in this fucked-up situation I had put myself in all because I was looking for love.

My legs felt like two strands of cooked pasta as I stood up. The muscles burned in every part of my body like I'd worked out for ten hours without stopping, the result of the all-night pacing I'd done back on my cellblock. My lawyer stood next to me, clutching my right elbow as if he could sense that I was about to take a spill onto the courtroom floor. My lips curled from the wave of nausea that crept up from the pit of my stomach to my esophagus.

Judge Graves took her seat. There was nothing attractive about the judge. And I wasn't just thinking that because she was about to decide the fate of my life. She was small and hunched over like she was about to look for something on the floor. I could tell that the lump that had settled between her shoulders as easily as a camel's grew was just what was meant to happen to her as she got older. Judge Graves reminded me of a witch I had seen in this book, *Hansel and Gretel,* when I was back with my Nana. When I was still allowed to attend school. If I remembered right, the witch in the book ate kids or something like that. Judge Graves did too. To me the judge looked like she smoked ten packs of cigarettes a day. I knew a smoker when I saw one. That drawn-up, ashen, purplish-toned skin. Those square, grey, stained teeth. Those burnt-tipped fingers and greenish, grey fingernails. I had lived with smokers all my life. Judge Graves probably hid her pack-a-day habit from her family and friends. Of course they'd be too bourgeoisie to recognize the signs of a chain smoker. I pictured Graves spraying something minty into her mouth and using that stink of White Diamonds perfume that old ladies wore just because Elizabeth Taylor made it. That was a quick, fleeting thought—me wondering if Judge Graves had family who cared about her.

She waved her wrinkled hand and motioned for everyone to be seated. "Except for the defendant and her counsel," Graves growled, that distinct smoker's rattle bubbling in her throat.

My lawyer gave my elbow a quick squeeze. I ignored him.

"Counsel, I am going to address your client directly. No sense in prolonging this with silly motions to dismiss and the like. Your client has been convicted by a jury of her peers and I am prepared to sentence her today. Is that understood?" Judge Graves announced.

My attorney said, "Yes, Judge," and let go of my arm like it was a venomous snake.

I stared straight at the judge. My thoughts were racing like the cars at the Daytona 500.

Jury of my peers? I hardly thought five old white ladies, two white men, two Hispanic ladies, one Chinese guy, one black dude who slept the entire trial, and one old black lady who kept crying whenever somebody mentioned the victim counted as a fucking jury of my peers. There wasn't one black girl on there who had been through the shit I had been through. Not one chick who could at least say, "Damn I see how that could have happened." Jury of my peers my ass. My legs were moving but I wasn't making them move. I also couldn't make them stop moving.

"Miss Jones, the crime you have committed is abominable to say the least. In my opinion, you don't ever need to walk the streets again. You crossed not only legal boundaries, but you trampled all moral and civil boundaries I could think of. Trust is something that you earn and in light of the situation no one on God's green earth should ever trust you again. Under New York State sentencing guidelines this court is prepared to sentence you to life in prison without the possibility of parole. However, it is under your due process of the law that we give you an opportunity to tell me, and this court, why I should not render the most punitive sentence available to me under the guidelines. You can tell me why in your own words I might have leniency on you and maybe sentence you to twenty-five years to life with the possibility of parole. What that means is maybe one day some parole board will have mercy on your soul and let you back onto the streets.

"Before I render a final sentence you will also have the opportunity to present members of society who can speak on your behalf, to tell me why they think I should have leniency on you during this sentencing. Miss Jones, I must tell you that just as it is your right to bring forth others who can speak for you, it is also the victim's family's opportunity to tell me why I should put you away for the rest of your natural-born life. Under this process it is their right as well. Do you have any questions?" Graves grumbled, looking over the edge of her thick oyster-shell frames. All of her words resounded loudly off the hollow oak-covered courtroom walls.

The gravity of what she was saying felt like a 1,000-pound anchor around my neck. I realized that the small dashes of light fluttering at the backs of my eyes were just me starting to get dizzy. A few sighs could be heard from the back of the room. I swore I could feel the heat from all of the eyes boring holes into the back of me. I could only imagine what Cheyenne must've been thinking and doing right then when she heard "the victim's family." Probably crying and biting her lip. I knew her so well. I had seen her when I was first led into the courtroom. Still pretty. Still way more conservative than I had ever been. She never took her eyes off of me. Aside from the first quick glance, I couldn't look at her directly, so I lowered mine.

"Miss Jones, after I hear you out I have the discretion to formulate a sentence as I see fit according to the sentencing guidelines. Whatever sentence is imposed, you will be remanded to the State of New York for the duration of your sentence. We are prepared to hear your statement. So I ask, do you have anything you would like to say to the court or the family members of the victim who are present in the courtroom today?" Judge Graves continued.

I licked my dry, cracked lips. I was prepared to recite the long apology I had rehearsed over and over again with my lawyer. I had let some of the girls on my tier hear it. They had said they would've given me a break if they was the judge. Picture that, any of them ever being a judge. We lived in fantasy a lot in jail.

I opened my mouth several times to speak. Finally, when the words were about to come, I heard that familiar raspy voice exploding in my ears.

"Hmmm, I told you, bitch. I told you! You wouldn't amount to shit! You was never shit, you came from shit, and ain't never gonna be shit either!"

It was Carlene. The sorry sack of shit that gave birth to me. A birth canal was what Carlene was to me. She surely had never been a mother. I felt like somebody had hit me in the chest with one of those big, metal sledgehammers they use at carnivals to hit the small ball into the bell at the top of a tall pole; the stronger the person the more effective the hit. I couldn't breathe. A flame ignited on my skin and my cheeks burned. A ball of fire that had been growing inside of me since I was a little girl finally exploded. I didn't turn around. I was afraid of what I might do if I turned around. My entire body shook. I couldn't stop my teeth from chattering. I willed myself to stay still although in my mind's eye I could see myself jumping over the wooden divider and wilding out. Anything I did now would just make sentencing worse on me.

The court officers rushed over to Carlene to make sure she was put out. The judge banged her gavel and screamed, "Order!"

I bit into the side of my cheek until I drew the sweet and metallic taste of my own blood. My chest heaved in and out. I swayed on my feet. The nerve of this bitch! My fists involuntarily curled so tight my bones felt like they'd bust through my knuckles. Tears burned at the backs of my eyes but I refused to let them fall. Carlene had gotten enough tears out of me. *Enough!* I screamed over and over in my head. The chaotic scene made the spot directly above my right ear throb with pain.

"Order!" Judge Graves yelled again as the crowd in the courtroom murmured about the outburst. "Order!" the judge yelled again, quieting the room once more. "Miss Jones?" Judge Graves continued, giving me the nod to speak my last words.

I was ready. I was motivated by the ball of fire sizzling in my chest. "Yes, Your Honor, I have something to say," I said, crumpling the paper in front of me. I could feel my 18-B, fresh-out-of-law-school attorney shifting next to me.

"What are you doing?" he whispered harshly in my ear. He knew then that I was not going to read the remorse speech he had prepared for me. He lifted his hand up to interrupt me. "Ah, Judge, my client—" my attorney started.

"Sit the fuck down! I have something to say," I boomed. I was not letting anyone else in the world speak for me. I had done that all of my life.

The judge seemed a little thrown off her game by the power of my voice. "Mr. Broughton, please. Sit down. Go ahead, Miss Jones," Graves ordered, her voice showing a hint of respect for me.

"Ahem, I am Kelsi Jones and I regret what I did so much, but I want everyone to know that I am a victim myself. Please allow me to tell my story," I said, choking back tears, although I knew none would come. I was all cried out. It was so quiet in the courtroom now you could probably hear a mouse pissing on a cotton ball. I had everyone's full attention now.

"What is a fucking childhood? Where I'm from child-hoods don't exist unless you mean a child trying to survive in the hood." —Kelsi Jones to her lawyer in response to his question during their first meeting.

Chapter 2

The first time I fell in love, I was eight years old and it was with my best friend's father. It was love, real love, the only thing I could equate with man-and-woman love. It was different from the love I had felt for my Nana; that's how come I knew I was in man-and-woman love with my best friend's father. I knew it because when he was around me, my palms would sweat, my heart would race, and I could always feel my cheeks flaming over. By the time I was nine, I could even feel something tingling between my legs around him. Not the kind of tingling that hurt, like when someone who wasn't supposed to touch you there touched you there. Of course he didn't know I was in love with him. I mean, I never told him or nothing like that. To him, I was just a kid—a kid who had become his daughter's best friend. A kid who he knew came from a fucked-up home and needed love and protection like a charity case.

Kevin "Big K" Turner had saved my life and was the first man to ever give a fuck about me. So, I secretly loved him in return. I loved his coffee-bean brown skin, dark, low-cut hair, his deep-set shiny eyes, and the way he dressed and walked. He was the man in Carlene's neighborhood, where she brought me to live in July of 1995 when I was eight. He was Cheyenne's father and she was my only friend. Big K was the only person I associated with love, aside from my Nana.

I never knew my father and I never really had a mother. If that's even possible. A kid with no father or mother. That was me. As the story goes, the day I was born my mother, Carlene Jones, who was fifteen years old at the time, was in the mirror, shaking her pregnant ass to Eric B. & Rakim's "Paid In Full," doing the whop when the labor pains hit her like a thunderbolt. I was making my entrance into the world, whether she liked it or not. After spending seventeen hours giving birth to me, Carlene never held me. She never looked at me. She refused to acknowledge that I was her child. Nana said Carlene didn't name me either. Carlene referred to me as "it."

"You take it and feed it. You hold it."

Nana says the white nurses at the hospital helped her come up with the name Kelsi. Nana didn't want me to be one of the Shenquauqas of the world. "Kelsi is a universal name," Nana always preached. "You can go anywhere with that name and people won't judge you before they meet you." Nana always had high hopes for me from day one.

Nana said I was the prettiest baby she had ever seen. "Girl, you ain't have one piece of birth trauma, uh-uh . . . No egg-shaped head, no swollen eyes, no pale skin . . . nothing. You came out just as pretty as you wanted to be. Smooth skin, eyes perfect, and a head full of pretty hair," Nana had told me when I was five. Nana said she stayed at the hospital, held me, fed me, and changed my diapers, which continued after we went home.

By the time I was two years old, I thought Nana was my mother, and Carlene . . . well I didn't think about her at all. I hardly ever saw her. She was like a distant cousin or a relative who popped in after a long car ride to New York from down South. Most of the time, when she came to the house, she slept the entire time and ate ravenously when she woke up. Carlene ran the streets, partying, and having a ball. Nana says Carlene was always a hottie. She got her cherry popped at ten, and it was downhill from there. From what I remember, at that time, Carlene was a shade lighter than the blacktop of the street, she had thick dark brown hair that was cut in a Salt-n-Pepa hi-low with the back shaved, and she always wore the biggest gold doorknocker earrings. She also wore rings on all of her brightly painted fingers like that man Mr. T from *The A-Team*. Carlene had a regular face, nothing exceptionally beautiful about it. Nana says Carlene's voluptuous body was what got her all of the attention. Those double-D-cup breasts, that reindeer ass, and her ability to use them to get what she wanted.

I was the complete opposite of Carlene. My skin was what Nana's old lady friends called "creamy caramel, almost yella." My hair was spongy, thick, but soft and would curl nicely with just a little bit of water and grease. It wasn't real long, but it was "a good grade," according to Nana. My eyes, Nana said, "is the only thing you got from that damn Carlene." My eyes were beady and kind of close together: the one thing that linked me to Carlene and also the one thing about my face I always hated.

The trouble started on my eighth birthday. I was flitting around the apartment Nana and I shared, waiting for my party guests to arrive. I had poked at my Cinderella cake four times already. "Kelsi, by the time the people get here that cake is gonna be poked full of holes." Nana laughed. I still don't know how Nana always knew everything. Maybe parents do have eyes in the back of their heads.

Everyone began arriving at the party around three o'clock; why I remember that time I don't know. I got so many compliments on the pink lace dress Nana had gotten me. I whirled around and around, like I was Cinderella.

"Let's sing 'Happy Birthday'!" Nana announced about two hours into the party. Everyone crowded around as I kneeled on one of the kitchen chairs, with the cake in front of me.

"Light the candles!" someone yelled.

"Hold on, let me get a match," Nana said, shuffling toward her bedroom. She always hid matches from me. "Just for your safety," she'd explain. As Nana looked for the matches, there was a loud knock on the door.

"I'll get it!" Nana's friend Ms. Bessie screamed. When she pulled back the door Carlene waltzed into our apartment like it was her birthright to be there.

She came in like a gust of cold air. The kind that took your breath away in the winter and made tears drain from the corners of your eyes. Carlene's clear plastic platform heels clicked against the ceramic floor tiles like firecrackers popping. I can remember it like it was yesterday. Her skin gleamed with Vaseline, shining like thick, freshly poured molasses, and her newly pressed hair was pulled into a greasy ponytail with baby hair lying flat with small dips in it around the sides of her head.

I was in awe of her. Carlene was always like a purple, sparkly unicorn to me or like a rainbow with gold at the end of it. Magical, yet unreal. I eyed her that day in amazement. I wished I had a sparkly, tight red dress like hers. I remember running my hands down my flat chest, wishing I had a set of knockers sitting up under my chin like Carlene did. To me, she looked like a movie star. The skimpy dress showed off much more than it covered, barely coming fully under her ample behind. I smiled at her. I wanted her to smile back at me.

She never did.

Carlene's eyes were dull. All of that sparkle was in her clothes, but none showed in her eyes. I had not seen her in a year and was kind of glad she had come to my birthday party. Nana, on the other hand, wasn't as happy to see Carlene. At some point, Nana had emerged from the back of the apartment with the matches. Nana's face had folded in on itself and her eyes hooded over. Nana's dislike of Carlene could not be contained. Her feelings of disdain were like those trick cans filled with rubber snakes: no matter how many times you closed the lid, it popped right open, letting the snakes jump out at you.

"Why you coming up in here looking like a whore?" Nana whispered harshly in Carlene's ear, trying to keep the partygoers from overhearing. "You ain't got no better clothes than streetwalker clothes?"

Carlene sucked her teeth and smirked evilly. "No matter what you say you can't blow my high t'day. It's my child's birthday and I came to celebrate," Carlene trumpeted; then she took a long drag on her Newport. Carlene walked over to the table, flicked her lighter, and lit all eight of my candles.

Nana dropped her matches on the counter and folded her arms. The singing ensued, but Nana never opened her mouth. I was the only one who could see worry and fear creasing Nana's perfect face.

"Now make a wish, big girl," Carlene sang, cutting her eyes at Nana. Nana stood off in the background, scowling; her jawed rocked feverishly.

I stood in front of my cake and with my eyes shut real tight I made the same wish I had made year after year since I could understand what wishes were. I would come to understand the meaning of one of Nana's favorite sayings: "Be careful what you wish for. God don't answer wishes, and fairies who answer wishes are the devil in disguise."

That night, when everyone left, I wondered why Carlene was still there, and so did Nana. Nana and Carlene weren't like the mothers and daughters you saw on TV. There would be no long talks, laughter, and trips to the mall together. I could tell Nana was agitated; she'd smoked a half a pack of Pall Malls in a matter of a few hours. I just sat in silence, playing with my new birthday gifts and stealing glances at my biological mother, who I didn't even really know. Carlene tried to make small talk with Nana, but it didn't work. Nana treated Carlene worse than she treated Ms. Ollie Mae, a nosey, gossipy lady at our church. Now that was bad, because Nana couldn't stand Ms. Ollie Mae.

Finally, Carlene had given up trying to make small talk with her mother. It got quiet for a little while—too quiet, if you asked me. Then, Carlene let out a long sigh, like air escaping a hole in a tire. She stood up and smoothed her dress down over her big butt. She interrupted the eerie silence by dropping a bomb on us. Carlene could've blown up Pearl Harbor with her announcement. Smacking her shiny, lip-glossy lips, Carlene used her inch-long red-painted thumbnail to flick something from under her equally long pointer nail and calmly said, "I wanted y'all to know that I'm gettin' married and I'm coming to get Kelsi when I do. We gon' start living like a family. She gon' have what I didn't have . . . a mother and a father." Carlene put the emphasis on "mother" and "father."

As young as I was, I remember feeling like bombs had exploded around me. My ears rang and my stomach knotted up immediately. I clenched my butt cheeks together to keep from shitting on myself. The floor even started shaking underneath me.

Nana jumped up, ready for battle. Nana's face was crumpled like one of those devil masks you see in the costume store at Halloween time. She moved in on Carlene like a lion about to take down a fine, sleek gazelle. Nana jutted a finger toward Carlene's face. "You ain't takin' this child nowhere! This here is my baby! You don't even have a damn place to live. Look at you! All shiny and bright to cover up the dirt and filth that lives in your soul. You ain't interested in being no mother to nobody. Pushing one out don't automatically make you the momma. You ain't interested in being a mother or decent woman, period!" Nana accused cruelly, her pecan face turning dark as it filled with blood.

I kind of felt bad for Carlene. She looked like Nana had slapped her in the face and kicked her in the gut with those words. I could see Carlene's neck moving as she swallowed a few times. She inhaled until her chest swelled. Then, Carlene bounced back quick, like she was used to Nana saying stuff like that to her. She raised one side of her mouth into an evil smirk. Her eyes went into slits and she started circling Nana, as if to say she wasn't backing down.

Carlene's heels clacked against the floor each time she said a word. "Let me tell you something." Clack. "Your insults don't work on me no more." Click. "I ain't a young, dumb kid who cares about what you think of me no more." Clack. "Let's not talk about who ain't fit to be a mother . . . *Mother!*" Click. Carlene stopped moving.

I guessed she was going in for the kill and wanted to stand her ground.

"You always trying to put me down in front of my child! I got a place to live, I'm getting married, and I'm taking my child with me! Ain't no courts ever gave you that baby. She's mine and you ain't using her to get no second chances in life. You had your chance to be a mother and you failed! You a failure just like the failure you raised!" Carlene spat, rushing over and getting close up in Nana's face.

Both of them seemed to be on the brink of hysterics. They stood toe-to-toe, eye to eye. I was hoping no one threw a punch. The tension swirling around the apartment was so thick I could've sworn I saw it circling red over the entire place. I continued to twirl the Cinderella figurine from my cake, my little fingers shaking as I tried to act like nothing was happening. But my thundering heart and flaring nostrils probably gave me away. My birthday dress suddenly felt scratchy and too tight against my skin. That was the first time I remember feeling afraid. Not scary-movie afraid, but deathly afraid, like something real bad was going to happen. The kind of fear that knots up your insides so bad you feel like pissing, shitting, and vomiting all at once. There was no more discussion about it that night. Nana and I thought nothing of it after Carlene left. Thought nothing of it, until the day Carlene came back to get me.

"No! I don't wanna go! Please!" I screamed through tears, holding on to my Nana's waist as tight as my little arms could grasp. I locked my fingers behind Nana's back to make my grip even better. The spot where I buried my face was wet with my tears and snot.

"You are my child and you are going where I go!" Carlene screamed, grabbing me roughly around my ribcage, tugging me toward her. I felt like my shoulders would pop out of the sockets from me holding on so tight.

"Please, Carlene! I'll do anything; just let her stay. Ain't no reason for you to take her now. She being raised right here with me. Don't be hateful; please leave this baby be, Carlene, just leave her be," Nana sobbed, holding on to me equally as tight. She wasn't going to let Carlene take me. I was sure of that, but I still held on as tight as I could.

"Don't make me call the police on you, lady! I did it once and I'll do it again!" Carlene warned, her voice a high-pitched screech that made the insides of my ears itch. "You making this harder than it gotta be. A child needs to be with the mother who gave birth to 'em. Not a pretender looking for second chances because they couldn't do it right with their own child they gave birth to. I'm telling you, I'm gonna call the damn cops!"

"You gon' have to call them cops tonight or kill me one, 'cause you ain't takin' this child from here unless it's over my dead body!" Nana announced firmly.

She wasn't letting go and neither was I. I just knew that would do it. Carlene didn't look like the type who was into having contact with the cops. She wasn't going to call no cops. Carlene tugged on my waist again and I felt like I was losing my grip. The bones in my fingers started cracking as I tried in vain to keep them locked together.

"Please! Nana, don't let them take me!" I screeched. I could feel my throat burning as I screamed as loud as I could. The salt from my tears was bitter on my tongue.

"Come on! Let go!" Carlene huffed, pulling some more. "She ain't none of your momma! I pushed you out into this world and if I want you with me then you gon' be with me!"

I buried my face deeper. I held my breath. I would have rather died from not breathing than go with Carlene.

"Miss, we gotta go. Why don't you just let Peaches take her child?" Carlene's new husband said calmly, his voice an even baritone.

I buried my face deeper into Nana's soft stomach when I heard his voice. I had forgotten that the scary-looking man had come there with Carlene.

"Fuck you and your Peaches! I raised this child. The momma didn't want her! Did your new wife tell you that? Did she tell you she ain't interested in being nobody's momma? Did she tell you she ain't nothing but a two-bit whore?" Nana screamed through tears.

I couldn't ever remember seeing Nana cry before then. I was still holding on so tight I could hear Nana's heart racing in my ear.

"Two-bit whore? Two-bit whore? If I'm a two-bit whore I was taught by the best!" Carlene hissed at Nana.

"Please! Carlene, let me stay! I'll call you Mommy from now on when you come; just please let me stay with my Nana!" I cried some more. The kind of pain I was experiencing felt like someone was dying in my arms. Every muscle in my body ached and my head was pounding. Just the thought of leaving Nana had me gagging on my tears and snot.

"You ain't gotta call me Mommy when I come, because you coming with me now!" Carlene screamed, her voice cracking.

I could tell she was hurt, maybe even a little embarrassed. Now that I think about it, maybe she felt betrayed by me, her only child, who was acting like she was the Grim Reaper coming to take me to hell.

"I believe the child's mother said to let her go, old lady," Carlene's husband growled loudly.

Next, I heard a click. When I looked up to Nana's face, I saw the end of a black gun resting on Nana's forehead. I squeezed my eyes shut and buried my face deeper into Nana's stomach. I inhaled her scent. Maybe something in my little mind told me this was final. *Dear God, please don't let them take me. I will always put my money in the offering at church from now on. I will not steal Nana's butterscotch candies anymore when she's sleeping. Please don't let them take me.* I said a quick, silent prayer. It wasn't enough.

The man lifted his gun and brought it down on Nana's head. I heard something crack. Then I felt something dripping on the top of my head.

"Oh, Lord!" Nana shrieked at first.

"Aggh! Nana!" I screamed too. We were moving all of a sudden. "God forgive them," Nana whispered as her body folded to the floor. She involuntarily released her grip on me as she went limp.

"Nana, wake up! You can't let them take me!" I still held on to Nana as tight as I could, but I was no match for the man's huge wrestler's arms. He swept me off my feet in one swift motion and carried me kicking and screaming to his rusty, old white ragtop Cadillac sedan DeVille.

He threw me into the back seat roughly and slammed the door. Then, Took, my mother's husband, walked calmly to the driver's seat and cranked the car up. I remember that the pungent smell of gasoline that engulfed the car made me dizzy. By the time I scrambled up from the seat, I saw Nana stumbling out of the building. She was going to fight for me. No gun butt was going to keep my Nana from fighting for me. I looked out of the dirty car window at my Nana, who was running beside the car with blood leaking from her head, as Took pulled away from the curb. Nana's face was covered with blood as she cried and screamed my name.

"Kelsi! Kelsi! My baby!" she screamed.

"Nana! Nana! Don't let them take me!" I belted out, putting my hands up against the glass. She couldn't keep up. At first, I sat and watched Nana from the window, but eventually I had to get on my knees to see her. The farther we drove, the smaller Nana got. I could hardly see her anymore. Suddenly Nana's silhouette just disappeared into the distance. I never saw my Nana alive again. I had lost the only person who'd ever really loved me.

Chapter 3

I had never been out of the Bronx in my life before Carlene and Took snatched me from Nana. I cried for the entire ride. Sitting on the hot, busted-up leather of Took's car, I could hardly breathe from the wind blowing in my face. Tears and snot were everywhere. I had white dried and crusted streaks extending from the corners of my eyes like war paint and running down my cheeks like the makeup on a sad clown. I continued to bawl out of control. I didn't care; I wanted my Nana. A few times during the eternity-long ride, Took turned his pale face around toward me and screamed, "Shut the fuck up, kid!" I had never seen anyone who looked like Took. His skin was so white it was almost transparent. His hair was thick and nappy, but it was a golden, brassy blond like it belonged on the head of a white person. Took's eyeballs were red with a black center. I pondered his features as I cried. I thought only white people had blond hair and pinky, whitish skin. At first, I thought Took was white, but his huge flat nose and nappy-ass hair quickly changed my mind. Anyone with red eyeballs had to be the devil, I surmised, but as I grew up I found out he was just what I heard people call albino.

I could smell the difference in the air between the Bronx and Brooklyn as soon as we crossed the bridge. I put my arm over my nose. The funny smell made me want to throw up. It was like the ocean mixed with garbage . . . Yeah, that was the best I could describe it. Brooklyn was flat compared to the hills I was used to in the Bronx. I hated Brooklyn already, no hills to ride my bike down. No bike to even ride. No Nana to watch me ride. I hated Brooklyn right away. Nothing good could ever come from this place. I had decided that at eight years old. Nana used to say, "Out of the mouths of babes comes the pure truth."

I was still crying as we pulled up on the strange block. My head pounded and I had to pee badly. I peered out the window at an orange and blue sign, posted in a small patch of grass, that read WELCOME TO CAREY GARDENS, N.Y.C.H.A. The building was very tall, not like the four-story walkup where Nana and me lived in the Bronx. There were so many people outside, kids and adults. I could hear music blasting from a large boom box sitting on a bench.

"Here comes the brand new flava in ya ear! Time for new flava in ya ear! I'm kicking new flava in ya ear!" The Craig Mack lyrics had everyone outside jumping.

"Ow!" Carlene shouted, raising her hands over her head and clapping. "That's my shit. This remix be having me going." She rocked her head up and down.

I just wanted to tell her to shut the fuck up. It wasn't nothing to fucking celebrate about. Nana wouldn't like me thinking about curses in my head, but I couldn't help it.

"The block is hot! That means that mean green for you, baby." Carlene giggled, leaning in to kiss Took's ugly cheek. She was like a different person all of a sudden.

Took was preparing to park the car so we could get out, but before he could bring it to a complete stop, three scary-looking people—two skinny women and a very sweaty-looking man—rushed toward Took's window.

"Yo, Took, man, where you been? I need a nick—"
The first skinny woman began stretching her balled fist
toward Took. She was quickly cut off.

"Bitch, can't you see I just pulled up! I got my kid
in the car and shit. Have some fuckin' respect, you
fiend! Get the fuck outta here until I park my whip!"
Took screamed at the lady. The skeletal lady and her
counterparts jumped back as Took purposely swerved
the car like he was going to hit them.

*I ain't his kid, I thought. I'll never be the kid of no
red-eyed devil.* However, since I never knew who my
father was, it did feel kinda good to have a man claim
me like that.

"Y'all gotta get out. I gotta go see Big K. I need to
re-up. I ain't got no more shit and as you can see these
fiends don't never rest," Took said to Carlene with an
urgency in his voice.

Carlene leaned over and kissed him again. I gagged
just looking at that nasty shit. "Go get that work, daddy.
I'll be waiting for you when you get back, so don't take
all long," Carlene said in a husky, trying-to-be-sexy
voice that made my skin crawl. Then she turned toward
me. Her face changed. It was suddenly crumpled like
she was smelling something real stink. "C'mon get out!
And wipe them damn crusty boogers off your face!" she
yelled at me.

I rolled my eyes and made a feeble attempt to wipe
the crusted snot and tears from my face. Wide-eyed
I exited the car, wondering what kind of life I was
about live. It was like a different world in front of that
building. There were at least sixty things going on at
once: people dancing, people arguing, people drinking,
people smoking, kids playing, kids fighting, babies
crying, babies sleeping. It was like all the people who
lived inside that tall building with all of those windows

were all outside engaged in some activity. They were all staring at Carlene and me now as we walked up.

Suddenly I felt embarrassed, ashamed of how I looked. I had never had to worry about that feeling while I was with Nana. But now, all eyes were on me. I had nothing but the clothes on my back. When they snatched me from Nana's, I was in what Nana referred to as "play clothes" so I wasn't even in one of my best outfits. The jeans I wore were a little too high and the T-shirt a little too tight. They were my last year's clothes that Nana made me wear around the house when we weren't going anywhere special. I had plenty of nice clothes at Nana's house, but Carlene hadn't taken the time to bring my clothes or toys, and Nana was too preoccupied with trying to keep me there to pack a bag for me.

As I walked toward the front of 2949 West Twenty-third Street—my new home—I looked around at all of the people as they looked at me. One set of kids caught my full attention. There was a group of girls playing double Dutch. "Ten, ten, ten, twenty, thirty, forty, fifty, sixty, seventy, eighty, ninety, one up, two, three, four, five, six, seven, eight, nine, two up!" They all sang in unison as one girl jumped in the middle of their rope.

One girl in particular caught my attention. She was turning on one end of the rope, and as I stared, she smiled. She was real pretty. Her hair was long and neatly done in a lot of ponytails. She wore yellow from head to toe and it seemed to bring out her Crayola-crayon brown skin. She kept her eye on me while she turned the rope made from telephone wire. I waved real quick and kept walking. I immediately wanted to get to know that little girl with the kind smile and kind eyes.

"Hey, Peaches, who you got there?" yelled an old, overweight woman wearing a housecoat. The woman's body spilled left and right on the bench she occupied to the left of the building's entrance. She was talking to Carlene, so it quickly became obvious to me that Carlene's nickname was Peaches. I thought it was just something Took called her. *I guess not.* Shit, to me Carlene looked far from a peach.

"This my daughter, Kelsi. I told you I had a daughter. What? You ain't believe me?" Carlene said dryly, but continued switching her ass into the building.

"She's a pretty little thing. Sure don't look nothing like you!" the lady replied, cackling and coughing at the same time after.

Carlene kept moving full speed ahead like she didn't want the lady to look at me too long. "Lula is so got-damn nosey. Always tryin'a make somebody out to be a fucking liar," Carlene whispered to herself as we stood waiting for the elevator. Carlene jammed her finger at the elevator button over and over like she didn't believe it would ever come.

For the first time since we'd left Nana's, I could tell Carlene was just as nervous about this new living arrangement as I was. She wouldn't look at me, but I could see her bottom lip quivering a bit. *Maybe she wants me to like her.* Carlene and I didn't speak a word during the elevator ride. I busied myself reading the words somebody had scribbled in black marker on the shiny silver walls of the stinky elevator: REEREE IS A SLUT. DANA SUCKS MAJOR DICK. YOUR MOTHER IN 6C IS UGLY. DAYDAY IS A FAGGOT. These were just a few of the things that stuck out to me. Nana probably would've covered my eyes to keep me from reading those bad words. Carlene didn't care.

Exiting the elevator, Carlene led the way. She rushed down the long, dimly lit hallway and I followed. The stale air assaulted the insides of my nostrils with a million different odors at once. I could smell the aroma of fried chicken, pee, fish, and garbage all rolled into one big whiff. As I passed one apartment, I could hear music blasting so loud the little knocker on the door vibrated. Another apartment had its front door wide open. The occupants inside moved around like they didn't even notice the door was open. Another apartment had huge dents in the door and bright yellow tape that said CRIME SCENE DO NOT CROSS in the form of an X across it. Seemed like the projects were going to be much noisier and busier than I was used to. What really got me was all of the garbage on the floor in front of the incinerator. *They gotta live here. How come they couldn't just pull the handle and put the garbage in?*

Apartment 4G—that's what the black letter and number on the door Carlene stopped at read. Carlene fished her keys from her pocketbook and opened the blue steel door. "Home, sweet, fucking home!" she exclaimed, stepping inside like she was introducing me to a palace.

Standing at the threshold, I raised my eyebrows, and covered my mouth. I felt a hard ball in my throat and something funny was going on in my stomach. Tears sprang up at the edges of my eyes. First of all the house stunk like garbage and dirty feet. Beer cans, soda bottles, clothes, Chinese food boxes, and any other item of garbage you could think of covered the floor. I used the back of my hand to wipe my tears and cover my nose at the same time.

"You better stop acting like you too good and brang yo' ass on in here. This where we stay so this is where you stay. Get all that other shit out of your mind. I'm ya mother," Carlene said, pulling me farther into the hellhole.

As I slowly walked in, my sneakers made low crackling sounds, as the soles stuck to the sticky, dirty tiles on the floor. The floor was a sickening shade of grey, but I knew the tiles were supposed to really be off-white. I examined my surroundings as I dodged the roaches scurrying back to their hiding places. There was so many of them they all couldn't find places to hide. "Eeeelll!" I screamed as one fell from some place high and landed on my arm. I started jumping and moving and swiping at my arms to make sure it was off of me.

"Bitch, you ain't ever seen a roach before?" Carlene hissed.

"Not this many and not on me," I commented, disgusted.

"Too bad! You better get used to living here because you sure won't be going back to live with that lady," she snapped.

"And my name is Kelsi," I mumbled sassily. Carlene had taken to calling me the B word and I was getting tired of it.

"I call you what I want to call you . . . *bitch*," Carlene retorted, getting so close to my face I could smell the Royal Crown grease in her scalp.

I didn't think she had heard me. I had finally moved far enough into the apartment to really access everything I was going to have to contend with. I was trying to find at least one thing that I might be able to live with there, but it wasn't easy. There was no furniture in the so-called living room. Sheets covered the windows instead of the nice lace curtains I was used to at Nana's house. A small, raggedy plastic folding table with one chair and one milk crate that served as a chair sat to the side of the small kitchen. The kitchen sink had dishes piled in it and to both sides of it. The dishes had food on them so old, black, green, blue, and grey mold grew in tall piles on some of the plates. The stove was caked with old brown and yellow grease. So was the wall behind it. I was scared to open the refrigerator; there were so many roaches around it I didn't bother. The kitchen had two ways to get in and out, so I exited on the side closest to the apartment door. I thought about making a run for it. But, where would I have gone? Being in Brooklyn was like being in a foreign country for me. I would've never figured out how to get back to the Bronx. Nana had kept me too sheltered for that.

As I stepped out of the kitchen, I had a clear view straight down a small hallway that led to the back of the apartment. I noticed that there was only one bedroom to the back of the apartment. *Where will I sleep?* I thought sadly, thinking about how I usually slept with Nana every night.

Carlene emerged from a darkened room at the back of the apartment. "You gonna sleep right here," Carlene huffed, dragging a dirty foam mattress into the empty living room. I guessed that answered my question.

"Listen, bitch, there are rules to staying here," Carlene said as she lit the end of a cigarette.

My jaw rocked as I bit down so hard my temples throbbed. *I told you my name is Kelsi!* I screamed in my head.

"First, don't touch the refrigerator and nothing in it unless you ask me or Took. You don't buy shit, you don't eat shit, unless we tell you to. Especially if you see a Pepsi in there, don't you ever, ever touch my Pepsi. Drink water! Kids drink water. If I decide to give you something else to drink, I will; if not, drink fucking water. Period. Don't touch the TV or stereo in my room. Matter of fact, don't touch shit in my room or go in there unless I send you in there or call you in there. Don't leave out this house without my permission or if me or Took take you out. You can't go outside unless I say you can go. There will be no fucking company in my house. These fucking kids around here are no good and I don't want them in my fucking crib. You got chores around here, so you ain't gonna be bored at all. You gotta do the dishes, and clean the bathroom, kitchen, and where you sleep at. Last of all, I see you growing up now, getting a little bit of buds for tits and rounding out to get a li'l bit of ass. Don't even think about looking cross-eyed at my man. That will get your ass thrown right outta here! Too many of y'all young bitches fuckin' people old man and then yelling 'bout somebody touched y'all or molested y'all. That shit don't fly around here so you better keep that li'l body to ya'self," Carlene rambled off, contaminating my breathing air with a cloud of smoke as she finished up.

I bit into the side of my jaw until I tasted the salty, metallic flavor of my own blood. My hands were locked into fists and my vision clouded over in shades of burgundy and red. Even as young as I was, what the hell made her think I wanted her albino man? I wasn't even old enough to think about boys my own age, much less a nasty-looking man like Took!

My first night there, I tossed and turned. I had never slept alone. I missed the scent of Nana's butterscotch that comforted me every night as Nana and I shared a pillow. Carlene didn't even give me a blanket, much less a pillow. I slapped at my leg as I felt needle-like pricks over and over again. Scratching them seemed to make it worse. I finally realized that there were bugs biting me on the dirty mattress. I got up and sat in the lone chair that sat outside of the kitchen. I used the milk crate to prop my feet up. I told myself I would sleep sitting up. It seemed like as soon as I finally fell into a fitful sleep, slouched to the side in the chair with my head on the dirty plastic table, Carlene was standing over me.

"Get up, bitch! We got a appointment today!" she screamed, shaking me hard.

Dazed, I looked up. The smell hit me first. It was like the nastiest underarm funk I had ever smelled in my life. I blinked my eyes a few times to get them to focus. They went wide. Carlene was damn near butt-ass naked, wearing just a small camisole. I crinkled my face and I wanted to hide my eyes. Nana had never, ever, let me see her naked. That was the first time I had ever seen a hairy cootie cat (that was me and Nana's name for a woman's privacy area). I immediately closed my eyes back.

"Bitch, I said get up! Now! I ain't gonna tell you again! I gotta be at face to face in a few minutes and you gotta be there too!" Carlene rasped, sounding like a monster to me.

I had no idea what she was talking about, "face to face." Nonetheless, I dragged myself up out of the chair. My neck ached and I could hardly turn it left or right. I guessed from the way I'd slept all twisted. I had slept in my clothes because, of course, Carlene hadn't bothered to give me pajamas. "I need a wash rag and towel," I mumbled to Carlene.

"Just wash your face with the one that's hanging in there. I gotta do laundry when we come back . . . if you hurry the fuck up and these people give me my check," she grumbled.

The bathroom was worse than the rest of the house if you asked me. I lifted my shirt over my nose as I surveyed how I would maneuver in that nasty-ass bathroom. The toilet seat was supposed to be light blue, but it was stained with yellow specs and brown streaks at the back. Behind the seat, on the white part, was hair, dirt, piss, and doo-doo stains. I pulled my pants down and squatted over the toilet, trying to be careful not to have my skin come in contact with the toilet at all. I already knew from the day before that I wasn't so great at it. Again, some of the pee drizzled down my right leg and on the back of my panties. To make matters worse, there was no toilet tissue. Carlene and Took had obviously been using newspaper and brown paper bag to wipe their asses. I wasn't doing that! I bounced a few times hoping I could drip dry.

I felt disgusting and wanted to take a shower badly. Nana had just let me start taking showers instead of sit-down baths when I turned seven. That idea quickly faded when I looked over at the bathtub. "Yuck!" I whispered, frowning until my cheeks hurt. I refused to step foot in that thing. It was black in the bottom with rings and rings of body dirt. It looked like it had not been washed in years. The edges had old, caked-on soap stains that would probably need a metal scraper to remove. The wall tiles were black in between and the faucets were caked with green and grey stuff. I turned back toward the sink and looked in the stained mirror. My hair was a mess and my face had red splotches on it. *Those bed bugs must've bitten me in the face before I got up and sat in the chair.* My eyes were crusty. I guessed the tears I had cried in my sleep for Nana had dried into crust. I reached up for the lone face rag that hung stiffly on the silver pole over the tub. I couldn't reach it, so I had to step onto the tub for a boost. When I snatched the rag down from the pole, I could tell it was dirty. It was so stiff it stayed bent in half like it was still hanging on the pole even after I had it in my hand. I swallowed hard. I turned on the hot water and stuck the rag under the stream. The water even seemed to repel from that face rag. Finally, I got it soft enough to wring it out. I reluctantly put it up against my face to wipe away the crust and sleep. "Agh, agh!" I gagged. That rag stank like somebody's ass! I threw it into the sink like it was a poisonous snake. I wasn't putting that thing back on my face.

I cupped my hands and splashed some water on my face. I looked around. I had no toothbrush either. There was no toothpaste in sight, but a box of baking soda on the back of the sink. I remembered that sometimes I would watch Nana brush her teeth with baking soda after using toothpaste. "That makes your teeth whiter," Nana told me once. I decided I'd use the baking soda and my finger to brush my teeth. I pulled back the top on the baking soda. "Ah!" I jumped and dropped the entire box on the floor. It was filled with so many roaches there was hardly any baking soda left. Tears immediately sprang to my eyes. I jumped at the sound of Carlene banging on the door. My heart was thundering.

"C'mon, bitch! This ain't no fucking beauty pageant. Wash your face and let's go! If I miss this appointment I gotta wait another four weeks for one," she screamed.

I felt hot all over. I cupped my hand again and got a little bit of water in my mouth. I swished it around and spit it out. I took some of Carlene's Royal Crown hair grease that sat on the back of the toilet and spread it on my face. That worked to get rid of the crusty streaks. I came out of the bathroom and Carlene was dressed and ready to go. *She didn't even wash up. Nasty, stink ass,* I said to myself. I would soon learn that Carlene was dirty in more ways than one.

We took two trains to get to Carlene's appointment. I fell asleep since I hadn't slept the night before. It was crazy how soothing the train was to me, even with all of those strangers on it. The noise, the slight swaying motion was comforting. It was the trains I would take to as comfort as I got older, too.

I was so hungry by the time we got to Carlene's appointment I had a pounding headache. My mouth was desert-sand dry and my lips were cracked. Carlene was bouncy and jittery like she had eaten a bag of sugar. "When we get inside don't ask me for shit out that vending machine or nothing like that. Don't speak to nobody unless I tell you to and I'll answer all the questions. You understand me, bitch?" Carlene told me, pointing a jittery finger in my face like I had done something wrong. I rolled my eyes at her. She was so ugly to me now.

AID FOR DEPENDENT CHILDREN. I read the sign in my head. That was the line me and Carlene got on. We were far back in the line, too. There were so many people there. I counted at least eighteen pregnant ladies and all of them had more kids with them aside from the one in their belly. Some of them had little babies and were pregnant again, too. How was that even possible? The line moved real slow, as one name at a time was called. My legs and the bottom of my feet throbbed, on top of the drumbeat of pain pounding between my ears. I was dying to go sit on one of the dirty orange, yellow, or light blue chairs that were situated around the walls. There were no empty ones anyway. It seemed like a lifetime before Carlene and I got to the lady behind the scratched-up Plexiglas window.

"Yes, I have a face to face with my worker Ms. Shelton today. She needed to see my child in person to give me the food stamp and check increase," Carlene said, using the most proper English I had ever heard her speak in the few times I had gotten to see her in my life. "Jones is my name. Carlene, and this is my child, Kelsi."

The lady swirled her chair around, checked something, and turned back to the window. "Have a seat. Shelton got six before you. Your appointment was for nine o'clock; you late, you go to the bottom," the lady said like she had said the same line one hundred times that day.

Carlene let out a windstorm of breath. "Fuck!" Carlene spat, grabbing my arm roughly and pulling me into a corner. She flung me into the wall and turned into me. She was covering me from the crowd so no one could see the fear dancing in my widened eyes. I couldn't understand what I had done wrong. "Bitch, you see what the fuck you did taking all long? Now we gotta wait in here all fucking day. I was gonna buy you something to eat . . . Now you ain't gettin' shit," Carlene hissed, her breath smelling like a swirl of shit and cigarettes.

I think that was the first time I felt that ball of fire in my chest get a little bigger. I would come to learn as I got older that it was anger inside of me that was growing like a well-watered plant. With hunger pangs tearing my insides up and that fire in my chest, I pictured a thousand ways I could kill Carlene that day. I was eight at that time, but those thousand ways would multiply into millions as the years went by.

Chapter 4

By the time we finished with Carlene's face to face, which, I found out, meant an in-person meeting with a welfare caseworker, Carlene had been given a stack of what the lady called "emergency food stamps" and Carlene could expect an increase of $175 plus back money in two weeks. When we left the office, I was moving slow. I was so hungry, I felt like I would faint. My merciful biological passage into the world finally stopped at a street frank vendor and bought me one frank, a grape soda, and a bag of Bon Ton plain potato chips. I remember that meal so clearly to this day because it was the first thing I had eaten since I'd been snatched from Nana's house. I couldn't even taste the food I had gobbled it down so fast.

When we returned to Carlene's building, I saw that same little girl again. This time she was doing the Hula Hoop instead of playing double Dutch. And, instead of all yellow, the little girl had on all red. I could tell someone cared about her. Her skin was shiny and clear. Her hair was parted in zigzag parts and she had pretty heart-shaped bubbles and barrettes adorning at least eight long ponytails. She wore a red top with sparkly silver hearts all over it and a red miniskirt. Her socks were folded down with red hearts all over them. She had on pristine white low-top Reebok track sneakers. The little girl stopped Hula-Hooping when she saw me looking at her. She smiled again and waved. This time, I smiled back and I waved again.

Carlene had stopped to speak to a guy, so she didn't have time to see me and the little girl waving and smiling at one another. The little girl motioned for me to come to her, but I was scared that moving would get Carlene's attention, so I shook my head no. The little girl tilted her head in confusion. Her shoulders slumped like she was disappointed, but then she stepped out of her Hula Hoop. She hung her Hula Hoop on the black metal gate that surrounded the small patch of grass in front of the building and walked over to me. As soon as she got close, I could smell the fresh scent of baby powder on her. She still had some showing on her neck, too. I immediately noticed the arm full of red and clear plastic bracelets she wore. I wanted them.

"Why was you scared to come over there?" she asked me.

She was even prettier up close than I thought she was looking at her from a distance. I was immediately embarrassed and felt inferior to her. I felt so ugly standing in front of that pretty little girl. "I don't know," I said softly. Looking away to make sure Carlene was still talking. I could see Carlene had that stack of food stamps out and she was in deep conversation with a guy who looked like he was dismissing her. Carlene looked like she was begging him for something.

"Is Peaches your mother?" the little girl asked, noticing me stealing glances at Carlene.

I looked down at my feet. I wished I could cover my dirty "play sneakers" so the little girl couldn't see them. I also wished I could blink and make Carlene just disappear. "What's your name?" I asked her, totally ignoring her question. I didn't want anyone to know Carlene was my mother.

"Cheyenne," she said. "I don't live in this building, but I come over here sometimes because it's a lot of my friends over here. I live in the real houses down Sea Gate."

I had no idea what she was talking about, "real houses," but I knew it was probably better than this building, or else why would she point it out so fast?

"My name is Kelsi. I live in the Bronx with my Nana, but I had to come here for a little while. I don't live in this building either," I said, feeling right away like I had to compete with this pretty little girl.

"I hope you stay a long time. I like you," Cheyenne told me.

She didn't even know me; how could she say she liked me? What about me did she like? I still had on my "play clothes" so they looked too small and they didn't match. My hair needed combing and brushing. My face was probably dirty and, to top it all off, I had spilled grape soda down the front of my shirt trying to drink it so fast, so I looked dirty as hell. Certainly not like someone this dainty, well-dressed, clean, sweet-faced girl would like.

"I like you too," I lied. Secretly I hated her: her clean clothes, her nicely done hair, and her pretty face. I could just imagine how clean her "real house" was, too.

"Can you stay outside for a little while?" she asked.

Don't leave out this house without my permission or if me or Took take you out. You can't go outside unless I say you can go. Carlene's words resounded in my ears. "I think I might be going back to the Bronx today so pro'ly not," I answered, lying again.

"Dag. I wish you could stay outside. I want some new friends. The girls around here be my friend for a little while but then they start getting jealous and talking about me and stuff and then we don't be friends no more. I'm bored out here by myself," Cheyenne complained.

I wanted to tell her to stop complaining. That at least she had nice clothes, nice hair, and a clean "real house." I looked over at Carlene again. She was finally exchanging something with the guy she had been talking to. A car horn sounded and caused me to look away. Cheyenne turned around too.

"C'mon, baby girl. We goin' to the rides," a man called from a real nice, big, shiny black Jeep-looking car.

From where I stood, I could see that the man had a neck full of thick gold chains and a crisp white shirt on. I couldn't really see his face. Cheyenne sucked her teeth and turned back toward me.

"I gotta go, Kelsi. That's my father. He don't like me to stay out here that long so he always makes up excuses to make me want to leave," she said disappointedly.

"What's the rides?" I asked her real quick before she left.

She looked at me with furrowed eyebrows. "You never seen all those rides just blocks from here? Coney Island . . . duh. You never went there?" Cheyenne said like it was something or someplace everyone in the entire world knew about but me.

"I told you I was from the Bronx!" I snapped, my jaw rocked back and forth. I wanted to punch her. The fireball in my chest was starting again. It just wasn't as hot as it was for Carlene.

"Even people from the Bronx come to Coney Island. On Easter, on Memorial Day and stuff like that. People get all dressed fresh and come to the rides. We are lucky to live right by the rides and we go all the time. Ask that lady you with if you can go. My father won't care," Cheyenne told me.

Was she crazy? Carlene would flip if I asked her to go someplace other than wherever she told me to go. "That's okay. I'm just going to stay here. I might be going back to the Bronx later anyway," I said with a straight face. That was just wishful thinking.

Cheyenne's father blew the horn again. She sucked her teeth. She started walking off, but she didn't go in the direction of her father's car. I thought she was going to get her Hula Hoop off the fence. She marched right up to Carlene and the guy. I crinkled my face in confusion. Cheyenne was saying something to Carlene; then she pointed to me and looked back at Carlene.

My body felt hot all over and my heart was knocking into that skinny bone in the center of my chest. Carlene shot me a dirty look from where she stood. Cheyenne marched to her father's car. Her father blew the horn again. I looked over to the car. He was leaning down looking in the direction Carlene was standing with the guy.

"Yo, Peaches!" Cheyenne's father yelled. He blew his horn again.

I was frozen in place. What was happening? I couldn't stop the sweat beads from running a race down my back. My underarms itched and so did my scalp.

Carlene turned toward the Jeep car with a fake smile and waved. "Wassup, Big K?" she answered with a fake song in her tone.

He waved her over. "Let me rap with you for a taste," he hollered out.

Carlene rolled her eyes at me. "I'll be right back. Stay right there," she grumbled to me evilly. She sashayed over to where the man she had called Big K, who I knew now was Cheyenne's father, sat parked in his big, beautiful, shiny Jeep car.

I watched as they spoke. Carlene was all smiles and giggles like she was talking to her schoolgirl crush. Cheyenne was in the back seat staring out of the window at me. She put her pointer and middle finger up and crossed them over each other. I didn't know what that meant. Carlene finally looked up from where she'd been leaning down, smiling into Big K's window.

"B . . . um, Kelsi! C'mere, baby! Hurry up!" Carlene called out, waving me over like the matter was urgent. It was the first time she'd called me by my name, which sounded more like an owner calling a pet than a mother calling her only child. I looked at her strangely. "C'mere and stop acting crazy, girl." Carlene laughed nervously.

Cheyenne was smiling and bouncing excitedly. I didn't understand none of what was going on. Whatever had made Carlene refer to me as "baby" surely had to be something or someone big. I made it over to the car.

"Kelsi, this Big K . . . Took's boss. His daughter wants you to go with her to the rides. I told Big K I was gonna ask you first. You wanna go?" She looked at me with a knowing, squinty-eyed glance.

I darted my eyes to Cheyenne who was shaking her head up and down, motioning for me to say yes.

"You don't have to go if you don't want to," Carlene said, like she was telling me to say no on the low. I felt the chest ball fire thingy again. I pictured it growing a little bigger inside of me.

"It's gonna be fun," Big K said, flashing a smile.

That was the first time I remember looking at him. His eyes were kind and relaxed. They were dark, but not scary dark like Carlene's. His skin was the color of the coffee beans Nana loved so much, and it was smooth and hairless. He had two shiny gold teeth in the front of his mouth that gleamed and sparkled when he smiled, and his watch had a huge face with rows of shiny diamonds going round and round in circles all over it.

"I ain't got no money to give," Carlene started, urgency lacing her words.

Big K threw his hand up in her face. "Don't insult me, Peaches. Ain't nobody asking you for no paper. I said *I* was taking shorty to the rides. Slow ya roll. What I look like asking *you* for money," he chastised, putting the emphasis on the difference between him and her. I mean, it was plain to see that there were big differences. Big K looked at me and softened his chiseled, handsome face. "What's it gonna be, little lady?" he asked in more of cheery tone than he'd just spoken to Carlene.

Carlene was moving her jaw furiously. Maybe that's where I'd gotten that from?

"I wanna go," I said softly, parting a nervous smile, not daring to look at Carlene. I didn't know if it was to make Carlene mad as hell or if it was to be closer to the kind eyes of Big K, but I said it again, louder the second time. "I wanna go to the rides."

"Yes!" Cheyenne cheered from the back seat, pumping her fist.

Big K laughed. "Calm down back there, cheerleader," he quipped.

Carlene was sizzling mad, I could tell. Her eyes were low and her nostrils moved in and out rapidly. She stepped back from the car like it was a big, black monster about to attack her. "And there you have it," Carlene mumbled while keeping a fake smile on her face. "Well then I guess it's fine with me. I ain't gonna go against the hand that feeds me right?" Carlene said, nodding at Big K and letting out a half-phony snicker after.

"Get in, little lady. This little one back here been waiting for you," Big K told me.

Cheyenne already had the back door open. I had to hold on to climb up into the Jeep car. I had never been in one before. Nana didn't drive. We walked or took the bus all over the Bronx when we had to go somewhere. Cheyenne hugged my neck like we had been friends for years. "I'm so happy you can come with us!" she whispered. It was strange to me, but I went with it. In my mind, if she liked me, her father would like me too. I had already decided that I loved him.

"What time y'all coming back?" Carlene asked, this time with attitude.

"It ain't gonna be that long. Just enough time for them to ride, play some games, and grab some grub. I gotta stop home and get Desi and Li'l Kev first. We do things as a family. You feel me?" Big K replied, like he was trying to send a message to Carlene.

There were no more words exchanged. Big K pulled off. I watched from the back window as Carlene stared after the Jeep car. I was silently praying that going to the rides would be worth whatever Carlene was going to do when I got back.

Cheyenne had been right. Her house was a real house. Her father had to use a little card to get into big black gates. The gates led to a hidden neighborhood with rows and rows of real houses. The houses all stood alone, not connected, like the buildings I was used to living in. There were grassy lawns out front with little brick structures around them. There were flowerbeds with yellow, red, pink, and purple flowers in them.

Big K turned the car into a driveway in front of a big pale brick house. There were tall green curved, spiral, and round bushes in front. Flowers surrounded the front walkway, too.

"C'mon, Kelsi!" Cheyenne said excitedly. "This is my house!"

I followed her out of the car in wide-eyed amazement. She ran up the tan brick steps that led to the beautiful beveled-glass front door. She twisted the gold doorknob and bounded inside. "Let's go to my room until they get ready!" Cheyenne instructed, waving me on to follow her.

I was moving slow, taking it all in. We walked through a grand foyer adorned with beautiful gold-framed pictures of Big K, Cheyenne, a little boy, and a real pretty lady. The house smelled like I would picture a home to smell in my fantasies—like rose petals and sweet candy.

"Cheyenne!" I heard a woman's voice call out.

That snapped me out of my reverie. Cheyenne was already on the steps heading to her room. She turned around and sucked her teeth.

"You took too long," Cheyenne whispered. "C'mon, now we have to go see my mother before we go to my room," she huffed, grabbing my hand and dragging me farther into the beautiful house.

"How are you going to try to go upstairs without introducing me to your company? How rude." A woman's voice filtered down the long hallway we were walking through.

I was busy looking up at the crystal chandeliers that lined the hallway while Cheyenne led me like a blind person through the maze that was her house.

"Mommy, this is my new friend Kelsi," Cheyenne announced.

I could feel my mouth hanging open, but I couldn't close it.

The woman walked toward me with a bright, gleaming white smile. "Ohh, you're very pretty, Kelsi. It's nice to meet you. I'm Ms. Desiree," the woman said, sticking out a beautifully manicured hand.

I smiled and shook her hand. She was the color of the Disney cartoon character Pocahontas. She was beautiful like a Native American, too, with slanted eyes, but not so slanted you would mistake her for an Asian. Her hair was long and dark, and lay on her left shoulder in soft, coiled tendrils. She had the most perfect mouth. Her lips weren't big and greasy like Carlene's; instead, Ms. Desiree had a small, heart-shaped mouth with a light tint of lip gloss on them. She wore a white tennis dress; her long, slender legs looked like she really played tennis for a living.

Cheyenne looked like the spitting image of Ms. Desiree. My heart raced as I touched her hand. I was already wishing that the beautiful woman was my mother instead of Carlene.

"That's Peaches' daughter," Big K's voice boomed from behind us. I turned around and took him in entirely. Big K was tall with strong arms. His shoulders were square, but not too big. I couldn't stop staring at his eyes. I had never seen a man with kinder eyes than his. He looked at his wife with such love. My heart was racing and I felt like I would throw up.

"Peaches . . . mmm, hmmm," Ms. Desiree said, looking back at me.

It seemed like they were speaking some secret language about Carlene, and I could tell from their silent signals it wasn't good. I wanted to run away and tell Ms. Desiree that I wasn't Carlene's daughter, that I belonged to my Nana, but I stood my ground.

"Either way, she's a cutie pie and you-know-who is all sold on this one," Ms. Desiree said, tilting her head toward Cheyenne. "Cheyenne, we're about to go, so why don't you and Kelsi go take a quick shower and change.

You have new stuff you can give her to wear . . . maybe matching but in different colors," Ms. Desiree said in an overly cheery voice. Again, she was sending some sort of silent-language signal to her daughter.

"I already took a shower today," Cheyenne pouted with her eyebrows crunched up. Her mother smiled and tilted her head again. I caught it. Obviously Cheyenne did too. Cheyenne immediately changed her facial expression.

"O-kaay," Cheyenne droned. "C'mon, Kelsi, I want to show you my room. Plus, we have to wash up and change before we get to go to the rides," Cheyenne told me.

I didn't fully understand it then, but as I got older I figured it out. There was no way the Turner family was going to take me out with them, looking the way that I did in my dirty play clothes. They had standards to uphold.

Cheyenne's bedroom was any little girl's dream. She had Pepto Bismol pink walls with white trimmings. She had a queen-sized bed with four long white posts and a pink canopy connecting them. She had a plush pink, white, and purple Barbie bedspread. Her curtains were Barbie and so was the throw rug on the floor. There was a tall dresser with crystal knobs and a grand standing floor mirror with beautiful white trimming. It was like something from a queen's castle.

"Let's find matching outfits like my mother said," Cheyenne said, stepping over to her double-door closet.

I couldn't even speak. I was too busy feeling the tornado swirl of emotions surging in my head. I felt jealous, inferior, happy to be there, sad to be there. I wished I was back with Nana, but that I could still be friends with Cheyenne. It was so much to think about. All I wanted to do at that point was lie down on that pink carpet and ball up into a knot.

When Cheyenne pulled back the doors of her closet, a lump the size of a handball formed in my throat. I had never seen anything like it, except on TV. Cheyenne had rows and rows of clothes—dresses, jeans, skirts, shorts, blouses, and T-shirts, all coordinated and hanging by color and style. She had stacks of shoe and sneaker boxes. There was a long hanging thingy with plastic shelves containing colorful headbands, pocketbooks, bracelets, and everything girls love inside. It didn't even seem to faze Cheyenne. Having so much seemed to be blah, blah, blah to her.

"Okay . . . my mother said to find stuff with tags. So here is four outfits. If you like them, you can have them. I don't even want them. I never wore none of it, so they are yours to keep," Cheyenne said with ease, tossing the color-coordinated outfits onto the bed.

I was blinking rapidly. It was like Cheyenne's closet was a store and I was on a free shopping spree. Even when I was with Nana, I never had it like that. There was so many skirts, dresses, and jeans in a rainbow of colors. Outside of the closet was the same.

Cheyenne had two huge Barbie Dreamhouses in either corner of her room. She had shelves on her walls with rows and rows of Barbie dolls all dressed in beautiful dresses. She had so many stuffed animals it was a like a jungle and a zoo in her room. She had a shelf filled with every board game you could imagine. A bookshelf filled with all types of books. Her dresser had a glass tray on it that held at least ten pretty crystal bottles of perfume. I walked over to it. Cheyenne had gold rings, chains, and earrings all laid nicely on her dresser as well.

My heart was racing and I didn't even know why. I picked up a thick, shiny gold necklace with XOXOs made out of the gold. "You like that? It's called an X and O link. My daddy gave it to me for my birthday. You know what Xs and Os mean?" Cheyenne said and asked all in one breath.

I quickly put the chain back down on the dresser. I shook my head no.

"For real? You don't know that Xs and Os means kisses and hugs? When Daddy gave me that chain he said he was the first man to every shower me with hugs and kisses," Cheyenne recalled dreamily.

I was suddenly aware that my lips were hanging open. This little girl had the world. I had nothing. I silently wondered who would be the first man to shower me with hugs and kisses. I scanned Cheyenne's room one more time to take it all in.

"Is your family rich or something?" I finally asked, my throat so dry the words hurt coming out.

Cheyenne stopped moving in and out of her closet and turned her full attention toward me. She smiled the same pretty, carefree smile she always put on her face. It was so effortless for her to smile. I remembered feeling effortlessly happy like that when I was with Nana. What a difference a few days had made.

"No, silly. My daddy works. He said we ain't rich because rich people don't have to work. One day he is gonna get rich and then me and my brother won't have to work when we grow up," Cheyenne explained as she continued to toss pretty items of clothing onto the bed. What she said made sense to me; rich people didn't work. But, her family still seemed rich to me.

Cheyenne and I both put on a pair of brand new jean shorts: hers was acid washed and mine were dark blue. She put on a purple T-shirt with a puffy rainbow on the front and I put on a pink one with a puffy heart on the front. Ms. Desiree did our hair to match, in six pony-tails each, with pretty bubbles and barrettes. Cheyenne gave me a brand new pair of high-top Reeboks, and although they hurt my feet a little bit I didn't dare say anything because I wanted them so badly.

We all went to the rides at Coney Island that day. Big K spared no expense. He carried a knot of money in his pocket, which he had no problem peeling from. We rode every ride twice. We played every game and had arms full of stuffed animals after. We had cotton candy, Nathan's franks, shrimp, soda, and huge swirly colored lollipops.

Ms. Desiree and Big K danced in front of the Himalaya ride while Cheyenne and I rode it forward and backward. I couldn't stop watching them. It was my first time witnessing love between a man and a woman. Big K held Ms. Desiree by the waist and hugged her from the back. He kissed her gently on her neck and acted like she was the only person there even though there were hundreds of people around. They picked Li'l Kevin up out of the stroller and held him between them, showering him with kisses. It was like I was watching a show on TV. The Turners were the perfect family.

When Cheyenne and I were done riding, we ran to them.

"Y'all enjoyed that?" Big K asked with his warm smile.

We both chimed, "Yes!" in unison.

As we walked around the rides, Big K held my hand on one side and Cheyenne's on the other side. He called us his girls the entire night. Each time he did, I got a funny feeling inside. I immediately loved them all. Each one of the Turners had touched me in a different way. I'd gotten so lost in being a part of their family that I had altogether forgotten that I had to return to the hellhole where I now lived. When Big K pulled his

Jeep car (which I learned was called a Range Rover) up to Carlene's building, my stomach immediately knotted up.

"You wanna go with me to walk her upstairs, Chey?" Big K asked Cheyenne.

She looked like she was about to cry. I was biting my jaw inside to keep my own tears inside. Cheyenne and I moved slow as molasses through a straw getting out of that car that night.

"Don't forget your clothes," Cheyenne said sadly. She grabbed a big bag of clothes and shoes she had picked out of her closet for me.

I held on to the biggest stuffed animal that Big K had won for me.

"Stop acting all sad. There's always tomorrow and the next day. It ain't the end of the world," Big K told us as he took an armful of my stuff from the rides to carry.

As soon as we all exited the elevator I felt flush with shame. The hallway stunk like burning hair and cat shit. Of course, there was a pile of garbage on the floor in front of the incinerator shoot.

Big K walked strong and confidently like the stench and dirt didn't faze him. I didn't have to lead him to Carlene's apartment either. He knew exactly where it was. Big K used the knocker and banged on the door like he was the police.

God, please don't let Carlene answer. God, please don't let Took answer. God, please let them be gone so I have to go home with Big K. I chanted prayers inside my head.

Big K banged again. This time he screamed out, "Peaches! Took!" Finally, the door opened a crack. The odor of rotting garbage mixed with bad fish wafted out of the apartment and shot straight up my nose.

I knew Cheyenne and Big K could smell it if I could. I looked at Cheyenne but she was just looking at the floor.

"Yo, Peaches, open the damn door all the way," Big K demanded.

Carlene opened the door a little bit wider.

"I'm bringing your shorty back," Big K said, peering inside.

Carlene had turned off the lights, I guessed so he couldn't see inside.

"Thanks for taking her," Carlene said dryly.

Big K looked at me pitifully like he was taking a stray dog to an animal shelter to be put to sleep.

"I'm gonna come see you tomorrow," Cheyenne said sadly.

I just nodded and stepped toward Carlene.

Big K handed her the bags and all of my goodies. I stepped inside of my reality and moved around in the darkness.

"Yo, Peaches. Clean up this fucking place. You got a real good kid right there. She don't deserve to live like this. What you do as an adult is ya business, but a kid don't ask to be here. I'ma be checkin' on that little one so you better do the right thing by her. Clean up this rat trap before I do something about it," Big K lectured and warned at the same time.

Carlene was shifting her weight from one foot to the next like she had to pee.

I felt that funny feeling inside again. It couldn't be anything other than my immediate love for Big K growing. I don't know which grew faster: my love for Big K or my hatred for Carlene.

Chapter 5

Big K kept the promise he made the day he took me to the rides. Over the next year, he checked up on me daily. He kept Carlene in line, which made life a little bit easier for me. Between Big K and the welfare caseworker, Carlene had no choice but to put me in school that September. I had turned nine years old the month before school started.

Cheyenne and I were definitely best friends by then. We never wanted to be separated. We shared everything. She didn't judge me based on Carlene. I stopped feeling jealous of her life and just settled for being happy to be a part of it.

During the school year Cheyenne and I got to see each other every day, even though she went to private school and I went to public school. I spent a lot of time with the Turners on the weekends, too, because Carlene and Took were too scared of Big K to protest.

The living conditions at Carlene's had only changed for a few weeks after Big K threatened Carlene, but I did what I could around the house to make myself feel better about living there. Big K also bought me a daybed with a clean, comfortable mattress and a pretty Barbie comforter set with matching pillows. I loved him more and more each day. I would secretly write him love letters, but then I'd use Carlene's lighters to burn them before anyone could read them.

It was June of 1996 when everything in everyone's lives went haywire. It was the first day of summer break from school. I remember like it was yesterday. An unusual heat wave had swept through Brooklyn. The weatherman said the heat index made it feel like 102 degrees outside. He warned old people and children to stay indoors. It was so hot the old oscillating fan Carlene had in my room did nothing but blow hot air. I wasn't allowed in her room where the air conditioner was. The heat kept me from sleeping. I had gotten up for the fifth time that night to stick my head in the cool breeze of the freezer door. It was the only little bit of relief I could get. As I dragged my feet and sweaty body back to my bed, I was startled by something moving in the dark. I jumped so hard a little bit of pee came out into my panties.

Took was sitting on the end of my bed. His pale, naked chest seemed to glow almost neon in the little bit of light that was coming in the window from the streetlight outside. I let out a long sigh.

"What are you doing on my bed?" I grumbled sassily. I hated Took and he hated me. We never had a good word to say to one another over the year I'd been there. He always let me know that I was a mouth to feed and a burden on him since Carlene didn't do shit around the house. I used to pray every day for him to leave the house. Most days he did, unless he was in the kitchen cooking something that required baking soda, boric acid, and sometimes he sprayed something real stink on his concoctions.

"Get off my bed. I'm sleepy and I wanna lie back down," I snapped.

Took patted the bed next to where he was sitting with his nasty white hand. I squinted my eyes in the darkness. He couldn't be talking to me!

"Come over here and don't make no noise," he whispered, sounding like a snake hissing. His command sounded like a foreign language to me.

I folded my face into a frown and folded my arms indignantly. *Is he out of his mind!*

"What? You stupid?! You better get off my bed right now! I'm not coming on the bed until you get out!" I said, raising my voice this time.

Took jumped to his feet. I jumped too because his sudden motion had scared the shit out of me.

Before I could move, run, put my hands up in defense, or anything, Took barreled into me like a bulldozer. I fell backward. My ass hit the tiled floor so hard my butt cheeks ached.

"I said to come here, bitch," he growled almost inaudibly. He grabbed me roughly by my arm and that was when I saw that he had a gun in his other hand.

A lot of pee escaped my bladder this time. Enough to wet my panties all the way through. My chest moved up and down like I'd just run a relay race. I couldn't catch my breath as I remembered that gun from the day he hit Nana with it.

"What'chu doin'?" I huffed, trying in vain to loosen his painful grip on my arm.

Took threw me on the bed roughly. He was naked except for a pair of boxers. He was so close to me I could see that the nappy, coiled hairs on his chest were the same ugly shade of brassy blond as the hair on his head. His nipples were pink and they stuck straight out like devil's eyes.

"Shut the fuck up," he huffed in my face. His mouth reeked of whatever he had been drinking. His entire body stunk like liquor, sweat, and the stuff inside of firecrackers.

"Ahh!" I started to scream, but it was short-lived. I felt a sharp pain across my face that sent the scream tumbling right back down my throat. My eyes shut involuntarily and little streaks of silver lights swirled around on the inside of my eyelids.

Took slapped me again, this time on the other side of my face. Something popped at the back of my neck and a sharp, stabbing pain shot down my spine. My arms and legs felt weak. My chest ignited with fire. *I'm gonna kill you! I'm gonna kill you!* a voice inside my head screamed over and over. No words came to my mouth. I felt buried alive because my brain was saying *run, fight, scream,* but my body would not listen.

Suddenly, I couldn't breathe. The smell of Took's sweaty hand filled my nostrils as he clamped it down roughly over my nose and mouth. I finally tried to kick my legs but his weight was too much. I was pinned down. Pain swirled through my head so badly I could barely open my eyes.

"If you fight it's gon' hurt. Relax and it won't hurt much," I heard Took's muffled words hot against my ear. He used one of his muscular legs to force mine apart. He was fumbling under me.

I felt his rough hand moving over my privacy. Nana had said to never let anyone touch me there. I couldn't fight Took. I couldn't move. I couldn't breathe. I heard Took spit then I felt his wet hand moving over me down there. He was fumbling again. I tried to moan.

"I got this gun right next to your head. If you make noise I'ma use it," Took panted into my ear.

I could feel dribble coming out of the sides of my mouth under his hand. There was more movement. Next, I felt something slimy up against my left thigh.

Took was grunting hard now. He was shaking like his nerves were bad. I could tell the slimy thing was in his hand now. He let out a sigh. After that he was pushing. His chest hairs were stabbing me in the face, like how the Brillo stabbed my hands when I washed dirty pots.

Took let out a long sigh. Then more animal grunts.

The sudden pain that filled my torso, abdomen, butt, and legs was indescribable. The best I can recall it now is that it was like someone sticking a thick, fire-lit tree branch up my ass and twisting it over and over again.

The grunts coming from Took was what I remember the most. He was like a horse after it had run a race, or a bull seeing red before it attacked.

I knew then that what was happening would change my life forever. I also knew that I would never allow it to happen again. I wanted Took to die. The last thing I remember was praying for God to strike him down.

I had to have passed out from the pain. The next thing I remember was waking up to Carlene's usual rant.

"Listen, bitch, if you think you gonna sleep and play with Cheyenne all day this summer that shit ain't fucking happening. Get yo' ass up and clean that kitchen and make something to eat," Carlene was going on.

It hurt to even open my eyes. My stomach felt like someone had cut me open and gutted me from the inside out. The heat was so thick in the room that my body fluids had my sheets completely soaked. When I finally opened my eyes, Carlene's naked ass came into focus. I was used to that by then.

Carlene had no motherly boundaries at all. Sometimes she didn't even close her door and I could hear her moaning and groaning with Took. Cheyenne told me those noises were from sex. She learned that from a fast girl on our block named Nasty Neecy.

"What the fuck happened to you? You sick or something?" Carlene rasped, terror etched on her face. "Where is you bleeding from?" she screeched, yanking the sheet all the way off the bed.

There was blood on my nightgown and I didn't even know it. I couldn't unfold my legs. I couldn't blink. I couldn't swallow. I couldn't lift my head. Everything I attempted to do sent butcher-knife stabs of pain through my entire body.

"Get up and go to the bathroom!" Carlene screamed, grabbing my arm roughly. She dragged me off the bed until my feet hit the floor. My knees buckled and I went down. I hit my chin on the cold tile floor. More pain swirled at the backs of my eyes.

"I know what you did now! I can see it and smell it on you! You fucked around with my fucking man didn't you? Oh, bitch! I told you I wasn't tolerating that shit! Get the fuck in the bathroom and clean yourself up! Now!" Carlene boomed.

Tears spilled out of my eyes. I think her accusatory words hurt worse than Took forcing his dick into my virginal opening. With each step toward the bathroom a fire raged under my navel.

"Wash every bit of him off of you! I knew you was gonna do this shit! I knew it! I guess your Nana ain't teach you no different than she taught me!" Carlene screamed some more. This time her voice cracked like she was about to cry.

I finally made it into the bathroom, and with what little strength I had I slammed the door. I plopped down on the toilet, but that made the fire between my legs rage even worse. I turned on the water in the tub.

When I sat down in the warm water, with the pain I felt I knew I would pass out again. I fought through it. "Agggghhhhh!" I screamed over and over again.

That fireball of anger in my chest had grown so big it exploded out of my mouth now. I had finally reached my breaking point in that house.

Cheyenne knew right away something was wrong after she knocked on our door and I said I didn't want to go outside to play with her. I would've never turned down an opportunity to see my best friend in the whole wide world. We had been waiting the entire school year for summertime so that we could spend every hour of every day together until we had to go to bed at night.

"I don't wanna go outside. I don't wanna go to your house either. Just leave me alone," I had snapped at her.

Cheyenne had walked away that day, shoulders slumped, on the brink of tears. I had been so mean to her. I felt horrible afterward, but I couldn't take a chance of her finding out.

Carlene had threatened me every which way that if I told anyone what Took had done to me, I would be dead. Carlene said she would take me away from Carey Gardens for good and I would never see the Turners again. The thought of not seeing Cheyenne, Big K, Ms. Desiree, and Li'l Kevin made me change my mind about going to the police on Took.

Even then I knew that a grown man fucking a nine-year-old was against the law. I mean, back then, I had reasoned with myself that even if it wasn't against the police law, it damn sure was against God's law.

For two days after what Took did to me, I didn't eat. I didn't drink. I didn't sleep. I didn't talk. I didn't cry. I didn't feel. I was just numb. I hardly moved from my bed. When I peed it hurt so bad that I would hold it until I just couldn't take it any longer.

Carlene would come into the front room where I slept and look at me like I was the lowest scum of the earth. She would curse, mumble, and then crawl her ass back into her room. She didn't go outside either. I could swear that she had aged ten years in those two days. Her face started looking sunken in and the skin on her neck looked loose like a turkey's neck. Her body didn't seem as filled out as it had; in fact, her reindeer ass was barely like a squirrel ass now. Her usually beautifully painted nails were chipped, broken, and brittle looking. Even Carlene's hair wasn't thick and shiny like it had been. I don't know if I hadn't noticed her losing all of her weight over the year I'd been there because I was too busy spending time with the Turners or what, but those two days I stayed in the house, seeing her as much as I did, I noticed that there was a drastic change from the Carlene who had brought me there and the Carlene I was looking at now. Carlene was boney, drawn up, and looked older than Ms. Lula now.

Took came and went like he usually did. Whenever I heard him put his keys into the door to come in, I would snap my eyes shut and pretend to be asleep. He didn't speak or stop in my room. He didn't use the kitchen to cook his stuff either. When my eyes were closed, I envisioned sixty different ways I could torture Took while he was awake.

On the fifth day of my isolation, Carlene finally left the house. With not so much as a word to me, she click-clacked her heels down the hallway and out of the apartment door. I knew Carlene was all dressed up in her saggy dress with no place to go. She hadn't even asked me if I was hungry or needed anything before she slammed out of the apartment. I was used to her neglect anyway. An hour after Carlene left, the door was rattling with someone knocking on it.

"Kelsi, I know you in there!" Cheyenne wasn't taking no for an answer. She had come to the door with her father.

When I pulled back the door, my heart felt like it jumped up into my throat.

"Ay, little lady, what's going on with you?" Big K asked, his infectious smile gleaming as usual. Cheyenne stood behind her father with her arms folded, dressed nicely, looking color coordinated, clean, neat, and beautiful as ever.

"Why you been giving my princess the cold shoulder and not coming outside or to the house? Did she do something to you?"

"I'm sick," I lied, dropping my eyes to the floor. I hated lying to Big K. I was not prepared to tell anyone the truth about what had happened. How would I have even formulated the words at the time? What would I have said to Big K, "Oh, I'm just sick because Took rammed his dick into me over and over again until I was bleeding and now I can hardly walk"?

"Oh yeah? What kind of sick? Let me take you to the doctor if you're sick," Big K said, as he looked beyond me into the apartment. I knew he must've been thinking where the fuck was Peaches. I wasn't exactly of age to be home alone.

"No . . . um . . . no! I don't need no doctor. I have medicine and stuff here," I lied again, this time a little more frantically.

There was no way I could let Big K take me to a doctor. I knew by the way I had to pee and make number two that there was something definitely wrong down there and a doctor would tell right away. They would ask me what happened and I would have to tell on Took. If I did that Carlene would take me away.

"Let me come inside and see what kind of medicine you got," Big K said. It wasn't a question or a real hard demand, but I knew he wasn't going to take no for an answer, especially from me.

I stepped aside and Big K and Cheyenne stepped inside. He looked around curiously. His usually kind eyes were now serious, dark, and scanning. He knew something was not right.

"Listen, little lady, why don't you throw on some clothes. I'll take you to the house and you can get dressed over there. We're going to your favorite place today," Big K said in the most comforting voice he could muster while trying to hide his obvious anger.

I knew he was fighting against it because his fists were balled so tight the tops of his hands were turning white and he was biting down hard on his bottom lip. There was no sense in saying no to his request. I knew by the way Big K started pacing up and down that he was not going to leave me there. I looked at the tears rimming Cheyenne's eyes as I limped around trying to get dressed. Even she could tell that I was never going to be the same.

Chapter 6

I ended up at Coney Island Hospital. As much as I screamed and begged them not to take me to the emergency room, Ms. Desiree and Big K took me anyway. The end result was I had to have my perineum stitched. That, as I learned at barely nine years old, is the area between a girl's vagina and rectum. I stayed overnight with Ms. Desiree right by my side. Cheyenne didn't really understand what was going on; her mother had just told her that I had gotten sick and needed to get better.

Ms. Desiree had cried and cried for me. "She's just a baby! What kind of monster would do that to a baby?" Ms. Desiree whispered to Big K through tears.

"Trust, it ain't gonna be left at this. Any motherfucker that would do this to a kid don't deserve to live," Big K said.

They thought I was asleep. Listening to them talk, I knew they really loved me.

Big K picked us up from the hospital the next day with Cheyenne and Li'l Kevin. None of us spoke on the way to their house. I felt too ashamed to speak. Ms. Desiree cried every time she tried to open her mouth to speak. Big K huffed, puffed, and cussed so he couldn't even speak. Cheyenne sensed that there was something terribly wrong so she just didn't speak. Li'l Kevin was only two years old so he could barely speak.

When we got to the Turners, Cheyenne and I went up to her room.

"Surprise!" she yelled as she pushed open the door.

My eyes lit up. The room was filled with balloons, teddy bears, and flowers.

"Daddy got all of these for you." Cheyenne beamed.

I inched into the room slowly, the stitches still making me walk funny. The doctor said they would dissolve on their own. I stood in the middle of the floor like a lost child. Hot tears ran a race down my cheeks.

"You don't like them?" Cheyenne asked, moving toward me.

"No, I love them. I love them a lot. I love all of y'all a lot," I cried, unable to control the floodgate of tears that had opened up. Cheyenne hugged me tight.

"We love you too, Kelsi, and we ain't never going to let nothing bad happen to you again," Cheyenne promised.

For the first time in my life, I believed someone's promise. Even Nana hadn't kept her promise to keep me in the Bronx with her. This time, something in my heart told me the promise was real.

Cheyenne was the one who told me about what had happened to Took. He had been beaten so badly, she said, his entire face was unrecognizable. All of his fingers had been broken and every tooth in his mouth had been knocked out. She told me that she'd also heard that whoever had beat up on Took had also shoved three broomsticks taped together up his butthole. Cheyenne had been the first one to start laughing when she said, "Up his butthole," and then I burst out laughing right behind her.

I laughed so hard at the end I was crying. I didn't feel sorry for Took, not one bit. But, for the weeks I stayed at the Turners, I often wondered about Carlene. Took was always the one who had made sure Carlene had stuff, like food, the medicine she took to keep from being sick every morning, and just basic things like soap to wash her ass. I could just imagine what Carlene was doing to stay afloat while Took was gone. After a few days of worrying about her I stopped thinking about her entirely. Out of sight, out of mind, I guess.

It was almost the end of summer before my body fully healed. I was finally well enough to go back outside with Cheyenne. Although every day I thought about what had happened to me, I put on a happy face and tried to be a normal nine-year-old.

Cheyenne and I were sisters in every sense of the word. Ms. Desiree treated us as equals, even when we got in trouble for giggling all night when we were supposed to be asleep. We would ride with Big K over to the projects every day. While he "worked," we would play double Dutch, hopscotch, Hula Hoops, Red light/ Green light, steal the bacon, and skelly.

Cheyenne and I were called Bobbsey Twins. We dressed alike. We acted alike. We liked the same foods. The Turners had essentially adopted me.

Most days, when Big K finished up his work at the building, he would take us to the rides. Sometimes, he would get finished early, go pick up Ms. Desiree and Li'l Kevin, and we'd all go to the movies and dinner in Sheepshead Bay. Those nights became my favorites because I got to watch how Big K loved all over Ms. Desiree. How he opened doors for her, held her hand, kissed her, and smiled at her like she was the only woman alive. I would make pretend I was Ms. Desiree and Big K was my husband instead of hers.

I could never forget the day when life as we all knew it came to a screeching halt. It was a blazing hot August day in 1996. I had just turned ten the week before; that is how I always remember it so clearly. Cheyenne and I were about to jump out of Big K's Range Rover with our matching Guess jean skirt outfits, Hula Hoops, and two bags filled with candy.

"Stay right in front, little ladies. I'm not staying that long today," Big K said as he parked up the Range Rover.

"Okay, Daddy," Cheyenne said as we giggled out of the door.

"Okay, Daddy," I whispered after her.

We started laughing harder. Big K parked and got out. I remember watching him walk with his distinct bop toward the building. I always watched him go in and come out with his money.

That day, as he walked closer to the door, something seemed different to me. There weren't half as many people outside like usual. Lula was even missing from her bench. Cheyenne was gabbing to me about something; she was nowhere near as observant as I was. I guess being raped had done away with the little carefree kid in me. I noticed everything and I was always watching people.

"Where is everybody?" Cheyenne finally asked, stopping for a minute.

I swung my head from left to right. My face was serious, my eyes scanning. I opened my mouth to respond but never got a chance. I had my eye on Big K's back and then boom!

It happened in slow motion. Big K yanked on the door handle of the building and as soon as he pulled it back we heard it. It was like thunder and lightning had struck. The rumble of feet came from everywhere, like a herd of wild elephants was trampling through the block.

"Police! Police! Don't move! Put your fucking hands on your head!" were some of the things we heard. Cheyenne whipped her head around and saw what I was already watching.

"Daddy!" Cheyenne screeched at the top of her lungs.

I grabbed her and pulled her down to the ground.

Loud flash bangs erupted around us. I could feel my heart hammering against my chest bone.

"Daddy!" she screamed again.

I held on to Cheyenne with all of my might to keep her from running toward Big K and the danger.

Police with long guns, short guns, helmets, and black bulletproof vests surrounded him. We watched in horror as they threw Big K to the ground face first.

I saw the blood explode from his face and nose. That was when I started screaming too.

"Big K! No! You can't take him! He didn't do nothing wrong!" I let out a guttural scream. "Don't hurt him!" Before I knew it I was on my feet racing toward Big K, Cheyenne hot on my heels.

I was scooped off my feet like a little ragdoll.

"Hey! Get out of here, little girl, before you get hurt!" a police officer chastised. Cheyenne was right next to me, flailing wildly as another officer held her. She was sobbing uncontrollably.

"Let her go. Let her go," I screeched.

Cheyenne was thrown right down next to me. We hugged each other tightly up against a fence and watched as Big K was hoisted up off the ground in handcuffs.

"It's gonna be all right, little ladies," was the last thing Big K said to us before he was thrown into the back of a waiting black van.

Sixteen other guys we knew from my building were also arrested and carted off like animals.

Cheyenne and me cried for two days straight after. I think Ms. Desiree cried for months, maybe years after. The final word about Big K's arrest was that Took had snitched on Big K and taken down his entire empire just like that. It was all because of me and the beating Took had been given by Big K and his workers.

Big K had risked everything—all because he had been protecting me.

"There are very few women who would love someone else's child exactly as they loved their own. But then again, there are very few women like my mother." —Cheyenne Turner to the prosecutor during their initial meeting.

Chapter 7

Cheyenne Turner

August 2010

"The court has heard from the defendant. It is now time for the court to hear from the victim's family," Judge Graves rasped. She had taken off her glasses and was pinching the bridge of her nose as she spoke.

I couldn't tell if she wanted to cry or what. I guessed Kelsi's story had touched the judge in some way. I hadn't thought about the years before my father got locked up in so long I found myself hanging on Kelsi's every word. Those were the best days of my life. I found myself tearing up as I recalled how much I loved Kelsi back then. She was truly like my sister then. I shook my head left to right trying to get my focus back. I had a very important job to do. A very important story to tell.

I tapped my brother on his shoulder. "Kev, it's our turn to talk," I said to him.

His fists were balled tightly, his mouth was pursed, and he rocked his legs furiously. I knew what that meant, but I still wanted to give him the chance to say something if he wanted.

"C'mon," I whispered harshly, touching his shoulder.

He wouldn't move. Getting a defiant teenage boy who had lost his mother to speak in front of throngs of people wasn't a battle I was prepared to fight in front of all of those people. Fuck it. I had to do what I had to do, with or without Kev.

I looked up at the judge with a simple, nervous grin on my face. I guessed it was all on me to speak on behalf of our family. As I inched out of the row where we sat, I suddenly felt the acids in my stomach burning. My dress suddenly seemed too tight and sweat lined up like ready soldiers at my hairline. It seemed like it took me forever to walk up to the little wooden podium where the microphone stood. The courtroom was eerily quiet although it was packed. I filled my cheeks with air, an attempt at staving off the wave of nausea that swept over me. I felt Kelsi staring at me, but I couldn't bring myself to look at her. She'd taught me a huge life lesson—there was nothing deeper than love turned to hate. I had loved her. I had loved Kelsi so deeply that now I hated her enough to kill her with my bare hands.

"Ms. Turner, are you all right?" Judge Graves asked, her eyes going low at the sides.

I cleared my dry throat, closed my eyes, pictured my mother's face, and shook my head up and down. I took a quick glance over at Kelsi then. She quickly averted her eyes from me. I knew she'd never be able to hold eye contact with me. She was a coward in my book.

"Yes, Judge. I . . . I'm fine," I spoke softly. I realized I needed to adjust the microphone so I attempted to move it. It made an ear-piercing screech. I jumped back.

The court officer raced over and fixed it. He put the microphone directly in front of my mouth. I used the back of my hand to wipe sweat from my forehead.

"Okay, Ms. Turner. When you're ready to speak you can address the defendant and this court. Take your time," Judge Graves told me. I nodded and closed my eyes.

"My name is Cheyenne Turner. The person everyone keeps referring to as the victim is my mother. Her name is Desiree Turner and she didn't deserve to die. She didn't deserve to be slaughtered for nothing. There are very few people in the world like my mother. I want to tell you all about the years leading up to her senseless murder because Kelsi told you hers, but we also have a story," I said, hearing my voice echoing off the courtroom walls. I was sure everyone was holding their breath waiting for my next sentence.

Chapter 8

That day in August 1996 that the police took my father; they also took our house. They trashed it before they took it though.

My mother explained to me that it was called "asset forfeiture." She said it wasn't the regular police; instead, it was the feds who had executed a search and seizure warrant on our place that day.

They had destroyed my room and almost every room in the house. They took all of our jewelry, clothes, fur coats, artwork, couches, and beds. They dumped out our cabinets, closets, and garage. They pulled up the floorboards and the carpets. I never understood what they were looking for when they took sledgehammers to the walls though. *Who hides things inside of walls?* I remember thinking when I saw the huge holes.

At nine years old, my family and my life had been devastated. There was no fixing it. Without my father, we had nothing but the few clothes my mother could salvage.

My mother had a small stash of cash that the police hadn't gotten to and someone from across town had brought her some money they'd owed to my father. None of that lasted long. We ended up moving to the sixth floor in Kelsi's building.

"Back to the projects from where we came," my mother had said the day we moved. She told me it had been the apartment my father had grown up in when he was a little boy. He'd kept it after his mother died. I had always assumed that we always lived in Sea Gate. I never knew we had ever lived in the projects when I was a baby.

At first, it was exciting living in the same building as my best friend. It was easy for Kelsi to just come upstairs to our house to play, eat, and do all of the things we liked to do. After a while, I realized that living in the building where my father used to work was terrible. I had never seen a roach in my life until we moved there. There were so many roaches Li'l Kev refused to walk on the floors in our apartment. He would scream until my mother or me picked him up and carried him everywhere. The constant noises in the hallway all night kept me up since I was used to living on a quiet, tree-lined block in Sea Gate. Kelsi told me I would get used to the noises, but I never really did. I just got used to not getting much sleep.

By the time 1998 rolled around, I was eleven and Li'l Kev was four. Like a faucet turned off, just like that, my mother had finally stopped all of her crying over my father.

"Look! Look at what I did for us!" she exclaimed, throwing a stack of papers onto our small wooden kitchenette table.

I picked up the stack first. I crinkled my forehead and looked at her strangely.

"It's college! I got accepted to college. I'm going to school for nursing," my mother said excitedly.

My eyebrows arched on my face. "Wow, Mommy! That's great!" I said enthusiastically. In my mind, I selfishly wondered what was going to happen to Li'l Kev and me while my mother went to school.

"I have to make things better for us while your father is gone. I wasn't on the system all this time and I'm not going on it now," my mother said that day. Then, as if she could read my mind, she broke the news to me and Li'l Kev that we would have to stay with fat Ms. Lula at night while she went to work and school. Ms. Lula and her house stunk like corn chips and ass. We hated every time we had to go there. My mother was too determined to let our complaints deter her.

As much as we cried, my mother held her head up high, left us, and pursued a nursing career. When my mother had a break from school, she would pack us all up—me, Kelsi, and Li'l Kev—and we would all take the same long van ride upstate to see my father. My mother would sacrifice everything to make sure she visited my father. If it was visit day for my father, my mother didn't care if she missed school, work, or we missed school. There was nothing more important than going to see her husband.

I could never forget the first time we visited him. He had only been gone for a month and I was missing him like crazy. My mother had dressed us all in our best clothes. She wore a pretty yellow and orange sundress that brought out her complexion. She had accessorized the dress with gold bangles and a pair of tan espadrilles. Kelsi and I dressed alike, in bright sundresses—hers aqua green and mine fuchsia.

My father was still on Riker's Island at that time. I remember that the guards at the jail treated us like animals. We were searched like thieves. Li'l Kev's milk had to be poured out of his bottle and my mother's pocketbook was dumped out.

"This is just stupid! We not in jail here you know!" Kelsi had sassed to the guards.

That was one of the things I loved about my best friend: she never backed down from a fight or confrontation, even with adults. When the guards had brought my father out to see us that day, he had chains on his hands and feet. He sat on the opposite side of a broken down–looking table, and after one hug for each of us we weren't able to touch him again. In one month, my father had changed drastically to me. He just didn't look healthy. His skin was dry looking, his hair had grown out into a small afro, and he looked way older than he had the day he was arrested.

I remember thinking that my father was dying inside that place, that he would never make it out of there alive. I had cried for almost the entire visit. I hated seeing my father in that stupid orange jumpsuit, when I was used to seeing him in nice, crisp name-brand clothes.

Kelsi, on the other hand, was overjoyed to see him. She even tried to hog my father's conversation from my mother.

Li'l Kev refused to even look at my father that day. If my father tried to touch Li'l Kev he would scream at the top of his lungs. Finally my father relented.

"Wassup with my baby boy? He forgot his old man already?" my father said, his voice cracking like he was about to cry. I guess as young as he was, Li'l Kev sensed that it would just be best to cut his ties with my father right away.

Not me; I held on to the hopes that my father, Kevin "Big K" Turner, was going to win his appeals and be home with us in no time. At least, that was what my father told us he was "working on" every time we visited him after that.

It wasn't until 2003, when I was sixteen years old, that I finally stopped believing in my father's appeals story. Seven years of the same old story had turned me into a cynical, bitter teenager who didn't believe in shit.

My father had been transferred from Rikers Island to upstate New York, which signaled to me that he was going away for longer than we expected. I was old enough by then to figure out that my mother had no more money to pay lawyers and that my father's street influence and connections had dried up, so none of his former employees came up off any money to foot his appeals bills.

When I'd done my own silly form of research, I found out that my father had been sentenced under New York's Rockefeller drug laws, and no amount of appeals could reverse the draconian sentencing guidelines that came with those laws.

Kelsi was the only one who faithfully accompanied my mother to visit my father. My mother didn't take Li'l Kev anymore because he never spoke to my father and made the visits hard on everyone. I had stopped going as well. It had become too painful for me to see my father aging ten times faster than if he'd been home. Seeing him in shackles and handcuffs, helpless, useless, had also taken its toll on me emotionally. I had suddenly found myself real angry with my father. I guess years of watching my mother bust her ass to become a nurse, all while keeping food on the table and clothes on our backs, made me resent him for leaving us.

My mother would act like she didn't get the memo that I wasn't visiting him anymore. The night before each visit, she would still try to get me to change my mind.

"Y'all need to go to bed so we can get up and get to the vans early. I like to find seats in the front so I can be first in that line when we get up there," my mother said as she stood in my doorway, a warm smile spread on her tired face.

I hated seeing her so tired all of the time. She worked twelve-hour shifts four days a week as a nurse at Kings County Hospital. Then, she would use her days off to either shop for things for my father or visit my father. I didn't know how she did it. To me, there was loyalty and then there was stupidity.

"I'm not going. But, you already knew this since I didn't go the last three times y'all went," I told my mother flatly.

She let out a long sigh. Her face went dark. "Cheyenne, I know it hasn't been easy, but he is still your father. You know that he would've never left if he had his choice. He is powerless right now, but it is not his fault. Kevin would've given his life to be here for us," my mother replied, her tone stern but soft.

She had been telling my brother and me the same thing for years now. I was tired of her making excuses for my father. I could not understand the kind of love my mother had for my father. Even though she had worked herself to the bone and had to live in the filthy projects, she never showed one ounce of resentment toward him.

I turned my back and pulled my blanket up to my neck. I was done discussing the issue with her. If I ever laid eyes on my father again, it surely wouldn't be while he was behind prison walls. That was final.

"Have it your way, Cheyenne, but he loves you more than he loves his own life," my mother chastised.

I sucked my teeth, wishing she would just turn off my light and get out of my damn doorway.

"Well, Kelsi, if you're going with me, be up," I heard my mother say, her voice filled with defeat.

The door clicked closed. I finally relaxed. I heard Kelsi rustling with her blanket on the other bed in my small bedroom. She was rocking; I could tell from the sound the mattress made. Kelsi rocked when she was mad.

"You know what, Cheyenne . . . I wasn't going to say nothing to you, but you are a fucking spoiled brat!" Kelsi said through gritted teeth.

I could tell her teeth were clenched as she spoke. I knew her so well. I popped my eyes open in response to her words. "No, correction, I *was* a spoiled brat. Now I live in the projects with the roaches and rats and crackheads just like everybody else!" I snapped back. I didn't mean for it to come out like that, but it was too late; the words had already left my lips.

Kelsi jumped up and turned on the light. Her eyes were hooded over and her face was folded into a snarl. I could see hurt etched on her forehead like a mask. She was moving like a boxer ready to pounce.

"What the fuck is that supposed to mean? Like everybody else like who? Like me? Oh, you won't go visit your father because he got arrested and *you*, Princess Cheyenne, was reduced to living the projects like Kelsi the poor bitch, daughter of a crackhead who lives with roaches and rats? You are fucking disgusting, Cheyenne! Your father was so good to you when he was out on these fucking streets! So what? You lived in a *real* house and now you have to live in the projects! So what? You don't have enough clothes to throw away or give to the poor destitute daughter of a crackhead! Oh, woe is fucking me, Cheyenne! Why don't you remember all the things he *did* do for you while he was here! How he loved you like no man ever will! How he gave you everything and risked his freedom to do that! How he loved your mother and showed you how a real man is supposed to love you! Why don't you fucking love him and appreciate him like I do and thank God he is your father instead of wishing every day he was your father

like I do? You fucking disgust me! I'm going home!"
Kelsi ranted, pointing in my face with every word like
she wanted to slap the shit out of me.

My eyes were as wide as dinner plates and my mouth
hung open. I couldn't even respond to what Kelsi had
said. She slammed my bedroom door and left. My
shoulders slumped and my chest felt like a two-ton
elephant was sitting on it. The tears came hot and fast.
I couldn't have stopped them even if I wanted to.

That night was the first time Kelsi and I had had a
real disagreement in all of the years we'd been friends.
That night was also the first time I realized how much
Kelsi really loved my father.

Chapter 9

"So how does it feel to be turning twenty-one and graduating from college all at the same damn time?" Kelsi asked me excitedly as she flopped down on the other bed in my room, which over the years had become Kelsi's bed.

I tilted my head to the side and smiled at her as I removed the last big bobby pin from my doobie. "It feels like I can finally go legally get drunk after all my fucking hard work," I answered her, giggling, as I shook out my long, newly straightened locks of hair.

We both laughed.

"Shit, I know that's right. But, fuck that, I turned twenty-one in August and I been waiting to get drunk with your ass. I need a fucking drink like nobody's business," Kelsi said, following up with a long sigh. She was staring up at the ceiling. I knew she was telling the truth.

Kelsi had a lot to deal with. Kelsi was beautiful, but she didn't think so. She was a little chubby around her stomach, but she had big hips and a big butt. Her face was pretty to me, but she always hated the acne that left dark marks on her cheeks. Kelsi kept her hair in micro-braids so that she could pretend she had long hair. No matter what flaws she pointed out on herself, I always thought she was beautiful. She let dudes treat her any kind of way. She had had many black eyes, broken ribs, and trips to the hospital over the years from dudes putting their hands on her. They took advantage of the fact that Kelsi didn't have a father around. I knew Kelsi was looking for love and acceptance from a man, but she didn't think so. She thought she played the "game" so well and that she was always "playing niggas." From my vantage point, she was the one who always suffered in the end. All I could do was love her through the rough times as her best friend, so that's exactly what I did.

"I'm real proud of you, Cheyenne. I can't front. You always been smart, beautiful, and driven. You ain't let shit stop you from getting that piece of paper. Especially no niggas. I always looked up to you. You way stronger than me, shit. I ain't even get that li'l high school paper. You got the big dog paper . . . degrees and shit. I'm amazed by your strength. Even when shit got fucked up at home you still fought through it. I love you for that power. That power I wish I had," Kelsi said, interrupting the quiet that had settled around us.

I lowered my eyes to the floor. Something inside of me felt funny. I was happy she had said those things, but sad for her. Kelsi's words threatened to make me cry. I knew she was speaking from the heart. I also knew she wished she had listened to me all of the times I was preaching to her about finishing high school and going to college.

"Awww, c'mon, *chica,* don't be getting all sentimental on me," I joked, sniffling back the snot about to run out of my nose. "Real talk, Kel, I look up to you too. Not many people can deal with what you had to deal with and still be in one piece. I mean I had my mother there by my side this whole time; you had to fend for yourself and I really don't think I could ever be that strong. Pat yourself on the back too. You're a damn survivor, girlie," I said, changing my tone to serious.

Kelsi rolled up on the bed and sat Indian style. "Well thank you, Chey. That means a lot coming from you, boo. Now enough of the sappy shit," Kelsi replied, clapping her hands. "What's the plan now? Ms. Desi said you got into some med school all the way in Texas?" Kelsi asked.

I bit into my jaw. I wished my mother didn't have such a big mouth. I wanted to be the one to break the news to Kelsi. I knew the thought of me leaving Brooklyn wasn't going to be so easy for her to handle. I had no choice but to be honest with her now.

"Yeah, I did get into the University of Texas at Austin medical program. It's real hard to get in so I'm kinda proud I made the cut. But, I don't know what I'm gonna do yet. I'm scared to leave my mother. Especially with Li'l Kev running the streets now," I said solemnly.

My brother was only fourteen years old and was already trying to build a reputation in our neighborhood. Everybody knew Li'l Kev was following in my father's footsteps, like it or not. Some people on the street gave him respect because he was my father's son, but other people wanted to see him suffer because of it. Kelsi lowered her head when I spoke about Li'l Kev. She knew how serious shit was getting with him.

"Yeah, I know. I was going to talk to you about that. I was with Scorpio the other night and Li'l Kev came to the crib talkin' about he was there to re-up. I said to him 'I know you ain't calling yourself selling for Scorpio.' Girl, he like to damn near cuss me out. Chey, I wanted to take a belt and beat his little ass. You know he's my baby brother too. I mean shit, I been around since the nigga was knee-high to a fly. Broke my fuckin' heart seeing him waste his life away when Ms. Desiree tried to keep y'all clear of the street bullshit. These fucking streets are mean, Cheyenne. They will swallow his little ass up," Kelsi lamented.

I was shaking my head in disgust. I knew Kelsi was right about Li'l Kev, but what about her?

"Neither one of y'all should be fucking with Scorpio," I replied quickly. I wasn't going to hide my feelings on that topic. "Scorpio is a fucking snake in the grass, Kelsi. He worked for my father back in the days and everybody around here says he was a part of the setup that took shit down. He was a part of the crew that got my father knocked. It was just crazy how fast he took over things. And, even as young as he was then, do you know how many times he tried to get at my mother after my father was gone?" I said to Kelsi seriously. I wanted her to know the kind of low-life she was dealing with.

She rolled her eyes and let out a long sigh. "Cheyenne, I've heard it all before. I mean, I fuck with Scorpio as a means to an end. That's it. Nothing more, nothing less. You think I don't know his history? I'm not trying to marry the nigga. He got fifty-eleven women out here in CI. But right now, this nigga is keeping clothes on my black-ass back. I ain't got nobody doing shit for me. I mean, look, I'm damn near living with y'all because Peaches' fucked-up ass ain't never did shit for me. Scorpio gives up the loot. I give up the ass and we got an understanding," Kelsi told me.

I guessed that was as honest as she could be. Kelsi was already known around our way for being a gold-digger and a user. We were the complete opposite when it came to that. Cheyenne Turner wasn't depending on a man for shit. I saw where that had gotten my mother.

"Well, why don't you do me a favor? Tell Scorpio to leave my baby brother alone. Tell him don't let Li'l Kev work for him or fuck with that business at all. I don't think my mother can take my brother getting knocked. She already suffered twelve years of heartbreak with my father," I said seriously, my voice trailing off.

It had already been twelve long, hard years since my father's arrest. Life had surely not played out the way I thought it would've back when I was nine years old.

"You think I haven't already tried that? Li'l Kev is far gone in that shit, Cheyenne. Believe me, my ear is to the street. He got his own thing going on and ain't nobody gonna stop that. Scorpio acting like Li'l Kev daddy now, teaching him the ropes, protecting him, and, most of all, influencing him," Kelsi said solemnly.

Hearing that shit broke my heart. We had a father. Absent or not, Li'l Kev didn't need no two-bit drug dealer acting as his father. An ominous feeling came over me. Nothing good could come of my brother being in the game. Nothing good at all.

"Surprise!" I almost jumped out of my skin when I walked into the Carey Garden's community center. My cheeks flamed over and my heart thundered with excitement. There were so many people huddled together. I didn't even know what to say or do at that moment. I was frozen, mouth and eyes wide.

"Aha! We got you!" Kelsi yelled as she ran straight into me with a big bear hug, breaking up the awkward moment.

"Surprise, baby girl!" my mother yelled, grabbing me and kissing me on my cheek. Everyone in the room starting laughing, talking, and cheering me on.

"Oh my God! I can't believe y'all got me so good. I really thought I was coming here for Tanya's baby shower," I replied, red faced. The crowd laughed. Cell phones were everywhere snapping pictures and video of me.

"Yo! You are so hard to surprise. You are mad nosey! All day you kept asking me where I was going, what I was doing, why I'm not coming with you to get your hair done. Then caught a attitude because I wouldn't tell you! Damn! You are one nosey-ass chick!" Kelsi complained jokingly. Ha! She was right. I thought she was brushing me off all day so she could be with Scorpio's dirty ass.

"Yes, Lawd! Hiding stuff from you is almost impossible. I had to keep everything for the party hidden in the nurses' lounge at the hospital," my mother followed up.

I gave my mother another big hug. She could never know how much I appreciated her.

"Well y'all both know I am a investigator on the low. Neither one of y'all can do anything without me so this was totally a surprise. Y'all did real good hiding this one from me," I joked. I was over-the-moon happy. I loved my mother and Kelsi so much.

It was definitely a party. The entire neighborhood was there. Even Ms. Lula, who had gotten so fat over the years it was hard for her to get out of her apartment, was there shaking her cane to the music. Some of my high school and college friends were there too. I couldn't believe my mother and Kelsi had pulled it off without me even having an inkling something was going on.

"What up, sis? Congrats on graduating and happy birthday," Li'l Kev said dryly as he gave me a quick tap hug. He acted like he was embarrassed to hug his own sister. I noticed he had about six dudes with him. I guessed they were supposed to be his thug entourage. Yeah, right. He was my baby brother. Period.

"Thanks, baby bro. But, you know we need to talk, right?" I said to him seriously.

He had not been home in three days. He had not been listening to my mother at all. My mother and me had been worried sick over him. I was glad to see him there safe and sound, but I intended on giving him more than just a piece of my mind when we were alone.

"Nah, we ain't gotta talk. I'm a man. I'm a'ight. Enjoy your party . . . nerd," Li'l Kev said, trying to make light of the situation.

I saw the strain on my mother's face as she watched our interaction. For her sake, I dropped the subject. For the time being.

The music was pumping. My mother had gone all out on the food. The decorations were beautiful. Everything was gold and purple. My mother always said those two colors together reminded her of royalty.

I was making my rounds, saying hello to all of my friends, when the music suddenly stopped. We all turned to see what had happened. I mean, stopping the music at a hood party was like keeping the earth from rotating. I saw my mother standing next to the DJ setup.

"Hello! Hello! Can I have everyone's attention please," my mother said into the DJ's microphone.

We were all facing her. The room got quiet. I looked at my mother and she still had it. All of the years of hard work and sleepless nights had done little to her beautiful face. Of course she had gained a few pounds, women do as they age, but she still had a nice stomach, legs, and round hips.

"Today is a very special day for me, my family, and especially for my daughter. I don't think God could have blessed me with a better daughter. Cheyenne, you are kind, smart, beautiful, and all a mother could ask for in a daughter and best friend. I am very proud of you. We have been though a lot as a family but you never left my side." My mother choked out her words. I was already crying.

Kelsi swiped at her face trying to make sure no one saw her tears. Li'l Kev rolled his eyes and put his head down. He was trying to hide his emotions too.

"I wanted to give you this party as your coming out. You are a woman now. There are things you will learn as you get older. I will be here for you through it all. So, with that said, I wanted your twenty-first birthday to be more memorable than you could've ever imagined. I have one more surprise for you," my mother said behind the bright smile that danced on her face.

Hushed murmurs immediately spread over the crowd like a wave. I could hear some people whispering, "She's gonna get a car," and "Maybe it's the keys to a new condo."

My eyebrows were raised into arches. My mother had done enough for me. She had paid for my entire college education, books, food, clothes, and everything. She had told me I did not have to work while I went to school. I knew that had taken a financial toll on her. I'd watched her work overtime shifts, come home, get five hours of sleep, and head right back to work. All for me and Li'l Kev. I just couldn't imagine her giving me much more.

"Cheyenne, for years I have wanted to give you this gift. I prayed and I prayed about it. Well, today, I can finally give it to you. Come on in!" my mother yelled into the microphone excitedly.

My face crumpled in confusion. We all watched as the door at the right of where the DJ was set up opened slowly. The room was pin-drop quiet. Then loud cheers, yells, ohhhs, and ahhs erupted in the room.

My eyes flew open as wide they could go. I felt hot all over my body. My stomach curled into a knot. Tears sprang to my eyes.

"Oh my God! It's Big K! Big K!" Kelsi was the first one to acknowledge him verbally. She dashed for him and ran into him for a hug.

He smiled and returned her embrace, but he never took his eyes off of me.

I couldn't move. My feet were rooted to the floor. My mouth was suddenly cotton-ball dry. I hadn't laid eyes on my father in the six years since I'd stopped going to the visits. He was the same, but different. I tried to remember the last time I'd seen him, but my mind drew a blank. I was blinking rapidly, but I could tell I was crying. His silhouette was blurry as the tears obscured my vision. I put my hand over my chest; my heart was racing painfully against my chest bone. I was choking on my own breath now. *Daddy? Is that really you? My daddy?* I was saying in my head, but the words wouldn't come.

"Congratulations, baby girl," my father said, his voice just as deep and soothing as I remembered it. He grabbed me and pulled me into him.

I finally took enough air into my lungs to keep myself from passing out. I swallowed the tennis-ball-sized lump that was lodged in my throat. I didn't know what to say to him or how to react toward him.

"Daddy," I finally croaked out breathlessly.

My father kissed the top of my head and squeezed me harder with his huge, muscular arms. He was bigger than I ever remembered him being. He also had a full beard. I could feel the beard hairs on my head.

"Yes, baby girl. It's your daddy. I'm home. I'm finally home," he said. I could tell he was crying too. "I've missed you so much. You're so beautiful. I'm so proud of you," my father spoke into my ear.

I inhaled his scent and silently thanked God he was back. When he finally let me go, he wiped away his tears and mine. He held me out in front of him and took a good look at me.

"Wow! What a lucky man I am to have such a beautiful baby girl," he huffed, like his breath had been taken away. I smiled. He still had some of the qualities I remembered.

"Where's my little man at?" he asked me, scanning around for Li'l Kev.

The crowd opened up so my father could go embrace his son. Li'l Kev was standing with his little crew talking like nothing was going on. He acted like his father being home didn't faze him one bit. Li'l Kev's face went stony when he saw my father moving toward him.

My heartbeat sped up again.

"What's up, Junior?" my father said proudly, stretching his arms out to embrace my brother.

Li'l Kev sidestepped. His eyes went into slits, his lips pursed. He looked my father up and down like he was a stranger in the street.

"Yo, nigga. My name is Kev. I ain't none of your Junior," Li'l Kev spat, scowling and poking his chest out toward my father.

The entire room watched the exchange. My mother stepped over.

"Kevin! Don't you dare be disrespectful! No matter what has happened, he is still your father," she interjected.

I could see the hurt on my father's face, yet he still smiled. He never took his eye off Li'l Kev.

"Nah, it's all right, Desi. I understand. I got penance to pay to my li'l man. I got years to make up. I'm willing to put in the work," my father said, a fake smile painting his face.

"Nah, nigga. You don't owe me shit. The streets is my daddy now. I don't need no just-free-nigga trying to tell me how this is done," Li'l Kev growled, brushing past my father and mother.

His crew of cronies gave my father dirty looks as they followed Li'l Kev out. I felt hot with embarrassment for my father. He wasn't used to that kind of rejection, especially publicly. When my father left Coney Island, he had been a man who commanded respect from everyone . . . family or not.

"Kevin! You come back here. Kevin!" my mother screamed at my brother's back. Tears were running from her eyes. She must've felt the same shame and embarrassment that I felt on behalf of my father. I wasn't even a man and I felt emasculated for my father. It must've been something for my father to take the high road in front of all of those people.

"Let him go. Things will get better with time. I'm no stranger to challenges," my father said as he shoved his hands deep into the pockets of his jeans. "This celebration is about my baby girl anyway right? So let's party. There's a lot of things to be happy about today!" my father cheered. The crowd agreed and the party started back up. I watched him closely after his fake pep talk. I could see my father's jaw going square. His homecoming wasn't going to be as happy as he thought.

Chapter 10

That first night my father was home our apartment seemed much smaller than it had in years. My father's presence took up more space than any of us was used to. With the exception of Li'l Kev, we all sat around talking the night after the party.

My father had aged a lot in twelve years. His newly grown beard was sprinkled with grey hairs and he was starting to lose his hair in the middle of his head. Still strikingly handsome, a few lines had begun to branch out from the sides of his eyes. His teeth were not the bright white I'd remembered them always being when I was a kid. He'd gained a lot of weight, but it was all solid muscle. Everything about him seemed foreign to me. His voice was louder; his body was bigger than when he'd left. The only thing that didn't seem to change were his expectations. My father thought things with all of us were the same as they had been in 1996 when he left our family. I could tell he was going to have a hard time learning that he was no longer the center of our world.

My father's was the first voice I heard when I awoke the day after he came home. I guess it felt strange since I wasn't used to hearing a man's voice in our house. I could tell that he wasn't alone. I was correct in my assessment.

When I padded into the kitchen in my robe and slippers, my father and Kelsi were up together. They were so engrossed in their laughter and conversation they hadn't even heard me approach. As I walked closer, I could see the side of Kelsi's face. She was glowing like a teenager meeting her first love as she spoke to my father.

I raised my eyebrows at the sight of them.

"Y'all up early," I said, my voice still filled with remnants of sleep.

Kelsi's face was turned away from where I stood now. When she heard my voice, she jumped like I was a ghost she wasn't expecting to see. I thought her reaction strange, but I put it out of my mind. My father smiled. He was a bit jumpy and jittery too.

"Hey. Baby girl," my father sang, quickly pushing away from the table. He came over and kissed me on the cheek. "I hope we didn't wake you up. Kelsi was just telling me all of the Peaches stories I've missed. Boy, I tell you, gone for twelve years and some things ain't change one bit. That Peaches is something else . . . always has been," my father rambled. Something was funny about his voice.

Nervousness mixed with trepidation is the best I can describe it now. At the time any suspicions I had went as fast as they came. Why would I suspect my best friend and my father? That was crazy!

They sure didn't seem like they were talking about Peaches. All that laughing. Ain't shit funny about how Peaches is whoring herself out and smoking all of the crack she can find, I was saying in my head as my father and Kelsi broke up their little powwow. Kelsi had never joked with me about Peaches. Mostly she avoided speaking about Peaches at all.

"Where's Mommy?" I asked my father, looking around. I wanted my tone to show that I didn't appreciate all of his and Kelsi's laughing and reminiscing without my mother there. Especially since I hadn't gotten a chance to have any alone time with my father yet. I also thought reminiscing, laughing, and sharing light moments should have been for my mother to be doing on her husband's first full day home from a twelve-year bid.

"That crazy lady went to work. Can you believe her?" Kelsi answered right away.

A flash of heat spread through my body. I shot Kelsi a look. She ignored me.

"Hmph, her husband just came home after all this time and she agreed to work someone's shift for them instead of staying home. Not me; I would be locked in a room somewhere laid up with my man for days . . . Even my kids wouldn't be able to get in or interrupt our flow," Kelsi continued, trying to sound like she was joking.

I could hear the disgust underlying some of her words when she spoke about my mother leaving to go to work. I tilted my head to the side, squinted a little bit, and gave Kelsi the side eye. I didn't like anyone talking about my mother. Kelsi of all people knew that about me.

"Um, she is not crazy. She has a *job*. Which is more than I can say about a lot of people. Plus, I'm sure she had good reason to go in today. I guess she figured he's home now and he ain't going nowhere, with nobody else, so why not make the money. It's probably just for a few hours anyway," I grumbled defensively.

I thought I sent the message to Kelsi and my father. She was quiet. He had a big dumb grin on his face.

I grabbed a breakfast shake out of the refrigerator and started back toward my room.

"How about we go down to the rides today," my father yelled out as I walked away. I didn't know if he was trying to make light of the tension-filled exchange that had taken place or if he was serious.

I paused for a few minutes. *He can't be serious. How old does he think I am?* I rolled my eyes without letting him see me.

Kelsi didn't say a word. She had to be thinking what I was thinking. *He has clearly been gone too damn long.*

"Um . . . yeah. You've been gone way too long. The rides are no place to go nowadays. Half of them are gone or broken down. Nobody dares eat at that Nathan's anymore. Trust me, nothing around here, including the rides, is like it was in 1996," I lectured, trying to keep the obvious disappointment out of my voice. I immediately felt sorry for my father. This transition home wasn't going to be easy if he continued to live in the past.

It only took three weeks after my father was home for shit to hit the fan with my brother. Li'l Kev came in the house with his key one night after being gone for more than a week.

My mother was in the kitchen. Kelsi and I were in my bedroom gossiping. My mother's screams erupted loudly through the apartment.

"No! Kevin! Oh God! No!" she belted out.

Kelsi and I scrambled up off our beds and ran to the front of the apartment.

"Let him go!" my mother screeched just as Kelsi and I rounded the corner.

That's when I saw them. My father had Li'l Kev down on the couch, choking him around the neck with one hand.

"Daddy! Daddy!" I screamed, rushing over to the heap of bodies.

"You wanna act tough? Huh, huh? I'm gonna show you tough. I ain't these boys out in the street. I'm a man who just did twelve years with real motherfuckers who did real things on these streets. You ain't so fuckin' tough now, Junior," my father growled as he clamped down harder and harder on my brother's neck.

Li'l Kev was making a low hissing noise. I could tell his oxygen was completely cut off. Kelsi was pulling one of my father's arms and I was trying to push his massive body.

My mother was screaming, but I can't even remember what she was saying in the chaos. My brother was turning a sickening shade of burgundy. I knew my father was powerful enough to take the life right out of Li'l Kev's scrawny, fourteen-year-old body.

"Big K, please. Please let him go. I don't know if I could take you being gone again," Kelsi said soothingly.

I remember clearly that, even amid the chaos, I had looked at her strangely. Something inside of me felt weird. I couldn't place it then. Besides, there was just so much going on.

My father slowly released his grip on Li'l Kev's neck. My brother rolled onto the floor, holding his neck. He coughed and wheezed, trying to get his lungs to fill back up with air.

My father stood over him. My father's chest was rising and falling rapidly and his fists were curled so tight his knuckles paled. "Now, li'l nigga. The next time I speak to you nicely, you speak to me nicely. I can't make up for the lost time, but that don't mean I'm gonna be disrespected by my own young'un," my father huffed, his nostrils flaring. My father began walking to the back of our apartment.

My mother rushed over to Li'l Kev. "Kevin? Kevin? C'mon, baby, it's okay. It's okay," she comforted him as she lifted Li'l Kev's head and put him in a position she said would help oxygen go to his brain faster.

I was silent. I guess I was still shocked. I had never seen my father get violent in my life. After he was locked up, I heard stories about how notorious my father was on the streets, but at home, he had been nothing like that. I guess time and circumstances change everything. From that day forward I realized my father was definitely a changed man.

Chapter 11

Things with my parents changed after my father choked Li'l Kev that day. With my brother gone from the house, probably for good, my mother and father argued incessantly. Kelsi and I had no choice but to listen.

"You think you the man around here, Desiree! You dish me a little allowance like I'm a fucking kid. You take me shopping like I'm a fucking woman. I can't put food on the table and you fucking let me know it every single day! I can't even get niggas in the street to throw me a fuckin' bone in this game, even though I was the one who fed their asses back in the nineties! Do you know what that's like for me, Desi? Do you?" My father's booming voice had yanked me out of my sleep.

I popped my eyes open, noticing that the sun wasn't even up yet. *What they arguing about now?* I thought, my mind still fuzzy with sleep.

"Kevin, you need to forget being in the streets! You are forty years old, not twenty-something. If you feel inferior because I work every day, pay the bills, and do what needs to be done around here and for you, go find a real job! I've done nothing but try to make you feel at home since you've been here. Yes, I leave money for you, just so you don't have to feel like you don't have. Of course I bought you clothes; what else would you have worn? All of your outdated clothes from the nineties? I'm the breadwinner. So fucking what? Get over it! Kevin, I'm not going to stop doing what I have become accustomed to doing out here without you," my mother screamed back. She was never really the type to raise her voice so I knew that she had to be pretty upset with my father right then.

"Doing without me? Without me seems to be a fucking theme around here! Yeah, seems like you became accustomed to doing a lot without me. A whole lot without me. You think I don't see? Who is the motherfucker in the Beemer who picks you up every day? Huh . . . huh . . . Desi! Who the fuck is that! I bet you he made it all good around here without me!" my father boomed. He was definitely changing the tide of the argument.

My interest had been piqued. I had never heard of someone with a BMW picking my mother up for work. *What is he talking about? He's crazy. Mommy has never had another man besides him,* I defended her in my mind. My father was definitely out of fucking order with his accusations now.

"Oh please, Kevin. That is a doctor from my job, who happens to be kind enough to come to this fucking hellhole to pick me up and take me to work. I don't see you volunteering to get me there. You've been home two months; not once did you even ask me about my work. Not once did you ever ask me how hard it was for me to become a nurse . . . a head nurse at that!" my mother responded.

Doctor who takes her to work? Oh shit. I never knew my mother got a ride to work from a man. I could see how my father could take that wrong. After all, we did live in the projects. Doctors coming to the projects in nice whips were taking a risk. A man who took a risk like that on a woman wasn't just trying to be helpful.

"Nah, I haven't asked you because you're too busy being gone all the time. When you are here you want to sleep or do whatever it is you like to do. I can barely get time to fuck my own wife. You know what that's like? Huh? Nah, you don't, Desi. I've been gone twelve fucking years. Twelve years I spent yanking my dick, dreaming about the day I could touch you again.

Hold you in my arms like I used to do! And in the two months I've been home you've barely kissed me, much less fuck me! You know what that does to a man?" my father yelled, his voice cracking.

I wanted to just cover my ears and never listen again. Those project walls were so paper-thin, even if I had plugged my ears with cotton balls I would've still heard every word.

"That is unfair, Kevin. What you're accusing me of is unfair. Just like you've been gone twelve years, I've been alone for twelve years. I haven't had a man in my bed. I haven't looked at another man. I haven't been intimate with anyone, except you, during those cold, horrible conjugal visits. So, I'm sorry if I've gotten accustomed to going without sex, love, intimacy, but that's what I had to do to survive the soul-stirring lone-liness I've suffered for twelve years! You've changed too, Kevin. Your touch is not the same. You are not the same loving, tender, caring man who left me in 1996. Kevin, you may not want to hear it, but everything for us has just changed." My mother was crying now.

I could hear that her words were coming through sobs. Thinking of my mother in pain made me hurt inside. I heard my father open their bedroom door and slam it. I pictured him stalking down the hallway and out of the apartment. Then, the apartment door slammed loud enough to shake the entire place.

Kelsi walked over and got into the bed with me. She hugged me tight from behind. I closed my eyes and let my tears drain onto my pillow.

"Shhh, don't cry, Chey. It's gonna be all right. Married people fight. They just have a difference on the way they see things now. After a little while, things will fit together for both of them. They are gonna be happy just like back in the days when we used to go to the rides. When Big K would kiss up and love up on Ms.

Desi every minute they were together. That will happen for them again," Kelsi whispered to me.

I had to wonder if what she was saying was right. Were things ever going to be the same for my mother and father? I didn't say anything in response to Kelsi. I just took comfort in my best friend being there for me. Being there for us . . . like we'd done for her so many times over the years.

One of the saddest days of my life was the day I had to leave to go away to medical school in Texas. I had decided to leave Brooklyn amid all of the turmoil going on in my house. I couldn't stand to see my parents at odds. My father was turning into an angry, bitter person, which was not how I wanted to remember him. My mother had retreated into a workaholic, and when she was home, she didn't speak much. My brother, well, he was completely out of the house. He would see us occasionally, but only when he had watched my father leave the building. I couldn't stand knowing that the streets had taken hold of Li'l Kev's life. I knew for sure that my mother had worked hard to make sure we turned out better than that.

Kelsi was in deep with Scorpio and, on the low, she was still making sure no-good-ass Peaches had food to survive.

I didn't have anywhere to fit in all of that chaos. Most days, I felt lost, like I didn't belong anywhere. I used to throw myself into my schoolwork, but since I had graduated, I didn't even have that. The decision to leave hadn't been that hard once I weighed my options—go away to med school or stay in the projects and deal with everyone else's drama.

"I'm going to miss you, Chey," Kelsi said, swiping at her tears angrily like she wanted to beat herself up for crying.

I threw a folded pile of clothes into my big purple suitcase without looking at her.

"When you've been with someone every single day for twelve years, which is most of our lives, you can't even imagine yourself one day without them," Kelsi continued.

I stopped putting things in my suitcase and turned toward her. "I love you so much, Kels. I'm going to make this doctor thing happen so our lives can be better. You will always be my sister; no amount of distance can ever change that," I said through tears.

Kelsi broke down. She flopped back on her bed and sobbed. Her shoulders quaked as she let the racking sobs take over. I sat next to her, pulled her up, slid my arm around her shoulder, and cried right along with her. I guess now I know that was the last real, true friend exchange we were going to have before the proverbial shit hit the fan.

Li'l Kev didn't come see me off, but he sent one of his cronies with a package for me. I slid it into my oversized carry-on bag and decided I'd open it when I got to the airport that day. My father didn't come to the airport either. I was glad, because the tension between him and my mother was enough to make me want to throw up every time. Kelsi, of course, decided to stay back as well. She said there was no way she could see me disappear into the airport and not lose it. We joked that she would be screaming so loud that the airport security would be hogtying her and carrying her away like she was a terrorist.

It was just my mother and I. She'd chartered a cab service to take us to John F. Kennedy Airport. We left two hours early so that my mother would have time to sit with me before I went through security. Once I was checked in, we found a little restaurant that was right outside of security. I didn't have much of an appetite.

My mother's eyes were so sad. "I'm surely gonna miss you. My baby's first time away from her mother in her life." My mother started the conversation first. She let out a windstorm of breath. "I can't believe you have grown up so fast," she said, dabbing at her tears with the cloth napkin from the table.

"Ma, I thought we wasn't going to do the sappy thing," I complained. I had cried enough for one day.

My mother put her hand up and smiled. She sniffled back her snot and wiped the last of her tears. "Okay, okay. I did promise. I'm just telling you how I feel, baby. One last thing: just know I am so proud of you that if I could afford to write it in the sky I would. You are the strongest little girl on the planet and I know you'll make me proud. There is nothing in this world that can match my love for you. I don't want you to think about anything going on at home. Just work hard and become the best doctor on the planet," my mother preached before the waitress interrupted us.

I never replied to my mother's little speech because I didn't want to cry anymore. I should have. I should have told her thank you for her kind words. I should have said something. I had no way of knowing that would be the last face-to-face conversation I would have with my mother. I mean, had I known that, I would've told her this:

"No, Mom, you are the strongest person I know on earth. You came from the bottom and you made it all work for you. You are one of the most influential women in the world and if I could I would get on every media outlet in the world, on top of every mountain, and anywhere people could hear me and say my mother, Desiree A. Turner, is the most remarkable woman on the planet and I love her more than life itself!"

That's what I would've said to my mother had I ever gotten the chance to see her beautiful face again. But, instead, I was robbed of that opportunity.

"I thought that my father would love my mother forever, after all she had done for him." —Cheyenne Turner

"I thought Big K would love me forever, if I did this one thing for him." —Kelsi Jones

Chapter 12

Kelsi Jones

Cheyenne left that day, leaving me with a huge void, a hole in my life so big that nothing or no one could've ever filled it. I had moped around the apartment for hours alone. Being alone forced me to look back on my life. I was twenty-one years old, the daughter of a crack whore, a high school dropout, and the sex toy of the local drug dealer, who treated me like a piece of shit under his Prada shoes. I would do anything for a quick buck, including suck dick, fuck in public places, and let myself be passed around for enjoyment. I had the typical, stereotypical, hood chick's story. My life was the shit urban novels (the only kind of books I ever read) were made of. I even thought about writing a book; but I knew I didn't have the patience or discipline to sit at no computer and type my story out.

I was in Cheyenne's room, on my bed. Yes, if you didn't know by now, I had my own bed in the Turner home. I heard the apartment door slam. I figured it was Ms. Desiree coming back from the airport. I had so many questions for her about whether or not Cheyenne finally broke down at the airport or if Cheyenne had sent me any parting messages. I wrapped myself in my robe and went toward the front of the apartment.

"Oh shit!" I jumped. I had bumped straight into Big K. "You scared the shit out of me," I gasped as I stumbled backward.

"You ran into me, so how I scared you? There you go again, walking with that head down," he joked.

I smiled.

"Pretty girls are not supposed to walk with their heads down. I told you that before," he chastised playfully.

I blushed.

He changed his course and we both headed into the living room/kitchen area. That was the first time I felt that old feeling again—that overwhelming closeness and tingling inside for Big K that I used to feel when I first went around him as a kid.

"So how did things go with Cheyenne at the airport?" I asked, grabbing some orange juice from the refrigerator.

Big K frowned so hard his eyebrows dipped between his eyes.

"I didn't go with them. I thought you knew that. Cheyenne probably didn't want me there anyway. She's her mother's child. I can't compete there," Big K said sadly. "I thought for sure you would go," he said, his tone more like a question than a statement.

I stopped pouring the juice. I gave him an equally strange frown.

"I couldn't even take helping her pack without crying all over the place. No way I was going to make it in the airport. I would've been a damn blubbering fool out there," I answered.

"Yeah, same here," he said solemnly. "I didn't want to crowd her mother either. You know? I already feel like the outsider around here. I wanted to give them their space and time before she got on that plane," he replied.

I could hear the hurt in his voice. Something flashed red inside of me. *How dare they leave him out of such an important event! They are both selfish bitches for that!* I ranted in my head.

"So, tell me about you. I have been so caught up in getting my family to want me here that I haven't even had time to find out how you're really doing. I mean, with Peaches all fucked up and . . ." Big K started.

I twisted my lips and he stopped talking.

"Damn . . . I never realize how awkward it is when someone asks me how I'm doing. I'm so used to people not really giving a fuck or either they just know what's up," I replied, pushing the glass away from me as I suddenly lost my desire to drink the juice.

"I always cared though. Since Cheyenne met you, I've always cared about you . . . a lot," Big K replied.

I smiled. I noticed he said he cared, but never said he cared about me *like a daughter.* Maybe he felt the same tingly, man-and-woman love for me that I felt for him. At least that was how I took his statement.

"I know you did. I always felt that you cared. I never stopped feeling that even when you were away," I said, my voice going low. I wasn't able to look him in the eyes. I felt so vulnerable at that moment.

He reached over and used his hand to lift my chin up. "I already told you . . . pretty girls don't walk around with their heads down. No matter what the situation is, you hold your head up high . . . always," Big K said, letting the kind smile I remember from back in the days spread across his face. I hadn't seen that smile since he'd been home. I felt powerful that the first time I saw it was while he was speaking to me and not to Ms. Desiree.

Big K and I talked for hours that first day Cheyenne was gone. I bared my soul and told him everything. I held nothing back about my past relationships. Who I fucked in the neighborhood. How many times I had been pregnant and had abortions. I told him all about my abusive relationship with Scorpio. And, most revealing of all, I disclosed to Big K all the trouble I still had with sex after what Took did to me. I talked to Big K that day like he was a licensed professional therapist. Never once did I feel like he was judging me. In fact, the way he listened so intently made me feel a deeper love and respect for him. It wasn't like a father/daughter love and respect either. It was that mutual respect that two adults have for one another when both have nothing else to hide.

"Nigga, is you loyal to me or ya washed-up-ass pappy?" I heard Scorpio bark loudly.

I was upstairs in his bedroom with pain pulsing between my ears like someone was hitting a gong right upside my head. "Mmmm," I moaned, so hung over I thought I was dreaming.

"Huh! Answer me, li'l nigga! I ain't got time for games! I'm hearing in the streets that ya washed-up-ass daddy been trying to step on a nigga toes out there and your soft ass just playing the passive role!" Scorpio yelled some more.

"Nah, man, you heard wrong," I heard Li'l Kev's quivering voice.

I knew then I wasn't dreaming. I jumped up so fast that my pounding head threatened to send me right back down on the bed. I stopped for a minute. "Ugh," I grumbled, feeling like vomit was about to creep up my esophagus. I took a deep breath and powered through the throbbing pain in my head and gut-wrenching nausea in my belly. I grabbed one of Scorpio's T-shirts to cover my naked body.

"I think this li'l nigga ain't got the heart to take care of his pops. This nigga stuntin' like he wanna be the next Big K out here, yet he letting his old-ass pops fuck up the business!" Scorpio said to the crowd of dudes sitting around watching what he was doing. "I think this li'l nigga might deserve to take this L in the name of his father!"

When I got to the steps I had a full view. Scorpio had a gun to Li'l Kev's head, while Li'l Kev sat cowering and crying in one of Scorpio's white leather chairs. I don't know what came over me. All I had on was a T-shirt and a thong, but I flew down those steps like a bat out of hell. I didn't give two shits about my safety. All I knew was that a member of my family was being threatened and I wasn't having it.

"What the fuck are you doing?" I boomed as I plowed straight for Scorpio. Even he had to look at me like I had lost my fucking mind. "Take that fucking gun out of his face! You know he is like my fucking little brother!" I growled.

Scorpio turned his six foot three inch slender frame toward me. When he swept his long dark brown knotty dreads out of his face, I could see that his charcoal black face and big, soup-cooler lips were crumpled into a snarl.

"Who the fuck is you talkin' to, bitch?" Scorpio barked.

When he called me "bitch"—the name Carlene had been calling me since I was eight years old—I just about lost it. I jumped on Scorpio and dug my nails deep into his skin.

"Leave him alone! He's a fucking little kid! Leave him alone!" I screamed as I bit down into Scorpio's shoulder.

"Get this crazy bitch off of me!" Scorpio belted out.

Suddenly, I felt my body being hoisted in the air. I felt a few of my ribs crack as I hit a wall.

"This dumb bitch musta lost her rabbit-ass mind t'day!" Scorpio lifted his Timberland boot and brought it down on my chest.

Pain rippled through my body like waves on the ocean at high tide.

"You tryin'a disrespect me in front of all my niggas? Huh, bitch?"

Another kick from his boot, this time it landed square in my pussy. I felt vomit come up out of my mouth.

"You staying up in they camp, too. I'm feedin' your fiend, nasty ass. You probably fuckin' this nigga right here!" Scorpio barked. This time he grabbed a handful of my hair.

Even with my body racked with pain I wasn't going out like a punk bitch. I was still spitting and kicking. A fire raged inside of my chest bigger than those uncontrollable wild fires that happen in California.

"Get the fuck off me," I gasped, slobber and vomit spewing from my lips. I swiped at Scorpio again; this time I took five fingernails full of skin off his neck.

"Ahhh! This bitch cut me," I heard him growl. I saw the blood on his neck right before he used his gun to hit me across my face. My lights went out. Blackness is all I remember after that.

I woke up the next day in Cheyenne's room in the worst pain I'd felt since Took raped me. My head felt like somebody was sitting on top of it hitting it with a hammer. My body felt like a 2,000-pound person was sitting on me. When my eyes fluttered open I immediately snapped them shut. It hurt so badly. My right eye wouldn't even open all the way, but I felt tears draining out of the side of it. I tried to take a deep breath and even that hurt like hell.

"Hmmm," I moaned. The small vibration from my moan sent pain through my throat and neck.

"Hey, Kels. I'm glad to see you awake." I heard Ms. Desiree's soothing voice coming from somewhere on my right, but I couldn't see her. "I have something you can take for the pain, but it's going to knock you right back out."

I swallowed hard. That hurt too. I slowly shook my head up and down. I needed the pills right away. I didn't care if that shit knocked me out for sixty days; I could not take the pain all over my body.

"Okay. Let me go grab you some water," Ms. Desiree said.

I closed my eyes again for a few minutes before I felt the presence of someone else in the room. I forced my one good eye open. Pulsating stabs of pain shot through my forehead again. I winced.

"Don't try to open your eyes for me. I'm here." Big K's voice filtered into my ears.

I let out a painful sigh. I shut my good eye. I was embarrassed for him to see me like this.

"Who did this to you, Kelsi?" he asked.

I thought the question was strange. Didn't he know? Hadn't Li'l Kev been the one to bring me home after the fight with Scorpio? Who had finally saved me from Scorpio's wrath? How many days had passed? My mind raced, which intensified my headache.

"They just left you for dead in front of the door. Desi found you on her way out to work . . . in this condition. You could've died out there like that. You're pretty banged up. I wanna know who did this shit to you," Big K whispered harshly. I could tell without looking at him that he was flexing that strong jaw.

"Where's Li'l Kev? Is he okay?" I mumbled through my swollen jaw, the smell of my own breath making me want to gag.

"We haven't seen him. Rumor in the building is he knows who did this shit. They sayin' Li'l Kev might have been there when this happened to you and ain't do shit to protect you. I'm looking for that little punk, too. Now I'ma asked you again: who did this shit to you?" Big K responded. I closed my one good eye. I had to because tears were running out of both eyes now. *Not again!* I was thinking.

Chapter 13

Between Big K and Ms. Desiree, I was up and on my feet in a month. She had wrapped my ribs so that they could heal and he had sat guard dog by my side every day when Ms. Desiree had to work. I heard Carlene came by once, but it wasn't to see how I was doing; she just wanted to borrow some money, as usual. Big K told me he had run her off with some of his old-school threats. We had a good laugh behind that.

The first full shower I took after Scorpio's assault felt so good. Even the initial painful pinpricks all over my skin from the hot water hurt so good. I spent more than an hour letting the water beat over my tender body. When I finally turned the water off, I pulled back the shower curtain and just as I did . . .

"Ahh!" I screamed. I was so startled I almost slipped and bust my ass in the wet tub.

"Oh shit! Kelsi! I thought that was Desiree in there," Big K yelled in response.

I was buck-naked right in front of him. I couldn't even reach my towel; it was too far away. I was too shocked to think to cover my nakedness with the shower curtain. My heart hammered in my chest. It seemed like everything was happening in slow motion.

He was stuck on stupid staring at me, but he didn't turn and run away. I was stuck on stupid letting him take in an eyeful of my body. It seemed like an eternity before either one of us did anything.

"Shit! I'm really sorry about this. I'm so sorry," he kept saying as he backed out of the bathroom and slammed the door.

I stepped out of the tub on wobbly legs. *Maybe I need to just take my ass to Carlene's and stop staying here. Especially because Cheyenne ain't here and Ms. Desiree is always at work,* I thought. My brain felt scrambled. I wrapped myself in a thick, plush towel, but I still felt like it wasn't big enough to cover me. I stood in the bathroom an extra twenty minutes gathering my thoughts. I looked at myself in the mirror that hung over the bathroom sink. I touched the remnants of the scars that remained on my forehead and above my lip.

"You need to get your life together, Kelsi," I whispered to myself. I didn't even know where to start when it came to getting my shit together, but I knew the way I was living was destructive for sure.

I opened the bathroom door slowly. I peeked my head out real quick and dipped back into the bathroom. My chest was rising and falling. I peeked out one more time, then darted for Cheyenne's room. I made it into the room without running into Big K.

Once I was in the room, I flopped down on the bed and, oddly enough, I smiled. Big K had seen me naked. I smiled at the thought. As sick as it sounds, I smiled and smiled some more.

Two nights after the bathroom incident with Big K, I awoke to another one of Big K and Ms. Desiree's arguments. They had been arguing way more often since Cheyenne and Li'l Kev were gone from the house. Sometimes I thought me being there when their own kids had left might be awkward for them. I thought maybe I should just go home and deal with my crack-head mother . . . Good, bad, or indifferent, Carlene was what God had given me.

After a few minutes of Big K and Ms. Desiree scream-ing back and forth I heard the apartment door slam shut. Either Big K or Ms. Desiree was gone.

I lay there for a little while, wondering who had stayed and who had gone. I looked at the clock. It was 4:42 a.m. My curiosity finally got the best of me. I got up and walked to the kitchen faking like I wanted something to drink. The entire apartment was dark. I flipped on the kitchen light. That's when I saw who had stayed.

"Damn, I was trying to be quiet and not wake you up. Could you tell by all of the yelling how hard I tried?" Big K joked, smiling even though I knew he was really stressed.

I smiled at his little joke. He had been at the table, in the dark, with his head down. I pulled up a chair, set my glass of juice on the table, and joined him.

"I could barely hear anything," I lied jokingly. We both laughed.

Big K was shaking his head from side to side like the weight of the world was on his broad shoulders. He looked at me and let out a windstorm of breath. "You know it's fucked up when a man comes home after twelve long years of being locked up with motherfuck-ers who act like animals every day, and feel like he wants to be back in the lockup. Twelve long-ass years of fighting, clawing, praying, politicking, fighting some more, just to stay in one piece so he could come home to his woman and kids. But when he gets home, he can't even fit in with his own family. Everybody is a stranger in their own home. He can't fit nowhere in their lives at all. You know how fucked up I am behind this? Nah, you wouldn't know. Nobody knows what it's like to have your manhood tested by your own flesh and blood," Big K said sadly.

I felt a twinge in my stomach. I could feel the pain in his words. I couldn't even imagine what it must've been like for him inside that prison, dying to get home, only to come home to an ungrateful-ass family.

"It might take them some time to adjust. They got so used to living on their own," I comforted him softly, choosing my words carefully.

The truth was his family members were all resentful that they had to fend for themselves after Big K got locked up. The selfish-ass Turners had been used to being spoiled by the lifestyle they lived when Big K was on the outside. They had no use for him now. Not me. I didn't see things the way Ms. Desiree, Cheyenne, and Li'l Kev saw things. In my eyes, Big K was still the man. He was the same motherfucker who used to feed the hood on Thanksgiving. He was the same nigga who would take other people's kids to get school clothes.

I was able to hold on to the good deeds Big K had done for me before he got locked up. I was able to hold on to them so tight that I was the only one who really treated him with the respect that the man of the house deserves. I held tight to every last good deed he'd done for me. I mean, he had really risked everything to get revenge on Took for me. With those memories fresh in my mind, I was able to stay loving Big K even after twelve years of missing him.

"Time to adjust! They had twelve years to think about shit. I mean, how is my fifteen-year-old son so deep in the streets that I can't say a word to him? How is my daughter so far removed from me that when she calls from Texas she forgets to ask to speak to me? And, my wife . . . Man, listen, truth be told, she doesn't even want me to touch her. You know what that's like for a man? A man like me who always lived and breathed for his family? Every risk I took back then on the come up was to make shit better for all of them. Not for me . . . for them!" Big K lamented, hitting his chest with his hands. He spoke so powerfully I was moved to tears.

I touched his arm gently. "If it makes you feel any better, I always have and always will appreciate you. You are the only man who has ever shown me any love," I said sincerely. I lowered my head and stared down at the table. That was the damn truth as raw as I could deliver it. It was the first time I had told Big K how I felt about him.

Big K grabbed my hand. The warmth of his skin against mine sent stabs of heated sparks up my arm and down my spine. Something jumped inside of me. Right at the core of my being, his touch let me know there was something between us. There always had been something between us. He was old enough to be my father, but the connection could not be denied. It was immediate. It was magnetic. It was undeniable right from that moment.

There was an awkward, silent pause. I can't say for sure who made the first move after that, but one of us certainly did. The next thing I remember, Big K's tongue was parting my lips. I gladly opened my mouth to welcome his tongue inside. It was warm and tasted like Big Red cinnamon gum.

Our tongues did a wicked dance with one another. Heat engulfed my entire body. My sore ribs ached, but Big K's touch hurt so good. The achy feeling throbbing through my torso intensified my desire for Big K. His hands were moving all over me so fast I couldn't tell what he was touching at any given moment. I didn't feel like myself. I felt ravenous. Wild. Freaky.

I reached down and grabbed a handful of his manhood. *He's your best friend's father.* The thought flitted through my mind. I ignored it. He was the man I'd always loved from the time I could feel that emotion. I clamped down on his swollen member.

Big K let out a gasp. I moved my mouth to his bottom lip and sucked on it as I massaged his throbbing bulge.

"Oh shit!" he gasped. "What are we doing?" he whispered as he pulled my T-shirt over my head, exposing my bouncy C-cup breasts. He hoisted me onto the table. The glass of juice I had poured earlier shattered to the floor. Neither one of us cared. I eased back, my entire body trembling. Big K leaned in and took a mouthful of my left areola.

"Oh God!" I huffed. My breasts were my weak spot.

Big K suckled both of my breasts until I was ready to explode.

My head fell back as he moved his mouth down to my navel. My body quaked all over. My pussy was soaking wet. As he removed my panties, I could feel my own juices leaking down my butt crack.

"You okay?" he whispered as he continued his journey downward. We were really doing this! I was more than okay; I was in fucking la-la land!

"Oh God! Yes! Yes!" I huffed barely able to get my words out. My mind was blank. Nothing was registering except that pure feeling of ecstasy that had come over me.

Big K put his warm mouth over my clit. My thighs fell apart, inviting him to taste me, lick me, and suck me. He flicked his tongue over my dripping hot box rapidly. Then, in and out. In and out.

"Ahh! Ahh!" I panted. I had never been handled like that. He was moaning too.

"Please! I want you! I want you so bad!" I groaned out, my words labored like I'd been running on a treadmill.

Big K lifted his head from between my legs.

I heard the elastic on his boxer snap. I knew he was exposed. I shut my eyes tighter.

Big K grabbed me with his strong, muscular arms and slid me toward him.

I wrapped my legs around him. "Agghh!" I belted out. He had entered me. His dick immediately filled me up. I felt a little bit of pain shoot through my pussy, but it quickly subsided into pleasure.

"Huh! Huh! Huh!" he wheezed as he rammed his body into my pelvis with the vigor of a jackhammer. Big K moved so fast I was slipping off of the table. I tightened my legs around him. That forced him deeper into me. I could swear his dick was touching my cervix.

"Oh God!" I gasped as he ground into me.

I bit into his neck. I didn't mean to, but I couldn't help it.

Big K hoisted me up and moved me over to the couch without taking his dick out of me. He moved carefully with his boxers around his ankles.

"Your shit it so good! So good!" he wolfed through labored breaths.

We made it to the couch without falling. He laid me down on the couch and kneeled in front of me. He pulled me closer, which caused me to feel his thickness way up inside of me. Big K moved his hips in circular motions as he held on to my hips. He wanted to make sure I felt every bit of him. I wanted to make sure I pleased him. I wanted to do what Ms. Desiree couldn't do. I wanted to be the best woman. After all, the best woman wins . . . right?

"Yes, grind it. Grind this pussy! It's your pussy! I'm not giving it to nobody else ever again. It's all yours," I huffed. I don't know what had come over me. I was possessed by the deep love I had for him. I couldn't help it. He had taken over my mind and body.

"Oh . . . fuck me! I'm right there! I'm right there!" I panted now. I could feel a few drops of dribble escaping the sides of my mouth. Big K had my fucking mouth watering. I had never felt the feeling I was having right then. None of the punk-ass dudes I had fucked had ever hit the right spot. The overwhelming feeling invading me was like what I would imagine a sunburst to actually feel like. As if spurts or flashes of sunlight was exploding inside of my groin. Then it happened. It all burst.

"Ahhhhh! Yes! Ahhh!" I screamed over and over. I had just experienced my very first orgasm and I knew it.

"Arrrggg!" Big K followed right after. His body completely relaxed. He moved out of me. His dick was still hard. He collapsed onto the floor while I was still on the couch. Neither one of us said a word. We both knew we had crossed a boundary that we could never take back. I think we both knew that we never wanted to take it back either.

Chapter 14

After that first time, Big K and I fucked every chance we got. As soon as Ms. Desiree left for work. Right before we knew she'd be home. Sometimes we had quickies while she showered. It was foul. It was risky. It was exciting. At first it was a game to me, but it quickly became obvious that I was in love with this man. If he had asked me to jump off the f Verrazano Bridge to prove my love, I would've asked what time and from what point. Anyone who couldn't understand where I was coming from after going unloved almost my entire life could kiss my ass.

Two months after our love affair started, I got up one morning and found Big K at the kitchen table with a stack of papers in front of him. I smiled at him, but he didn't smile back.

"Good morning to you too," I said sarcastically.

"Check this shit out," Big K said, sliding the stack toward me.

"National Benefit Life Insurance Company." I read it and looked at him quizzically.

"Desiree took out a $1.5 million policy on me. She also made me the beneficiary on her $2 million policy. She gives me these fucking papers and tells me to sign them. She don't discuss them with me or nothing," he ranted. He seemed stressed, like he thought there was some sinister reason for her taking the insurance out on him.

"So, what's wrong with that?" I asked. I wasn't tracking with him. A lot of husbands and wives had insurance on each other. He looked at me seriously.

"She also gave me these," he said, sliding some more papers toward me.

I read them over and my heart began racing wildly in my chest. *She's buying them a house? In Long Island? What about me? How will I see Big K?* My mind raced like crazy.

"She's trying to get us up out of these projects. The only place I've ever know is Coney Island," Big K complained. He never said anything about not being able to see me anymore. I mean, I was grown now. The chances of Ms. Desiree inviting me to move into their new house with them would probably be slim.

I was quiet.

"You know what two million could do for us right now? Me and you? We could get rid of everybody. We could really be together for good. I would have enough to be a real factor in the game out there. I could put my investment up and triple that shit in no time. I could take you with me to another country where we could live like a fucking king and queen off that, baby girl," Big K said dreamily.

Those were the words I'd been dying to hear. Big K speaking about us having a future together. As insane as it might've seemed at the time, I was longing for that.

"You hear me, baby girl? That money could free us," he said as he pulled me onto his lap. He wrapped his arms around me and massaged my breasts.

I closed my eyes and smiled. I could actually picture us living together happily ever after. I was quiet while I dreamt of what it would actually be like to have our love on public display instead of all of the sneaking around we were doing.

"Too bad Desiree would be in the way of our dream. I mean, she would have to die before I got that shit," Big K said solemnly.

"Yeah, we might as well forget it. She's the picture of health. She won't be dying no time soon," I said dismissively. I stood up from his lap. I was uncomfortable all of a sudden. We were getting a little too bold for our own good.

"Even people who are the picture of health die. They could die in accidents. They could die in a robbery gone wrong. I mean, good health ain't got shit to do with it. Especially when you live in the projects. Especially when your husband and son was in the game and made enemies, you feel me?" Big K replied.

I crumpled my eyebrows as I listened to him. *What the fuck is he trying to say?* I asked myself silently. He didn't keep his intentions a secret for long at all.

Right after that Big K fucked me in the shower. He fucked me so good I had gotten nauseous and threw up afterward.

"Damn, I fucked the shit out you huh?" he asked as I hurled over the toilet. "Either that or your ass is pregnant with my seed."

A cold feeling shot down my spine when he said that. In all of the time we'd been having sex, I hadn't even realized that my period was missing. *Kelsi! What the fuck is wrong with you! What are you doing!* I screamed in my head.

Big K grabbed me from the back and fucked me some more.

When Ms. Desiree came home that night, I faked like I was asleep. I heard her come to the room and tiptoe back out when she saw that I was asleep. I listened as she took her shower. Then, I heard it. I was frozen. Paralyzed by anger. That fire sparked up in my chest and I could hardly control my breathing. I lay there listening as Big K had sex with Ms. Desiree. I immediately hated her. I hated her for being his real wife. I hated her for being able to fuck him while someone else was in the apartment. I hated her for having what I thought was mine. That night, I pitted myself against Ms. Desiree. She was now my enemy.

Every day for three weeks Big K worked his magic on me. He fucked me. He fed me lies. He pumped me up and he made a plan. We would be together forever. He would love me forever, if I did this one thing to make sure.

The night Big K gave me the 9 mm Glock, he handed it to me and said, "This is what is going to make things for us official. We won't have anybody to worry about and we will have the money we need."

I took the gun, stuffed it into my bag, and left the apartment. I had had five shots of Patrón that served as my liquid courage that night. I had tried to clear my muddled mind. I couldn't allow myself to think about my Nana, who I had missed dearly. I couldn't think about my friendship with Cheyenne. I couldn't think about my past. I couldn't think about my piece-of-shit mother. I couldn't think of anything except being with the man I had always loved. Finally getting love from somebody was motivation enough for me. I started to fantasize about the future Big K and me would have. Being able to walk down the street holding his hand. Being able to marry him in a church. Most of all, being able to give birth to the baby I was carrying and celebrate with Big K like parents of a newborn should. Those fantasies propelled me to do what I did.

I can't remember much from that night because I have purposely put it out of my mind. But just like Amy Fisher, I know that I pulled the trigger to do away with the wife of the man I loved. I was finally going to have someone of my own. At least that's what I had convinced myself. As crazy as it may seem now, I had actually felt like I'd done the right thing for everyone involved.

Chapter 15

Cheyenne Turner

When the house phone rang in the middle of the night I immediately knew something was wrong. My mother was the only person who called me at the apartment I shared with a roommate in Austin, Texas. Anyone else contacted me on my cell phone, which hardly rang these days.

"Cheyenne," Amber, my roommate, called out to me in the darkness of my bedroom.

"Hmmm," I moaned. We had an early start the next day with our first round of exams upon us. Neither one of us wanted to be up that late.

"The phone is for you. It's your father," Amber grumbled, annoyed. I flung my blanket off of me, wishing that we had spent the few extra dollars on a cordless phone instead of the stupid landline that plugged into the wall. "Thanks," I groaned out as I brushed past Amber, stomping my way to the living room.

"Hello?" I huffed into the receiver. It was my father for sure. My heart stopped beating for a few seconds. "Daddy? I can't understand you. What are you saying?" I asked urgently. I was definitely jolted into full wakefulness now. Something was wrong, that much I knew. My father was sobbing into the phone. I had never heard him cry.

"What? What are you saying? Something happened to who?" I asked, my voice going high-pitched.

Amber was standing in front of me now. She was moving her lips to silently ask me if everything was okay. I put my hand up in a halting motion to her.

"Okay, calm down," I said, my voice cracking now. I heard my father take a deep breath. He started speaking again. I was finally able to understand what he was saying.

"Something bad happened to Mommy?" I asked calmly at first. My face crumpled in confusion. There's no way something bad could happen to my mother. Then what he was telling me had finally settled into my brain. "Something bad like what? No!" I screamed.

My father had said, "Cheyenne, your mother is gone." I collapsed. There was no way I could live without my mother. She was my whole world.

I still don't know how I made it from Texas to Brooklyn in one piece. Amber came along to make sure that I got there safely. She was just a sweetheart like that. The entire trip home was a blur. Amber and I didn't talk much, but our unspoken body language let me know that I wasn't imagining things.

My mother was dead. I wasn't going to believe it until I saw it. No one knew anything about the circumstance surrounding her death, except she had definitely been murdered. Kelsi never called me after I spoke to my father. She never called my cell while I traveled. I just figured she was probably just as distraught as I was.

When I arrived at my building there was a candle-light shrine outside dedicated to my mother. My father met me outside. As soon as I stepped out of my cab, I just started screaming. It was real. My mother. My best friend. My whole world. Was gone. Dead.

"Hi, baby girl," my father greeted me with a forced smile. I looked around at all of the people outside. All of the candles. It was real. My mother was dead. Murdered.

"Who would do this? She never hurt nobody! She never hurt nobody! Why?" I screamed. "Why?" I caught a glimpse of a few people from the neighborhood crying and wiping their tears away.

My father grabbed me and held me. I dropped down to the ground where they had placed candles and teddy bears in my mother's memory. I could not stop screaming.

I don't remember how and when they were able to get me upstairs, but I do remember walking into our apartment and collapsing again.

Kelsi finally showed up after I had been back in Brooklyn for about three hours. I was lying on the couch with a cold compress over my eyes when she came in. She rushed over to me.

"Oh, Chey, I'm so sorry." Kelsi bent down and hugged me. "I'm so, so sorry," she repeated. My floodgate of tears started up again.

"Why! Why! She didn't deserve this! She was a good person," I sobbed.

"I know. I know. She didn't deserve it. I'm so sorry. I'm so, so, sorry," Kelsi cried. I had no idea at the time what she was sorry for, but it wouldn't take that long for me to find out.

The day after I got home the detectives showed up at the house. Detective Brice Simpson was the detective who stood out to me. He was strikingly handsome with a well-groomed mustache and goatee. His hair was cut low with waves that were perfect. He seemed like any other guy from our neighborhood. He even wore jeans with a nice V-neck sweater instead of a suit and trench coat like most detectives I knew about. He did all of the talking. After the introductions, the white detective with Detective Simpson mostly took notes.

"Your mother was shot in cold blood. There was nothing taken from her. We found all of her jewelry, wallet, everything intact. When we see things like this, we think it's personal," Detective Simpson told us.

My father shifted on the couch where we sat huddled together.

"Is there anyone you could think of who would have something personal against your mother . . . your wife?" Detective Simpson asked.

I shook my head vigorously back and forth as the tears started up again.

"Man, my wife was a gentle as they came. Nobody would want to hurt her," my father answered on our family's behalf.

Detective Simpson gave him a look. "What's been going on at home? Any drama? Any conflicts?" Detective Simpson asked.

"Nah, man. Everything here was peachy. We are a close family," my father quickly answered.

Kelsi sat across on the loveseat across from Detective Simpson. He looked over at her. She lowered her eyes and started swinging her legs in and out. I knew her so well.

"Well, my . . . He just recently came home from being in prison. My brother is on the street selling drugs . . . working for a dude who is my father's known enemy. She basically has lived with us since we were kids because her mother is on crack and used to really abuse her," I rambled, letting out all of our family secrets.

Anything that would help the detectives find out who killed my mother.

Detective Simpson was quiet for a few minutes.

"So you've been gone to medical school in Texas? Your brother is gone from the home? Who was here? Just your parents?" he asked, his forehead creased.

"And my best friend who, like I said, has been basically living with my family," I said, looking over at Kelsi.

She stopped swinging her legs in and out.

"Excuse me. I need to use the bathroom," Kelsi said as she jumped up from the couch. She rushed to the back of the apartment and slammed the bathroom door.

"I guess she's emotional huh?" Detective Simpson asked.

I shook my head in the affirmative. "To give you some clarification on the type of person my mother was, she took care of her, Kelsi, like she was her own child. How many women can you say would do that? There is no one I can think of, for any reason in the world, who would just shoot my mother down like a hunted animal," I told him. I laid my head on my father's shoulder.

Detective Simpson took a deep breath. "Cheyenne, I usually don't make promises when it comes to my cases. But, I'm making the exception for you. I promise you I will find your mother's killer, and when I do, I will make sure that person never sees the light of day again," Detective Simpson told me with feeling. He shot my father a squinty-eyed look. Then he stood up.

"Thank you. I really appreciate it. Trust me, my mother didn't deserve to die like that," I said through tears. I stood up and shook Detective Simpson's hand. I looked in his eyes and I saw a sincerity I had never seen from anyone other than my mother. I knew then that he was going to solve the case.

"I would've bet my life and lost if you told me that Kelsi and my father were the ones who plotted to kill my mother." —Cheyenne Turner's final statement at the sentencing

"I will never forgive myself for hurting the only family I ever had. I just wanted to be loved forever." —Kelsi Jones's final statement at the sentencing

Chapter 16

Kelsi Jones

August 2010

"Life without the possibility of parole. Life without the possibility of parole."

The words kept replaying over and over. Loud gasps rolled through the crowded courtroom. Reporters burst out of the courtroom doors so they'd be the first to report the story.

I didn't even react. I didn't cry. I didn't get weak at the knees. I stood there while Judge Graves read me the riot act for what seemed like the one hundredth time. I kept my head up high; after all, pretty girls didn't go around with their heads down. I deserved it. After reliving everything I realized just how much I deserved it. All of my life I had blamed others for any mistakes I made, but it was me. I was the one who had pulled that trigger. I was the one who had slept with another woman's husband after that same woman had been more than a mother to me. I had tried to steal her life. I was finally able to take responsibility for my actions. I did it and I deserved to rot in prison for the rest of my life. I didn't turn around after the sentence was handed down. The court officers flanked me on either side. They'd come to take me away. I didn't have the courage to turn around and look at the faces of the ones I'd hurt. I never wanted my son to see my face. Although he was only a few months old, I knew it best that he never have to grow up ashamed of his biological mother like I had. I was sure that Cheyenne was going to give him a good life. Cheyenne loved me at some point in our lives. She was just like Ms. Desiree: selfless and like a saint. My son was her baby brother and after I'd given birth to him, in my heart, I had named her the godmother, just like we'd planned it as kids.

I kept my head up all the way back to the courthouse holding cells. My attorney was the last person I saw that day. He handed me a sealed envelope and told me to open it when I was alone. I stuffed in down my panties since I knew that once I got to the jail they'd take it away. When I was finally alone with no guards breathing down my back, I opened the envelope. There was a card inside. I opened it. I immediately recognized the handwriting.

Kelsi,
You are not like my daughter, you are my other daughter. Here is your set of keys to our new home. I told you that I would always be here for you. Well, I meant it. Now get to packing! ☺
Love Always,
Ms. Desiree

That was it. I fell to the floor. I had nothing left. I curled my body into a ball and closed my eyes. I finally relived what I'd done. My eyelids were like a movie projector as I watched it unfold.

Chapter 17

Kelsi Jones

I waited for Ms. Desiree to get off work. Just like I'd practiced with Big K, I waited for her to go into the parking lot where I knew she'd wait fifteen minutes for a ride home.

Big K had timed it all out for me. He had been watching Ms. Desiree at work for months because he thought she was cheating on him with some doctor. He was the one who told me which stairwell to hide in near the elevator she would take to her ride's BMW.

She had her bag flung over her arm and she was humming a tune when she got off the elevator. At that moment I wondered what the fuck she could be so happy about. She was buying a house and trying to leave me behind! That's what I told myself.

I took my last swig of Patrón from the flask Big K had given me. I winced as it burned my chest going down. I can't lie; it eased my nerves a lot. I fingered the Glock that I had in my hoodie jacket pocket. *It's now or never,* I told myself. I stepped out of the darkness.

"Waiting for someone?" I asked in an eerily low voice. Ms. Desiree jumped so hard she almost tripped and fell.

"Ah! Oh my God! Kelsi! Why would you scare me like that?" Ms. Desiree huffed, holding her chest in a clutch-the-pearls manner. "What in the world are you doing here? And how did you . . . ?" she rambled, her voice still trembling from the scare.

"Don't talk. Please stop talking," I demanded. I felt the alcohol taking over my speech. My heart hammered so hard I felt short of breath.

Ms. Desiree's eyes went wide. She had seen the gun before I intended for her to see it. "Kelsi! What are you do—" she started.

"Shut up! Shhhh! Don't talk I told you! If you talk it will make this harder!" I growled at her. I looked around.

Big K had told me to keep my back to the left where the camera was. With the black hoodie on, I'd look like a robber.

"Okay. I won't," Ms. Desiree whispered. "But think about—"she started again.

"I'm done talking. I said shut up!" I hissed, this time I pushed the gun toward her chest.

Ms. Desiree started blinking rapidly in response. She was too shocked to speak. Tears started falling from her eyes. "Why?" she mouthed.

Even in the haze of my intoxication, I felt something in my heart burst. I felt myself about to give in to emotion and run away. I had come too far for that. Now that Ms. Desiree had seen me with the gun she would report me to the police if I left things as they were.

"You could've walked away and left him with me! Why didn't you just do that? You tried to move to a house and leave me!" I said through my own tears now.

Ms. Desiree was shaking her head from side to side. "Please, Kelsi. What is the matter? Are you on something?" Ms. Desiree whispered. Her lips trembled so fiercely she couldn't even pronounce the L in please. "Can't we talk about this? I . . . I . . . can . . ." she murmured, tears dancing down her cheeks.

I heard a noise on the other side of the parking garage. I jumped. Ms. Desiree went to open her mouth. I guess she was going to scream. That's when I panicked. I had gone over the time that Big K had given me to get the job done.

"Oh shit!" I huffed. Boom. Boom. I pulled the trigger twice. The sound of the gun exploded in my ears. I didn't anticipate it being so loud. I immediately felt nauseous. I went deaf in both ears. I couldn't concentrate on the pain throbbing at the center of my eardrums. I took off running as fast I could go. As I ran, the hood flew back off of my head. I knew then that one of those surveillance cameras in that parking garage was going to get me. I couldn't worry about that. I ran and I ran until my body finally gave out.

Chapter 18

Cheyenne Turner

August 2010

There were so many news reporters outside of the courthouse after the sentencing. Li'l Kev and I had all types of microphones and recording devices being shoved into our faces. I didn't have anything to say.

We stood behind the prosecutor while he took the opportunity to speak about how justice had been served. Through the crowd, I saw his face. He was fighting his way toward us. Finally, he started up the courthouse steps. He had a serious look on his face. My heart skipped a beat. I balled up my toes inside my shoes.

"Congratulations," he said, grabbing my hand and giving it a squeeze. I was fighting back my tears.

"Thank you for keeping your promise," I whispered to Detective Brice Simpson.

He squeezed my hand again. "Thank you for letting me," he replied.

I felt an inner peace come over me. *Everything for a reason,* I thought. *Everything for a reason.*

The last I heard about my father, he'd been murdered six months after his conviction for the murder of my mother. I didn't attend his funeral. I received a package a month after with a stack of letters he'd written to me and Li'l Kev. My brother and I sat together and burned them in the backyard of the home my mother had bought before her death. We burned the letters without ever reading them. A month after that, I received a check for $1.5 million from National Benefit Life Insurance Company. I was the beneficiary on my father's insurance policy. My mother was still looking out for us.

Torch

Chunichi and Meisha Camm

Chapter 1

Mental Interrogation

"Shall we begin?" the strange-looking woman asked.

Her hair was grey and stringy and her clothes were old and crumpled. She was a frail old woman who looked as though she should be at home knitting or making cookies instead of here with me. Nevertheless, I played along.

"Yes, I've been ready." I nodded my head after taking a sip of my warm Sprite in a can.

"My name is Dr. Gilman. I'm the chief resident psychiatrist for this facility. Do you know where you are?" she asked as she pulled out a notepad and pen from the desk drawer.

"I am at the Virginia Psychiatric Institute," I replied.

"What's your name?"

"Angela Farmer."

"Angela, do you know what day is it?"

"Today is Tuesday, first thing in the morning."

"Do you know why you're here?"

"I'm here because I stabbed my mother, Pamela Farmer. But not only did I stab her, I strategically mapped it out. I was sure to place the knife perfectly so that I did not hit any major organs or arteries. I wanted to be sure she stayed alive long enough to feel every part of her body slowly burn after I lit the flame and set her ass on fire," I said with a satisfied grin across my face.

Dr. Gilman seemed unmoved by my story and continued with her interrogation. "How old are you, Angela?"

"I'm twelve years old. How old are you, Dr. Gilman?" I returned the question. I was starting to get quite bored with this stupid question and answer game.

"Let's stick to me asking the questions, please," Dr. Gilman quickly redirected me. "You seem a little advanced for a twelve-year-old. Tell me a little bit about your education. "

"Well you seem a little old for the position you're in, but you don't see me asking about your credentials," I spat back.

"Again, Angela, please just answer the question," Dr. Gilman said with a blank face.

"Fine. I've spent a lot of time reading. I've been reading my grandma's old encyclopedias since age four when I first learned to read. It's my only way of escaping the terrible place we call life," I explained.

"Please explain why you feel life is so terrible."

"Life is unfair. Some people are just lucky enough to be born into greatness while others are born into hatred, poverty, and illness. Then, we're taught to thank this great spiritual being, God, for our blessing and pray to Him for our shortcomings. Now you tell me, does that make sense?"

"Hhhmmm . . . interesting thought," Dr. Gilman said as she scribbled on her notepad. Then she continued, "So, do you feel you were treated unfairly by God?"

"Yes." I nodded my head.

"With that said, do you feel bad for what you did, or do you feel it was justified?"

"No, I do not feel bad at all. If this God being and heaven and hell really exists, then my mother was going to hell, right? So me killing her only made it so she could dance with the devil quicker than she expected," I said with little emotion.

"Angela, tell me a little bit about you," the doctor suggested.

"I will tell everything you need to know, but first you have to agree to become me," I bargained.

"I'm not sure I understand what you mean." The doctor seemed a little apprehensive of my request.

"Close your eyes and imagine yourself a six-year-old little girl. Not the average happy six-year-old playing with dolls, but a dirty six-year-old who hadn't had a bath or a decent meal in weeks. Picture yourself wandering into a neighborhood crack house with twenty dollars' worth of food stamps going to buy a ten dollar rock for your mom's crack addiction, then stealing from the corner store just to have a snack to eat.

"Now imagine yourself at age seven. Crack is no longer good enough and Mommy has turned to heroin. At night, you sleep on a pallet of old newspapers in a cold apartment because Mommy has sold not only your bedroom furniture but all the furniture in the apartment. Your only friend since birth is a raggedy Minnie Mouse doll and eventually Minnie was taken away too.

"As if your mother and best friend being taken away isn't enough, envision at age nine your virginity is taken as well. It's traded for fifty dollars worth of drugs. At ten, you finally think things are getting better when Mommy finds a boyfriend. He puts the family in a nice apartment with furniture and provides clothes and food. You're going to school and finally starting to make a few friends, but everything has a price. Soon, things turn dark again when you began getting raped by Mommy's boyfriend almost every day after school. You tell Mommy but she doesn't care because her boyfriend pays the rent, electric bill, and keeps her drugs coming regularly.

"Imagine at eleven years old, the boyfriend is gone but so is Mommy. For a week, you didn't eat anything because Mommy got her tax return and went on a drug binge and left you home with no electricity or food. At twelve years old, imagine Mommy dressing you up nicely and putting makeup on you, then handing you over to three men in exchange for drugs. She smiles and assures you everything will be okay as she walks out of the room and closes the door behind her. For hours these men beat and rape you. Then, when it's all over and you're crying uncontrollably and begging for an explanation your Mommy dearest smacks you and orders you to stop crying because she has a bad headache. When you refuse, she locks you in a closet for three days."

I paused as the emotions from that day began to take over and my eyes filled with water. I struggled to continue my story. "As you lay in darkness for seventy-two hours in your urine and feces with hunger pains shooting through your body, your hurt turns into fury."

"You can stop now. I've heard enough!" Dr. Gilman yelled. She opened her fearful eyes with tears streaming down her face.

I quickly wiped my tears and began to smile because I knew I was getting to the best part of the story. "So to answer your question, no, I do not feel guilty." I continued, totally ignoring her request to stop, "As my mother's body was burning I laughed. Every time she begged for mercy I kicked her in the stomach and then in the face. I'm glad for what I did," I explained with a huge smile on my face and breathing hard. This rush of energy came over my entire body. This newfound energy made me feel powerful.

"Our session is over," Dr. Gilman said, jumped up from her chair, ran toward the door, opened it, and signaled for me to leave.

"Enjoy the rest of your day," I said as I rose from my chair and skipped out the door merrily.

The door slammed behind me.

Chapter 2

A Day in Court

"Angela Farmer, please rise," the judge ordered.

I didn't know what to expect next. The timid little six-year-old inside of me was so afraid. I hid my head behind my lawyer's arm.

"Your Honor, may I have a small recess with my client?" my lawyer requested.

"What does recess mean? Is this when we go outside and play? I thought that was only at school," I said to her, tugging on her sleeve.

"It means you and I will talk alone for a few minutes," she whispered back to me.

"Yes, I will call a fifteen-minute recess. After we reconvene, I would like to speak with Ms. Farmer in my chambers," the judge requested.

"No," I shouted out.

"Your Honor, with everything Angela has been through, she does not feel comfortable being around anyone of the opposite sex. Besides, an agreement has been reached between my client and the prosecution," my lawyer explained.

"Very well. Ms. Farmer will not have to speak with me in the chambers." He nodded.

During the recess, all I could think about was if I was going get to go home. For nearly two years, I'd lived in the psych ward waiting for my case to be over. I had no place to go if I got out, but I was ready to be released. My maternal grandmother died years ago and my mother never mentioned any other relatives to me.

"Ms. Farmer, do you realize what you have done?" the judge asked after court was back in session.

It was as though those words brought out a new being in me. I dropped my lawyer's hand that I'd been holding so tight. I stood up straight and looked the judge in the eye as I responded. "Yes. I have saved my life and been given a gift of not ever being abused again in the process," I said proudly with no remorse. I knew I was too young to be tried as an adult.

My lawyer looked down at me in shock as she tugged my sleeve and gave me a stern look that read "shut up."

"The prosecution recommends no jail time," the judge said reluctantly.

I looked at the judge and gave him a satisfied smile.

"The prosecution and I have agreed to a reasonable sentence," my lawyer stated.

"Let's hear it," the judge said, obviously unhappy with the option my lawyer and the prosecution had arranged.

"Ms. Farmer will plead no contest. Her record will remain sealed and placed into the juvenile system. Upon turning eighteen years old, the record will be destroyed," my lawyer explained.

"Do you understand how you will plead?" the judge asked me.

"I do understand," I said.

"How are you feeling?" the judge asked.

"Failed," I said.

"Explain please, young lady." The judge seemed intrigued by my statement.

"The justice system failed me. I told neighbors how I was being abused. I even stopped a police officer in his patrol car eating his lunch. I begged him to take me with him, but he didn't. I realize now that it's not as if no one believed me, it's just that no one cared enough to do anything about it." I gave my statement.

"We're here now," Ms. Frazell, my lawyer, said as she attempted to give me a hug.

I turned away. Who cared if she just won a court case for me? She was still a stranger in my eyes.

"Angela, may I ask you one more question?" she asked.

"Yes."

"Do you know the names of the men who hurt you?"

"Just as I told the detectives, I don't know their names," I lied.

The police were still trying to find the men who my mother let rape me years ago. I guessed they were having trouble finding them. I didn't care either way. I knew their day was coming—with or without the help of the police.

Chapter 3

A Place to Call Home

"Where are we?" I asked the social worker while clinging to the seat belt of her SUV. We'd pulled up to a home that was unfamiliar to me.

For the past months, social services had been trying to find any known relatives of mine to possibly adopt me. Even though my story gained local television attention, no one had come forward. I have been living with my social worker, Betty Hill. She was good to me. More importantly, she didn't ask me a lot of questions about what happened in my past.

"Well, you're in the city of Suffolk. It's a little country. A new environment will be good for you. Someone wants to adopt you. Angela, take a chance and open up your heart. Not all people are bad," she expressed before getting out of the truck and heading to the front door of the house.

I watched as she knocked on the door and it swung open. Betty was met by a woman wearing a big old smile. She turned back and signaled for me to come. I took my time getting out of the truck. I slowly walked toward Betty with my head down.

"Hello, Angela. Please come right in," the friendly woman said.

"Hi," I replied. The palms of my hands were becoming sweaty.

"Hey, Mrs. Miller, I know we're a little early. The weatherman called for rain. I wanted us to get here wet free," Betty explained. Then, the both of them started laughing.

"So, you're just going to leave me," I said. My heart was beating so fast. Betty was only the person I sorta trusted.

"Not at all. Come sit down before you get yourself all worked up for no reason. I'm going to stay the next few days while you transition to this household."

"Angela, you don't know me and I don't know you. I'm here to help, that's all," Mrs. Miller said.

"If you don't like it here, you can come back with me," Betty stated.

"Okay." I nodded my head.

"Now that we have talked about the business for today, it's time for some fun. I will take your bags and put them in your room. Follow me, this way. On the bed, I placed a T-shirt and a pair of overalls for you. We're going to milk some cows and feed the chickens before it gets too hot outside," Mrs. Miller stated.

I walked into my new room and looked around. There were dolls, stuffed animals, my very own TV, and a selection of DVDs. I pulled back my purple curtain and peeped out the blinds. I noticed the farm filled with all sorts of animals. I didn't even notice it when we first pulled up in the driveway. I took off my clothes and put on the overalls Mrs. Miller had laid out for me. A few minutes later she knocked on the door.

"You ready?" she asked.

I didn't respond. I just followed her on to the barnyard.

Not only did we milk the cows and feed the chickens, I also collected their eggs and fed the pigs.

"A week ago, some piglets were just born. They were so cute," Mrs. Miller told us as we fed the pigs. As we worked she told us funny stories of her growing up on the farm. Before you knew it, we were done.

"You ladies, go get washed up for dinner," Mrs. Miller instructed us.

She had prepared tender roast beef with gravy, baby carrots, and melt-in-your-mouth mashed potatoes. The rolls were so buttery that I wanted another one but didn't ask. I didn't want her to think I was greedy. I had a great day. Helping out on the farm made me feel like I had done something good. As we were eating the front door opened.

"Hello, everybody," a man said.

My heart was beating so fast. I wasted no time jumping from the table and running upstairs into the room I was to call my own. I hid in the closet and quickly closed the door.

"Angela, come out," Betty instructed.

"No," I yelled from behind the closet door.

"Please, honey, he won't hurt you. George is my husband. I've been married to him for over twenty years. He has a gentle soul," Mrs. Miller pleaded.

"All men will hurt me. That's all they want to do!" I shouted between cries. When I called her Mrs. Miller, it didn't occur to me till then that the title "Mrs." was an indication she was married.

The trio left the room and I cried myself to sleep. It felt like hours had passed. I woke up to them whispering outside of my bedroom door.

"Joyce, maybe this isn't a good idea. This girl may be damaged beyond what we can do to help. I didn't retire to deal with this," George stated.

"No, we're doing the right thing. Angela needs us. She needs love. Honey, you had to have known there was going to be some resistance at first," Mrs. Miller explained.

"She's right," Betty said.

"I hope this works," George said before opening the door. None of them came into the room. I cracked open the closet door. A teacup yorkie came running my way. I opened the door all the way. The dog started licking me.

"Did you have an enjoyable nap?" Betty asked.

"Yes. What's the dog's name?" I asked, changing the subject.

"Angela, you will have to decide that. She is all yours," George said.

"With that doggie comes responsibility," Mrs. Miller urged.

"By the way, it's a girl," Betty added.

"I will pick up after her. I promise," I said, holding my new puppy in my arms. "I will call her Fera."

I was starting to think maybe living with the Millers wouldn't be so bad after all.

As the days passed, I grew pretty fond of my new family. Before long it was time for Betty to part. She stayed over a week before she headed back home. I overheard her on the phone telling her sister that she used her vacation days to stay with me. I was grateful someone was finally starting to care about me.

Chapter 4

Self-discovery

"So, tell me, how was your first day of high school?" Joyce eagerly asked me as I walked into the kitchen to grab an apple.

"I made a lot of friends," I said, smiling. I was attending Nansemond River High School in the ninth grade. This was my first day in high school. For the first time ever, I was properly prepared for school. Instead of being an outcast, I fit in with every other teenage girl in the school.

"Glad to hear it. What about your studies? Do you like your teachers?"

"I've got plenty of homework. I need . . ."

"Honey, I already picked up your school supplies. I know the school said wait until the first day, but I wanted you to be ready and prepared for the enormous amount of homework those teachers give to you," she said. We both started laughing.

"Joyce, thank you for everything," I expressed before Fera ran up to me, wanting me to pick her up.

"You're welcome," she said as her eyes filled with tears.

"What's wrong? I didn't want you crying. This is a happy time," I said as I wrapped my arms around Joyce.

"No, it's not you. With everything you have been through, I've seen a positive change in such a short time. I'm happy to be a part of it. Angela, this is the fresh beginning of the rest of your life," she announced.

"Yes." I nodded. I gave her a hug.

"Here," she said, handing me a cell phone, laptop, and a printer. My eyes started to get bigger.

"Child, you need a cell phone for emergencies. Type-writers are outdated. You need this laptop for your homework. When I ran out to the bank this morning, I drove by Best Buy. A sale was going on and there you have it."

"Thank you," I said, smiling.

"Hush up, now, Fera. Angela has to do her homework. You're coming outside to the barn with me," Joyce said to Fera, who was constantly barking for attention.

"I don't mind working in the barn for an hour or so. Besides, it's therapeutic to me. During lunch, I got half of my homework done," I offered.

"Okay, I will meet you there in a few minutes," she said, carrying Fera with her. She loved that dog just as much as me.

I went to my room and set up my laptop and printer on my wooden desk. Then I plugged up my new iPhone to the charger. I threw on my overalls and boots and headed to the barn to meet Joyce.

It didn't take long for us to finish up our work in the barn and get dinner prepared. By the time we were setting the table, George walked in from work.

"Joyce, please stop feeding that dog rib eye steak. You're going to kill her before she reaches two," George commented as he headed toward his seat at the dinner table.

I laughed. At times, these two were comical. Most of all, I saw the love they had for one another. I didn't remember my father and my mother never spoke of him. The times when I did work up the nerve to ask her, she smacked me across the face. She told me I was messing up her fun time. But I knew what she really meant was I was blowing her high with my questions. I never could understand what was so terrible about my father, who was so disturbing for her to even discuss.

After eating dinner I helped Joyce clear the table, and washed dishes; then I headed to my room. I turned on the radio and stumbled upon the group called TLC. Their song "Waterfalls" was playing. Meanwhile, I grabbed my laptop and hopped in the bed, researching a Web site that could potentially help a person locate any known relatives in the United States. I had always been curious about who my family was. My mother, with her evil ways, purposely left so many unanswered questions about our family and her past.

With an unsuccessful attempt at trying to find a known relative, I quit researching. The singer R. Kelly's song called "Your Body's Callin'" began to play on the radio. I began to surf some pornography sites. It was my secret addiction. I slid my hands beneath the covers and into my panties to massage my clit. It gave me a feeling that I'd never experienced before. My head fell back onto my pillow as I moved my pelvis in motion with fingers around my clit.

"You ready for bed?" Joyce asked, nearly scaring me to death. After knocking on my bedroom door she entered before I could say to come in.

Lucky for me, my hands were hidden beneath the covers. "Almost. I'm doing a few review questions for my biology test tomorrow," I lied. "By the way, tomorrow will you take me to get a library card? I was looking online earlier at a few books that I would like to read," I continued.

"Sure, let's go right after you get off the bus," she agreed.

"Good night," I said.

"Sleep well. You're going to strike an A-plus on that biology test tomorrow," Joyce said, then exited the room.

I got out the bed and went to the bathroom to get prepared for a night's sleep. As I brushed my teeth the images of the pornography site and me touching myself kept plaguing my thoughts. I tried to shake it as I turned on the shower and hopped in. But as I washed my body the temptation became so overwhelming. I could no longer control myself. I propped one leg on the side of the tub and began to massage my clit just as I'd seen the woman on the porno Web site perform with pleasure. The more I rubbed it, the better it felt. It got so extreme that I got a sudden euphoric rush all over my body. It was a feeling I'd never felt before. I was paralyzed in bliss. I took a few deep breaths as I gathered myself. As I washed up, I was starting to feel ashamed of what I'd done. It was a horrible act. Sex was terrible in my book. How could I actually enjoy something like that when I'd been raped so many times? I began fighting with myself. The timid little girl in me cried uncontrollably, the horny whore in me wanted more, and I hated that it happened. My mind was spinning and I felt like I was losing control.

I grabbed my razor and began to slice my thigh over and over again. The sight of the blood made all the noise stop. There were no more voices in my head. The little girl was gone, the whore was gone; it was only me. I rinsed the blood from my leg and watched as the bloody lather went down the drain. Then I got out of the shower and put on my nightclothes and went to bed. It didn't take long before I dosed off to sleep.

It seemed as soon as I'd gotten into a deep sleep a noise coming from the living room woke me up. I opened my door with Fera in my arms. George had a golf club in his hand and motioned for me to be quiet. My heart started racing as I watched him quietly creep down the stairs. I went to see if Joyce was okay. She was hiding in a corner of her bedroom. I gave Fera to her.

"Get the hell out of my house," George commanded someone.

I rushed downstairs to grab a knife out of the kitchen. Neither George nor the burglar dressed in black noticed me. I stood in a dark corner as I watched George hit the burglar across the back with the golf club. The burglar went down but got back up. George swung again with all his might but his next hit missed the burglar by a hair and landed the golf club on the hardwood floor instead. The burglar rushed George and they both tussled on the ground. That's when I noticed the burglar had a gun. He hit George in the face with the butt of his gun.

Without thinking I approached the burglar from behind, pulled back his head, and sliced him in the face with the butcher knife. I caught him right above his eyes. A few more milliliters and he'd been sliced from eye to eye. Blood instantly began to stream down his face. He yelled out in pain and struggled to his feet but he couldn't see past the constant flow of blood. I picked up a lamp and started hammering down on the burglar's head. I kept hitting him over and over again. George, Joyce, and Fera were my family. No one was taking them away from me!

"Angela, stop," Joyce begged as I continued to hit the burglar over and over again. By this time, the police had arrived. The police officer had to pry the lamp out of my hand.

The paramedics took George to the hospital. He only had a concussion, but the burglar wasn't so lucky. He was pronounced dead on arrival. My countless blows to the head had killed him. Once again, with my help, justice had been served. The police had been looking for that burglar for months. He had robbed at least ten other homes. I was cleared of any charges. The police immediately ruled it self-defense. Once again, this rush of adrenaline came over me so much I believed I could have lifted a car up. The feeling was so powerful and I craved more of it.

The next day, Joyce had a security system installed in the house. We never spoke of that night. I made it clear that I couldn't talk about it.

Chapter 5

Life Moving On

Four years had passed since I moved in with Joyce and George and I turned into what our fucked-up society would call "the pretty little girl next door." Joyce and George were so proud of me making honor roll every year, but they didn't know it was because I'd screwed just as many people as I made A's. Although I was labeled as the perfect kid, there were times I felt another person would take over my body and lead me into a sexual tantrum. Then, there were those times when I felt like a little child, afraid and alone. Nevertheless, I managed to flourish into a young adult and keep my peculiar behavior under wraps. At one point, I thought my parents had caught on to me. Out of nowhere one day, Joyce and George came to me and said they thought it would be a good idea for me to speak with a counselor about my past. Although I was reluctant, I agreed just to please them. I overheard Joyce explaining to George that she didn't want my messed-up childhood to affect my adulthood. I knew Joyce was genuinely concerned about my well-being so I met with the counselor as she instructed.

I walked downstairs and into the living room. Joyce was in the rocking chair with Fera in her lap, humming a song. Throughout the years she did this at times, always looking at a picture hanging on the wall. Once I asked who he was and she replied, "A younger version of George." I never asked again.

"Call me after your session. I want to know if you're going to feel comfortable with this counselor," she instructed.

"Yes, ma'am," I replied, giving her a hug and then petting Fera on her head.

On my first visit, I wasn't sure what to expect, but I had already decided I would not tell her about my sexual cravings or my self-induced torture afterward. I'd cut myself so much that I could not wear short skirts or shorts without using Dermablend concealer to cover my scars. Surprising enough, my first session with my counselor was a piece of cake. From that point on I had no worries. I met with my counselor once a week.

My sessions with her consisted of conversations about my anger, bitterness, resentment, and pain. She had classified me as having severe anxiety when I felt as though my life was threatened. Funny thing was, even after all those sessions I still had not forgiven my mother for what she did to me. What mother would allow their child to live through recurring torment? The things my mother said and did to me constantly haunted my mind. I could remember telling Joyce that I didn't know how to forgive. I never asked to be born. Many times I felt I was better off being left at the front entrance of any hospital than raised by my mother. Anytime Joyce thought I was feeling down she continued to let me know that God had a plan for me and I was here for a reason. Even though I still hadn't decided whether I truly trusted and believed this "God" most people seemed to worship, I accepted what Joyce said.

When the night of my eleventh-grade ring dance arrived, Joyce was more excited than I was. That night, I realized that I rejuvenated Joyce's life. Before I arrived she had all the complaints of old age: forgetfulness, fatigue, aches, pain. With my companionship, she had a vibrant glow and was lively like a young adult. Fera and I kept her busy.

While Joyce thought of how exquisite I would looked dressed like a young queen of Jordan, I rehearsed in my mind all the different sexual tricks I was gonna do later into the night. Joyce bought me the dress three months prior to the date of the ring dance. She was definitely a planner and always taught me to start early and never be late for nothing.

"Close your eyes," Joyce suggested after she entered into my room.

"What is it? Do I have a bug on me or something?" I asked.

"Child, hush up. You look just like—"

"Like who?" I asked, cutting her off.

"Umm, the cartoon character from the Disney movie, *The Princess and the Frog*. Green is definitely your color. You're truly a queen in the making. Tonight is your night, so, Angela, please enjoy it."

"All right." I nodded my head.

"Now, you have made me lose my train of thought. Back to what I was saying: close your eyes, for the second time," Joyce instructed.

"Yes, ma'am."

"Now, you can open your eyes." After I opened my eyes, George came in with Fera dressed in a dog version of my dress. She looked so cute as she rushed toward me and hopped into my arms. In her mouth was a key.

"Go ahead, grab the key, baby," George said.

"What's this key for?"

"Think about it," Joyce said, grinning.

Immediately, I started screaming. "Where is it?" I yelled, full of excitement.

"In the garage," George said.

They followed me as I ran full speed down the stairs. Inside the garage was a brand new Toyota Corolla. I literally jumped with joy.

"Thank you so much," I said, giving them both hugs.

"You're welcome," Joyce said.

"No more carpooling with Julie and Becca," I said.

"Plus, you can go to the store, bank, and run all my other errands for me. I'm getting too old to run the streets all the time," Joyce added and we began laughing.

"I need to finish getting ready. Karl will be here in less than twenty minutes," I said, then headed back to my room.

Thirty minutes later, the doorbell rang. George greeted Karl at the door. Then, he led him into the living room. Seconds later, I made a grand entrance. All eyes were on me as I came down the stairs. I took my time walking in the four-inch heels I had on. I wasn't accustomed to walking in heels, plus Joyce was nearly blinding me with the constant flash of her camera. She was worse than the paparazzi.

"Just a few more pictures," Joyce said as we continued to hear the sound of her flash from the camera. She had old-school cameras and refused to upgrade.

My mouth was beginning to get sore from smiling so much. I was used to sore cheeks from giving head but holding a constant smile triggered some serious pain. It's unreal what a male will do for just a little bit of head.

After Joyce released us, Karl and I got into the limousine to be en route to the Virginia Beach Pavilion where the ring dance was being held. It had an early nineties theme for the event.

Once arriving, I realized Julie and Becca were already there with their dates. We went to the bathroom to talk privately. They both had plans to have alone time with their boyfriends. My heart began pounding, hoping I wouldn't be faced with that same option. I wasn't ready for Karl to touch me and especially not kiss me. My thoughts were on sex, but it wasn't with him.

"Can I have this dance?" Karl asked after I came out of the bathroom.

"Yes, you may," I said, taking his hand. The DJ began playing "Forever My Lady" by Jodeci. My mind instantly flashed back to my days in the projects. My mom would play that song all the time.

"So after we leave here, what's next?" he whispered in my ear as we danced.

"Home for me," I quickly responded.

"Well, I thought maybe we could get a little bit closer," he said while touching my butt.

I quickly grabbed his balls and pulled them tightly toward me. "Are we close enough now?" I asked while gritting my teeth.

Karl was having trouble talking so I finally let go.

"My apologies, Angela. I was way out of line," he admitted.

"Your apology is accepted," I said. The song "Electric Slide" came on. Karl regained his composure. I flashed him a smile and we started doing the infamous Electric Slide dance.

Later on that night, Karl dropped me off. A special someone by the name of Jeff picked me up. It was perfect timing. I was waiting in the bushes for only ten minutes. Jeff was attending William & Mary. I met him at a bookstore. It was his sophomore year majoring in architecture. Jeff offered to take me to my ring dance but I didn't want Joyce asking me a lot of questions.

Jeff was Greek, packed with muscles, with wavy, curly hair and a smile that could make a girl feel so special. Me, on the other hand, I looked at Jeff as a sexual toy. I did dirty nasty things with him. That part of my life had to be separate. Jeff had a juicy, long dick. When his tongue caressed my clit, he made sure to grab my hips when he knew I was about to pop in his mouth. His strokes were deep and hard. Jeff could always take the sexual frustration edge off. That night, we did it at his parents' house at least three times. They were out of town for the weekend. He made sure to have me back at a respectable time. I hoped Joyce didn't suspect a thing.

Chapter 6

The Big Day

"I now call Angela Farmer," the principal announced. The crowd went wild.

Throughout my high school years, I had countless friends. Ms. Miller, my social worker, Ms. Frazell, my lawyer, and the honorable judge from my case all made an appearance at my high school graduation.

"Thank you," I said while shaking most of the school officials' hands. The principal gave me a firm grip. He knew my history and always told me I would be successful. I was determined to beat the odds and not let the past eat away my soul.

After graduation, George and Joyce gave me a surprise graduation party and paid for a seven-day cruise to the western Caribbean. Julie and Becca were invited to come along. Becca's mom and grandmother would be going with us as well.

Each morning, we arrived to a new place as the sun welcomed me after I stepped out on the balcony. The only thing I bought for myself was a ring in Belize that resembled a coral reef. It intrigued me. Each day, I sent postcards to George and Fera to show where we were.

With Joyce close by, I kept my sexual behavior under wraps. For the majority of the trip, I didn't give a guy the time to even talk to me. I just didn't want to. At times, I don't want to be touched. On the last night of the trip, I couldn't sleep because I had a nightmare about my mother locking me in the closet. I needed to get some air and kept reminding myself it was only a dream. I was so grateful for what I had and was excited about starting school. In my heart, I wanted to stay on the correct path and not let my demons overcome me.

"Anyone sitting here?" a voice asked standing next to me. I was by the pool. On the other side some people around my age were laughing and taking pictures.

"No," I said.

"May I?" he asked.

"Sure." I nodded my head.

"Hi, my name is Gil," he said, extending his hand. He looked to be in his mid-thirties and the clean-cut type.

I liked the clean-cut type.

"Angela," I replied, shaking his hand.

"Nice to meet you."

"So what brings you out here so late?" I asked.

"It's the last night on the ship. I wanted to see the stars one last time. I've never been out of the country so this was an experience for me. I came with some buddies of mine."

"I came with my family. I'm hungry. Do you want to grab a slice of pizza?" I asked. The pizza stand was open twenty-four hours a day.

"Okay," he agreed. As we were walking together, his phone continued to buzz.

After three slices of pizza and more conversation with me just listening about his life story, I got a funny feeling in my stomach. Something wasn't right. I quickly ended our short-lived pizza date and returned to my room.

It took me a few minutes but I remembered his face when we all boarded the ship and at three of the resort areas we were docked at. Maybe, I couldn't prove it, but this man had been watching me or someone within my group. The next day, my guard was up. I didn't see him anymore. All of us arrived safely at home. Fera jumped into my arms.

Chapter 7

Going Back

When we arrived back from our cruise, my mind was on one thing and one thing only—the sweet taste of revenge. Becca's mother was a registered nurse and owned a home health business. While we were on our cruise, I heard her mother and grandmother talking about picking up a new case for a woman named Yvonne Cumberland who had a son named Harvey Cumberland. Becca's mother wrote down the information on a piece of paper, but I took it and placed it in my pocket while no one was looking. I couldn't resist. I had to strike on this lovely opportunity that had literally fallen right into my hands.

The next night I was headed out to execute my plan.

"Where are you headed to?" George asked with his nighttime beer in his hand.

"I'm going to catch a late movie with Becca," I lied.

"Have fun. I'm going to be in the bed and catch the Jay Leno show. The comedian Jamie Foxx is going to be on tonight. The man is hilarious," George said as I slid right past him and headed to the garage. He didn't even look up as he spoke. I jumped into the car feeling a little guilty for lying to George about where I was truly going, but it was a necessary evil.

Years had passed but I still remembered the neighborhood where I lived with my mother. After all these years had passed, the sign Diggs Park in bold red letters was still bent over to the side, still covered in rust. Even the smells were the same. *Wow, the guy Mommy used to buy her drugs from is still working the block. I thought he would have invested in a reasonable retirement plan by now,* I thought as I passed the familiar face. All grown up, no one even recognized me. I got out of the car and headed toward an apartment building with medical scrubs on.

I knocked on the door.

"Well, hello there. I sure appreciate you coming to take care of my mother," the man said after opening the door.

"You're welcome, Mr. Cumberland," I responded with a smile.

"I just need to get some rest and check on my dog," he explained while heading toward the living room. It looked as if he was going to put his shoes back on.

"I'm going to check on Mrs. Cumberland," I said while putting on latex gloves.

Within minutes, I approached Mr. Cumberland from behind and quickly pulled his head back. I pulled out my knife and cut his forehead right above his eyes. Blood was pouring down his face.

"I just want to get a little closer. Remember you said that to me while raping me when I was a little girl, Harvey Cumberland?" I whispered in his ear.

I never forgot the names of those men. The police couldn't provide the justice that I was so desperately seeking. So I took the law into my own hands. That always worked better for me anyway.

"Now, wait a minute, stop. That was a long time ago. I had a bit too much to drink and I was high on a combination of drugs. The night got carried away."

He paused and grabbed his eye. "I can't see," he whimpered.

"That's what I wanted for you to do, just stop. Now look who's whining."

"Listen, I'm sorry for what happened to you, Angela," he pleaded.

"If you were that sorry, Harv, then you would have turned yourself in to the police along with the others. I hope you said good night to your mother," I replied before finishing the job.

I got out my large blow torch from my bag and lit up his whole body. He was dead with his skin as crisp as a kettle-cooked chip.

"One down, two to go," I said as I packed up my items and walked out the front door.

There would have been three more individuals but something happened. Unfortunately, my mother's boyfriend who raped me repeatedly after school died in a motor vehicle accident. It was in the newspaper. After reading the article, I felt cheated. I craved to hear his screams of agony and whimpering before he took his last breath of life.

Chapter 8

A New Beginning

"Hello, people. My name is Professor Surry. This is biology 101. Please pull out your schedules and make sure you're in the correct classroom at the correct time and with the correct professor." He paused a moment and looked at us over the rim of his glasses "Either we are all in the right place at the right time and with the right professor, or no one has the balls to actually get up," Professor Surry continued.

"You will learn a lot in my class, and if time permits we'll spend a few days in the cadaver lab to give you all an opportunity to earn some extra credit. My rules are simple. Show up to class and do the homework. We're all adults here, so I'm not holding anyone's hand. With that said, if you already have your book, please turn to page sixty-seven. If you don't have your textbook, I advise you to get one or share with the person next to you. This is the first year that the biology textbook will be launched online. If that works better for you so be it. Any questions?" he asked, then gave that same creepy look over the top of his glasses again.

I looked around the room. Not a single hand was up.

"Now, let's begin," he announced.

This class seemed to drag on forever. I began to look out the window and my mind wandered as the professor spoke in a monotone voice. I began to wonder if I would graduate college, let alone with a biology degree.

I didn't want to disappoint George and Joyce. I knew she would be so proud to see me graduate college. I would never forget the look on her face when I received my high school diploma. If it weren't for them, who knew where I would be? Joyce always insisted I had my personal angel looking down on me.

Even life was now better than I'd ever imagined. I often could still hear my mother's words echoing in my mind: *This is the life God gave you so you may as well get used to it!* One of the many things she would mention to me was that I would be destined to stay locked up in that small, cramped apartment in the projects and eating three-day-old Hamburger Helper. At the time that was really the best meal I could get. As I began to think about my past a sudden rush of anxiety came over me. My heart began to race and my hands were shaking. I felt like I couldn't breathe. As a reaction I stood up. When I stood up, I knocked my books off my desk. Papers scattered everywhere. I was so embarrassed.

"On that note, class dismissed," I heard Professor Surry say as I hurried to pick up my books and papers.

I fell to the ground on my knees and quickly shuffled the papers together. I noticed a pair of brown leather loafers in front of me.

"Here you go."

I looked up to see Professor Surry standing before me with my books in his hands. "Thank you." I stood up and grabbed the books from his hands. Then, I quickly looked away.

"Are you all right? You look a little pale," he mentioned.

"Yes," I said, still refusing to look him in the eyes.

"I call it the freshman jitters. Relax, it's your first day." He smiled then walked away.

Now, I just needed to hear Joyce's voice telling me everything was going to be all right. Her voice represented the good in my life. My mother's lies represented the evil. It was a constant battle going on in my mind of which side I would choose.

After classes, I rushed home. Fera met me at the door as soon as I walked in. Joyce and George were both gone, but I knew it wouldn't be long before they came home. I went to my room, tossed my book on the floor, and grabbed my laptop.

Fera insisted to be on my lap while I was online. She was patiently waiting for me to rub on her belly. Next, the whines came, but I continued to ignore her. She was the most spoiled dog that I knew. Joyce and I took the award for making her that way.

I heard someone knocking at the door.

"Come in," I said before turning around to see who it was.

"Hey, honey, what are you doing?" Joyce asked.

"I'm just e-mailing Julie and Becca, telling them all about my first day at Old Dominion."

"All right. Dinner will be ready in an hour," she said.

"What are we having?" I inquired.

"Fried chicken. I want to try out the new skillet I bought exclusively from the celebrity chef Paula Deen's cookware line," Joyce said, proud of her new cookware.

"I can't wait to taste it with a few dabs of Louisiana Hot Sauce." I laughed.

That was one perk about being at home. Before entering college, Joyce and George suggested that I live on campus, but I wasn't ready to leave home yet. After all, who would cook me dinner? And there was no way I could leave my Fera behind. I gave her a big hug and sat her down on the floor.

After turning back around to face my laptop, I finished e-mailing my two best friends. Becca was attending Hampton University and Julie was accepted to Virginia Commonwealth University in Richmond, Virginia.

I jumped in the shower to get freshened up for dinner. Joyce didn't allow dirty hands at her table. As I bathed, I looked at the many marks all over my thighs. A certain feeling of shame came over me as I ran the washcloth over my legs. Thank goodness, the marks were hidden to Joyce's eyes. She would first lay hands on me and pray to God to get the demon out of me; then she would make me continue my therapy sessions.

I hurried and rinsed the soap from my body and got out of the shower. After drying off, I grabbed my Victoria's Secret Amber Romance body spray. It only had a few drops left. I sprayed those few squirts on my neck, arms, and legs. Then, I threw the bottle away. Normally, Joyce would have a new spray, body wash, and lotion set waiting for me but money had been tight lately.

Since Joyce and George were recently retired and forced to live on a fixed income, I knew extra money wouldn't be handed out to me. Besides, whatever Pell school grants didn't cover for tuition, George and Joyce were paying out of pocket. I felt bad when the total of my schoolbooks came to a whopping $600. So there was no way I was going to ask for something like Victoria's Secret fragrances.

As I got dressed in my Victoria's Secret pajamas, I realized just how privileged I was. It was time for me to get at least a part-time job and help out a little bit. Earlier in the day, a classmate of mine, Heather, told me about a place called Pearl. It was an upscale spa not far from Shore Drive in Virginia Beach. She'd recently been hired there and figured that would be a perfect spot for me. I had no other choice but to take her up on the offer.

Chapter 9

Interview

"Thank you for calling Pearl; would you be so kind and hold please?" I could hear the receptionist say as I walking up to the counter.

"Yes, how may I help you?" she asked me after I approached the front desk. Calm and serene music was playing in the background. A scent of cotton freshness filled the air. I could have closed my eyes and taken a nap in this place. I felt so at peace there.

"Hi, I'm here to see Antonia. I have an interview at three o'clock," I stated.

"Your name is Angela, yes?"

"Yes." I nodded.

"I'm so glad you could make it. I'm Antonia. Please have a seat in the waiting room and I will be with you shortly." She pointed to a room beside the receptionist desk.

I walked into the waiting room and was met by a sixty-inch flat-screen television. It was turned to the CNN news channel. A small concession table sat in the corner. Espresso, tea, Italian sodas, juice, and water were offered. Also, there were shortbread cookies, crackers, cheese, and grapes perfectly arranged on the table.

"Would you care for a glass of champagne?" a tall, slender woman with a dark tan asked me.

"No, thank you," I said, then noticed Antonia walking up.

"Ahh, Angela, I apologize for the wait. Please, let's go into my office," she said while shaking my hand.

I immediately picked up on the Coco Chanel perfume she had on. Joyce wore the same perfume. She reserved it for those special nights she and George went out dancing. She said the perfume made her feel sexy.

"Have a seat," Antonia said.

"Thank you." I nodded, sitting down in the elegant chair before me. Her office depicted the Renaissance age of Italy with her wall full of paintings. The chairs were made like masterpieces. They were accented floral upholstered armchairs in dark oak.

"Heather told me you were beautiful. A picture of you wouldn't do you justice. Now, let's get down to business. I need a girl in the afternoon to answer phones and schedule appointments. I pay three dollars above minimum wage. Is this something you can agree with?" She got straight to the point.

"Yes; when can I start?" I asked full of excitement.

"Today, if you brought the white shirt and black pants and black shoes that I instructed you to bring."

"Yes, I did," I said, holding up the small duffle bag full of clothes.

"Well, in that case, you can start right now. I need a copy of your driver's license and your social security card so you can begin giving your hard-earned money away to the government. This is what they like to call taxes. Personally, I think it's legalized robbery." Antonia and I both laughed; then she continued. "There is a bathroom down the hall. You can change clothes there. Next to the bathroom is a closet; please bring up some shortbread cookies. Last but not least, here are your very own pair of pearl earrings. If I like you, I will buy you a pearl necklace. This officially makes you part of the team. Guard those pearls with your life and don't come to work without them. Got it, newbie?" she asked while giving me a playful smack to the butt.

"Yeah, I got it." I gave her thumbs-up with a smile.

"Welcome to Pearl, my darling. Call me Tony or Antonia. I will meet you at the front desk in thirty minutes. Meanwhile, you're welcome to look around," she said.

After I changed my clothes in the bathroom, I went to the closet to grab the shortbread cookies as Antonia had instructed. The door shut behind me. I couldn't help hearing a moaning sound coming from the back of the closet. I moved closer to the sound and moved out of the way some supplies on a shelf. There, I found a small peephole in the wall of the closet. Out of curiosity, I looked in. I could see a woman who looked as though she had just finished giving a man a massage. I watched quietly as she inched toward his dick. She began to kiss his thighs then moved toward his balls. Seconds later, she was licking his balls and stroking his penis. Next, in a sudden motion, his dick was engulfed in her mouth. His moans became louder. She stopped and climbed on top to ride him. He grabbed her tightly around her waist as she thrust her pelvis against his. With every stroke, she was pounding her pussy on his dick even harder. The man climaxed within minutes. The woman climbed off of him and began to clean him up.

Even though I was in shock from what I'd just witnessed, my pussy was undeniably soaking wet and I had an overwhelming urge to have an orgasm. I found a spot in the corner to sit. I propped open my legs and placed my hand inside my panties. As I pictured the image of the woman riding the man's dick, I massaged my clit quickly back and forth. I needed to cum and fast. What seemed like a minute later, my body was shaking with pleasure. I took a moment to gather myself then prepared to leave the closet. I realized what was really going on. This business was soliciting for sex. I knew that was probably how Antonia made her real money. I had to wonder, *should I even be working at a place like this? So this is what Becca calls a happy ending.*

"Angela, darling, did you find the cookies? I might have forgotten to pick up some at the store," Antonia said after opening the closet door.

Startled by her entrance, I quickly yelled, "I got them," while holding them up and smiling.

"Wonderful. Now let's get you on the phone," she said.

"Great," I said with a smile.

I decided to try this newfound job out for a while. It paid decently. Besides, I was the one snooping. I knew I would never agree to have sex with a client.

Chapter 10

Moving Along

Two years had passed with me strolling through college, only putting in a few late nights. Things were progressing just as I planned.

I had moved out of Joyce and George's home and into a cozy apartment near Town Center in Virginia Beach. It was hard to go but Fera and I were ready to be on our own. Of course, we would go visit every Sunday for family dinner. At times, Fera cried for Joyce. For a while, I felt a little guilty about taking her baby away from her. They slept together every night. Now, Fera and I slept together.

Antonia had promoted me to be the manager of her spa. Since my promotion, she was hardly even there. As long as the money was right and the girls were safe, she didn't have a care. It didn't take me long to realize that her so-called "spa" was really operating as an upscale cathouse. There were beautiful girls wanting to get paid and men obliging them with cash and credit cards.

There were times I still watched from that peephole in the closet. It was my little secret. My mind drifted to a world of lust and sexual satisfaction. I had begun to think about sex as much as I'd thought about the revenge on the men who raped me when I was younger. It was almost as though I was obsessed with sex and revenge.

I'd spent months researching the whereabouts of Sam Burns and Timothy McCall, the two other men who raped me when I was a child. Those memories had never left my mind. Mentally and emotionally, I have been tortured over and over again each day. I knew from my research that both of them remained good friends to this very day. At times, I wondered if that event held their friendship so tightly after all these years. It turned out Harvey Cumberland, the first man I killed, left his best buddies a large sum of money. With it, those two opened up a bar called Jazz. Fortunately for me, they worked late nights. For months, I had been carefully watching them at the bar and it was finally time for me to execute.

I was camped out in my car across the street dressed all in black. When the night was dying down, I crept over behind the building of the bar. I even wore Depends underwear just in case I would be out here for hours. Since that awful night they raped me, I'd been dreaming of this moment of revenge.

"I'm going to take the trash out and I'm outta here," Sam said while opening the door. He kept the door cracked open. I assumed because he had more trash to take out.

It was my chance to strike. I was able to slither into the bar. I quietly located the circuit breaker and turned the knobs to a downward position to turn all the lights off.

"What the hell!" Timothy blurted out.

I never forgot the sound and tone of each of their voices. I was laughing inside with my knife in one hand and my infamous blow torch in the other, knowing the sheer joy I was going to experience while slaughtering them. I could feel someone coming. An adrenaline rush came over me. I caught Timothy from behind, jerked his head back, and cut him right above the eyes. He immediately dropped to the floor, lying on his back. He yelled out in pain while grabbing his eye.

"Shut up!" I said. I stepped on his dick, grinding it with my sneaker. I cut his throat and cut his wrists.

"You remember me. I'm Angela Farmer."

"I'm so sorry. Forgive me. Have mercy on my soul. Jesus wouldn't want this."

"You want to play the Jesus card. Well, I'm here to tell you, the Lord isn't here tonight but the devil is. Go join your friend Harvey and burn in hell," I said before lighting the blow torch on him. As I remember, Timothy was the lookout guy, too. So as a bonus, I cut out his eyes and left them at the bar.

Sam was still upfront counting money and listening to music from his cell phone. He didn't hear the commotion in the back. I got down on all fours and inched my way closer to him. I was on the other side of the bar where he couldn't see me. Finally after twenty minutes, Sam called out to Timothy. My adrenaline was rushing to the point where I was shaking. I took a deep breath.

He came out from the other side of the bar to head toward the back of the restaurant. I stuck out my leg so he would fall, and ignited the blow torch, starting with his face first. Timothy was the worst of all of them beating me repeatedly. I started cutting him with the knife everywhere. I wanted him to suffer for the rest of the night.

"Who are you?" he asked.

"Doesn't everyone want to know that tonight?" I laughed.

"Take whatever you want."

"What I want is your soul to suffer for eternity," I screamed, kicking him in the stomach.

"Stop, please, I got a wife and kids."

"They will grow up without a daddy. Angela Farmer is my name. Your friends along with yourself know what you did to me."

"I thought you died," he said, barley able to talk.

"No, I'm still here. As for you, it won't be the same case." I took out a bottle of peroxide out of my bag and poured it all over his body. He screamed in agony.

"Stop please," he begged.

"Wow, the same words I said to you as a little girl." I continued to torture him for another hour.

"Say hello to my mother when you arrive in hell," I said.

When there was little fight left in him, I stabbed Sam in the heart. He died instantly.

Driving home to my apartment, I felt no mercy. My only concern was curling up with Fera and studying one more time for a history exam.

Chapter 11

Nightmare

"Let me in," he said.

"No," I replied and starting running away as fast as I could to my secret place in the closet of Pearl.

"All I want is you," he assured me.

"A massage isn't the only service you have been arriving in this facility for," I said.

"Believe me, I get massages and leave. There is nothing more. You know you want me." He brought his lips closer to mine.

My mind struggled for half a second as I turned my head. Logically, a voice said no, but a deep-set urge inside me said yes. The man gently grabbed my chin and turned my face toward him and he leaned in for a kiss. This time, I didn't resist.

"Mmm," I said and closed my eyes right before we kissed.

"You've been watching me for a while," he whispered as he ran his fingers through my hair.

Although what he was saying was true, I didn't say a word. My mind started to drift back to the many times I'd watch his massage sessions through the peephole in the closet wall and masturbated at the same time. He started undressing me slowly. Again, I didn't resist. Once I was completely naked, he paused and looked at my entire body as if to take it all in. I began to feel self-conscious and grabbed my clothes in an attempt to cover up my scars. He grabbed my hands to stop me. Then, he got on his knees. I watched as he kissed my thighs with loving care and licked the multiple cut scars on my thighs. He slowly worked his way up my body, kissing and licking every inch on the way. When he stood to his feet, he nibbled on my neck. He never removed any of his clothing. He kept his suit on, only unzipping his pants. I closed my eyes tight as he pressed his dick against my vagina. My mind flashed back and forth.

"No!" I yelled and pushed him away.

The child inside of me didn't like this experience. It brought me back to the horrific rapes I'd experienced as a kid.

"Sssssshhh . . . it's okay," he whispered as he squeezed my ass tight and pushed his dick inside my vagina.

"Aaaahhh!" I yelled out in pain but I wanted him to continue. It was a pleasurable pain and I liked it. I finally relaxed totally and let him in. I was tired of playing the cat-and-mouse game. We began kissing again. It was more as if his tongue was chasing mine. He couldn't get enough of me. With each stroke, I wanted more and more. Within minutes, I reached my climax.

"Mmmm." I gave a relieving exhale then felt a jolt.

I opened my eyes and looked around.

It was only a dream. I woke up to Fera licking me on the cheek. Julie, who was visiting for the weekend, was on the computer playing the game *Sims* and laughing her head off.

"Hey, sleepyhead," she said.

"How long have I been asleep?" I asked.

"Just for a couple of hours. That dream must have been steamy. I could hear little moans coming from you," she mentioned.

It was quite amazing and deep inside I wished it wasn't a dream but I was too embarrassed to say.

"I collected the mail for you. I think that letter you've been waiting for has arrived. I have to run now, but call me and let me know what it says," Julie said, then gave me a hug.

"Thanks; you can let yourself out," I yelled to her as she walked out of the room.

I rubbed my eyes and gathered myself. I needed to be fully awake for this letter. I'd been waiting for months. I took a deep breath as I opened the letter titled Virginia Laboratory of Clinical Research. I read the first few lines: We are glad to inform you . . . That was all I needed to read. I knew from those words that I'd been accepted.

"Yay!" I screamed at the top of my lungs, startling Fera. She began to bark as I yelled.

I grabbed my cell phone to call Joyce and George. The phone rang several times but neither one of them answered. I figured they were probably on the farm but I couldn't wait for them to call back. News this great had to be shared right away, and even better in person. So, I grabbed the letter and Fera and hopped in the car and headed to Joyce's home.

Chapter 12

The News

"Joyce, I got accepted to a research lab," I screamed as I busted through the front door with my Fera in my arms and the acceptance letter in my hand. No one was home; although, Joyce's car was in the driveway. My cell phone rang.

"Hey, David, how are you?" I asked in an upbeat voice. He was Joyce's nephew.

"Angela, hey, I'm at the front door. Will you let me in?" he asked.

"Sure," I said before hanging up the phone.

"Hi," I said, greeting him at the door. "I'm not sure where Joyce and George are right now—"

"I know where they are," he said sharply, cutting me off and leading me to the bottom step of the staircase to sit down.

"Where are they?"

"Angela, listen to me carefully. Joyce was in an accident. They went to the Kroger grocery store. George went in and Joyce decided to stay in the car. Out of nowhere, a drunk driver hit the car. Joyce is hurt very badly. It's possible brain damage. George is all right," he explained and then snatched my keys away.

I stood up but my knees weakened. I sat back down. Joyce was hurt and I couldn't even move.

"I need to go the hospital," I said with tears coming down my face.

"They are at Obici Hospital. I'm going to take you, now. Angela, you are in no condition to drive." David's words began to slur and echo in my head.

The room started to spin. I couldn't breathe. I didn't know what to do. At a time like this, I knew Joyce would pray. I gave up on God a long time ago but I was willing to call on His name for the sake of Joyce. In my mind, I began to pray for God to heal her. I had to wonder if I was I being punished for killing those men who savaged me.

"Please drive fast," I demanded after David had approached the highway. "Where's Fera?" I asked, almost forgetting about her

"I put her in the doggie crate in the kitchen. She will be fine 'til we return to the house," he said.

Sweat was pouring down my face. The minutes seemed endless but we finally pulled up next to the hospital entrance. I managed to get out of the car. I didn't take two complete steps before everything around me became silent, and my vision slowly left me and suddenly everything went black.

Chapter 13

Awakening

I awoke to a doctor shining a light in my eye. *So this is the end huh? I never knew if this heaven place really existed and if so I never imagined there would be a place for me,* I thought.

"Angela . . . Angela." I heard a male voice call out to me.

"God, is that you? Am I in heaven?" I managed to say softly.

"Get the doctor. She is in room five now," he said to someone.

Soon, I heard heels clicking toward me.

"Angela, my name is Dr. Seymour. You're not dead, honey. You have been in the hospital since Friday. I need you to nod your head slowly so I know you understand the words that I am speaking to you," she instructed.

I nodded my head as I struggled to focus my eyes. As things became clear I was able to see. George was standing next to the doctor. I sat up slowly and looked around the room. I didn't see Joyce.

"Where's Joyce?" I asked.

No one responded. It was as though I hadn't said anything at all so I asked again. "Where's Joyce, George? Answer me," I demanded.

The room went silent, and with the exception of the male nurse quickly coming in to take my vitals, everyone sat motionless.

"Where is she?" I yelled angrily.

"She is in the room across the hall," George finally replied.

"I want to see her," I said as I struggled to rise from the bed.

"Now, just a moment, Angela, please. We need to talk," a familiar voice said.

I looked up to see my therapist entering through the door. "I don't want to hear what you have to say. Joyce needs me right now! Where is Fera? What day is it?" I asked.

Again the room was still and no one responded. I was beginning to get beyond irritated. "Somebody answer me," I pleaded.

"Fera is at the house. David and his wife are there keeping her company. Today is Sunday," George explained.

"Give me a few moments and then I will let you see Joyce," the therapist, Dr. Gunter, bargained with me.

"Listen to her," George added.

"Angela, you have a severe anxiety disorder. The worst kind I have ever seen. Due to your condition, you have been in a coma state for several days. I wrote you a prescription for a drug called Ativan. When these attacks happen in the future, you need to take the medication. When you are discharged you will get a prescription for the medication. Also, I urge you to continue therapy sessions with me or another psychologist. The rape and the abuse from your mother have deeply affected your past and present, but please don't let it affect your future."

"Are you done, now?" I asked while getting out of bed to enter into the hallway to find Joyce's room. George assisted me with putting a robe on.

"Joyce," I called out as I entered the hospital hallway.

"Follow me," George instructed.

I walked closely behind George. The halls were quiet and there were only a few people around. I looked at the large rooms with glass sliding doors. All the patients seem near to death and barely holding on to life. My stomach filled with butterflies as I began to wonder what kind of state Joyce was in.

George stopped in front of a room with similar glass doors as all the other rooms we'd passed. The curtain was drawn so I couldn't see inside. "This is Joyce's room." He pointed. I took a deep breath and walked in.

"You woke up," Joyce said in a whisper as I walked in.

Her voice was weak and she looked just as sick as the other people I'd seen in the rooms before hers. She had a tube in her nose for oxygen and multiple IVs stuck in her arms. I was hoping it looked worse than it really was.

"Joyce, when are we leaving? I just want to go home," I said with tears in my eyes and leaning down to hug her.

"Baby, I'm going home, just not quite yet. Sit down; I want to talk to you."

"I'm going to take such good care of you. All these years of helping you cook won't go to waste," I said, holding her hands. We both laughed together.

"Yes, you do know how to run my kitchen. First, I need to explain some things to you. Angela, I know you've gone through a lot in your life and you experienced some really bad things as a little precious girl. For so long you thought no one loved you and you were alone. Well, you weren't alone. George and I have loved you your entire life."

"My entire life?" I interrupted Joyce. I was confused by her statement.

"Angela." She squeezed my hand tight. "George and I are your paternal grandparents. Your father was our son. He was one of the youngest men recruited in the FBI. The first week on the job he was killed by an assailant. Your mother didn't handle it well. She went into labor the day of the funeral. She wasn't able to attend and blamed you for not seeing your father, George III, one last time. Your mother ceased all contact with anyone. We had no idea how badly you were being treated and attempted many times to reach out to our only grandchild. Your mother had schizophrenia. Her drug use made matters worse," Joyce explained.

I sat in silence as I tried to absorb all the things I was hearing. Tears began to fill my eyes and my heart ached literally.

"Here are some pictures of your father," George added, then handed me an envelope.

I remained silent. I couldn't form any words. I didn't know what to say or how to feel at the moment.

"So this is the same man whose portrait hung in the living room for all these years?" I managed to ask.

"Yes," George confirmed while nodding his head.

"Before you ask, we didn't tell you because we weren't sure if you could handle this type of delicate information. We showed how much we cared by raising you. Yes, the first decade of your life was pure horror, but the next one, I hope you feel we brought joy and enriched your life."

"Yes, you did." I finally managed to force out some words, then burst out into tears and began to cry uncontrollably.

"From the bottom of our hearts, we apologize for not telling you sooner," George said.

"I love you," Joyce said and squeezed my hand hard again.

Tears were streaming down her face. The monitor that sat beside her began to beep fast and loud. Moments later, the nurses ran in. George pulled me aside, sat me in a nearby chair, grabbed my hands, and looked me directly in the eyes.

"Your grandmother has a bad heart. We discovered this a few years ago. The accident has taken a toll on her body. She has been struggling since we got here," George explained.

"What are you saying?" I asked, although I knew exactly what he meant.

"It's time," George said to the nurses who struggled to keep Joyce alive.

He led me over to Joyce's bedside.

"Angela, it's time. I'm going home to heaven. I'm going to ask God if I can take over being your angel." She forced out the words.

A sudden feeling of peace came over me. It was as though I knew Joyce was leaving this earth. George and I both kissed and hugged her. Within seconds, she took her last breath and fell into an everlasting, peaceful sleep.

"She was waiting for you. She didn't want to be revived initially but she asked that the nurses resuscitate her until she got to see you one last time. She didn't want to leave you without the chance to say good-bye," George said with tears in his eyes.

Chapter 14

Sorrow

Six days, eight hours, twenty-four minutes, and fifty-nine seconds later, we laid Joyce to rest. I refused to look into the casket. I wanted to remember her as she was: warm, vibrant, and full of life. George and I decided for her to wear a pink dress she wore most of the time when they went dancing. A pink rose was placed in her hair. It was surreal that she was even gone. For days, Fera continued to go to Joyce's bedroom, looking for her. Every time she did that I would break down in tears.

Even though at first there was some resistance, the church finally agreed to let me have Fera be present during the funeral. Joyce would have wanted it that way.

Julie and Becca were right by my side. My old social worker even showed up to be there for me. To my surprise, Heather and Antonia sent flowers to the church. People from high school who I hadn't seen or heard from in years made an appearance. It meant a lot to me that people cared about my grandmother and me. The choir sang the song "I Feel Like Going On." I could barely stand. George had to literally hold me up.

He was trying his best to put on a strong front. Deep down, I knew he was hurting even more than me. They had been married longer than I had been alive.

There wasn't a single seat left in the church. I knew but I didn't realize how much Joyce had impacted the community. She had helped so many families get on or get back on their feet.

"Let's not be sad and weep into the night. Instead, let's rejoice her death," the preacher suggested, looking directly at me.

At the end of the service, we all marched out. The open casket sat at the door of the church so people might view the body as we exited. The family exited first. My heart raced as I got closer to the church doors. I knew Joyce's pale, cold, lifeless body would be waiting there for me.

"Are you sure that you don't want to get one last glimpse of her?" George asked.

"Yes, I'm sure." I nodded my head.

The repast was held at the house directly after we left the burial site. I was sitting in the kitchen at my grandparent's house, barely able to speak. So many people were giving me their condolences but I wasn't even listening. It's not that I didn't want to, I just couldn't. Life had become a blur. I didn't know what the next day or the next minute would bring. All I knew was that Joyce, whom I loved so dearly, was gone. Tired of the constant aggravation, I walked out to the back porch. I figured a little air would make me feel a little better. Fera followed me outside.

"Angela, please eat something," Martha suggested. She was one of Joyce's best friends. I hadn't been outside a full five minutes before she spotted me. Martha had been sitting on the swing, smoking a cigarette, when she noticed my presence.

"No, thank you," I said, shaking my head.

I began to get short of breath and everything began to spin. I needed to lie down. I went upstairs to my old bedroom to take off my black dress. Afterward, I stood in the mirror and looked at my naked body. I stared at the multiple scar marks on my thighs. Then, I grabbed the razor that was sitting on the top of my dresser. My initial thought was to slit my wrists. After all, I had nothing more to live for. Then, Fera ran in the room and sat beside me. I was so deep in my thoughts that I totally ignored her. Then, she began to whimper. There was no way I could ignore that. I picked her up and dropped the razor to the floor.

I finally took an even longer look at myself, wondering, *what am I doing? What am I supposed to do now?* I started to feel like I was losing it and Joyce's death was going to consume me so much that I may have spiraled downhill. Being on the brink of insanity, I grabbed an Ativan and popped it in my mouth, then lay down for a much-needed rest.

Chapter 15

Tension

"I'm going to erupt in your mouth," I assured him with his head buried in between my legs.

"I'm ready and can't wait for you to do it again," he lifted his head up long to whisper.

The alarm clock sounded, waking me from my sleep. I woke up and removed my hand from between my legs, realizing I was only dreaming.

"Damn it, I was dreaming again!" I said to no one in particular, then hit the off button on the alarm clock.

Periodically, I would have this dream of having steamy sexual encounters with the same man. Funny thing was that I could never see his face. All I seemed to get a glimpse of was his smile. I flipped on the television to get a look of the weather for the day. That's when I read across the screen that the university was closed due to bad weather. That was music to my ears.

I went to the bathroom and started the shower as I brushed my teeth. The entire time all I could think of was my dream. The constant thoughts of that dream were causing sexual tension to build up inside of me. As I got naked for the shower, I began to touch myself. Just then my cell phone rang. By the time I reached the phone it had stopped ringing.

I checked my voicemails and it was my therapist I had been seeing. She was still calling me. I figured

George was probably putting her up to it. They were so afraid that Joyce's death would cause me to act out and possibly hurt someone or myself. Little did they know, I hadn't laid a hand on anyone but myself, and that was in the most pleasurable way possible.

After a quick shower, I decided to go to the store to pick up a few items. Fera was running out of her doggie treats. She would have a fit knowing her favorite chicken bones were all gobbled up. I dressed warmly and threw on snow boots. The streets were snowed in so I would have to walk around the corner to the store. When I reached my destination, there were only the store clerk and manager there. I guessed we were the only ones brave enough to chance going out in such bad weather.

"Excuse me, do you carry chicken treats for petite dogs?" I asked the manager, who was stocking up the shelf with salad dressings.

"Yes, I think so. Let me check in the back," he replied. "What kind of dog do you have?" he asked as I followed him.

"A teacup yorkie," I answered as I continued to follow.

As I watched this young man, the urge I was feeling from this morning was increasing. I felt like I couldn't fight it any longer. I wanted to run to the women's restroom and masturbate in hopes that it would provide some sort of relief.

"You can wait here or continue shopping. Don't worry, I'll find you," he suggested, interrupting my moment of extreme sexual tension.

"I will hang out here," I said, smiling.

I watched the movement of his tight, round ass as he walked. For some reason, I began to place his face on the faceless man in my persistent dreams. Almost instantly, that sexual urge I had earlier in the morning was back. The urge was so strong that I actually glanced around to see if there was a bathroom nearby that I could go in and please myself.

After he went into the back, I waited a few minutes. I glanced around again for a visible restroom but there was none in sight. I placed my oversized purse in front of me as I gently rubbed my hand between my legs. That just couldn't give me the satisfaction I needed. I felt like I was going to explode inside. I headed into the stockroom in the direction I'd seen the manager go. When I walked in, he was kneeled down, looking through boxes. He turned around and got up.

"Ma'am, it's not recommended that customers enter the stockroom. Liability purposes," he explained.

I totally ignored the statement he made. My mind was on more pressing issues. I came closer to him and I gave him a kiss. At first, he looked confused and pulled back slightly. I grabbed his face and kissed him again. This time, he wanted more. His tongue felt warm as he kissed me passionately.

"Where's your office?" I whispered in his ear.

"Over there." He pointed as I rubbed on his dick.

I'd never had an experience like this before, but I'd played it over so many times in my head. With the constant dreams, the demonstrations I watched through the peephole at Pearl and with all the pornos I'd watched, I felt like I'd seen enough to teach a class. It was as though I was a self-taught professional.

I gently tugged on it as I led the way to the office. I took down his pants and motioned for him to lie down on his desk, not bothering to clear out the countless piles of paper on top. I pulled up my trench coat and placed my panties in my coat pocket. He struggled to take out a condom. I quickly placed the condom on his dick, not hesitating to climb on afterward. Both of us could hear the store clerk paging him over and over again. Neither of us cared. I had to come and so did he.

It was quite painful as I forced my wet pussy down on his erect penis. Slowly, inch by inch, we moved in unison, pushing his dick deep inside me. It was a pleasurable pain, like nothing I'd ever felt before.

"Your pussy is ssoooo tight," he said as he squeezed my ass tight.

Once he was fully inside me, my thoughts drifted back to scenes from multiple dreams and pornos I'd seen. I thrust my hips back and forth, giving my clit a pleasing feeling. It didn't take long for me to reach my climax. We both panted. It was an indication we had come. Without a word, I lifted my body and slid my panties back on.

"Now, about those chicken treats. Did you find them?" I asked while tightening the belt of my coat.

"It's in the boxes near the long shelves," he said, panting.

"Thanks." I nodded.

"Take a couple of bags free of charge," he suggested.

"No; I appreciate the offer. You work just as I do. Missing inventory won't get you that yearly bonus," I said and walked out of the office.

Chapter 16

Visitors

"Welcome to Pearl, how may I help you?" I greeted the gentleman. The line was getting backed up.

"I have an appointment with Amanda. I'm a little early. It's my first time," the man explained.

"Please, have a seat in our guest area. There are complimentary refreshments, as well. You're welcome to them," I replied.

"If you don't mind, may I pay upfront? When I get done, I have some other business meetings to attend to," he said.

"Of course, sir. Let me just take a peek at the package you're receiving today," I mentioned.

"Do you take all major credit cards?" he asked.

"Yes. Your total will be $575," I said as he handed me the card, not caring about the figure I gave him. After a short while, I escorted him to his room.

All of the sudden, the FBI came barging in the facility. My hands started shaking badly and my armpits were sweating.

I was shoved into a room until they were ready to speak with me. Women and men were close to bare naked being hauled to the nearest police station. It was so humiliating. While waiting to be interrogated, I still had my cell phone. A few years back, the owner, Antonia, and I had established a special language. I sent her a text to a private cell phone line saying the Chanel perfume had ran out. It truly meant law enforcement had raided the place.

Pinned to me was a woman who was sobbing about her husband finding out about her indiscretions. She had been a regular client, always requesting Thomas. A few months earlier, she blurted out he was the only man who knew how to satisfy her. I knew the employees were selling pleasure and sheer fantasy. I just never envisioned Pearl getting raided.

The FBI officer dragged me to Antonia's office.

"Aah, I remember you little one from years ago on the police force. My last name is Goldman. What would have your grandmother thought of you working here, Ms. Farmer?" she started to ask me.

It was becoming rather difficult not to retaliate. I had to remain calm if I wanted to walk out of here. Fortunately, for me, Antonia gave me intensive training on these situations having the potential to get out of control.

"Leave my grandmother out of this," I said, finally acknowledging her.

"You go from milking cows to knowingly working for an upscale whorehouse," the agent said, obviously trying to strike a chord with me.

"What can I help you with?" I inquired.

"The head of Pearl, Antonia," she stated.

In my mind, I laughed. The FBI was going to put in countless hours to track Antonia. This wasn't her first go-round with them. The agent, Goldman, appeared to have a personal vendetta against her. *Let the games begin.*

Mostly, everyone was taken to the local police station for questioning. No one truly knew where she was. I didn't even know. Later into the night, we were released.

Chapter 17

Aftermath

I later found out Antonia and the establishment of Pearl owed back taxes totaling over $1 million. It was the true reason why Pearl was raided the previous week. From the time I sent her that text, I still hadn't heard from her. Of course, all of her phone numbers were no good anymore. Because I'd pretty much been running Pearl, nearly all of the employees and clients were looking for me to pick up the pieces. The loss of Pearl was hitting us hard. I was barely able to pay my rent. Sad thing was, I didn't know what I was going to do, either. Working in this kind of business doesn't guarantee a severance package.

Janet, another of the employees, told me that she didn't have money for daycare. I felt bad. Jacob from security left me voicemails saying his house was going to be foreclosed on. Their burdens were beginning to become mine. A lot of Antonia's workers had been with her for years. It was wrong how she just left. No one knew where the hell she was. She could have been at her beach house in Los Angeles while everyone was suffering. As for myself, my brain had grown tired of trying to figure it out. I was on my own, now.

This day, I made it a point to refer all calls to voicemail first thing in the morning. I had another exam to study for and I wanted to go check on George. I would go by every Sunday and cook him a meal. In honor of Joyce, I would make fried fish. It's a funny story. The first time I learned to fry fish, Joyce gave me a thirty-minute lesson on it. That same day, she hosted the church picnic. I fried at least a hundred pieces of fish, slaving over hot grease for at least ten hours. She would always tell me work does a body a whole lot of good. I laughed to myself as I thought back to that story.

A knock on the front door interrupted my trip down memory lane. I realized it was Heather, a classmate and coworker of mine. She graduated last year with a chemistry degree. She vowed to find a cure for Parkinson's disease through obtaining a job doing clinical research. Well, grants ran dry and the research jobs were scarce and most required a master's degree before you could even apply.

"Hey," I said after opening the door.

"May I come in for a few minutes?" she asked.

"Yes." I nodded.

"Have you heard from her?" she asked, referring to Antonia.

"No," I responded. She knew I wouldn't lie to her.

"What if this matter is more serious than we thought?"

"You could be right," I agreed.

"I've been thinking. Don't judge me, but I made a spreadsheet of all the men who made appointments with me. Plus, I managed to escape with the appointment book," she explained.

"What do you have in mind?" I wondered.

"We could try to go in business for ourselves. Angela, you have the charm and charisma to get the clients in the door. I keep them coming back. I have got bills to pay. The local grocery store isn't even hiring. Think about it and please let me know," she expressed.

"I will." I nodded. She left soon after our conversation.

On the way to see George, all I could think about were the pros and cons of going into business with Heather. My options of making ends meet were limited too. Besides, I couldn't dare ask George for any money.

"Ouch," I yelped as the grease from the skillet popped me on the arm. Fera came from the living room to see if I was okay and to see if I was going to give her another baby carrot. Of course, I gave her another one.

"Angela, are you all right in there?" George asked from his recliner chair in the living room.

"Yes," I said. My mind kept drifting about the conversation I had with Heather earlier. It was such a risk. *Can she and I really pull it off?* I thought as I flipped the last piece of fish with the spatula.

Chapter 18

Sunday Afternoon

"Your meals are tasting better and better," George commented, nodding his head.

"Thanks. Joyce made sure I was going to learn how to cook." I giggled.

"Hey, boss. I'm done out here. The tractor is ready to go," Larry, the handyman, said after entering the dining room.

"Thanks," George said.

"Would you like a plate to take home?" I asked.

"No, I don't want to impose."

"I insist. We have plenty of food," I replied.

"All right, I'll take a little plate home," he agreed, knowing he wanted the food in the first place.

It took no time to make a hefty plate to go and walk outside with Larry. Besides, I needed some fresh afternoon air.

"Can we take a walk?" I suggested, motioning to the door.

"Sure," he agreed.

"So how are things?" I asked him.

"Well, you know. I'm taking it day by day. It's still unreal Sheila and the baby died on the operating table. It's been over two years but I still struggle with it every day. About two weeks ago, I managed to go out on a date," he explained.

Larry had been working for George even before I came along. It started as a part-time job in the beginning. As business grew, Larry never left. He's five years older than me. When I was younger, I would watch from my window him working on the farm. I had to admit a few times he probably caught me staring.

Sheila and Larry had been high school sweethearts. You know, the couple everyone loves to hate. For a while, they struggled to conceive a child. Her pregnancy went smoothly. She was so happy at the baby shower. While Sheila went into premature labor, she suddenly fainted. Her heart stopped. The autopsy report came back with a rare heart condition.

Now, Larry was just trying to make it day by day. In an instant, his family was dead. After the funeral, I wondered how he got out of bed. He would be on the farm working for hours just so he didn't have to go home.

"How did the date turn out?" I asked.

"A disaster, because all I did was talk about her. George said take all the time I need. That man will never get over Joyce passing away. That woman truly had his heart."

"Yes," I agreed.

This was the right opportunity for me to make my move. I slowly moved close to him and nestled my hands in position to rub his chest and move up to his shoulders.

We stopped next to the barn to watch the sun set. He had been coming to the house for years and had always been respectful to Joyce and me. Deep down, I thought Joyce told him my story. When he looked at me, I could tell he felt pity for me.

"What are you doing?" he asked after I got behind him. He seemed sort of startled.

"I'm going to relieve some built-up tension for you and me," I assured him, guiding him into the barn.

By this time, the sun had set. I took off the sundress that I had on to be completely naked, no panties or bra. I motioned for Larry to take off his shirt. The hay in the barn served as a bed for us to lie down together. I climbed on top of him and continued to rub his chest. I playfully put my breasts in his face. I started playing with my clit to give him a show that only he could watch. The next thing I knew, his tongue was sucking on my clit. It was as if he was pulling my orgasm even closer to his mouth. I came so hard that it felt as though the ground was moving with me. Larry laid me down, and took off his pants and boxer shorts to enter into my nectar walls. Each stroke was hard and immersed. After we both came, a small period of silence moved in.

I put my dress back on.

"Angela, that was beautiful," Larry said while trying to hug me.

"Stop," I said.

"What! I don't understand."

"Stop, leave me alone."

"You let me make love to you and now you're looking at me as if I'm trash."

"Larry, leave me alone!" I screamed with tears in my eyes.

When I walked back into the house, I grabbed Fera. She was asleep in George's lap. He was asleep as well. I put my hair in my face so he wouldn't notice that I had been crying.

"You gone already?" he asked after hearing Fera whimper.

"Yes, I've got a long day tomorrow," I explained.

"Bye, Angela. I'll see next week. I love you."

"I'm looking forward to it. I love you, too," I said and walked out of the door. I didn't see Larry anywhere in sight. I couldn't deal with what just happened. I stormed to the car and placed Fera in her car crate. She was whimpering because she could tell something wasn't right with me. What I wanted to do was just drive and get lost into a song.

After an hour or so, I ended up at Heather's door. I knocked on the door. I knew it was late but hopefully she would be home and answer.

"So do you have an answer for me?" Heather asked, yawning, after she opened the door.

"Yes." I nodded.

"Come in here so I can hear it," she said, eager to see if I would take part in this business plan.

"Okay, I will agree to this for only a while," I stressed to her.

"I understand how you feel. I myself want to do this temporarily as well," she stated.

"All the tools and resources are within our reach."

"Explain while I make some popcorn," she said.

"We have everyone's number from Pearl. We will decide who is useful or not. First thing is the location. A few days ago, Jacob, who was one of the top security guards, called and said his house was in foreclosure. I spoke to him. His duplex is the house in foreclosure. He kicked both of his tenants out for nonpayment. We will start small and use his house. In a few months, I will be aiming for us to be in some sort of building. What do you think so far?" I asked.

"I like it so far. You're the brains in this operation. Do you want soda, juice, or water?" she asked from the kitchen.

"What kind of soda do you have?"

"Italian soda. You have a choice of lemon or blood orange."

"I will take a small glass of blood orange," I decided.

"You're in luck. I have kettle corn tonight," she said.

"Hip hip hooray," I replied.

"I will be saying that when my first student loan payment is paid on time." She snickered.

Later on that night, I lay in my bed thinking about what was going to happen. I could feel the pressure on my shoulders already. I knew those people I wanted to hire back were going to be depending on me. I wasn't sure I could handle it.

Chapter 19

School News

At times, I felt as though I shouldn't have been born during my era. I preferred the early 1930s and 1940s, when life was much simpler, mixed with a mother who truly loved me. Even after so many years, I often still wondered why she just couldn't love me. I couldn't remember one time when she hugged me or said I love you. Funny thing was I had more loving memories with my second-grade teacher, Ms. Old, who paid more attention to me than my own mother.

Trying to find my car in the university parking lot was a nightmare at times. I couldn't tell you how many times I would forget where I parked.

"Excuse me, are you Angela Farmer?" a woman asked as I was getting into my car leaving class. The school parking lot was noisy because so many people were trying to leave.

"Yes," I said, wondering where I knew this woman from. She looked familiar.

"Hi, I'm Maureen Saunders."

"What can I help you with?" I inquired, now wondering if she was one of the FBI agents who had approached me trying to find the whereabouts of Antonia. I was going to make sure that my answers to the few questions I allowed her to ask me would be short and to the point.

"I'm looking for my birth mother. I've been searching for quite a while. You were listed as next of kin to
Pamela Farmer. I'm your half sister," she explained
and then gave me a hug.

I pushed myself away from the grips of her arms.
My stomach began to turn after hearing her say my
mother's full name. I hadn't said that name in years.
My surroundings were spinning. I broke out in a cold
sweat and my hands began shaking.

"Are you all right?" she asked.

"Yes." I nodded. I quickly reached into my purse to
grab an Ativan pill.

"You sure?"

"I'm positive. You just hit me a lot of unexpected
information. I mean I never knew you existed," I
responded.

I tried to gather my composure. I wasn't really sure
how to receive Maureen. A part of me was thankful I
wouldn't be so alone in life. Yet another part of me felt
George, Joyce, and Fera were all the family I needed.
I quickly rummaged through my purse to pop a pill in
my mouth.

"I have proof. Here is my birth certificate and I have
a few pictures of her. She gave me up at the tender age
of fifteen. My adopted parents were great but I have
always been curious about my mother and father."

I examined the birth certificate. We didn't have the
same father. I couldn't bear looking at the pictures. The
sight of my mother made me nauseous. I didn't care
whether it was a young picture of her or not.

"This is a lot to take in," I said, taking deep breaths.
The medicine was finally kicking in. I was ready to ride
the wave of relaxation.

"So where is our mother?" Maureen wanted to know
so desperately.

I pondered before answering her, *Should I tell her the truth? Or should I lie? If I tell her the truth, I may run the risk of not having any type of relationship with her.*

"How did you find me?" I asked, changing the subject.

"I hired a private detective."

"Do you mind if we go sit down?" I asked her while pointing to a bench nearby.

"Okay," she agreed.

"Tell me about yourself. We will get to your mother later."

"I'm thirty-two years old. I'm married with two kids, Jordan and Jade, with a dog named Chewy. I work for an accounting firm. I have always loved numbers. And you?"

"I'm twenty-two years old. I'm graduating next week with a biology degree. I have a dog named Fera, who I love dearly. I recently was laid off by my employer. The economy got a hold of the company," I lied. I was too embarrassed to tell her how I really made a living. "Do you have pictures of your family? I'm sure your children are beautiful," I said in an attempt to switch the subject off me.

"Yeah, they're my cutie pies," Maureen replied, reaching into her purse, pulling out her wallet, and showing me the most recent school pictures of the kids. She told me about the kids as I looked at the pictures.

"You're a good mother. I can tell."

"Did our mother raise you?" she asked.

"I was in her possession 'til the age of twelve. Then, my paternal grandparents raised me," I answered her in a roundabout way.

"I have longed to know what she looks like now and where she is in life," Maureen commented.

"Listen, your mother was mentally ill. She suffered from being bipolar and was a drug abuser. With this deadly combination, my childhood was unbearable. She beat me, would leave for days. Ultimately, she hated me and to show it she let three men rape me at the age of twelve. After I was raped, she locked me in a closet for days. I almost died. I stabbed her repeatedly and set her body on fire. Your mother has been in hell for quite some time. If you must go visit, she is at the Woodlawn Cemetery in Virginia Beach. Before you ask or if it may cross your mind, I don't feel bad for what I did and never will."

Maureen ran to a nearby garbage can and began to vomit. I followed her.

"I'm sorry that I don't have a better happy ending for you, but this is the truth and I hope you can handle it," I said with a straight face. "How could she have done that to you? Who would treat a little child so cruelly?" She cried even more.

"I don't know. I've asked myself that same question many days and sometimes several times a day."

Maureen asked me to go to the cemetery with her but I couldn't bring myself to go. We exchanged numbers and I agreed to have dinner with her before she left to go back home to Charlotte, North Carolina.

That night I couldn't sleep. Meeting Maureen and being forced to speak about my mother unleashed a deep-rooted anger and I couldn't let it go. How do you forgive someone for such a despicable act?

I decided to take a drive so I could at least attempt to clear my head.

It was late but I was craving a sweet latte from Starbucks. There was one in our area that stayed open 'til midnight. It hit the sweet-tooth spot. Since it was on my way home, I stopped at a gas station to fill up so I wouldn't have to do it in the morning. Tomorrow morning I had my last exam and would be fighting traffic going to Old Dominion University for the last time to attend a class anyway.

"Where is she?" a man's voice asked.

"What?" I asked as I turned around to see who it was. He punched me in the face. The gas clerk was on the phone. It was just him and me out there.

"You don't get to ask me questions. Antonia owes me money. I was there when the feds raided the place. I paid for a night totaling over a thousand dollars and all I got was a damn backrub. Tell her I want my money back," he instructed me.

My face was throbbing. I immediately noticed the night clerk was jamming to the music coming from his earphones. Suddenly, he shut off the OPEN sign lights and turned on the CLOSED sign lights. The wave of adrenaline came over my entire body. I quickly grabbed my knife from my shoe and sliced this man's forehead and the side of his face. He fell to the ground, not being able to see. I quickly removed my blow torch from the trunk of the car and beat him in his face with it.

"You won't ever touch another woman again. Not even your wife," I said, noticing his wedding ring. "Does your face hurt?" I asked.

"Yes," he whimpered.

"Good. My face hurts now since you punched me in the face. Say it louder," I instructed him while I beat him over and over again. He was a prick named Tommy. I gladly ignited the blow torch and used it all over his body. All I could see in my mind was my mother's face. Then, he died. It was so dark that I hoped no one saw a thing.

Chapter 20

Grand Opening

Our grand opening went better than I imagined. Staying up all night was easy when you're constantly being handed cash. The last client appointment was scheduled for five in the morning. Some men preferred quickies before heading off to work. After giving everyone their earnings for a night's and early morning's work, enough was left over for me to deposit some cash in the ATM.

After pulling out of the bank parking lot, I stopped by Hardee's to pick up breakfast for the night crew. Heather and I chose only twelve people to come on board with us.

Before I could get out the car, the security guards were taking out the biscuit-sausage-and-bacon-aroma-filled bags. I myself wasn't that hungry. Part of me felt guilty for what I was doing. I could see Joyce now shaking her head, wanting to slap me with a side of a hearty lecture. On the other hand, it felt good to know I was helping people get their bills paid and have food for their families, including their pets.

Exhausted and grateful that I could sleep for the majority for the day, I was getting into the elevator to go up to my apartment floor. All of a sudden I heard Craig. He was my neighbor's son and came to check on her most of the time. Agnes Murphy was a sweet woman who would bring Fera doggie treats. She would bring me pastries and cookies from Sugar Plum Bakery. That was before she was diagnosed with Parkinson's disease. Now that I thought about it, I hadn't seen her lately.

"What am I supposed to do?" he hissed into his cell phone. His back was turned so he didn't notice me creep around the corner. "She has it. Give me one last night," he insisted, taking the stairs.

I knocked on my neighbor's door several times and there was no answer. Fortunately, she gave me a key, which was in one of my kitchen drawers. After entering my apartment, I went into the kitchen, quickly rummaging through the drawer. I found the key and dashed out the door.

I turned the key. The stench of urine from the apartment was damn unbearable. I found Agnes tied up with rope in the middle of her living room with a washcloth tied to her mouth. She was so pale.

"Ms. Murphy," I called out while untying her. The ropes were so tight that her wrists were covered in blood.

"Help me, please," she pleaded.

"I'm going to help you. Can you tell me what happened?"

"Craig is in trouble with those gamblers again. He wouldn't let me go until I gave him the money to pay off his debt. I have been here for a week or more tied up. I couldn't keep track of the days. I can't believe my only son would do this to me," she sobbed.

"Everything is going to be all right," I insisted.

The first thing I did was grabbed some of her clothes and her medicines. I found a suitcase under her bed. I walked her over to my apartment. I let Agnes soak in the tub and gave her a bath. She was too weak to eat so I managed to find some chicken broth in the pantry along with some crackers. I had to make her drink at least six to seven water bottles. Within hours, Agnes fell asleep with Fera right by her side.

Rage came upon me. At times like this, I got so angry that even my vision was blurry. How could a son treat his mother like garbage over money! He was going to torture her until she gave him the money. Agnes mentioned this wasn't the first time he had threatened her, but he had never done anything like this to her. This time, she stood her ground and refused to bail her son out.

While she slept, I turned on the television in the living room: "This is Wendy Morgan from news channel four. Good evening; we start first with the mysterious death of an unidentified man. He was found several weeks ago burned to death at a gas station. Police do not have any leads at this time. If you were a witness to this vicious crime, please call the crime line at 1-800-425-8973," the news reporter stated.

Chills went down my spine. This was the first and would be the last time that I ever made the news.

Agnes continued to sleep. Nightfall arrived and I headed back to her apartment and waited and waited in the same chair that Agnes was tied to with one of her wigs on and her clothes on.

Finally, the door cracked open. It was Craig. The aroma of alcohol mixed with that stench filled the air.

"Mom, please just give me the money. They will kill me if I don't come up with it," he begged.

"I have the money. It's in the car," I explained. Then, he untied me.

"Good, because I parked right next to your car," he said.

We took the back way entrance to the garage. Thankfully, no one was outside. I started walking slow as

Agnes did. Craig was so drunk. He couldn't tell that I was far from his mother.

"Get in your car and I will bring it to you. No more money. After this, I want you out of my life," I said.

"Mom, this won't happen again," he said with spit drooling down his mouth.

My knife blade was already in position to attack. I cut him right above his eyebrows and stabbed him in the stomach. "You belong in hell. Those guys you owe money to won't be able to get you now," I whispered in his ear while taking the blade from his stomach. Then, I revealed my face to him. He gasped for air and quickly took off in his car.

The next morning, I called the police. By this time, Agnes wasn't pale at all. The paramedics still insisted they take her to the hospital. She told the police exactly what she told me.

"Officer, Ms. Murphy insisted that I don't call the police, but I had to do something," I explained.

"We do see a small number of parental abuse cases. You did the right thing by calling us," the officer responded.

While there, the police confirmed her son Craig was found dead at the river docks, stabbed to death. The police chalked it up to the men he owed money to. Meanwhile, I called Agnes's sister in Connecticut to come down for a few days. The next call I made was to a cleaning company. When she arrived home, I wanted her apartment to be spotless.

The doctors wanted her to stay in the hospital for at least a week for observation.

"I can't thank you enough, Angela. Thank you for rescuing me," Agnes said.

"You're welcome," I replied, giving her a hug with my mind on Joyce. I missed her so much.

Tomorrow, I would get some much-needed rest.

Chapter 21

Lunch

"Hey," I said, giving Becca a hug after the waitress seated me.

"Hi," she said.

"Sorry I couldn't make it to your graduation," she mentioned.

"Becca, you had emergency spleen removal surgery. Even if I had the ceremony in the hospital cafeteria, you wouldn't have been able to make it," I replied. We began to laugh.

"You're right," she added.

"Besides, a friendship with me shouldn't be based on whether you're there for every major event in my life. A real friend is there every day in spirit. We live miles apart but I have picked up the phone and you have stayed on the phone all night hearing me cry about losing Joyce. The next morning, you had to be work at six. That's a true friend."

"Thank you. So how do you feel, college graduate? Not to mention you graduated a semester early. "

"Joyce and George are proud of me. I'm showing my mother and will never stop showing her that I became something," I stated.

"Yes, you did." She nodded.

"What are you having for lunch?" I asked.

"I want the Moroccan chicken salad with no avocados," Becca said, pointing to the entrée on the menu. We were at California Pizza Kitchen at Town Center.

"Good choice. I think I will have the spinach and artichoke pizza," I noted. I was grateful to be eating an early lunch since I was starving.

"Have you been nightmare free lately?" Becca asked.

"Yes, up until three days ago. I notice that if I don't have enough sleep, the nightmares come back. They are getting worse," I explained. My heart started beating fast.

"Hi, I'm Sara. What can I get you ladies to drink?" the waitress asked.

"Raspberry tea, for me," Becca replied.

"Ice-cold water. Please hurry," I suggested. The room was starting to spin.

"Are you all right?" Becca asked.

"I will be." I pulled my medicine bottle out of my purse so I could take my anxiety pill. I took a deep breath while my hands clinched the table.

"Do you want to leave?"

"No, I'm not going to spoil the fun," I replied. My pill was kicking in now.

"All right."

"As I was saying about the nightmares, they are getting more intense. I am running in the dream with my mother chasing me. She has a belt in her hand. I'm younger, too; around the age of ten or eleven years old. The other night, she was chasing me and I came to a cliff. It was either jump or endure the beating from her. Then, I woke up soaked in a cold sweat," I explained.

"Here are your drinks, ladies," the waitress announced, placing them on the table.

"Thank you," we both said in unison.

"Have you told this to the psychiatrist?" Becca asked.

"No. I only see her if I need a medication refill."

"You don't like her?"

"She is too abrupt and wants me to confront my feelings. These days, I can't even speak of my mother without popping a pill. "

"Find another doctor."

"I will. It's not high on the priority list, right now."

"I'm going to the bathroom. I will be right back."

"Angela?" a voice called out.

"Larry," I spoke.

"Do you mind if I have a seat where you're sitting?" he asked.

He was dressed in his work clothes. Larry was such a hard worker that I wouldn't have been surprised if he had contracts with several restaurants in this area. He was a contractor. Working on the farm became a side job for him.

"Well, I'm with my friend Becca. I can chitchat for a few minutes. How are you?" I smiled.

"I'm baffled, to say the least. We had sex in the barn and I simply don't hear from you. I leave several messages and texts and still no answer."

"What do you want from me?"

"Conversation. Maybe, you could have picked up the phone at least one time. We need to talk."

"Larry, talk about what? We had sex. Damn, it was good. You want some more. Right now," I added, rubbing his leg. I was getting horny.

"No, Angela. I'm not going to be a sex buddy to you. I thought maybe you cared for me a little."

"Listen, I can't be in a relationship. I don't want to talk all the time . . ."

"But you will have sex with me. I'm not that kind of guy. What I am is a man who needs more than that. I want to get to know you even more. You're a beautiful and caring person," he explained.

"Larry, I'm damaged. There isn't a fix or a cure for people like me. Besides, I don't need your pity on me," I screamed. Then, I quickly lowered my voice.

"I know all about what happened to you. Angela, you will overcome what your moth—"

"Stop right there. Leave me alone. This conversation is over," I demanded. Larry got up and walked out of the door.

"Who was that?" Becca questioned as she returned to the table.

"He is one of George's friends out here working a job and came over to say hello," I explained. "Tell me and provide all the details about the brand-new marketing job you already have landed," I suggested, desperately wanting to change the subject.

I quickly wanted to get my mind off the conversation with Larry. He just wanted to fix me and make me better. Life didn't work that way. I murdered men, bad men, preferably.

Chapter 22

News

Last Sunday, George urged me to go along with him for a routine doctor's appointment, so I did. Lately, he had been acting not himself. Usually, George was immaculate head to toe. One day, he didn't have his socks on. As was the same for me, he just really missed Joyce. It had been a little over a year.

I suspected George wanted me to go to the doctor with him so I could be relieved that he had a clean bill of health.

I didn't get any sleep last night. My body wouldn't go into rest mode.

"George Miller." The nurse called us back into one of the doctor's offices. I had been here before when I was a little girl. Joyce and I would sit in the waiting room as we ate cinnamon candy and sang church songs. She loved the Clark Sisters. Cinnamon candy was one of her favorites.

Twenty minutes passed. I could barely keep my eyes opened. There was a light tap on the door.

"Come in," George said.

"Hey, tough guy," Dr. Knorr said to George.

"Hey, Doc." George snickered.

"Angela, I haven't seen you in years. How the heck are you?" he asked, giving me a hug.

"I'm doing well, and just trying to figure out my next move after graduating college."

"Graduate school on the horizon for you?" he asked.

"Maybe," I added.

"What was your major?"

"Biology." I nodded my head.

"Pre-med. The state of Virginia has a large shortage of doctors, especially in family medicine," he suggested.

"I will think about," I said.

"Mr. Miller, how are you feeling?" the doctor asked.

"Doc, I'm feeling great."

"You should be. Your EKG, blood work, and urinalysis all came back within normal ranges. Also, I gave you a referral to go see a neurologist. I have test results back from that."

"Yes, you did. That doctor was strictly business. He didn't have much of a bedside manner," George added.

"I will have to speak with him about that. You are the fifth patient to tell me the same thing this month. At the neurologist there was a mini mental-state exam that you had completed. Based on the test results, you didn't do so well."

"This man is in his sixties. The only exam he should be performing is which chicken is the best to sell to the local grocery store," I said. We all began laughing.

"On a serious note, the test revealed that you have early stages of Alzheimer's," the doctor revealed.

"What! I can't lose George too," I said. My heart began to race and my palms were sweating. My hands were shaking. I sat down in the chair and started taking deep breaths.

"She needs water," George said.

"I will get some water." The doctor quickly dashed out of the room and returned with a Styrofoam cup of water. George reached into my purse to get out a pill. I took a deep breath. My hands wouldn't stop shaking.

"Do you want me to continue?" the doctor questioned.

"Yes." I nodded.

"Angela, I know that is a lot take in all at once. Do you need to leave the room?" he asked.

"No, I will be okay. I need to hear this too." I nodded my head.

"Very well, then. George, I recommend that you don't live by yourself anymore. That large farm and all those animals are a huge responsibility for you. I suggest that you may want to consider living in an assisted-living home. I have prescribed a drug called Exelon for you. It has been sent to your pharmacy already. It will slow down the progression of the disease," he explained with pamphlets and brochures in his hands.

I began to cry so much that my face was hurting. George and the doctor were comforting. I felt guilty. George was the one who had the condition, not me.

"George, I want to see you back in my office in a month so I can evaluate this new medication."

"Sure thing, Doc."

"Angela, it was nice seeing you again. I apologize for the circumstances," the doctor explained, shaking my hand and then George's hand.

"Listen, Angela, I know the cards of life you have been dealt have not been the best. I'm going to be all right," George expressed while I was driving.

"How so? One day, you won't even know my name," I sobbed.

"Think positive. Right now, I'm thinking about my future. At this very moment, I want to go down to Marlene's Cafeteria for something to eat. "

"Okay, we will head there now."

"Angela, I've been working on a farm all my life. I need to retire from it. This is a good opportunity for me to downsize. Just promise me that you will always keep the farm and its land in the family."

"I promise." I nodded.

At lunch, George and I looked over the brochures of some of the assisted-living homes. He even wanted to go visit one today after lunch.

"Good afternoon. I'm Darcy, the property manager here at Pinehill Manor Homes. What can I help you with?" she asked while shaking both of our hands.

"Hi, we're here to view an apartment. My grandfather would like to find a cozy unit to call home," I said.

"I can definitely help you with this request. How many bedrooms were you looking for, sir?"

"Probably about two," he said.

George loved the apartments. It was in the heart of downtown Chesapeake. Plus, he was only fifteen miles away from my apartment. He decided to put down a deposit on a unit. While he and the manager discussed business, I went to go look around. I walked around only to find a rosebush. It was beautiful with white roses. The complex was surrounded by rosebushes.

I heard a faint yell coming from an apartment on the main level. "Stop," a woman's voice said.

I looked in the apartment to see a maintenance worker of the complex and a young woman in the kitchen.

"My grandmother will be home any minute. Just go and leave me alone."

"I have had my eye on you, little lady, for quite a while," he said while taking his pants down. I knocked on the door and ran away to divert his attention.

"You had better keep your damn mouth shut," he instructed her.

He ran out and started fixing a hole in the ground as if nothing happened.

Later on that night, George had decided to sell the animals to the highest bidder. He wanted to enjoy life and take a break. I didn't blame him. Hard work was in his blood. It would feel strange to see George relaxing. Before you knew it, he would be telling me that he met a special woman at the grocery store on senior citizen discount day. These changes were going to be hard for me. The animals represented George and Joyce. She was gone. I didn't know if I could bear to see George wither away in front of my eyes.

I decided Fera and I would be staying with George tonight.

"Do you need anything? I need to make a quick run to the store," I informed him.

"No, I'm fine. All I need is a good night's rest. I have got a big day ahead of me tomorrow."

I was on my way back to Pinehill Manor Homes to search for that piece of trash. I waited for hours and didn't see him. Tomorrow was a brand new day.

Luckily, the next night he was there. I spotted him in the main office gathering up trash. With my knife in its rightful position, I was ready to deal with him.

I parked my car near the trash can hoping he would be coming my way. He was listening to his iPod. Adrenaline came over me. My body even began to feel hot. I came from behind, jerked his head back, and sliced him right above his forehead. He began to scream.

"Shut up," I whispered while grabbing him and slowly piercing his throat with the knife. "Do as I say and walk to the sound of my voice until I say stop." About a half mile down, there was new construction and a manmade hole was in the middle of a dirt pile.

"Let me go," he begged again.

"No; you have a taste for young girls. Did you give your victims mercy? How many?" I asked.

"What?"

"Tell me how many there were. I'm not going to ask you again," I assured him.

"Twenty-two," he said while peeing in his pants.

"Did you kill anyone?" I asked.

"No, I swear. Please, let me go," he begged again.

His face was covered in blood. I took the torch out of my backpack and lit his body up with it. He fell to the ground. With my black gloves on, I rolled his body into the hole.

Knowing George he would still be up. I made it just in time to watch old episodes of *Saturday Night Live* with him. Fera greeted me at the door.

"Hey, baby," I said after picking her up and petting her.

"What did you get from the store?" George asked.

"I got a few things for myself but I picked up Ben & Jerry's crème brûlée ice cream, your favorite. I noticed you were out of it," I said while taking it out of the plastic grocery bag.

"It's just what I'm in the mood for. Thank you, Angela," he replied.

"You're most certainly welcome," I said, handing him a bowl of ice cream and a spoon.

Little moments as these I hoped George wouldn't forget. Time likes these I needed to cherish the most.

Chapter 23

Business

"I was pondering whether we should recruit new girls," Heather suggested while she was using the elliptical machine at the gym.

"I don't know. More people mean more money coming out of our pockets. Plus, you and I have hearts. Heather, I refuse to be in this business longer than I need to. Our distorted vision of helping people will make us want to stay longer in this tangled web of providing pleasure," I replied before taking a sip of my bottled water and wiping off the sweat on my face with a hand towel.

"Come on, just think about it. I met these girls at the nail salon. They're students just trying to make extra money. Besides, I don't need them to actually have sex with clients," she said.

"What else would you have them do?" I questioned.

"Maybe just have them for dating services only. We could make it clear with the clients: no extras. I'm sure Jacob wouldn't mind finding a few nice gentlemen to escort them on the dates. Of course, the client will not know or realize someone is watching from afar."

"We are still putting out more. This time, we will be spending more money on security expenses. Besides, we haven't reached our goal for a down payment on a building. We are so close, though," I added.

"Well, I'm just trying to appeal to the fellow consumer."

"How old are these girls?" I asked.

"They told me eighteen and nineteen. My gut tells me they're probably fifteen and sixteen trying to explore a new adventure," she said.

"No one under the age of eighteen will work for us!" I screamed.

"Angela, what the hell is wrong with you? Keep your voice down," Angela requested.

"Young girls have no idea what they want. They are so impressionable at their ages," I said, shaking my head, in tears.

"Angela, what happened to you—"

"Don't!" I warned, cutting her off.

"Who hurt you as a young girl, or maybe a little girl?"

"You don't know what you're talking about," I said.

"Angela, at times you have dozed off asleep at the so-called desk in Jacob's house. I have heard your ramblings of the 'no's' and the 'stops.' Plus, I will never forget your whimpering cries in the night," she explained.

"I gotta go. See you tonight," I said before grabbing my towel. The room was spinning because I had not eaten anything. My hands were shaking. After I got outside of the building, I started taking deep breaths. I ran to the car to pop a pill.

Chapter 24

Changes

I was staring at myself in the mirror. Now, I realized what it meant when a woman said she had bags under her eyes. I hadn't slept in days. The nightmares were increasing. My back was against the wall to seek treatment. Maybe the psychiatrist could help me. Having anxiety attacks shouldn't have been an addition to my lifestyle.

The shrink wanted me to face my fears. To be honest, I was too petrified to uncover what lay deep in my mind, heart, and soul.

Today was moving day for George and the animals. Between two farmers, the animals were divided up. George could buy a small townhouse with the profit that he made. He tried to offer me some money but I declined. The way I saw it, he and Joyce saved me. The least I could do was take care of him.

George had been diagnosed with Alzheimer's disease. Looking back, I did remember some minor incidents. On a Sunday afternoon, George couldn't remember his way home after leaving a church service, and a few times he forgot to feed the pigs and chickens. I had noticed that his new medication only slowed down the progression of the disease. It would be heart wrenching if one day he simply didn't recognize my face or little Fera's face anymore.

Since Heather could handle a night without me, I stayed with George in his new apartment. To his face, I acted like I was so happy for the new change. Deep down, my heart longed for the way things were growing up. Joyce would have never agreed to leave the farm. She would have continued to work until the day her body wouldn't let her anymore. Still, the adult in me understood that George deserved to be happy.

Chapter 25

Road Trip

I was heading down I-95 to Charlotte, North Carolina to visit with Maureen's family. I didn't come empty-handed. I baked a raspberry tart. Joyce always taught me ladies must always bring a gift when being invited to someone's home as a guest. When I was young girl, she and I would have our very own tea parties. There, she would teach me the proper etiquette at the dinner table. It took many pleadings, but, eventually, Joyce would let me start wearing her hats to the table and getting dressed up. I loved pretending with her that she was the queen of Suffolk and I was the upcoming princess being groomed to one day have her throne.

Two exits away from my destination, I stopped at a nearby rest stop to use the bathroom. It was a quaint rest stop with picnic tables and a small convenience store set up around it. As I got out of the car, I noticed my tire was flat. *Damn it.* I didn't want to be late to Maureen's house.

"I can fix it. Do you have a spare?" a gentleman asked, approaching me and pointing to the tire.

"Yes, it's in the trunk." I nodded.

"Give me a few minutes and I can get you on your way, young lady. I have four daughters. My middle one is probably around the same age as you. If they were in some kind of distress, I would want a kind-hearted man to help them too. In fact, I'm waiting on two of my daughters and my wife to come out of the bathroom, now," he explained.

"Thank you. I'm Angela, by the way," I said.

"My name is Norman," he replied as we shook hands.

After making small talk with Norman for a few minutes, his family came out of the bathroom. His family was so nice and warm to me. His daughters were lucky to have them as parents.

Years ago, I revealed to Joyce that I was curious about my father. She mentioned to me he would have been proud of me. Maybe he was looking down from heaven watching over me. As memories play back in my mind, Joyce did drop hints of the truth.

"Thank you. I really appreciate your help," I said and got back into the car to pull off.

An hour later and with one more exit to go, I thought I heard state police sirens.

"Ma'am, I need your license and registration," the state trooper ordered me after I slowly rolled down the window.

"Yes," I agreed, handing over what he had requested. The car was beginning to spin slightly. My body temperature began to rise.

"Ma'am, your state inspection sticker has expired. It's only been seven days so I'm going to let you go. Also, you were not wearing your seat belt," he explained.

After he finished talking, I revealed to him my matching plum-colored bra and panty set. I started to unbutton my petite polo shirt. I unclipped my bra in the front. The woods were right behind us. I quickly ran into the woods. He followed me. I quickly took off my jeans. He unbuttoned his belt to take down his pants. He ran his fingers from my neck all the way down to my feet. His tongue began playing with my left nipple. He picked me up to ride me against the tree.

"Harder," I demanded.

It was over before it began. It was the best quickie I've ever had. I came so fast and so did he.

"Wow," he said, watching me adjust my clothes to a decent manner.

"Have a nice day," I said, heading to the car, and then pulled off.

I had finally reached Maureen's house.

"Please come in," Maureen greeted me at the door. Thankfully, the events of the day didn't throw me up off schedule.

"May I use your bathroom?" I asked while handing her the tart that I had prepared. I wanted to wash my face and freshen up before meeting the rest of her family. Baby wipes and travel-size soap, washcloths and deodorant did wonders for me.

"Of course you can. Go straight down the hall then make a left," she explained.

When I went to use the bathroom, all I could think about was my mother and how Maureen would ask me more questions about a woman who was a monster. She longed to understand our mother even more. I couldn't give her the answers she wanted to hear.

"You can do this," I said before looking in the mirror at myself, taking a deep breath, and stepping out of the bathroom, heading toward the living room.

"Who is this lovely little lady?" I asked, giving Maureen's daughter a hug.

"My name is Jade," she said.

"My name is Jordan," her son said. I gave him a hug as well.

"Well, it's nice to meet the both of you," I replied.

"Angela, this is my husband, Tom," Maureen said. I shook his hand.

"This is a real treat for you to visit us," he added.

"Thank you. The road trip was nice coming up."

"You didn't tell me that you were a baker. I can't wait to cut into that tart you made," Maureen said.

"My paternal grandmother taught me how to cook, bake, fry, and sew," I said. We all started laughing.

"Well, dinner is ready," Maureen announced.

"I'm hungry," Jade said, running to the table. We were all seated.

"Lord, let us give thanks for this meal and please bless the hands that prepared it. We are truly glad to have Maureen and Angela united. In Jesus' name, we pray," Tom said.

"Amen," everyone said in unison.

Maureen had made pork loin with roasted vegetables and mashed potatoes. I was glad because I needed something hearty on my stomach. I hadn't really eaten all day.

After dinner, I helped Maureen with the dishes. Afterward, we went and sat down in her study to talk. "Thank you for inviting me to dinner. You have a lovely family and home," I said.

"You're welcome. I'm hoping you can come more often. So who has Fera? You could have brought her with you," she added.

"She is with one of my friends. I didn't bring her because I didn't know how your family would feel about a dog running around the house. "

"The kids have been begging Tom and me for a dog. The next time you make it this way, please bring Fera so we can get some practice time in." She giggled.

"I will," I agreed.

"So, Miss College Graduate, what are your plans?" Maureen asked.

"I'm still figuring that part of my life out. A degree in biology can steer you in so many different directions. Right now, I'm doing an internship at a clinical research lab."

"Do you like it?"

"I love it. I wish the lab department would create a position for me."

"Determination and hard work met with the right opportunity and timing will land you the job you want," she suggested.

"The powers that be there know I'm striving toward that goal," I said.

"Do you have any pictures of her?" she asked, quickly changing the subject.

It felt as though a knife had cut through the conversation. Based on her tone, I could tell she wanted to drill me with questions probably as soon as I handed her the tart. The few times I had talked to Maureen on the phone I never allowed her to ask me questions about our mother. I wanted to answer them in person, one time and one time only.

"No, I only left with the clothes on my back the night that I killed her."

"Where did you live?"

"We lived in a tiny apartment in Norfolk. I don't ever remember having furniture except a kitchen table. Anything valuable she would just sell for drugs. "

"What was her drug of choice?"

"Crack, and if she scraped up enough money, it was heroin."

"Did she ever use drugs in front of you?"

"Yes, plenty of times. She was proud of it. Drugs were the only things that made her happy."

"Did she ever show you any kind of affection or love?"

"No. When she was there she either ignored or yelled at me. There was no in-between. She left me alone, a lot. At times, I was left overnight, too," I explained.

Maureen began to cry. "I just still can't believe this," she said.

"Maureen, I know it's a lot for you. Deep down, you were looking for maybe some kind of angelic mother, but that simply wasn't the case."

"Have you been back to the apartment?" she asked.

"No," I said, shaking my head.

"How was childhood after?"

"It was wonderful. My grandparents loved and nurtured me. I still think of my grandmother every day."

"How is your grandfather doing?" she inquired. I had already shared with her that George had been diagnosed with Alzheimer's disease.

"I haven't talked to him much, these days."

"Why? I thought you two were so close."

"We are close. Lately, he has been so busy. The assisted-living home offers a lot of activities for the residents."

"That's a good thing," she commented.

"Yes, it is."

"May I make a suggestion? I will tread lightly."

"Yes, you may," I said.

"Go over there and surprise him with dinner."

"I have done so, but he wasn't home so I just left fried chicken, mashed potatoes, and turnip greens on the counter for him."

"That was nice of you. I'm sure he appreciated it. What about our maternal grandparents? Where are they?" she asked, shifting the conversation again.

"I don't know," I said, shrugging my shoulders.

"Angela, are you all right? Your forehead is sweating."

"I'm just a little hot. Do you mind getting me a glass of water?"

"No. I will be right back," she said, leaving the room.

Just in case I couldn't get through the conversation, I placed an Ativan pill in my pocket. I quickly popped it in my mouth.

"Here is your glass of water. Also, I cut two slices of the raspberry tart with a scoop of vanilla bean ice cream," she explained, handing it to me.

"Thank you."

For the next few hours, we finally talked about Maureen and her life. She wanted me to meet her adoptive parents. I agreed to it for her. It took a lot for me to go back in time to answer her questions honestly and wholeheartedly. I looked forward to the next trip.

Chapter 26

Unleash

"What a day!" I said after walking into my apartment. Fera immediately ran up to me. She wanted to be picked up.

"Hey, you," Heather said after turning around in the chair to face my direction.

"Thank you for keeping on her for me," I said.

"No problem. I already fed and walked her. I have only been here for a few hours. I have been online searching for graduate schools," she expressed.

"Did you see any schools that you may be interested in?"

"No, I haven't yet. Wouldn't it be grand to find a school that offered scholarships? My student loans, now, are already kicking me in the butt."

"Heather, one thing I know about you is that you are definitely not a quitter. If there's something you want you go after it. Keep searching; you will find something," I assured her, giving her a pat on the shoulder.

"You're right. Speaking of something I want, there's something I've been meaning to talk to you about," she said.

"I'm all ears," I said, sitting down on the couch. She sat down next to me and began crying. I had never seen Heather cry at all, even when we were all hauled off to jail. "What's wrong?"

"Angela, do you believe in love at first sight?"

"No, not really. Love grows over time. I do believe two people can have chemistry or a spark in their first encounter together."

"I believe in love at first sight."

"So tell me, who's the guy?" I asked eagerly.

"You're assuming it's a guy. Angela, it's you who I have always loved. Since the first time I saw you in class, I gave you my heart. I'm in love with you," she explained, placing her hand on my thigh, and then reached over to kiss me.

I quickly turned my head and moved over to give me more space between us. "Heather, I can't do this. I had no idea you felt this way."

"I've been hiding it for years. Only Adrianna, one of the girls who used to work at Pearl, confronted me about it. That day, I couldn't stop staring at you," she whimpered.

"You are one of my best friends. I love you like a sister. I want to continue only a friendship with you, but is that something you can handle?"

"I guess. I'm going to have to," she said.

I reached over to the glass table to give her a Kleenex tissue. "Come on, I'm going to go put Fera in her doggie crate. Why don't we go grab some frozen yogurt at Skinny Dip?" I suggested, trying to lighten the mood up.

"Okay," she agreed.

I opened the door and a man more like the size of a gorilla stood in the doorway.

"Can I help you?" I asked while trying to remember where I put my pocketknife in my purse.

He pushed his way into the apartment. Fera began barking uncontrollably. Heather and I started running toward the bedroom. He grabbed me from behind and injected something into my neck. The next thing I knew, I passed out.

Chapter 27

Surprise

"Angela, wake up," a voice said. It was coming from an intercom.

"Heather, darling, wake up," the voice said again.

I awoke sitting in a chair at a table. The guy who barged in my apartment, along with three other men, was there in this warehouse. My heart started racing. I didn't have any pills on me. I was convinced these men were going to rape us. Who were they? Why did Heather and I have to become their victims? The door opened.

"Ladies, my apologies for all this commotion," a woman's voice said.

"Antonia," I said, still groggy from whatever that man injected me with.

"You both have been checked for wires. I have to take necessary precautions. Those feds are on my tail once again."

"What did that animal inject us with?" I asked.

"It was just a small dose of a sedative. Angela, I knew you wouldn't come willingly." She giggled.

"What do you want from us?" Heather asked.

"I don't want anything from you, for now. I only have a few questions."

"How long are we going to be here?" I asked, getting the questions rolling first. It was cold and the smell of must and mildew lingered in the air.

"I assure you, only for a little while. Listen, girls, you two, honestly, were some of my best workers. I apologize for what happened. As you know, I owe the IRS a crap load of money and they want it yesterday. The feds have built a rather strong case against me. Do you hear what I'm saying?"

Both of us nodded our heads. I had to pee so bad that I was going to go right there and then.

"Have the feds or any type of law enforcement tried to contact you in anyway?"

"No, they have not," Heather said.

"We were all questioned the day Pearl was raided. You can't tell the feds or police anything you don't know. Antonia, you taught me that."

"Well, someone from Pearl is testifying against me. I'm going to figure it out," she said.

"It's not us. Can we please go, now? Fera is probably worried about us," I said.

"Fera is in a safe place. If you get through this small demonstration we are about to conduct, I will give her back to you, safely. If you don't pass, Fera's throat will be the first one that I slice. You see, ladies, I'm facing twenty years to life in prison. I'm not going to prison or any other hole those pigs want to stick me in."

"I will kill you if you hurt Fera. Antonia, she is an innocent dog who has done nothing to you."

"Settle down, Angela. This is the way of the business. Fera has your heart and I have to be assured that you or Heather don't have my freedom at stake."

"What the hell do you want us to do?" Heather asked.

"Take a lie detector test."

"Let's get on with it," I said.

"Great. We shall get started."

Heather and I took the lie detector test. Now, we were waiting for the results. Antonia let us use the bathroom. I would have rather peed outside. The stench in that rusty stall was unbearable. I knew I hadn't been talking to police but I couldn't say the same for Heather. I began to take deep breaths. Then, I went back into the interrogation dungeon. I didn't even know what time it was.

"Well, ladies. You passed. Thank you for your loyalty," Antonia said, tossing me a package.

"What's this?" Heather asked.

"I'm a little short on cash. All I could spare was five thousand. Use it however you wish," she explained, giving us hugs. The next thing I knew, one of her guards handed me back my dog.

"I didn't lay one hand on her. I promise," he assured me. Fera bit his finger.

I was so angry that I kicked him in the balls. He fell to his knees.

"Tony, she is a firecracker just like me. Leave her alone. Good-bye, ladies," Antonia said and walked out the room.

We were injected again in the neck. The room went black. The next thing I remember was Heather, Fera, and me being placed back at my apartment. It was the next morning. Sunday, that is. We both decided to take a shower and then go to breakfast at the Village Inn. I gave Heather some clothes to wear. We were both around the same size.

Before we went, I called a locksmith to have the locks changed. Also, I made a mental note to have a security system installed.

"What a night!" I said after the waitress took our orders.

"I'm just happy we made it alive. Antonia is a psychopath," Heather commented in a low tone of voice.

"She is a psychopath who loves money. With the five thousand, we should divide it up between everyone and just say it's a bonus."

"I agree." Heather nodded her head.

We both hoped to never encounter a visit from Antonia again.

Chapter 28

Annoyed

"Good morning, how are you?" a gentleman asked.

I just sat in the waiting room of the Checkered Flag Toyota superstore on Virginia Beach Boulevard, hoping this oil change wouldn't take long. I had to get down to the lab and I didn't want to be late.

I had clients calling, wanting to make appointments during the day and getting frustrated with me because I couldn't oblige them. Every client knew from the beginning that we didn't operate during the day. Whatever the men and women did on the side was their own personal business.

"Morning." I nodded, yawning.

"You don't remember me, do you?" he asked.

"No, I don't," I said, shrugging my shoulders.

"I'm your grandfather's insurance agent. I assessed the prices of the farm animals and accidentally spilled hot coffee on the kitchen table," he explained.

"Yes." The coffee brought it all back. "Yes, I do remember, now. Nathan, right?" I asked, extending my hand.

"You got it. Watts is my last name," he said, shaking my hand. Nathan was clean-cut in his suit. His height was over six feet. I liked a man who I had to look up to.

"What are you having done to your vehicle today?" I inquired.

"I'm getting a tune-up and having the brake pads replaced. I travel so much I have to make sure my 4Runner truck is safe."

"Ms. Farmer," a voice called out.

"Yes, that's me," I said, waving my hand.

"Your vehicle is ready," the car technician stated.

"Thank you. I will be right there."

"Well, Angela, it was nice running into you. If you have some time today or maybe this weekend, I would love to take you out for a nice evening for dinner or even lunch," he offered.

"Thanks, but my schedule is swamped."

"If you ever need me for insurance purposes, let me know," he said, pulling a business card out his pocket and handing it to me.

"Oh, yes, I will make sure to tell my grandfather that I ran into you," I said before walking up to the counter to retrieve my car key and pay for the service.

Now, I went home to change my clothes into scrubs. It had been another long, profitable night. I was going to make it to the lab on time, after all. I hated being late for anything.

After leaving the lab, I headed over to George's house, thinking about Fera. I was getting worried about her. She hadn't eaten anything in days. She wouldn't even eat peanut butter, which was her favorite treat. Yes, I gave my dog people food including carrots, spinach, and raw string beans. My little one loved her vegetables.

Fera had been staying with George to keep him company. I was on my way over there to pick her up. While en route, I stopped over at PetSmart and purchased an adorable brown outfit with matching shoes. I loved dressing my doggie up. She was getting up there in age. Lately, I'd noticed that she had been moving a little slower. Normally, I took her out twice a day to do her business. It was mandatory to take her out at least three times a day, now; otherwise, she would poop and pee on the carpet.

I knocked on the door and waited a few minutes. I knocked on the door again. I had a key to his apartment but using it would be a last resort. A third time I knocked on the door, but this time harder. Many bad thoughts were running through my mind. George could have slipped in the shower and accidentally hit his head. My heart started pounding. I had no choice but to use the key. I quickly opened the door and let myself in. Fera instantly came up to me so I could hold her. *One down and one more to go,* I thought.

Music was playing in the background. It was Nat King Cole's song named "Smile." I walked into George's bedroom and he was dancing with another woman. My mouth dropped. No wonder George had been getting me off the phone sooner than usual, claiming he was trying out new recipes. Yes, but, George was trying out his recipes with someone else.

"My grandmother is more beautiful than you will ever be," I quickly commented.

"Angela, please show some respect," he suggested.

"Hello, Angela. Do you remember me? George talks about Fera and you all the time," Betty said, opening her arms for a hug. She was my former social worker who introduced me to Joyce and George.

"Lady, don't come near me! So were you cheating on Joyce with her?" I demanded to know.

"Of course not. After she died, we became reacquainted," he replied, shaking his head.

"I don't believe you!" I screamed.

"Lower your voice and show your grandfather some respect," Betty said.

"How could you do this to us?" I asked, completely ignoring her comment. "George, you will never see Fera or me again!" I shouted with tears in my eyes, with my breathing getting heavy.

"Calm down, Angela," George said.

"How could you? Joyce hasn't been dead for two years yet."

"Was I supposed to wait?"

"Yes, you should only be with Fera and me. Besides, I know I can cook better than her. All you need is food, television, and a reclining chair."

"You can't give the love I have for him. This has all happened so suddenly," Betty added.

"He doesn't love you. George has and will only love Joyce," I screamed while making my way out with Fera in my arms.

"Joyce is gone. I have to move on with my life," he said.

"No, you don't!"

"I deserve to be happy," he said.

"Fine, be happy. You have made your choice. How quickly you forget about Fera and me. We have been your family. Not her," I said before storming out.

Chapter 29

A Walk

I headed over to the house in Suffolk. Usually, I went by there a few times a month to retrieve the junk mail and to make sure the house was all right. George decided to leave most of the furniture in the house because he simply didn't have enough room in his apartment. He had called me a few times but I didn't answer, nor did I call him back. It was a bright sunny morning and I didn't want to ruin the day by arguing with George.

"Good morning, Ms. Dubler," I said as I waved to her.

She lived across the street from us. For the holidays, she always made a lemon chess pie, which I loved.

"Hello there, Angela. How is your grandfather doing?"

"He's hanging in there and loving that new apartment of his."

"I'm glad to hear it. Please tell him I said hello."

"Yes, I most certainly will," I said as I walked away.

I walked into the house. Immediately, I heard something coming from upstairs. As I moved closer to the stairs, I realized the noise was coming from the attic. I quickly ran to my old room to grab a flashlight. I always had one under the bed just in case the lights went out. Over the years, they had a tendency to do that.

Slowly, I let down the ladder to enter into the attic. I went up those stairs. I hated going into the attic. It was always so hot up there. I immediately spotted three squirrels running amuck. They quickly scattered, hiding behind boxes. I noticed a hole on the side of the house which was obviously where they were coming from. Dead or alive, I wanted them out of the attic. I called Larry. He was able to fit me in to patch the hole up. In the meantime, I called a wildlife company to catch the squirrels. They came out to set the traps. Inside each trap was food. Within two hours, the squirrels were caught unharmed. Larry pulled up shortly after they left.

"May I have a seat?" Larry asked.

I was sitting on a bench feeding the ducks. There was a lake behind the house. George, Joyce, and I would sit out here for hours to talk.

"Yes, you may," I agreed.

"How have you been?"

"I'm doing all right. Listen, Larry, thank you for coming out to fix that hole," I said sincerely.

"You're welcome."

"If you came to this bench to give me another lecture about what happened in the barn, I'm really not in the mood to listen," I stated.

"I'm not going to speak of that again."

"Good," I said with a sigh of relief.

"I did want to talk to you about George, though," he stated.

"What about George? He's with Betty now, having fun."

"Yeah, he is, but he misses Fera and you. Angela, make things right. That's all I'm saying."

"Are you hungry? I'm in the mood for Earlene's. I know you won't let me pay you for fixing that hole so at least let me take you to a late breakfast," I suggested.

Earlene's was a restaurant staple in Suffolk for the past fifty years and it was one of Larry's favorite spots.

"Okay," he agreed.

"Good, let's go. I'll drive," I said as I pulled my keys from my pocket.

There, Larry and I talked about all the funny memories on the farm. He told me the first time he milked a cow it kicked him. My favorite part was getting fresh eggs from the chickens.

"Thank you for coming to brunch with me," I said after pulling into the driveway back at the house.

"You're welcome."

"After talking to you, give it some time, I will probably have a change of heart and go visit George. I just can't stand seeing him with another woman. Betty doesn't fit my family equation," I explained. "Would you like a cup of coffee before you go? Knowing you, I'm sure you have a few more stops to work at today."

"Yes, you're right about that. I think I will have one cup."

We got out the car and headed into the house. I prepared the coffee and poured him a cup.

"Sugar and cream . . . just the way you like it!" I said as I walked toward the table where he sat.

"Thank you," he said after I place the coffee mug on the table.

"No problem. How's work going?"

"It's going very well. I'm getting more jobs, which means I have to hire more people. I just signed a contract with CVS pharmacy. The corporation wants one built here in Suffolk and another one in Chesapeake," he explained.

"I'm glad to hear everything is going wonderful for you." I patted him on the shoulder. "Wow! Under a lot of stress?" I asked, noticing his shoulder was tense.

I began to rub both of his shoulders to work out the kinks.

"Mmm," he moaned. Larry dropped his head and closed his eyes.

"I can work out those tense spots," I whispered in his ear, then gently licked the lobe.

I began slowly kissing him, moving my lips down the side of his neck then to his lips. His lips felt warm. Larry gripped me in his oversized arms and pulled me closer to him. We kissed passionately as we started taking off all our clothes. I wanted every piece of clothing off him. I wanted him completely naked. Besides, getting a glimpse of those abs made me even more wet.

Larry turned me around, starting gently kissing the back of my neck while rubbing my hair. He moved his hands to my breasts and cupped each of them, squeezing them tight. I could feel his manhood pressing against my bare ass. With the left hand still gripping my breast, Larry moved his right hand between my legs. I moaned as he massaged my clit. With my vagina dripping wet, Larry removed his moist fingertips and, in a single motion, he turned me over, picked me up, and placed me on the kitchen counter. While kissing again, his dick reacquainted itself and the stiff pumps began.

"Wait, Angela, this isn't right," Larry said, pulling out of me. I quickly pulled him back in.

"Don't stop, please. You know you want it. Now, come and take it," I instructed, lying back down on the kitchen counter.

Larry couldn't resist. Even though what we were doing may have been wrong, at the time it was pleasing to us both. So Larry gave in to temptation and continued to have sex with me until we both came simultaneously.

After sex, we decided to take a shower together. Larry washed me from head to toe, paying special attention to each part of my body. He was so gentle with every touch.

"Angela, I like being with you," Larry commented as we both were putting back on our clothes.

"Likewise." I smiled.

"May I ask you a question?" Larry asked; then he continued, "Will you tell me what happened to you? I only know bits and pieces."

"No, I can't talk about it right now." I quickly reached in my purse for a pill. My entire body started shaking.

"Are you all right?" he asked.

"Yes, I will be. Just leave, please."

"I can't leave you like this . . ."

"Please, just go. I will be fine," I said, walking slowly to the couch.

I lay on the couch and within minutes I was asleep. An hour had passed before I woke to the sound of my ringing phone. It was Larry but I refused to answer. I had three missed calls from him. *Men can be such slow thinkers,* I thought as I pressed the end button on my phone, sending Larry to voicemail. Larry hadn't realized yet that if he didn't bring up the issue of my mother, I would be more willing to let him stay in my company. I felt bad that Larry felt that I used him for sex. The truth was that I really did. When those uncontrollable sexual urges took over, I had to oblige them. By chance or coincidence, Larry just happened to be around at that particular time.

Later on that night, I head over to Jacob's house. This was the house that we were using for work until we could afford something else. I called it the unofficial Pearl. Fifteen people were on the schedule for tonight. I was tired and not up to working but the job had to get done. I was sure to brew plenty of coffee to keep me awake throughout the night and early morning. After work, I had an interview scheduled. A position for a research lab technician was available. My appointment was at nine a.m. sharp. There were ten other candidates gearing up for the job and I was determined to come out on top.

While en route to Jacob's house, my phone started ringing.

"Hello?" I answered right away.

"It's Heather."

"Hey."

"Get over to the house, now," she instructed.

"I'm on the way," I replied.

Then she hung up the phone. I knew something was wrong by the tone of her voice, but things we could say over the phone were limited so I didn't ask any questions.

I hit the gas pedal. Within ten minutes, I arrived at the house. I rushed in. Everyone was downstairs in the living room sitting down.

"What happened?" I yelled in a panic.

"It's Adrianna. I told her to wait so someone else could be with her."

"You're still not answering the question."

"She got here early and so did one of the clients. He tied her up and raped her. He left before anyone else got here," Jacob explained.

I fell to my knees. This was a real-life nightmare. Jacob helped me back up to my feet and sat me in a nearby chair.

"Where is she?" I asked.

"Upstairs," Heather stated.

I quickly ran upstairs and held her in my arms. I knew she needed my support.

"Do you want to go the hospital?" I asked.

"No, please, don't make me go. I want to forget this night ever happened. Besides, I took a hot shower and washed his filth off," she said.

"Adrianna, I'm so sorry," I cried while squeezing her tight.

"It's okay. It's not your fault."

"You don't have to do this anymore," I stated.

"I have bills to pay."

"I know but this line of business could cost you your sanity. Why don't you take a week off and think about it? I'm going to text to your phone a rape crisis center hotline. They offer counseling services," I explained.

"Thanks."

"Here is five hundred dollars. It's not much but hopefully can get you through the week," I said, handing her the money from my pocket. It was all the cash I had on me.

Jacob followed Adrianna home to make sure she got there safely. I wanted to call it a night but the others wanted it to be business as usual. I had never experienced the down side of the business. I later found out some of the other men and women working for Heather and me had been raped, tortured, and beaten as well in past experiences. This all was just too much for me to absorb.

My stomach started to churn. The room started spinning. Feelings of guilt over Adrianna and the memories of that night I was raped flashed back in my mind. The room got dark and I passed out.

"Angela," Heather's voice spoke softly.

"Yes," I answered, groggy.

"Are you all right?" she asked.

"I'm going to be fine. Give me a minute. I left my purse in the car. Will you bring it to me, please?"

"Yes," she agreed and brought my purse to me.

I quickly got out the medicine bottle and popped a pill in my mouth.

"Thanks," I said, slightly relieved.

"You're welcome. You know, Angela, I've finally figured out what happened," Heather stated.

"Oh good." Heather's statement was music to my ears. "Tell me what happened tonight. Why wasn't anyone else here with Adrianna? Someone should always be here at least an hour before a client comes." I asked for answers.

Little did everyone know, Heather and I had installed video surveillance cameras inside and outside of the home. So even if no one talked I knew I could get at least get a license plate number on the culprit.

"I'm not talking about tonight. I'm talking about you. Angela, you were raped or someone did something very bad to you," Heather said.

"Not now, Heather, please," I said as I attempted to get up from the chair and walk away.

"I'm here if you want a shoulder to lean on," she said, following close behind me.

"I have to go. Take all the profits from tonight. I didn't do any work tonight anyway," I said while walking toward the door to leave.

"Angela, please stop avoiding the subject," Heather insisted while gently rubbing my arm.

"I can't do this right now. I'm fine," I said, grabbing my arm back then rushing out the door.

When I finally got in the car and out of sight of the house, I began to cry. I sobbed all the way home.

Chapter 30

Peace Offering

"What's wrong with Fera?" I asked the veterinarian after blood and urine tests were performed.

"She has a kidney infection, which explains why she wasn't eating. Here is a prescription for an antibiotic," he explained.

"Will this reoccur?" I asked.

"I'm hoping that it will not. If she's not acting her normal self, not eating or urinating, bring her back in two days," he instructed.

"I will do." I nodded while petting Fera. I was so thankful it wasn't anything serious. Fera was getting up there in age. Her not being by my side would seem unreal to me.

"Fera's rabies shots are due to expire," he noticed while looking at her chart.

"Let's go ahead and take care of it. Also, I want to put a microchip in her. Just in case she gets lost, I will find her," I commented.

"All right. I will send the tech right in."

"Thank you."

The vet petted Fera on her head and walked out of the exam room. Within minutes, the tech walked in. Fera cuddled under my arm and attempted to hide as she got closer. As much as I hated to hear Fera whimper, I grabbed and handed her over to the tech. Fera's constant cries were killing me, so I left the room.

After the bill of $342.54 was paid, we left the vet's office. While walking out the door, a German shepherd was barking at Fera. She was so frightened that she started trembling and peeing all at once.

"Barry, down, boy," the dog owner commanded.

I looked up and it was one of the clients with his wife and kids. Little did his wife know that he had an appointment with two women that very night. The double lives people lead. They are only inches away from being crossed over.

I went home to give Fera a bath and put on the cutest pink outfit I could find. The medicine seemed to be working. She was acting like her old self again by running around and getting into every and anything.

I had a change of heart. I packed a box with most of the food and drinks that I would need for the evening for George's house. Fera and me headed out the door.

I turned the key to open George's condo door. He was sitting in the living room on a recliner, watching the evening news. Betty was in a robe, looking as if she just got out of the shower. I took a deep breath hoping I could actually play nice. I quickly noticed in the living room that all the pictures of Joyce were gone. My forehead began to tense up and I could feel beads of sweat forming on my nose and forehead. *This woman thinks she can just come in here and take over house,* I thought as I scanned the room to see what other changes she'd made. I originally assumed she was only staying a few nights every once in a while, but at that point I felt that she actually lived with George.

"Hey," I said to George.

Fera ran past me and jumped in his lap. He laughed as she hopped up and down, licking him all over his face. George and Fera were so happy to see one another.

"Angela put that smell-good stuff on you. Didn't she?" George cooed to Fera as he petted her in attempt to calm her down.

"Hello, Betty," I greeted her.

"Hi, Angela. Honey, we weren't expecting you."

"I know but I'm here now."

"What do you have there in the box?" she inquired.

"It's dinner for tonight.

"What are we cooking?"

"I already cooked the collard greens. They just need to be heated up. I'm going to bake a few sweet potatoes, slice them open, and smother cinnamon butter on them. Joyce taught me how to make that kind of butter from scratch," I bragged.

"What's the main dish?"

"It's fried catfish. I bought it from Dean's Fish Market. George prefers their market because they clean the fish so well."

"May I help?" she asked nicely.

"No, thank you." I responded just as nicely and headed into the kitchen.

I enjoyed the fact that Betty was a little uncomfortable with me coming over at all. I had a key. As bad as she wanted to, she couldn't say a word to me. This was my grandfather and my territory.

"Give me thirty minutes and dinner will be served," I said while placing fresh rolls on a pan to be baked.

"So what can I get you two to drink? I made fresh tea and lemonade," I advised.

"Lemonade for me," Betty said.

"Tea." George nodded then headed toward the table.

I returned with the main dish and followed with the side items. As soon as the food was on the table, George quickly decided to say grace. I guessed he wanted to avoid getting me to do the task. I believed he feared I would say something slick out of my mouth. He was probably right!

"So, Angela, how's the lab going?" Betty asked, attempting to make conversation as we ate.

"It's going well," I commented.

"Did you get that position?" George asked.

"I will find out in another week. With so many possible candidates, it's taken awhile to interview everyone."

"George talks about how you love working there."

"Yes, I do, but for right now, it doesn't actually pay the bills," I said.

"Times are tight and everyone is on a budget," Betty commented.

"Yes, Betty, you're absolutely right about that, which brings up what I wanted to speak to George about."

"We're listening," Betty said.

"Well, George, my lease is up in two weeks at my apartment. I want to come here and live with you. How nice it would be just the three of us," I suggested, looking down at Fera while she was eating her bowl of baby carrots and spinach.

Betty choked on the lemonade that she was drinking. Inside, I was dying laughing. Did she really think that she was just going to come in and take over my grandfather, who happened to adore me, without a fight?

"What about the house in Suffolk?" Betty asked.

"The deed on that house is in my name only," I replied.

"Angela . . ."George said, giving me an annoying look.

"What are you looking at me for? Since she was making suggestions, I wanted to point that tidbit out to her," I admitted.

"Let's just have a peaceful dinner," he said.

"All right." Betty nodded her head.

"It's too far away from the lab and George," I stated, returning to the subject at hand.

"I figured young people would appreciate their own space. This apartment is small," Betty said.

"Four is a crowd. Besides, I plan to put anything I'm not using in storage."

"Or you could use the Suffolk house," George said.

"I never thought about that. Thank you, George. You've always had my best interest at heart," I said.

"You know I love you."

"I want to apologize for the way I treated Betty and you."

"It's all right. I already forgave you two weeks ago," he said.

"I understand that you're still grieving over your grandmother," Betty said.

"Thank you for accepting my apologies," I said.

"You're welcome," they both said in unison.

"May I move in with you?" I asked.

"Of course, my home is your home, always," George expressed.

"Thank you," I said and gave him a hug.

"You're welcome." George snickered.

I noticed Betty was giving him a nasty look. I refuse to let her take over but I would not be disrespectful to her. Later, I discovered she actually lived across the hall from George. I was happy to know she had her own place.

"I'm going to decorate to put a modern touch on the place," I said as I looked around.

"Whatever you want, Angela. I'm just happy to see you smiling again. Do me a favor," he said.

"What's that?" I asked.

"Don't burn a hole through my credit card." We both started laughing as he handed it to me.

Chapter 31

No Deed Goes Unpunished

Since the incident at the business, I had been keeping an eye on Adrianna. I even gave her another paid week off. I told her to consider it a mini vacation. Guilt still lingered in my heart after what happened.

Over the years, I learned that patience was an acquired trait. For the past three hours, I had been waiting for Donna, a client of mine, to meet me at Starbucks. Normally, I would have left after thirty minutes but she had vital information that I desperately needed. Plus, she called and kept me updated. She was stuck at work. Someone didn't show up to take over her shift. Donna worked at the Department of Motor Vehicles. The night Adrianna was raped, I retrieved and viewed the surveillance tape. I was only able to get a glimpse of the license plate of the culprit. I knew Donna could help me put the pieces of the puzzle together and find our guy.

"Sorry for the delay," Donna said after she approached my car.

"It's okay. I understand. Besides, you're doing me a favor. "

"Well, here it is. This transaction shall never be discussed again," she said, handing me over a folder.

"Of course." I nodded, then handed her an envelope. In payment for her service, I gave her half off a night of service with our best guy, Cole.

"I will see you later. The kids are already calling me, asking what we're eating for dinner. It's the story of my life." She giggled, heading back to her car.

"Make spaghetti. It's quick, easy, and makes for plenty of leftovers," I suggested.

"Hmm, says the woman who doesn't have any children. I will think about that." She laughed again and pulled off.

Inside the folder was the driver's license of the man. His name was Gary Richardson and he lived in Virginia Beach.

I drove over to the address on the driver's license. His home was in the heart of the quiet suburban community of Great Neck. I parked in front of a house a few doors down from the address and watched as he drove the same car from the surveillance video into the driveway of his home. It took all I had to restrain myself from pressing the gas and running him over after he got out his vehicle.

My cell phone rang.

"Hello?" I answered.

"Hi, Angela," Adrianna greeted me on the phone.

"Hey, I should be at my apartment in an hour. We're still on for tonight?" I asked.

"Yeah, I just finished working out. I will be over shortly," she said.

"All right. I will see you later," I responded before pressing the end button on my cell phone.

After watching the guy check his mail and head into his home, I pulled off and headed home. It killed me to see that guy just go on with his life as if he hadn't worry in the world when he was a freaking rapist! I drove home deep in thought.

***

There was a knock at the door.

"Come on in," I said after opening the door.

"Thanks for helping. It was hard for me to ask because I have a lot of pride," Adrianna admitted.

"It's no problem. Now, let's crack those books open," I replied.

After three long hours, Adrianna had a better grip on calculus. I had some leftover shrimp and linguine that we devoured and then did a few more practice problems.

"So how are you feeling?" I asked, eagerly wanting to know where she was mentally with the whole ordeal.

"I'm having nightmares," she admitted.

"You can see a counselor."

"I'm too ashamed."

"If you change your mind, I know of plenty of resources that you can reach out to. What are your nightmares about?"

"It's the same events of that night. He ripped my clothes off and raped me. Except in the dream, I managed to get his mask off his face."

"What does his face look like?" I asked as if I didn't know already.

I was curious to see how the man looked in Adrianna's dream. I grabbed a piece of paper and pencil as Adrianna began to describe our culprit.

"He was in his mid-thirties with a touch of grey hair, and looked as if he hadn't shaved in days with an overgrown 'college cut.' His eyes were blue. He had huge ears. I noticed a birthmark on his face. It was on the left side of his chin. His right hand looked as though it had been burned in a fire," she explained in detail.

By the time Adrianna was finished describing him, I'd made a mock police sketch of the guy in her dream. "Is this how he looked?" I said, holding up my rough sketch.

"Yes," she responded, then held her head down.

"You know, Adrianna, it's good to talk about your feelings," I said as I rubbed her back gently.

"I guess so. For now, I'm done. I need to get home and get plenty of rest before I take the exam at eleven o'clock tomorrow morning," she said.

I walked Adrianna to the door and watched as she got into her car safely and drove off. After she left, I compared the sketch I'd drawn to the actual driver's license of the culprit. It was amazing how the two were so similar, all the way down to the birthmark on the right side of his face.

For the next two weeks, I studied this man's schedule, deciding when, where, and how I was going to strike. He was married with two small children. An older woman lived with them. I assumed it was one of their parents. Richardson worked for a power plant company in Newport News. He left for work at twenty minutes after four faithfully every morning.

I planned my execution very carefully. Killing Richardson would be the ultimate gratification. Dressed in black equipped with a matching black pack, I surveyed around his work building to make sure there were not any visible cameras. I made sure both of my license plates were covered up before parking in the back of a nearby run-down hotel. I watched as Richardson pulled up. As I crept up closer to the car, he was singing along with the music playing on the radio with his eyes closed. Within no time, I hopped in the car. He didn't even notice me until I sat down in the back.

"Turn the music off," I demanded, feeling a rush of adrenaline.

"What!" he replied.

I pulled out my knife and pressed it into the side of his face. "Can you hear me now?" I asked.

"Yes." He nodded, turning pale.

"Turn the music off," I repeated and he immediately did so by pressing a button.

"Music is off. Please just take the car. I will give you my wallet," he begged.

"I don't want your car and I don't want your wallet, Mr. Richardson," I explained, slowly slicing into his throat.

"What do you want?"

"Your heart to burn in hell. She never did anything to you."

"Who? What are you talking about?" he asked in a panic.

"The young girl you raped."

His eyes immediately looked down with a guilty look. "She was a whore working in a whorehouse. So what about that spells rape? She wanted it. Most of them do," he said cockily.

"Is that right? Is that how you rationalize it in your mind?"

"Yes. I'm looking into your eyes and I can tell that you want it, too. Come on, relax, let's take this down a notch and climb in the back seat for some fun," he offered.

"No," I yelled.

"You may want to reconsider your decision," he said and then attempted to reach for the glove compartment. I gave him a hard blow to the temple with the back end of my knife.

"Okay, okay, okay," he screamed while holding his head.

"Hold your arms up," I demanded.

This time he did exactly what he was told. I had to confirm what Adrianna said about the burn. Yes, it was there.

"Richardson, there may have been a chance I'd let you live if you had shown a little remorse, but obviously you don't feel guilty at all for your actions. Tonight, your family is simply going to have to eat dinner without you," I said.

There was no way he was going to be set free and run. I was just trying to get into his head. It worked because he begged. He repeatedly begged and I laughed.

I cut him with the knife right above the eyes. This gave me enough seconds to climb over into the passenger seat. I got the urge to carve his eyes out. He screamed in agony. I laughed again. Seeing him suffer gave me so much joy. I opened the glove compartment to see what was in there. It was a small pistol. I grabbed it and cocked it.

"Get out of the car," I instructed.

"I can't see," he whimpered.

"I'm not telling you again."

He managed to get out of the car. I pressed the button to open the trunk on my way out. I pushed him toward the back of the car. I pressed the tip of the gun into his balls and instructed him to get into the trunk. I wasted no time pulling out my torch from my backpack and lighting Richardson's body up.

The James River was close by. The fog was thick that early morning. I drove along the coast until I found the perfect location. I placed the car in drive and let it glide into the river.

It was still dark outside. It wasn't time for the sun to make its presence known. At a nearby tree, I quickly changed my clothes into sweats and placed them into my backpack. It took me thirty minutes to get back to my car. To people who had noticed me, it appeared as if I was taking a morning jog.

I smiled the entire drive home. I was pleased to know that I had gotten justice for Adrianna and maybe even for myself, too. To many, I could be painted as a serial killer, but I truly saw myself as a vigilante.

Chapter 32

The Verdict

At the lab, a bouquet of gardenia flowers was sent to me by none other than Nathan Watts, the insurance agent. Also, he sent a dozen of fresh-baked cookies of various flavors. It was a hit with my coworkers. We all loved to snack. He'd called and sent me texts several times. He was pursuing me hard and not giving up without a fight. I found that rather cute. After all, I did find the guy rather attractive. Not only that, he had such a good heart. I'd seen it many times in the way he treated George.

I grabbed a cookie and admired my flowers, then grabbed the card that was embedded. It read:

I just wanted to brighten up your day.

Nathan

Well, you can't stop a man from trying, I thought as I placed the card in my purse. Then I grabbed the flowers as I left the lab for the day. I had to admit that I loved the chase.

Lounging on the couch with Fera was one my favorite pastimes. Working all day at the lab and then staying up all night to collect money and watch over the women at the business was beginning to take its toll on me. Heather continued to put the bug in my ear for us to finally get a building. To be honest, I didn't want to deal with a monthly loan, clients, employees, payroll, and everything else that goes along with having a legit business.

I turned on the television to the news. They were running a segment on a dog show that would be held at Chesapeake City Park. Next, the news reporter was interviewing a widow sobbing about the loss of her husband. I tuned in. The lady was none other than the widow of Tommy, the prick who I killed at the gas station.

I felt a moment of sadness as pictures of his children flashed across the screen and his widow cried. She had no idea she was married to a monster. I never understood how bad people attempted to portray good lives. At some point, good and evil always collided. His wife wanted the killer brought to justice. *Unfortunately, that will never happen,* I thought, giggling to myself then turning off the television.

All of a sudden, I felt a wave of nausea come over me. I barely made it to the bathroom to vomit. After I was finished and brushed my teeth, I started thinking about everything that I ate. All I could remember eating was a bowl of oatmeal for breakfast and a turkey sandwich for lunch. I had the stomach bug before. This definitely wasn't the stomach bug. All I could hear was Joyce reminding me to always keep peppermint candy and saltine crackers around. It cuts down on the nausea. I ran to the pantry. Fortunately, I did have a bag of peppermint there. There were no saltine crackers. I immediately ate two peppermint candies. Fera ran over to me in the kitchen to make sure that I was all right. I decided to make a cup of ginger tea, hoping it would settle my stomach. I didn't have any soup and I surely didn't feel like going to the store.

Within minutes, the tea kettle started whistling. As I poured the tea, I began to think long and hard, racking my brain trying to figure out what could be wrong.

"Oh my God! My period was late. That's why I'm sick!" I yelled and dropped the tea kettle.

I ran out of the house with Fera in pure adrenaline and headed to the drug store. I didn't want to waste any more time thinking about my last period or calling a girlfriend to actually discuss the matter.

After I left the drug store with three different brands of pregnancy tests, I raced back home. I gulped down three bottles of water. All three of the pregnancy tests came out positive. I knew I had slept with two men since my last period but I was sure to use condoms. Then I remembered . . . Larry. The last time I had sex with Larry the condom broke. I told him not to worry about it because I had planned to take the morning-after pill, but the next day it slipped my mind. I was certain I was pregnant with Larry's child and I damn sure wasn't going to tell him. He was already trying to save me. Me being pregnant with his child would send him over the edge. Larry wanted to be the one who played the role of savior from my abusive childhood. Not to mention, his wife and child died. He would be overjoyed to get a second chance at fatherhood. I couldn't deal with that. I was certain to have been at least six to seven weeks along. I made sure to be so careful. I couldn't believe this was happening to me! I regularly got tested for STDs and always used condoms.

The next morning, I made an appointment with a local abortion clinic in the area. The Web site stated that they were very discrete. Mentally, physically, emotionally, I wasn't ready for a child. I didn't want to tell anyone because I wasn't interested in hearing anyone's opinion. I knew the baby's soul would float to heaven and Joyce would watch over that child for me. One thing for sure was there wouldn't be a next time. I would be more responsible and take better precautions.

"Ms. Farmer," the nurse called me back. "How are you doing?" she asked.

"I'm okay and ready to get this over with," I explained, handing her the $400 in cash.

The nurse went over how the procedure would be performed and gave me an opportunity to choose other options. My mind was made up.

"The doctor will be in shortly," she said and then closed the door.

I changed into the exam gown and minutes later, there was a knock on the door.

"Angela, I'm Dr. Moran. A pretty girl like you shouldn't be in a place like this. I don't ever want to see you back her again," he said after he and the nurse came back into the exam room.

"Yes, sir." I nodded my head.

"Lay back, open your legs; this will be over soon," he explained.

I chose to be put to sleep. I didn't want to remember or see anything. As the anesthesia kicked in, I dozed off to sleep.

"We'll be waiting for you," Joyce gently spoke, holding a baby in a green blanket.

When I awoke, it was all over. After lying down for an hour, the nurse called a cab to take me home. I didn't want to run the risk of someone spotting my car in the parking lot, especially Larry. I never knew what city he was working in. Larry has already been hurt too much in his life. I didn't want to add to it.

Over the next two days, I took some time off at the lab. Fera and I headed to George's house. I could tell in his voice over the phone that he had something to say.

When I walked in, I knew Betty would have her behind plopped on the couch. It was as if it were her permanent spot. She looked at me as the enemy attempting to kidnap George rather than a granddaughter. I realized it was partially my fault because I had been so unkind to her. Moving in with George was truly never an option; I only said it to get under Betty's skin. I had begun to accept George obviously enjoyed her company. Deep inside, I don't want him to rot away all alone. Betty made him feel vibrant and alive.

"Hey," I said after opening the front door and putting Fera down. She ran over to the recliner chair to sit on George's lap.

"Hello there," he said.

"Where's Betty?" I asked.

"Her sister is visiting for the week. She is out shopping with her now."

"That's nice," I said, grateful I could talk to my grandfather alone for a change.

"Angela, I'm glad you're here. I need to tell you something."

"What's wrong?" I asked, thinking the worst. My heart started beating quickly.

"Well, I know one day I won't be in my right frame of mind, but today I am. Joyce and I reviewed your case file. It was despicable what those vultures did to you. It was Joyce's idea but we started a class-action suit against the city of Norfolk for not protecting you. Do you remember the officer you told to help you?"

"Yes," I said.

"Well, he documented it. Each time his superiors wouldn't do anything about it. The suit settled about ten years ago. Angela, after attorney fees, you were awarded one hundred thousand dollars. It's been sitting in an account earning interest all these years. Take that money and make some good out of it. Honey, I'm so sorry what happened to you," he expressed, holding my hand.

"What was the name of the police person who ignored my cries?" I asked, not even caring about the money.

"I can't tell you that, Angela."

"Why?"

"I know you killed those three men who hurt you," he whispered.

"I . . ."

"You don't have to explain anything to me. Joyce never figured it out but I did. That night you told me that you were going to see a movie with Becca, I followed you. I saw everything through the window. We will never speak of this again. I understand why you did it. Sometimes, people truly get what they deserve," he said.

I began to weep in his arms. "Am I a bad seed?" I asked.

"No, of course not. You're beautiful, a college graduate, and going to make some man happy with that cooking of yours." We both started laughing.

"I can cook a little," I admitted.

"You're just being modest. Speaking of men, that young man Nathan Watts has dropped plenty of hints to me that he likes you. He has been by the apartment a few times just to check on me. Angela, he is a good man. I think you should give him a chance," George suggested.

"Maybe." I nodded.

"I'm in the mood for Mayfield vanilla ice cream. I just brought some from the store the other day. Go run in the kitchen and make us some bowls. Plus, I made sure to get my Fera some frozen doggie treats. I couldn't leave her out of the fun," George said.

Chapter 33

Chance

I stared at myself in the bathroom mirror as I thought about all the things I'd done and all I'd been through in my life. I knew there were evil people who roamed the world, but me, I was just a product of my environment and my mother's psychotic behavior. The effects were devastating and many would have never made it this far, but I did. I beat the odds of becoming a junkie or a whore just like my mother.

Sure I had my downfalls but I lived as a productive member of society, contributing to the justice system in my own little way and striving for success at the same time. I began to think about what the future held for me. Just as George had promised, he gave me the money. I continued to let it sit in an account.

Initially, my only goal was simply to run an upscale whorehouse, but as time had passed, I had a change of heart. I was tired of staying up late. Being in the sex business came with a price. I was tired of the late nights and the constant stress and worry. Every night, I was on edge. I constantly monitored the patrons in an attempt to protect the employees and make sure that money was right. I was beginning to want a real life where I didn't have sex with different men all the time. The sexual urges had begun to decrease. My routine visits with the therapist had a great impact on my life.

I knew leaving the business would be a huge change but, like always, I was up for the challenge. There was a lot of planning ahead of me so I started by giving Nathan a call.

"Hello?" a voice answered me.

"Nathan," I said.

"Hey, so you finally called." He laughed. I could tell he was smiling through the phone.

"You broke me down." I laughed then continued, "I'm only kidding."

"Do you know when you have some time to get together?" he asked.

"Yes; are you in the mood for a sugar rush?" I inquired.

"I like my fair share of sweets."

"On Saturday morning, meet me at Sugar Tree Bakery," I suggested.

"Okay, I know where it is. What time?" he asked.

"Are you an early bird?"

"Matter of fact, I am," Nathan confirmed.

"Great. Let's meet around nine o'clock in the morning."

"Agreed," he said.

"I will see you then."

"Looking forward to it," he said before hanging up.

After speaking to Nathan I prepared dinner and got ready for a long night at work.

To my surprise, the night ended early and profitable. Sooner rather than later, I was going to have to tell Heather that my heart wasn't in the business anymore. Little by little, I had been teaching her the business side of running an upscale whorehouse. So if she decided to continue the business on her own, she would be more than ready. As we counted the money and did the checks and balances for the night, I started small talk with Heather.

"So how's the lab these days? You haven't spoken about it in about one whole day," Heather said, laughing.

"You think you're so funny. Are you getting tired of me talking about the lab?" I asked.

"Hmm, a little. I know you love working there," she replied.

"Yes, I do." I nodded.

"It's where your heart is."

"Correct. In fact, I will be working more hours. I have to admit that it's hard juggling this and the lab."

"Angela, you're a morning riser. I'm a night owl. We are who we are," Heather stated before we locked up the house and left.

I headed home to take a hot shower and catch a quick nap.

The alarm clock went off. I got up to prepare for my date with Nathan. I decided to play it simple with a fitted T-shirt and jeans and sneakers. Still exhausted, I drank a Red Bull on the way to the bakery. I didn't want to be yawning in Nathan's face. I walked in and was in awe of the morsels of pastry goodies laid behind the glass. I definitely had my eye on a raspberry bar, two shortbread cookies, and, my favorite, an elephant ear: a glazed doughnut that is shaped into an ear.

"Do you know what you want?" Nathan asked, startling me. I began to wonder just how long he was standing over me, watching me bent over.

"Yes, I sure do." I smiled at him.

"Give me a few minutes and I will be ready. What do you recommend?"

"You should definitely try a shortbread cookie and a lemon drop."

"Okay," he agreed.

After ordering our baked goods, we ordered two cups of coffee. We sat on the bakery patio and talked for hours. I was really enjoying his company. Plus, he kept his hands to himself the entire time. Even more impressive, I kept my hands to myself. Not one time did I find myself having an outrageous sexual thought or overwhelming urge to seduce him.

Luckily for us, there was a park near the bakery. We walked around the park and talked, joked, and laughed to burn those calories off we just put on. Nine o'clock in the morning so easily turned into one o'clock in the afternoon that we called it a day and agreed to meet again soon. I had to admit, I couldn't wait to see him again.

"Will you keep me waiting long before the next time that I see you?" he asked while I got into my car.

"I won't. I promise," I assured him. He gently held my hand. It was a nice gesture, I thought, driving away.

I was on my way to Heather's apartment. It was time I let her know my plans to quit the business.

"Come in, the door is open," Heather announced before I even had a chance to ring the doorbell.

"Stranger danger," I commented as I opened the door and walked in.

"Well, I saw you coming into the parking lot." She giggled then continued, "Hungry? I can make some sandwiches."

"No, thanks. I just came from Sugar Tree Bakery, high off of sweet treats. I bought some of your favorites, including their infamous petit fours," I said, handing her the box of goodies.

"Angela, thank you so much," she said before opening up the box.

"We need to talk," I said, walking over to the couch.

"About?" she asked, nibbling on a petit four and sitting down on the loveseat.

"I want out of the business."

"I saw this coming," she said.

"How did you know?" I asked.

"Your demeanor has changed, especially after Adrianna's rape and you getting the lab position," she commented.

"Yes, you're right. That did play a major part into my decision," I admitted.

"What about me, Angela? I still can't get a job. I have a master's degree now and that doesn't mean shit. Our line of business, excuse me, my line of business now is my only source of income. I'm not going back to Dallas to my mother's house looking like a failure," she cried.

"Dry your tears before I start crying too."

"Angela, I can't do it without you. You're the brains. I'm not."

"Yes, you can do it. I have written down everything for you and something else, too," I explained, reaching into my purse. I handed Heather $10,000 in cash.

"Angela, I can't take this."

"Yes, you can and you will. Think of it as a cushion until you figure out what you want to do. In my heart, I don't feel as though you want to run a whorehouse for the rest of your life, either."

"Maybe you're right. For now, it works for me. These bills come in every month and they go out getting paid. It's discouraging when the movie theatres are not even hiring."

"You will find your way. Besides, we will always be close, just not business partners anymore. I'm handing you the torch." I gave her a reassuring smile.

"Yeah, it's the torch full of problems," she commented, laughing.

I felt relieved after talking with Heather. I had finally walked away from our business. That was another chapter closed in my book of life. Things were coming along just as planned.

I spent the rest of the week putting things in motion for the other life changes I had planned. At the end of the week, Nathan and I decided to go to the Yard House, a new restaurant all the local blogs have been buzzing about.

We made small talk as we waited to be seated at our table. I made sure to look exquisite. Nathan made me feel so secure. I felt as though I could tell him almost anything. I could tell he felt the same. Little by little, he started revealing things to me.

"How was your day?" I asked.

The waitress took our drink order.

"Great. I sold three insurance policies and I went to visit my Aunt Victoria."

Nathan's parents died in a car accident at a young age. His aunt and uncle raised him and his younger sister. That's all I knew up to this point.

"How is she doing?" I asked.

"Today was a better day. She and my uncle were always chain smokers. Now, it just caught up with her. She has a mild case of emphysema with an oxygen tank tagging along with her. The doctor urges her to stop smoking. When no one is looking I know she still sneaks a cigarette every now and then. After my uncle died, she honestly hasn't been the same. The sparkle in her eye is gone," Nathan explained.

"What happened to your uncle?" I asked.

"He was found dead stabbed and burned to death."

My hands started shaking as if I was in a panic. "What's your uncle's name?" I asked reluctantly.

"His name was Timothy McCall. He was a decent man and raised us as if my sister and I were his very own children."

"Your last name is Watts."

"Yes, he was my mother's brother. Her maiden name was McCall as well. Then, she married my father and his last name was Watts. You're looking at the third generation of Watts men to sell insurance. My blood-line just has a knack for it," he said lightheartedly.

"You're going to do the same thing to me," I said and ran out. Nathan ran behind me. I managed to get outside. He gently grabbed my arm.

"Angela, what's wrong? What did I say or do that upset you so much?"

"You're going to hurt me just like the others. Don't touch me!" I screamed and ran across the street.

My head was spinning. I was beginning to lose my balance. I needed my pills but I'd left my purse in the restaurant. I refused to go back. All I wanted was to get as far from Nathan as possible so I kept running. My sight became blurry and there were spots in front of my eyes but I couldn't stop running. My hearing was diminishing, but I could hear several car horns in the distant. Still, I couldn't stop running. All of the sudden, I felt an enormous force and excruciating blow on the side of my body. Before I could realize what had happened, everything went black. I was hit by a car.

Moments later, I felt a gentle nudge. I opened my eyes to witness Joyce dressed in a white robe holding a baby, this time in a yellow blanket. I gently rubbed the baby's cheek. I reached out to hug Joyce and didn't let go for a long time.

"Why did you leave us? We needed you," I sobbed.

"Baby, it was my time," she explained.

"Where am I?" I asked.

"*You're caught in between life and death,*" *she said and pointed down. There, I could see doctors and nurses trying to revive me.*

"*Joyce, I want to go with you,*" *I pleaded.*

"*No, this isn't your time,*" *she replied, shaking her head.*

"*She's right, Angela. This isn't your time,*" *another voice said.*

It was my mother. She was covered in flames. I reached to choke her. The flames were hot and burning my hands but I didn't care. I refused to let go. I wanted to kill her and make her suffer over and over and over again as she had done to me.

"*I hate you!*" *I screamed so loud that I could barely talk. Joyce tried her best to get me off of her. I kicked her, spit on her. It was though I turned into an enraged animal.*

"*Stop it, now!*" *Joyce commanded.*

Out of breath, I stopped on Joyce's command.

"*Angela, I'm so sorry,*" *my mother confessed.*

"*No, you're not sorry. I don't believe you. Why are you even here? The devil let you loose for the evening?*" *I yelled, still enraged.*

"*Please forgive me,*" *she repeated.*

"*No, I will never forgive you. Go back to hell where you belong,*" *I said. All of a sudden, a force pulled her down and she was gone.*

"*Angela, you have to stop killing or you may end up in hell just like your mother,*" *Joyce advised.*

"*This rage of anger comes over me. I can't control it.*"

"*Yes, you can control it. You have to forgive if you truly want to be set free and move to the next chapter of your life. God forgives so you must as well! I am with you always watching over you. Now, this little baby girl of yours will be watching as well. Remember that. Allow peace to come into your heart,"* she urged while walking into the white light.

"No! Joyce, please don't leave!" I begged.

I tried running behind her but my legs couldn't move.

"When will I see you again?" I asked as I watched her walk away.

"You are destined for enormous opportunities to help others. Tell George I love him and that Betty don't have nothing on my cooking. Kiss Fera for me," she said.

In a flash, she kissed me on the forehead. I kissed the baby on the forehead.

"Joyce, please don't go," I repeated over and over again.

I awoke to George and Nathan standing over me. Nathan had this look as if he knew my pitiful story.

"Angela, I didn't know my uncle along with the others had done such horrible things to you. I'm so sorry," he said, holding my hand.

"Get away. I never want to see you again," I screamed, crying, yanking my hand back.

Both George and Nathan walked out of the hospital room. Then, only George returned.

"How are you feeling?" he asked.

"I'm in pain," I said.

"You should be with the way that car hit you. Nurse, my granddaughter is in pain. Would be so kind as to bring her some medication for relief?" he asked the nurse who happened to be walking by my room.

"Yes, I will be right there," the nurse replied.

"I saw her."

"Who?"

"Joyce."

"Are you sure you saw her?" he asked.

"Yes, I did."

"What did Joyce say?"

"She said that she loved you and Betty doesn't have anything on her cooking." We both started to giggle.

A few days later, I left the hospital with a mild concussion, a broken leg, and many bruises. I couldn't work for two months, which gave me plenty of time to think. While lying up on the couch with Fera on my chest, I decided I wanted to do something meaningful with my life. I wanted to help those who had a troubled childhood like my own. After weeks of pondering, I decided to start a group home for young girls who had been abused, abandoned, and/or mistreated. I was going to use the money that George had given me to turn Joyce and George's farm home into a safe haven for women.

My new lease on life was an ongoing process. With continued therapy with a new therapist, I'd faced my past and learned to control the many psychological effects I battled. I stopped cutting myself altogether. Although the sexual urges to just have sex with any man had subsided the urge to kill men who hurt women were still prevalent. I would try not to strike again. My knife and torch were always close just in case.

As for now, I couldn't face Nathan. The last thing I wanted was for him to feel pity for me, and to come in between him and his beloved aunt and uncle.

I heard the door lock turn. I knew it was Larry. I trusted him enough to let him have a key to my apartment for the time being. He was here to take me to my therapy session. He had been an angel taking care of me. Being cooped up in an apartment for an entire month drove me crazy. Tension built up.

"Where are you?" Larry asked.

"In the kitchen," I replied.

"Wow. What a welcome," he said.

I was not dressed for the therapy session. In fact, I wasn't dressed at all. I was totally naked. I moved closer to Larry to kiss him on the lips. I nibbled on his neck. He unbuckled his pants while I reached for the condom on the kitchen counter. It had probably been awhile for Larry too. Both of us needed to relieve built-up tension. He picked me up and laid me down the kitchen table. He entered into me. I closed my eyes to enjoy his deep strokes of sexual bliss.

"Now I'm going to take a shower before we leave. Care to join me?" I asked when we finished having sex.

Larry picked me up, carrying me to the bathroom. He not only washed me down but also massaged my back.

An hour later, we headed to my appointment.

"Will you be all right?" he asked before driving off.

Larry had an important meeting to attend. He was trying to land the contract for renovating all the Buffalo Wild Wings restaurants in the Tidewater area.

"Yes." I nodded before closing the car door. Besides, I didn't want him to miss out on an opportunity like this because of me. I cared a lot about Larry. He was a true friend.

I slowly managed to get into the office building by myself without any help. It was just the way I wanted it. I had to start doing things on my own to regain my independence. Julie, Becca, and George had all pitched in to care for me.

The office was on the first floor of the building. I walked in through the door and let the receptionist know that I was present.

"Angela?" a voice called out. I turned around to see none other than Nathan Watts. *I hope Larry and him didn't cross paths or even see each other,* I thought while looking at him, surprised that he was here.

"Nathan."

"Please don't say anything. I just wanted to let you that I'm here for you. I've been waiting for you and I'm going to continue to wait to get another chance with you. It hurts but I understand why you responded the way you did at the restaurant," he explained.

"How did you find me?" I asked.

"Let's just say George is in my corner." We both started laughing.

"Well, first, I apologize for being hateful to you. Nathan, you didn't do anything to me."

"Apology accepted," he said before hugging me.

"I will call you tonight, I promise," I assured him.

"I look forward to it," he said before leaving the office.

"Angela, Dr. Gunter is ready for you," the receptionist said. I followed her to therapy room.

"How are we, Angela?" the therapist asked.

"Great." I nodded.

"I have been reviewing your chart and you have made some remarkable progress."

"Thank you."

"Today I want to try hypnosis, if you're willing," she suggested.

"Okay, if you think it will help," I said.

"Yes, I think it will get a breakthrough for you." She nodded her head.

"Agreed."

"Let's get started. Now, have a seat and lie back in the chair. Listen to the sound of my voice. Close your eyes and count back from ten," she gently instructed me.

"Ten, nine, eight, seven, six, five, four, three, two, one . . ."

There was a rather long pause.

"Lie back, lie back, lie back. That's what those men would say to Angela when they did those vicious things to her."

"What's your name?" Dr. Gunter asked, uncovering a multiple personality.

"Lucy. I don't believe we've met. I am Angela's protector by any means necessary," she announced in a stern tone with a cold look, jumping up from the couch. Then, she shook Dr. Gunter's hand.

"Is there anyone else I need to meet?" the therapist inquired.

"Yes, I'm the only one you haven't heard from. My name is Pia. I could tell you stories of all the sexual encounters I've had. What fun," she commented in a sultry voice, batting her eyes and twirling around.

"Pia, tell me more about yourself," the therapist suggested.

"She is already gone. The only one that you will actually get stories from is me, Lucy!" her voice said after closing her eyes for a few moments only to reopen them again.

"All right."

"Are you ready to begin? The only ground rule I have is that the subject of Larry is off-limits. He's the only man I have ever loved and I will not discuss our relationship with you," Lucy informed her. "So with that being said, are you ready?" she asked again.

"Yes," Dr. Gunter said.

"Now, let's get started," Lucy said while lying back down on the couch.

Church Girl

Ni'chelle Genovese

Chapter 1

Bittersweet Introductions

Small white candles flickered on a table off to the side. Inhaling, my senses were bombarded with the scent of lime and coconut.

What in the Lord's name kind of sacrificial mumbo jumbo was this? Tay never lit candles or did any of that romantic foolishness and he especially didn't do it after the baby. We got it in when we could and suffered when we couldn't. There were candles everywhere and they made shadows shift and dance on the walls.

He came to me out of the shadows that were dancing in the corner. It was as if he were a shadow himself. The lone dark figure strode toward me and fear paralyzed my feet—froze my vocal chords. It wasn't until he was standing over me that I got the nerve to look up. I was afraid I'd see the face of death in those shadows, finally coming to take me away. But, there wasn't anything cold or deadly about the man who seemed to have appeared out of the darkness.

He was so tall I had to strain my neck to look up into his face. He smiled and the darkness melted away like fog in the sun. I smiled a shy smile back and instantly fell in love with his cinnamon brown skin, perfect white teeth, and deep dimples. He stretched out his hand and directed me to have a seat in a chair that seemed to have appeared out of nowhere. I smoothed

the back of my dress and did as I was instructed. I
was mesmerized as this tall tree of a man knelt down
before me. His head was bald and looked baby smooth
to the touch.

There was a knowing light in his grey eyes that
reassured me in the quiet darkness. My breath caught
in my throat as he slowly trailed his hand up my
inner thigh. He didn't break eye contact. His fingers
followed the tiny goose bumps that rose on my skin
like they were Braille instructions. He wasn't shy or
nervous; it was as if we'd known each other forever,
and I was his. I held my breath as he looked away
from me to lower his head.

His lips touched a sensitive spot on the inside of my
ankle and it felt like I'd been hidden away for years in
a cold, dark cave and his touch was my first sunrise.
I closed my eyes, silently telling myself, Girl, breathe
before you fall out. His lips felt like warm honey as
they trailed wet kisses up my calf and inner thigh.
The heat from his long fingers scorched my skin
as he began slowly pushing my panties to the side.
Involuntarily my head fell backward and a soft moan
somehow snuck out from between my lips just as I felt
his lips close in on my clit.

Oh, Lord, this nigga was not playing around. He
went straight for the gold. My hands had a mind
of their own and somehow they found their way to
his ears. I caressed them, dug my nails into the skin
around them, and then I was holding on for dear life.
He was busy introducing himself to my pussy. Telling
her she was his favorite color, and she was his favorite
food, and how much he'd missed her. He said all that
with his tongue in between softly licking and sucking
on my clit. My body was loving his introduction and
I pulled harder on his ears, begging for him to tell

my pussy his life story. Hell, he could tell her about nuclear physics if he wanted to, just as long as he didn't stop.

I moaned again, but this time the sound alarmed me. It sounded like I was outside of my own body, like the moan came from someone beside me. I glanced down to see if he'd noticed, but the lighting in the room had changed. The shadows were back and darker than they were before. It was too dark for me to see him, but I could still feel the warmth of his hands and his mouth. I was getting closer and closer but something was pulling me away, throwing me off. There was an odor in the room that I couldn't ignore any longer. It smelled like sour sweat and old urine. I opened my mouth to breathe but couldn't get air. Panicked, I tried to tell him to stop, but I couldn't see him and his head was no longer in my hands. Reaching out for him my arms only caught cold, empty air, and I felt a sharp pain across my cheek.

My eyes jerked open. Someone's hand roughly covered my mouth. My senses were coming to me too slowly. It was cold. It was dark. My heart was speeding in my chest as the haziness of my dream faded. The rough wool blanket on the floor underneath me felt scratchy against my bare skin, but the good feelings were still there. My storyteller was still talking; I just couldn't see who it was. I was about to cum and my head rolled back against something cold, metal, and hard. I reached out again and my hand came in contact with long, thick hair.

Smack. It was too dark to see the hand that struck my face.

"You better stop that shit and be quiet." The voice trailed off as I felt warm breath and fingers spreading me open.

I froze. It was a woman's voice. Where the hell was I and who was she?

Shock and confusion were the only things that kept me still long enough to fall back under the spell of her lips. My mind was reeling and the slow throb building between my thighs was clouding my ability to think clearly. Without warning she sucked my clit hard between her lips and as if on cue my body and mind exploded at the same time. Like lightning, everything hit me in a flash.

Six months ago I was arrested for embezzlement. The FBI came to my office, handcuffed me, and read me my rights in front of my employees, some of whom were people from my church. Did I do it? Of course not, but I should have known from the smug looks on the agents faces down to the disapproving glares of people I worshipped with—that I'd already been judged.

Apparently I was a millionaire to the tune of around $2.5 million and I didn't even know it. "Ghost money", is what I'd started calling it since no one seemed to know *where* the hell it had vanished to. Transia, was my company. I'd started it my senior year in college. After taking out a small business loan I bought a shipping container and leased a Mac Truck. My fiancé drove the wheels off of that thing and we undercut the prices of nearly every competitor in the area until we had enough customers to afford another truck. Those two trucks turned into a fleet that serviced the entire U.S. shipping anything from Audi's to office equipment.

It's bad when you have to learn about your alleged crimes one by one, piece by piece as they're laid out in front of you like a mine field. Every time you acknowledge a 'mine', a small explosion goes off in the heads of everyone listening, and the shrapnel spells out the word *guilty*.

Yes the company is mine. Yes the invoices are mine. Yeah, that account has my name on it, but it's not mine. Boom.

"Over the course of four years, you invoiced three specific and I dare say affluent warehouses for transit charges, weight fees, and container rental. All of *your* paperwork shows that this happened. When the warehousing records for those companies are pulled it's peculiar that there were in most cases no pickups by Transia on those days. In addition to that, in the event there was a pickup the amount on *your* paperwork doesn't match the inflated invoices that these warehouses received *and* paid." Brimmer the prosecuting attorney stated in his condescending high-pitched nasal tone.

The public defender I was assigned turned out to be about as useful as snow to an Eskimo. His off white dress shirts were stained yellow at the armpits, drawing attention to the rivers of garlic scented sweat that rolled off him at each proceeding. We'd gone over my case briefly; he'd simply nod causing the third chin underneath his second chin to jiggle in agreement. There was no way to explain how funds were wired to various accounts in my name or how invoices were sent out at nearly triple what they should have been.

Where is my wonderful fiancé Dontay you're probably wondering? Dead, I hope. No, I shouldn't think like that. Especially since I hadn't spoken to him and I don't know what happened. Me and God are still working on this forgiveness thing as you can see.

Jabber Jaws my public defender would only tell me but so much, but Dontay was picked up on separate charges and tried separately. They had him for stealing cargo, as well as "assisting me." That idiot sold me out as a plea bargain, he admitted to everything—damning me in the process. That bitter little pill of information settled itself in my stomach and began to slowly poison me with anger from the inside out. I'd sacrificed so much for love and at the end of the day; love didn't give a damn about me. The only good thing I'd gotten out of love was my daughter Jada.

My parents were overly religious, like church on Sunday, Wednesday, & Friday religious. I wasn't even allowed to associate with boys *after* I'd turned eighteen.

"You keep your eyes on The Father, and *nothing else*." Momma would say with a slap across the back of my head every time she'd catch me staring out the window at boys.

It was like the sound of a fuse being lit or something similar to the gritty head of match running along the smooth flint runway on the back of a book of matchbox. That's what it was like the first time I saw Dontay and he saw me. If I were the ship this fool had to have been my Captain, yes he was my Noah—because that's how serious we were. There was a time when I would have gone against every single biblical scripture I'd ever been taught if he so much as frowned. I mean commandments were broken, sins were committed and there was all kinds of hell and hedonism going on when we were together. In the aftermath of it all we made another life, procreated *and* all of it transpired under my mother's unconsenting roof.

It was so extensive, this emotionally unyielding physically mind-blowing me every which way kind of love that every time we saw each other it was like falling in love all over again. A sensual fuse of feeling would be lit *literally*, and we only had seconds to figure out who'd be the victim of the resulting passionate explosion. Full of sin we were and at all times. We were divine together but never anything good. When you love as hard as we loved there ain't no amount of praying in the world that can stop the jealous fights we'd have.

Jada was three now and Dontay had missed the first two years after she was born because I was weak in my spirit and in my faith. I cheated on him in anger and I've regretted it every day since. He eventually forgave me, said he couldn't live without me, and I forgave him as well. We fell back into our routine like synchronized swimmers.

At the end of the day my forgiveness cost me, as I was sentenced to six years in the East River Correctional Facility in Suffolk, Virginia with the option for parole in three. My parents had disowned me when I'd gotten pregnant, because even though I wasn't killing anyone or doing drugs I was still living in sin. I'd managed to take what little I'd had back then and do something. Now, despite everything my life was being ripped away from me slipping through my desperate fingers like smoke rings.

Welcome to my life, ladies and gentlemen, or what's left of it.

Chapter 2

Night Dreams and Day Mares

I lay momentarily dazed by both pleasure and pain as I remembered where I was and what got me here. I hated falling asleep. Whenever I slept I'd dream of being home with my baby girl, or I'd see Dontay's smiling face and we'd be at the house having dinner or making love. Whenever I'd sleep, Aeron, my cellmate, would take the opportunity to let it be known that as long as I shared this cell with her, I had to share my body as well.

"Go 'head, princess. Tell momma she the G-O-A-T." Aeron lay down on her side in the shadows facing me from the bunk across the cell. A smug grin was spread across her face. This was routine with her. First she'd take it, then she'd gloat about it. Fighting her was pointless. I was all of five feet two inches and about 120 pounds soaking wet. Aeron was five feet ten inches, thick for her size, and strong. If we were in different circumstances I'd say she was actually not bad looking. Those different circumstances would have to be me being a member of the opposite sex, however, because as it stood there was nothing attractive or sanctifying about what had just occurred.

She had a soft, oval-shaped face, with strong, high-arched brows. She didn't do like most of the Puerto Ricans who shaved theirs off and drew them in. I was sure in another lifetime and another place she could probably pass for a model with her small waist and perfect features. But her eyes told a different story. Her dark hazelnut brown eyes were always stormy, always angry, as if she were coming from an argument or on her way to handle one. She had a way of squinting and raising her eyebrow as if she were daring me to defy her. Defeated, I shifted my cotton prison uniform back on my body and made my way off of my makeshift pallet on the floor. I moved cautiously toward the bottom bunk where she was lying. We'd had a disagreement earlier when Aeron swore I was looking at another inmate too long. Her punishment was to make me sleep on the floor with nothing but a thin wool blanket. I sighed before answering her, my body felt stiff and sore.

"Yes, you are the Greatest of All Time. Can I lie down please?" This was our custom. She was bigger and stronger, she was highly respected by the other females in the unit, and as long as I was hers, as long as I was with her, I was safe.

She moved to the side and I scooted onto the bunk in front of her and tried my best to ignore my humiliation. There's nothing to describe what I went through daily knowing my body wasn't mine. I was raised by the church and these homosexual acts, whether I was a willing participant or not, still felt like a huge stain on my soul. I'd beg for forgiveness and deliverance but it was like I was stuck in a hamster wheel. Every day it would all take place all over again.

It was a Tuesday and normally I would be getting home from choir rehearsal around this time. On Wednesdays after work I'd go to the church and work with the teen Bible Study group, and on Mondays, Thursdays, and Fridays I assisted Sister Patterson with the women's ministry. Those days seemed like a lifetime ago, when it was such a hassle to get out of my office some nights at a reasonable hour.

I'd debate about stopping and picking up something quick and easy or just ordering pizzas because I was too tired to cook. Dontay would complain but of course he'd been home all day and hadn't bothered to fix anything let alone thaw something out. But, my chunky little baby girl would eat anything; she was never picky when it came to food. The memories alone made my eyes and my mouth water. Church was such a huge part of me that no matter how much I prayed on my own, I didn't feel like the one-hour community sermon they held on Sundays in here was enough to get me back into God's good graces.

"You know I'll be gettin' out of here soon, don't you, *Mami?*" Aeron's voice broke into my thoughts, a warm whisper across the back of my neck. "You won't have anyone to protect you when I'm gone. I really do care about you. I don't want anything bad to happen to you."

I lay listening quietly. She didn't like to be interrupted so I was always careful to make sure she was finished before I'd speak. I'd learned that about her quickly after I'd impatiently rushed to answer her a few times. The sting of her hand would stop the words from forming right on the tip of my tongue. Now, I listened patiently and waited before I spoke.

Aeron was at the end of a five-year sentence for larceny, and I looked forward to and also secretly dreaded the day that I'd no longer have to share my cell with her. Because of my small frame and quiet demeanor, I got tried on a daily basis in here. I *used* to carry a Bible; it got knocked out of my hand and the pages were ripped from it. I *used* to wear a beautiful fourteen-karat gold cross around my neck: a gift from my mom for my sixteenth birthday. I got jumped in the showers for that. Everybody always wanted to mess with the "Church Girl," steal from the "Church Girl"; they knew "Church Girl" wouldn't fight back. I wasn't made for nobody's prison or jail. I wasn't even a criminal.

My first month was by far the hardest. I couldn't figure out if I was being blessed or if karma was just messing with me. Out of all the real 'threatening' cellmates I could have gotten, I was celled with a psychotic little Filipino woman with large, wild eyes and stringy blond and black hair that fell past her butt. I think her name was Reynoo. Well, that's what I called her anyway. I could never understand a word she said because her accent was so thick. The only thing I was certain of at the time was that we were going to starve to death, because the other inmates would steal every bit of food right off our trays during meals. I wasn't stupid. I knew if I so much as slipped a note to a correctional officer about it, I'd get beaten or stabbed to death for something like that.

My first night in our cell will be imprinted in my mind forever like the seal on all those 'ghost green-backs' that landed me in there. My stomach was in knots from not eating. I huddled on my bunk, watching in horror as Reynoo took her own feces out of the toilet and smeared it in the corners of the cell walls along the floor. She was crawling along on her hands and knees, singing softly in Tagalog. I buried my head under my pillow to try to block out the horrifying stench. I cried and prayed myself to sleep just knowing she was going to try to kill me before the sun came up. My family wouldn't even be able to have an open-casket funeral because she'd probably eat me or something crazy.

Four days later, after having absolutely nothing to eat and with no money in my commissary, I watched in absolute disgust as Reynoo gathered several huge roaches. My momma always called them things water bugs when they'd get in her house. They'd hide all day and as soon as company would come over or you'd find yourself in a comfy spot, they'd climb up the wall or perch on the ceiling just to fall and scare the living daylights out of everyone in the room. Everybody and anybody would call themselves gangsta until that water bug starts flying. I'd seen the manliest of men go to climbing on the couch, running around, screaming all girly and whatnot when there's a rogue water bug zipping around the house.

Reynoo managed to catch six or so that were drawn to her "shit traps." Hunger will make a person fast as all hell, because those things are no joke when it comes to running. She'd trap them in an old sardine can, placing the thin tin lid carefully in place and then hold it over a small candle. It's hard to describe the smell because of all the shit everywhere, but they surprisingly didn't smell any worse than roasting cashews. I could hear them in there scraping, clawing, and scurrying around for a few seconds, and then it would go silent.

For an entire week I lived off of that filth. I still gave thanks, I still prayed like I was supposed to. I even meditated and chanted. And then one morning, after I'd gone through the breakfast line as I usually did, I set my tray on the table and waited for the vultures to come. The line served apple cinnamon oatmeal, cheese eggs, grits, and a buttered biscuit that morning. I still remembered. They even used lemon-scented soap in the kitchen because it made me think of lemonade every time I smelled it. I knew it would only be a matter of time before I completely unraveled or died from some type of disease from eating an infected roach.

On that particular morning Stanika, one of the bigger girls, was one of the first to assault my breakfast. Ripe onion and ass: I smelled her before I saw her. She was what the correctional officers called a "habitual hose-down," notorious for never taking showers. Her residual funk would get to the point where they'd have to throw her into a holding cell and literally spray her down with the fire hose. I initially just thought she was nasty. I didn't find out until later she had a fear of the showers because she was assaulted and raped in there by a male correctional officer her first week in. The other COs stood by, laughing and recording it on their phones. Just so happened that a phone got stolen out of the CO's car not too long after and was sold to the highest-paying news team. Everyone involved was fired, fined, and punished.

She was in the process of reaching for my oatmeal and I was holding my fork in a death grip. Staring down at her fat grubby fingers, disgust registered instantly on my face at the black dirt accumulating under her nails. An image of her scratching her ass all day floated through my mind and instantly I could smell Reynoo's shit as if it were singed into my nose hairs.

The chatter in the cafeteria clashed against my eardrums sounding like the crunch of roaches as they echoed in my ears every night. No matter how many times I brushed my teeth each day, the dirty, charred taste of them still seemed to coat my tongue permanently from the night before. I hated the antennae and the fine hairs on their legs; they always got stuck in between my teeth and it'd take me all day flossing to get all the tiny segments out.

I was exactly one half of a heartbeat away from jumping off the deep end. Stabbing that fat heffa, and anyone else who dared take anything off my tray, seemed like the only logical solution. If I'd done what I was thinking, I was positive I wouldn't have made it out of the cafeteria alive. Thank the Lord, Aeron decided to come over when she did. She offered me her own tray and within the next hour I was out of my shithole hell of cell and moved to hers. I should have known her kindness would come with a price.

"Why so quiet tonight, princess? You don't wanna talk to momma?"

No, I didn't. I wanted to talk to my fiancé. I wanted to talk to my daughter, Asia. "I'm just tired, Aeron. I've got a lot on my mind," I quietly responded.

Satisfied with my answer, she put her arm around my waist and I lay quietly until I could hear the steady sound of her breath going in and out, indicating that she'd fallen asleep. Tears burned slowly down my face, soaking my corner of the pillow we shared. I cried myself to sleep, quietly asking God how I'd ended up in the hell I was in and wondering what I'd done to deserve it.

Hours later I was awakened by clanking and loud yelling.

"How many times have I told y'all bitches to keep it separated?" Officer Blakely was standing by the cell door.

She was a muscular, dark-skinned, mean-looking woman. Her face was always turned up in an ugly frown, like she smelled sour milk twenty-four hours a day and, as a result, her face was permanently scrunched up from the smell.

"I'm sorry, Officer," I apologized, sitting up, quickly pulling the course blanket up to my chin. I clumsily bumped Aeron in the process and I already knew she was probably glaring up at me for interrupting her sleep. None of this was my fault and yet everyone was taking it out on me. I felt like a weak sapling bowed down under a ton of snow in winter with all of its leaves dying for sun and the roots desperate for warm soil. All of this pressure . . .

"It won't happen again. I got cold and Aeron suggested I sleep in her bunk to stay warm."

"I don't give a fuck. You could tell me it felt like a northern wind was blowin' up a polar bear's ass up in there and I'd still tell ya keep ya ass in ya own fuckin' bed. One more of these and ya ass is in solitary." She turned and marched off.

"All that damn noise for nothing. Waking people up and shit. She need some dick or *something* up in her life. She'd be a lot nicer if she got her a good piece of ass at least twice a week. Who I gotta roofie or pay to dick her down?" Aeron threw a quick middle finger in the direction Officer Blakely had just stormed off.

Climbing over me off the bunk, she stood facing the mirror and started braiding her long, thick hair. She always wore two long braids that fell down either side of her head; they reminded me of Pocahontas. Man, my head was a hot mess. I self-consciously patted an itch in my own fuzzy cornrows. One of Aeron's homegirls from a different unit braided my hair up every Wednesday or Thursday and all it was doing was making my mess grow thicker and faster.

"Aeron, I need to call my baby sister. Can you get me a phone call please?"

I felt like I'd switched places with Jada when she'd bug me for cookies before dinner. My tone begging and my eyes pleading. I had no choice but to be reduced to this level and, ashamed, I could only lower my head and wait for her answer. I clenched my teeth, telling the stupid tears that I could already feel starting to burn with every blink to go away.

I needed to find out where they had Dontay locked up at. I needed to talk to him. There were so many unanswered questions, like why he did what he did and why hadn't he told me. What was I supposed to do; what were we supposed to do? Was he in some kind of trouble? He used to gamble; maybe he'd gotten in over his head and was trying to pay off a debt. There had to be a reasonable answer. I couldn't accept the fact that he'd just throw me under the bus and think he could get away with it. On top of that I had no idea what I should consider saying when I sat before the judge. My trial wasn't scheduled for another four months and it killed me not knowing when his trial was, or if he had copped a plea, had already been sentenced, or what.

"I got you, *Mami*. Now, give me a kiss and let's go eat breakfast."

I got up and gave her a small, emotionless peck on the cheek. Anxious to finally speak to a familiar voice again.

Chapter 3

War of Juarez

I dialed my little sister's cell phone number and my heart skipped a beat as it rang. Other than the first time I'd spoken to her, it normally went straight to voicemail, so I was shocked and excited.

"Leslie speaking. Who's this?"

"It's me, sweetie, hey." The sound of her voice brought tears to my eyes.

"Oh damn. Hey, Eva. I miss you so much. Are you okay?"

"I need to know where Tay is being held. Have you found out where they put Jada? I feel so cut off from the world in here. This court-appointed lawyer isn't helping me worth a damn, and they seized all my accounts so I don't have any way to pay for a better one."

Leslie giggled on the other end and spoke to someone in a hushed tone. "Boy, stop. I'm on the phone with my sister." She sounded so happy and completely distracted as she turned her attention back to me. "Look, I haven't found out exactly where Tay is, but I heard he might be in the Clinton jail. You know Momma and Daddy ain't want nothing to do with Jada. CPS took her, Eva. I'm sorry."

My heart slammed to a halt in my chest. My baby was with child protective services? My parents weren't shit. They were so Christian and so concerned about their reputation in the eyes of the community. When I was pregnant I'd asked for a few things for the baby and they blatantly ignored me. I'd never gotten any help from them back then and I damn sure couldn't figure out why I was expecting it now. God might have loved me in spite of all my sins, but I sure couldn't say the same for my own flesh and blood.

"Leslie, is there any way you can try to get custody of her? You are her aunt." My voice strained as I tried to speak through my tears. "I don't want my baby being raised by strangers. She doesn't deserve it. I don't even deserve to be here."

"Sis, I tried. But I'm only eighteen. They won't give me custody. I'll think of something, I promise. I gotta go. Class starts in a few minutes. I signed up for summer sessions so I can get ahead a little in this college game. Call me when you can and I'll fill you in on anything else I find out."

"Okay, I love you." Inside my heart was breaking into a million pieces. I felt hopeless as the call disconnected.

"What up, bitch?" a voice called out from behind me.

I cracked a half smile as Sayzano strolled over to me. She, I mean he, was one of the few people I felt safe talking to. All of the gay and transgendered inmates were housed together in a protective unit, but they were allowed to eat and come out onto the yard with the female unit.

"Hi, Say. I just found out my baby's with CPS and there's nothing I can do about it." My voice cracked.

Sayzano grabbed me up into a hug and for a second I forgot all about my problems as I was faced with the bigger problem of suffocating between his huge fake breasts.

"Don't you cry, baby girl. I know a couple niggas on the outside. You give me a few days and we'll work shit out. Okay?"

I nodded and Say held my face in between his large hands and looked me in the eyes.

"Look, we gonna go take out these cornrows and braid you up some fresh ones 'cause, bitch, you lookin' like a hot mess, and Say ain't friends with no hot messes. All Say's bitches is thoroughbred, first class, top shelf, neck breakers. Shit, we make haters hate themself. So bring ya ass." Say let my face go and threw his hands in the air dramatically before laughing.

I smiled for the first time in a long time and followed Say. I was momentarily blinded as we walked out of the building and into the yard. The sun felt different when I was feeling it from behind these brick walls. No matter how hard I tried, I just couldn't absorb its warmth. It was mid-July and nearly ninety degrees outside, but I felt as cold as January on the inside. As we approached the area lining the basketball hoops, I could see Aeron standing to the side, towering above most of the females. She gave me a worried glance when she saw me wiping my eyes with my sleeve. She covered the distance between us in several quick long-legged strides.

"Somebody been fuckin' wit' you again?" She was always quick to defend me.

"No, I talked to my sister. Everything's fine. I'll be fine."

Aeron took my hand and led me over to a picnic table. She realized what she was doing and released it quickly. The guards were funny about inmates and body-to-body contact. I sat down and she sat on top of the table with my shoulders between her legs. She pulled a comb from her pocket and started to unbraid my hair.

"Yeah, A, you unbraid that bird's nest and I'ma do it up real nice in just a minute. Say got some bid'ness to handle right quick." Having said that, Sayzano put his hand on his hip and pranced off.

Say was busy looking for his boo, a skinny little white guy we all called Milan. He had to be the prettiest man I'd ever seen in my life. Eyebrows always arched and his long jet-black hair was always pulled back into a cute little ponytail. I'd never in my life been around gay men before and never had any idea they could be so feminine. The way that man sashayed around the yard, one would think he was on a Paris runway.

The couple looked so odd yet extremely happy together. Say was tall and chocolate with high cheekbones. I guessed he looked like a real queen on the outside, rocking wigs and makeup with those big pillow breasts. Say had once described a few drag shows that he'd done and I smiled from just picturing it in my head.

I pulled some fresh cherries out of my pocket that I had saved from breakfast and popped a few in my mouth. I munched silently as I thought about life before I was locked up. Dontay and I used to always go pick cherries or hit the Strawberry Festival in Pungo. We enjoyed each other's company so much. He was my best friend. I was distracted from my thoughts and the show Say and Milan were putting on, kissing and cooing at each other, when I felt Aeron's breath beside my ear.

"*Mami,* I want to tell you something and I don't want you to get upset okay?"

What in the world did she want? To share me with another one of her cellies? Wouldn't be the first time. Or wait, maybe she wanted to tell me that she'd found some other chick to make her plaything. I didn't know why, but the thought instantly made me a little jealous. I squashed that emotion like an ant. I wasn't gay. I was only doing what I needed to do in order to survive in this place. If she moved on it would be hell without her protection, but God would see me through it.

"Well, what is it?" I tried not to sound impatient.

"My ex works for the sheriff's department in Virginia Beach. I asked her to run your *fiancé's* name." She spat the word "fiancé" out as if it were toxic. She hated thinking of me belonging to anyone but her. "She said she couldn't find anything in the court system on a Dontay James."

"What does that mean? My public defender said he was part of it. He and I were the only ones with administrative accesses to the system to make the kind of changes that were made."

Her hands stilled in my hair and I craned my neck to look back at her anxiously, waiting for her explanation.

"Do you think he could have plea-bargained or gotten off? Never even gone to prison? That's what I mean," she replied, giving me a solemn stare down.

My mind was a flurry of activity as I tried to process a thought it kept rejecting. He wouldn't. There was no way Dontay would do not do any time at all and leave me in here for years.

"Of course I'm sure. What you're saying is unthinkable, unfathomable, unbelievable, un . . . un . . . I can't think of any more 'un' words but you get my point." My voice was getting raspy and it hurt to swallow past the lump forming in my throat. I turned back around, content with staring at a patch of clovers growing next to the bench. A ladybug slowly trekked across one of the clovers and I'd have given anything to switch places with her.

Aeron rubbed my shoulder compassionately and said, "Anything is possible when money is involved. Money is the *un-doer* of millions of men and women.

Look through history; it happens all the time no matter the century or the currency. Money doesn't make a person evil, it just shows us who the evil ones really are, sweetheart."

Everything just seemed so overwhelming. Aeron's hand was still on my shoulder and I could tell she was genuinely trying to figure out a way for me to get all the facts. That made my heart warm toward her ever so slightly. At least someone in here cared about me.

"Oh shit," Aeron's outburst broke my train of thought as she tensed behind me.

I looked up to see what had her on high alert. Lord knows I wasn't ready for any more drama.

"Speak of evil and I guess it'll stride on over and say hello," Aeron snapped, focusing her attention on Juarez marching across the yard.

Say and Milan stopped chatting and posted up with their arms crossed and lips pursed up as they stood behind Juarez. It looked more like they were vogueing than protecting anything. I hid a small giggle at my two gay warrior guardian angels.

"What the hell you want, Juarez?" Aeron climbed from behind me to address her older sister. They were identical twins. Antonia Juarez was born five minutes earlier, so she claimed the title of being the oldest. When Aeron got caught she didn't dare say who her accomplices were. Antonia, on the other hand, decided she wasn't taking the blame alone. She was all too willing to take the witness stand and incriminate her sister for a lesser sentence. From that day forward Aeron never called her sister by her first name. Only by her last, to remind her that she was disloyal to her own blood. They were beautiful angry mirror images of each other.

"Hey, I come in peace this time. I just wanted to let you know I'd take good care of your, um, kitten when you get out of here," Antonia replied, shooting a slick grin in my direction.

A visible shiver ran through my body at the cold and menacing way she spoke about me. I didn't want to be taken care of by anyone, but I was sure I'd suffer a helluva lot worse if Antonia ever got her hands on me. Aeron bristled up and for a split second I thought she was going to go off and punch Antonia. But her release date was only a week away. She wasn't stupid.

"What?" Sayzano jumped in angrily. "Who the hell you calling a kitten? Ain't nobody got no damn pets up in here. You ain't taken care of no got-damn body, and I suggest you back da fuck off before I go Cleveland bus driver on ya Amazon ass. I ain't scared to hit a woman."

The yard fell silent at Say's outburst; everyone was anticipating a fight. Say started to go in before any of us could react. The guards ran over to put a stop to it before anything else could transpire. Say winked at me as he was being led to solitary, and Milan wailed like someone had just died. It became clear that it was all an act to diffuse the situation before Aeron got caught up.

Free time was cut short and we were all led back inside. Antonia shot me a look that made me feel physically ill. It would only be a matter of time before Aeron left and she got to me, and I had no idea what I could do to keep me from the hell that I knew was coming.

As we entered our cell, Aeron pulled me into a tight hug. Her sudden display of affection caught me completely off-guard.

"Don't let my sister scare you. She's always been more bark than bite. I promise." She leaned back, still holding me in her arms, and winked.

"Well big or small a bite is still a bite; it hurts all the same." I couldn't bring myself to return her hug and stiffly tried to pull myself away, but she wasn't ready to release me.

"Stop it. I'd give you a kiss to calm you down but I'm allergic to cherries. She isn't going to do anything that you don't allow her to do." She nuzzled the side of my neck with her lips before letting me go. A myriad of emotions swept over me. Regardless of Aeron's reassurance, the thought alone of Antonia scared the hell out of me, and I prayed God would see me out of this before I had to deal with that woman one on one.

Chapter 4

Model Inmate

Being locked up makes time drag. But, before I knew it, a week had flown by and Aeron was packing her things, chattering away and pacing around our cell in anticipation of being released in the morning. I'd still not heard anything else from my sister, and with Aeron leaving, the heaviness of my situation was starting to wear me down more and more.

"I just don't know what the hell I wanna eat first when I get outta here." Aeron was nervously playing with her hair in the mirror. I never realized how long it was until now. She rarely wore it out and I envied the way it fell like a black cloud around her shoulders in layers and stopped in the middle of her back.

"I think I'm gonna get my ass some salmon or a large cheese pizza. Hell, they can put the salmon on the damn pizza. Oh shit, and I can't wait to pour myself a big chilled glass of Rosé or Moscato."

Funny, she didn't strike me as the champagne or wine type. Learn something new every day I guessed.

Despite her chipper mood I chimed in sadly, "Well, just make sure you pour a little on the ground for me. I don't see me lasting more than a week without you."

I hated to admit it, but the realization that I'd finally be alone in here was facing me head-on and I couldn't see a bright outcome no matter how hard I prayed or recited my psalms. Antonia wasn't due to be released for another few months after getting in trouble a few times for starting fights in the yard. She'd gotten a reputation for being a troublemaker and having a short fuse; otherwise, she'd be getting out tomorrow too. Damn my luck.

"Aww, sweetheart, don't talk like that. I can do more for you out there than I could ever do in here." Aeron waved her hand around like she was addressing a grand hall. She walked over and looked up at me, her large eyes wide and excited, her voice filled with exasperation. "How many times do I have to tell you not to worry, *Mami?*"

"Aeron, this isn't worry. This is me being realistic." There was just too much for me to process at one time. I couldn't control the tears that fell from my eyes. I was usually so good at hiding my pain or my fear. Storing everything up for late nights when I would cry myself to sleep or in the showers where my tears could roll down my face unnoticed. Yet, this time I just felt so empty and so drained of everything, I couldn't hold them back.

Aeron stared at me in stunned silence. I buried my face in my hands and let go of all the pent-up emotion I'd been holding back. My shoulders were shaking uncontrollably as I felt every last drop of hope leave my body. The bunk sank beside me and I felt Aeron's arm wrap around my shoulders as she pulled me into her chest. I didn't know how long we sat like that. I also didn't know how the kiss started that put an end to my own assuredness about my sexuality.

We'd never actually kissed before. She'd kept most of our encounters controlled and as passionless as possible. My eyes closed and my mind actually went blank that never happened when Dontay used to kiss me. It was nothing like kissing a man. Her lips were sweet, warm, and soft just like mine. I could taste the salt from my tears as the tip of her tongue traced my bottom lip, timidly at first. It sent shivers along my cheekbones like someone was standing beside me running a feather across my face.

My mind was doing cartwheels bouncing around good and bad, right and wrong. *Bad touch, this is still bad touch.* My grown behind actually reverted to simple childhood logic as some kind of guiding light to keep me from getting lost. They teach you about sexual abuse and how to identify good touches and bad touches, but damn it they never said that a bad touch would feel good.

I couldn't breathe, yet I was breathing super fast at the same time. It was probably the pre-stages of hyperventilation. My lips parted ever so slightly, and she dove in. Our tongues touched. Aeron moaned against my lips. It was the softest, most feminine sound I'd ever heard her make and that sound alone sparked an instantaneous blaze that set my whole body on fire. What used to be the last thing I'd ever wanted from her was now the only thing I could possibly think about.

I'd never felt this way for a woman. My heart was pounding so hard I could feel its beat reverberate through my chest downward to a similar throb building between my legs. She shifted from my lips and drifted a warm, slow kiss along my neck, stopping to suck and lick on a spot just beneath my ear that I never even knew existed.

This is so wrong, I should stop her.

Stop her for what? You might not get this kind of attention for a long time. Might as well enjoy it. I lost out to my own mental argument as my body reacted to her caresses and the flood gates were opened. I could feel it through my thin cotton panties, dampening my cotton pants. I was sure as hell there'd be a wet spot on the bunk if I got up. This was nothing like I'd ever expected. Her hands were soft and warm like heated satin running across my skin. She lifted my shirt just enough to slide under and tease my nipples with her fingers through the thin fabric of my bra. I was literally melting. That's the best way to describe the things that her mouth and hands were doing to my body.

And just as soon as it all started, she stopped. The heat from her mouth was replaced by the cool air. I opened my eyes, confused. Angry at whatever this interruption was.

"We have to stop. As bad as I want you right now, I can't risk not walking out of those doors in the morning. If we get caught . . ."

"I know," was all I could muster up the strength to say.

"I promise if you don't let yourself waste away in here, I'll make it up to you okay?" She tenderly tilted my chin upward until my eyes locked with her deep brown ones.

"What do you mean?" I was confused and horny, and suddenly so damn frustrated the last thing I wanted to do was make false promises.

"Just promise me you'll hang in there. I know I wasn't the nicest to you, but I had to toughen you up. You'll see. Just be strong for me. Let's go to sleep."

I started to lie in my spot beside her on her bunk but she motioned for me to get in mine. In an entire three months together I'd never slept in my own bunk and the feeling isolated and empowered me at the same time.

***

The lights switched on, an indication it was morning. I stretched and almost fell off my bunk as my eyes focused on Aeron in the mirror. She was dressed in a pair of skin-tight black jeggings. I never followed fashion but the equally skin-tight tank top she was rocking looked like an Emilio Pucci design I once saw when I was on Nordstrom's Web site. Couldn't be; the top I'd looked at cost damn near $900. I mentally shook my head and shamelessly continued my visual scan, admiring her new look. Were those red bottom heels? Probably knockoffs, but either way she looked like she'd just stepped out of a magazine.

"Well good morning, my sweetness. Like what you see?"

I was staring in stunned amazement at the transformation she'd made. "Where the heazy did you get those clothes? You look beautiful."

"My cousin dropped 'em off. And don't say 'heazy.' I don't know why you just don't say 'hell.' We're all going there anyway." She rolled her eyes and huffed at me before continuing. "I couldn't be seen walking out of here in anything less than spectacular; believe it or not, I do have an image to uphold, *Mami*." She giggled and twirled like a little girl. Her hair spiraled around her like the women in the shampoo commercials.

I was momentarily shell-shocked by the fact that Aeron, the no-nonsense, take-charge, bad girl actually giggled.

"Well *hell*. I guess you'll be turning heads all up and down the cell block. You're gonna need an armed escort." I swung my legs over the side of the bunk and just stared at her in wide-eyed awe.

"You know, my first assignment as soon as I step foot on free ground is to look for your baby and your man. I promise. Okay?"

I could only nod as I climbed down off the bunk feeling drab and small compared to her. "You don't have to do anything for me. But I'd appreciate it." I refused to cry. There was no reason for me to cry and get all emotional over someone leaving who was practically a complete stranger who made me do unspeakable things. I took a deep breath. *Suck it up, girl. You ain't about to be crying over no grown-tail woman.* I pep-talked my tears away.

"Well ain't you just a fuckin' ray of sunshine? C'mon, princess, bring ya ass. Your damn carriage is waiting outside and it's blocking my damn gate." Officer Blakely's scrunched-faced self appeared out of nowhere and unlocked the cell door.

Aeron grabbed up a few of her things, telling me I could keep everything else, and she left. We didn't say good-bye, we didn't hug, and inwardly I couldn't help feeling like I'd just lost my best friend . . . perhaps even my lover.

Chapter 5

Some Company Loves Misery

I spent most of the day alone in my cell. It was almost time for dinner and fear and depression kept me from eating or joining everyone out in the yard. My stomach rumbled loudly in protest. I'd made up my mind to at least try to eat something. I was waiting for the cells to open when Officer Blakely's stank face appeared in front of my cell.

"Hey, princess, I thought you would get lonely so I brought ya ass some company." Antonia stood close behind her, holding a box filled with her belongings, a smug sneer on her face.

"What up, boo? You didn't think big sis was gonna let you sit and cry all alone did you?"

I stood in terrified silence as Antonia and Officer Blakely exchanged glances. I knew Antonia would pull this crap. I just figured I'd have at least a couple of weeks or a few days before Antonia tried to mess with me. I was in no way prepared for this.

Blakely unlocked the cell door and Antonia leered at me as she walked over and placed her things onto the top bunk.

"Y'all play nice," Officer Blakely said sarcastically as she gave Antonia a wink. "If I hear any yellin' from outta here I'll just assume it's a false alarm."

The key sliding the lock back into place sounded like a death sentence to my ears. I stood frozen, afraid to make eye contact, afraid to sit down, afraid to breathe.

"You gonna just stand there and play mannequin or you gonna get over here and help me unpack my shit?" Antonia's dark presence seemed to take up the entire cell.

"I'm sorry, I'll help you."

I didn't even bother telling her that the top bunk was mine. There was no point in starting any drama this early on. Ephesians says that we should be humble, patient, and gentle, and so I'd try my best to accommodate her intrusion into my world. I walked over and opened her small box of things, removing her hair brush and folded uniforms. I placed them in the spots where Aeron used to keep stuff on a small shelf over the sink in a corner. Antonia climbed up onto the bunk and watched me like a vulture staring down a small animal from the sky. I could feel the heat from her eyes following me. All the tension was making my hands shake and the muscles in the back of my neck were tense. I recited the Lord's Prayer over and over as I busied myself unpacking. I couldn't bring myself to even glance in her direction.

"You ain't that bad looking, ma. 'Cept for them ugly-ass cornrows. When you get done unbraid that shit. I'on't like it." She spat her displeasure with my cornrows as if it were disrespectful to have my hair in a way she didn't approve of.

"If I unbraid my hair, I don't have a flat iron or anything to straighten it out. It'll look crazy."

My body slammed up against the cell wall with so much force I saw bright spots. Antonia had jumped off the bunk and slung me so hard my teeth chattered. She stood in front of me, her fingers digging hard into my shoulders and her nails cutting into my skin.

"Bitch, did you hear me give you a muthafukin' option? You take that shit out. I ain't playing with your little scary ass." She released me from her grip.

I fought to keep my composure. It took everything I had to keep from crying. I nodded okay and walked on shaky legs to sit on the bottom bunk and started unbraiding my hair. This was going to be worse than I thought. I was delivered from the belly of the whale and dropped straight into the lion's den with no weapon, no shield, nothing but the Word to protect me.

When dinnertime came I was nothing more than a walking zombie. Antonia told me what to do, when to do it, and how. Say and Milan stared disapprovingly as I went to sit with Antonia's group of friends in the cafeteria. The most I could manage to do with my hair was run my fingers through it. My shoulder-length wavy afro was a mess and I was too ashamed to make eye contact with anyone. I barely touched anything on my tray. One of Antonia's friends kept smirking at me like my prison whites didn't exist. She stared like she could see me buck-naked and she was enjoying it way too much.

"Ay yo, Antonia. That's a cute li'l toy you done got yourself. How much for me to play with it for a little while?" Her deep, masculine voice echoed into the empty pit in the center of my stomach. It bounced off of my spine and vibrated up toward my ears as I stared down at my tray afraid to look up.

Antonia's arm thumped heavily around my shoulders as answered her. "Shit, you my people. For you—no charge. Just name the time and place."

Everyone at the table laughed and started making offers. Some were kidding while others were very serious. I could feel the tears threatening to come down, but I refused to cry. I stared at the food on my tray so hard I could see every grain in the dry-ass rye sandwich they served and I'd counted all twenty-two of my potato chips at least five times. The nervous tension I was feeling was taking its toll on me physically. My mouth dried to the point that I couldn't swallow. I quietly popped in a piece of gum and prayed it would give me some relief.

It was a torturous salvation when dinner ended. I managed to grab a few bits of fruit and some chips from my tray and put them in my pocket in case I got hungry later. I didn't know when these women would make their trades with Antonia for my body but for the moment I was just happy not having to face them anymore.

Back in our cell I lay on the bottom bunk intending to pray and meditate before the evening count.

"Da fuck you getting all comfy for? I didn't say you could lie down." Antonia leaned up against the cell wall and crossed her arms over her chest.

"What do you suggest I do?" I wasn't sure if she'd take my question as me being a smart ass and I couldn't hide the tremble in my voice.

"I suggest you get ova' here and show me what dat mouf do." She sneered at me, pointing to the ground in front of her, or did she point at her crotch?

My eyes widened in shock. I knew she couldn't be saying what the hell I thought she was. Aeron had never made me perform oral sex on her so I had no idea how or what to do. Lord Jesus . . .

"Um, I . . . I don't know how, Antonia." I stammered out my reply as I stared apprehensively down at the white tiles on the cell floor. I could feel the sweat beading on my upper lip and forehead from my nerves. Maybe she would lose interest if she knew I didn't know what the hell to do. Maybe she'd give up and just leave me alone. I was wrong. I could hear the fabric slide in the silence of the cell as she pulled off her cotton pants and panties. I made the mistake of glancing for just a second and caught her standing spread-eagle up against the wall. *Loooooooord Jesus, if you've ever delivered anyone please deliver me.* I prayed in earnest fervent silence. My lips moving quickly and silently.

"Guess you 'bouta learn then. Bring ya ass ova' here."

Never in a million years would I have ever pictured myself in this type of situation. If I said no she'd have probably beat me to death. If I did it, I didn't have any idea how to do it right so she'd have probably gotten pissed off and still beat me to death. Reluctantly I got up off the cot and kneeled in front of her. I hadn't made any kind of direct eye contact with her out of fear that I'd see a punch or a slap coming.

"Okay. Now, eat dis pussy like it's your last meal. You ain't eat dinner so I know your ass hungry." She grabbed me by the back of my head and pulled my face toward her.

I made the mistake of letting my eyes focus on her privates and my immediate reaction was to pull away. My face balled up in disgust. Had this heffa never in her life heard of a razor or Nair? I stared in horror at the tangled mass of curly black hair. I couldn't believe she seriously wanted me to put my mouth there.

Her hand was painfully tight around the back of my neck as she guided my face closer and closer until I could feel the soft, thick curls tickling my nose and my chin. The praying began in my head even though it felt more like a monologue.

Okay, I take every gay thought I've ever had back; forgive me, Father, because I can't do this. I know this must be some kind of punishment or lesson because I was having thoughts about Aeron but this is just not right. I'm used to a penis, and I can't imagine doing this to whoever whenever and especially not now. Why is it so hairy?

Cringing, the only thing I could think to do was squeeze my eyes shut and move my mouth in a Pac-Man motion. I was trying my best to not taste or get my tongue on anything. Antonia moaned and spread her legs farther apart at the contact of my mouth on her naked skin. I'd been trying to hold my breath and made the mistake of inhaling. I swear the scent of unwashed woman parts stung my nostrils, probably singed off every hair, and stained my upper lip. I felt a gag coming. Trying to hide my dry heaves as I fought for air made me lose all thoughts of the gum in my mouth and there was just so, so much hair. Before I knew it I'd actually managed to Pac-Man-style "nom nom nom" my gum all up into that mess. I stopped and leaned back in shock. Antonia looked down, trying to figure out what caused the interruption.

"What the fuck?" She yelled down at the tangled mass of bright pink watermelon gum intertwined all up in her black curls. I silently giggled as a slow smug smile spread across my face.

That'll teach your ass to try to force-feed someone when you ain't even got the sense to keep that mess tidy.

I already knew the blow was coming before it made contact and the world went black. But at least it was worth it.

Chapter 6

She Popped My Cherry

When I came to it was dark in the cell. I wasn't sure how long I'd been lying unconscious on the floor. I also couldn't believe they had done a count and didn't notice I wasn't outside my cell. Officer Blakely probably handled that, I was sure. I groaned; my head throbbed as I tried to sit up and timidly I glanced around for Antonia.

"You thought that was real fuckin' cute didn't you?" she asked calmly from her perch up on the top bunk. She sat there and stared down at me with an unreadable expression. It was nerve-wracking not being able to tell if she was angry, or feeling vengeful.

"It was an accident. I forgot about the gum. I'm sorry. I . . . I was nervous." My voice was barely above a whisper. Talking just felt like it would make my head hurt worse. Talking could also get me hurt a lot worse if I irritated Antonia.

She hopped down and I visibly cringed away from her.

"Well, princess, it's your turn. So strip the fuck down. I'm gonna teach you what to do, so next time you'll do me right." She shook her head disapprovingly. "Tsk tsk, my sister should have schooled you better than that."

I felt disgusted by the thought of her mouth on or near me. Even though she looked so much like Aeron, her persona and her demeanor made her ugly in comparison.

"Um, I need to pee. Can I freshen up real quick?" I asked nervously. Even though she ain't have a right to say anything, she sure as hell wasn't going to talk about my stuff smelling or tasting any which kind of way.

"Just hurry the hell up."

I was relieved after she barked out her approval with her face scrunched up in a frown. She turned, pulled a magazine from under her pillow on the top bunk, and adjusted so she could see it under a small slit of light that shone into our cell. I slowly made my way over to the toilet as my mind quickly tried to spin up some sort of plan. Curly black hairs were scattered all over the inside of the toilet bowl. Apparently Antonia had no choice but to cut all that gum out of her hair. I couldn't help but smile. My triumph was short-lived though.

"I *said* hurry da fuck up. I ain't tryin'a be up all damn night."

Antonia's harsh tone snapped me out of my moment. She put the magazine away and started undressing with her back to me, and I took that as a chance to clean myself up and also remove my uniform. I walked over to the bottom bunk and lay down. She stood over me with her arms leaning on the top bunk.

Please tell me why in the hell would she shave her stuff and not take a moment to shave those yeti bushes growing under her damn armpits?

She stood there staring down at me while I fought the urge to scoot as far away as possible. I was worried one of those little white deodorant clumps dangling from her armpit hair would fall and, given my luck, it would land right in my eye or something crazy.

"Damn, girl, you got some pretty-ass titties. Shame they always hidden all up under that uniform." A smile spread across her lips.

I'd started to say thank you, but wasn't sure if that was a real compliment or if I was supposed to take it like one. The entire situation just felt awkward and she didn't help standing over me staring like she was.

Without warning her heavy self fell on top of me and she kissed me while roughly running her hands over body up toward my breasts. I closed my eyes and tried to find the energy Aeron had sparked in me but it just wasn't there. They looked the same, but nothing about Antonia felt the same as when I was with Aeron. She pulled her lips away from mine and sucked and bit hard into the side of my neck. I winced and involuntarily my hands flew up to push her away.

Antonia just laughed and pinned my hands above my head as she slid her body in between my legs and bit hard into my skin everywhere that her mouth could reach. I clenched my teeth as tears slid out of the corners of my eyes, but I didn't dare scream or cry out.

When she was done with what I guessed was her crude version of foreplay, Antonia released my hands and sat back on her knees between my legs.

"Now, I'm gonna show yo' ass how to eat pussy."

My entire body tensed in anticipation of the pain I knew was coming. She palmed by butt cheeks in each hand and pulled my hips into her face. Her teeth grazed my clit lightly before her mouth fully opened and I was completely caught off-guard at the jolt of heated lightning that shot through my body. She stiffened her tongue and plunged it inside me as far as she could and all the air flew out of my lungs. Small white sparks discharged behind my eyelids that got larger each time her tongue slid out and back in again. The woman had to do some kind of oral-strengthening exercises on a regular basis. I could almost guarantee that she must have eaten pudding cups without a spoon damn near every day of her life. I mentally slapped myself to keep from begging her to keep going when she stopped.

"Damn, girl. You taste sweet as fuck. You got that good-good."

Her comments were so out of place. Was I supposed to say thanks?

Apparently, no, she didn't need a thanks. I was angry at myself for even enjoying what she was doing. Antonia moaned to herself like a fat kid in front of an all-you-can-eat candy buffet. She was in it more aggressively than she was a few moments ago and at that point I couldn't help it. Closing my eyes the little evil voice in my head began chanting, saying, *just let it happen*, over and over again.

Repeatedly she alternated between licking my clit and diving into my core with her tongue. Dear Lord, the woman was multitasking like nobody's business. The entire time her mouth was moving, she'd let go of my butt and with one hand spread me open so her mouth could get full access to every inch of me.

Her other hand stayed in motion tugging and teasing my left nipple, then over to do the same to the right. My body wasn't under my control anymore. In those moments every nerve ending under my skin was follow whatever orders her mouth gave them, and damn it if my legs weren't shaking. I pulled the pillow over my face to stifle a moan when I felt that painfully delightful stretching as two or three fingers glided inside me. She started stroking me in a "come here" motion that made the fine hairs inside my ears stand up. My eyes rolled back in my head and all I could do was feel. You could call me whatever instrument you want—with her hands and/or her mouth, she was playing the hell out of me.

My senses were clouded by pleasure and I failed terribly at trying to distract myself so I could listen in case any guards walked through. All I could hear were the sounds of my wetness as Antonia's mouth and hands drove me into a frenzy. All sense of reason completely left me in that moment and I let go and gave in to the throb that had begun to build between my legs. My entire body convulsed and I could feel my walls clench and tighten as I came harder than I'd ever thought possible. The heat from Antonia's mouth was driving me insane and everything felt extremely sensitive. I fought myself to keep from reaching out and pushing her away. She licked and kept licking everything, from my clit downward. I could hear her slurping up my juices. When she covered my opening with her entire mouth and licked and sucked hard the sensation sent me crashing into another spiral of spine-breaking spasms.

Antonia sprang up, her brow creased in surprised confusion. We locked eyes as her hand went to her lips. At first I thought maybe she had a hair stuck between her teeth. She opened her hand and held it up to her lips, spitting a cherry into it. I could see the muscles in her throat working and she licked her lips repeatedly as realization of what I'd done sank in. I slowly slid up from my position and stood beside the bunk. My legs were so shaky, I wasn't sure if it was from cumin' the way I did or from fear of what was about to happen.

"Looks like you got my cherry, Antonia." My voice was a low, shaky whisper as I stared her right in the eyes.

"What. The. Fuck?" Antonia was holding her throat and her face contorted as if she was in extreme pain.

From what little I did know about people with severe food allergies I gave her no more than a few minutes before her airway closed up completely.

"Call for help . . ." she choked out, looking at me pitifully.

I simply pressed my index finger to my lips, and shook my head saying no. "Just relax. I think this'll go a lot smoother if you try to relax," I whispered.

I quietly put my prison clothes back on and slid the remaining cherries from my pocket and laid them neatly on her bunk. What Antonia hadn't realized when I'd asked to pee was that I'd bitten a cherry in half and smeared the juice on my lips, my privates, and even popped half of it inside. I remembered Aeron once telling me that the only thing she and her sister had in common was their allergy to cherries. Who knew that tiny seed of information would wind up being so colossal?

You started this and now you need to finish it. If you stop now, you know she'll kill you for what you just did.

I grabbed the razor she'd used to shave with earlier and walked toward her with the other half of the single cherry in my palm. Her eyes widened in horror as I pressed the razor to her throat.

"I can finish this off and let you feel this blade run across your throat, or you can eat the other half of this cherry and die quietly."

I didn't have time for her to give me an okay. I didn't want to risk chickening out. I roughly shoved the cherry in her mouth and watched her fight to chew and swallow. If the coroner did an autopsy they needed to find that other half in her stomach so none of this would point back to me.

Antonia slumped forward on the bed, her face turning a pale white in the dim lighting of the cell. Her chest was heaving hard and she was starting to thrash around as her airway constricted. I sat on the toilet of our cell and watched her intently. I'd just committed murder. How lenient is heaven when it comes to letting someone in who's stained with so much sin?

Chapter 7

I Know Not What I Do

I was awakened by the loud clank and electric hum of the lights coming on. It was morning, time to face what I'd done. I glanced down from the top bunk and stared emotionlessly at Antonia's pale, lifeless hand hanging over the side of the bottom one where I'd left her. I couldn't move her back up top and there was no point in trying to. Anything done to a body postmortem was sure to leave a mark once the blood stopped flowing, and I didn't want to leave any evidence of foul play. I guessed nights of watching *Snapped* reruns on TV had taught me more about being a killer than I'd thought. Mentally I kicked myself for not making her climb back up before finishing her off.

The demon on my left shoulder was mocking the angel sitting on my right.

You did that. You sinned, you've broken one of the sacred Ten Commandments. But it's not like you had a choice. She would have eventually beaten your ass to death if you didn't handle her first. What's done is done. Repent and you'll be back in His good and merciful graces.

"Open up seventy-three! Open it up!" Officer Blakely rushed in and I sat up wide-eyed and dazed.

"What the fuck happened in here? I need a medic in zone two, cell seventy-three. Inmate down, we have an inmate down! Get a unit in here now!" She radioed for help and slid Antonia's body onto the floor. She was feeling for a pulse, looking for a heartbeat.

"What the fuck you do to her, bitch? I know your ass did something! You did this shit? What the fuck did you do to her?" Officer Blakely was hovering over Antonia's body, glaring up at me furiously.

Everything happening around me was a blur. Another female officer came out of nowhere and yanked me down from my cot. She directed me to stand outside of our cell. As a precaution I was cuffed: my hands behind my back, and shackles were placed tightly on my ankles. I could already hear the whispers going up and down the block. Mirrors were sliding out of several bars as some of the inmates tried to get a glimpse at all the commotion.

"Yo, yo, you hear that? Church Girl killed Antonia."

"That little scary-ass Jesus freak murked Antonia?"

"She ain't do that shit; she ain't crazy enough to do something like that. Antonia probably tapped that till she passed out or something."

I stared straight ahead, like I could see everything and nothing at the same time. My thought process was hell, maybe if I looked a little crazy the other women would believe I'd killed her while the guards would find the cherries and know otherwise.

At that moment Officer Blakely shook her head up at the other CO and radioed for the coroner to come up. She picked up the cherries that were beside Antonia's body and placed them in a Baggie, handing them to the other CO. She got up and marched toward me, scowling, her hand on her nightstick.

"I guess your ass ain't hear shit huh?"

Blakely stood eye to eye with me. One hand rested on her favorite weapon of choice, her baton, and the other on her radio.

"I think I might have heard something, but I chalked it up as a false alarm."

I couldn't help throwing her own words back in her ugly, fat face. I knew I'd said enough at that point, maybe too much. So I just shut up.

Officer Blakely rolled her eyes at me and directed her gaze back to Antonia's body. "I don't see no marks or bruises; there's no skin under her fingernails. Nothing indicating foul play." She looked at me again, her voice a questioning growl: "She was eating those cherries in there?"

"I don't know, ma'am. What she did or didn't do, eat or didn't eat was between her and the Lord, I imagine." I answered her in a singsong matter-of-fact tone.

My response almost sent her through the roof, as she leaned her scrunched-up bulldog face in closer to mine. She was so close I could smell her Listerine and coffee-scented morning breath. She roughly poked me in the center of my chest. Inwardly I flinched, but outwardly I didn't even blink at the gesture.

"We'll see what the coroner has to say 'bout that shit. Now, get your monkey ass back in there." Her eyes narrowed to dark slits and she hissed between clenched teeth, "Antonia was more important than you think. You all up on that praying shit. Well you better pray word don't come back that this shit wasn't an accident or I'm going to personally show you hell on earth, bitch." Droplets of spit flew from her mouth and landed on my cheek like flecks of hot lava. She grabbed my shoulders and roughly pushed me inside before unshackling me. I climbed back up onto my cot and lay back, crossing my arms behind my head and staring at the ceiling.

My nostrils flared in disgust but I didn't move a muscle. I just feigned the appearance of complete and absolute indifference. I heard the click-clack of Officer Blakely's shoes as she stormed off. They were carting Antonia's body away and removing her things, and I couldn't believe what I'd gotten away with. Murder.

Chapter 8

The Butterfly Effect

This would be my first breakfast alone since Aeron's release. My hands were clammy and it felt like I had a gazillion moths flying around in my stomach as we got in line to go to the cafeteria. No one was looking directly at me, but I could tell all the side eyes were definitely on me. I cracked my knuckles; it was bad habit from when I was a kid, but I was so nervous I couldn't help it. Lady, the inmate in front of me, flinched at the sound and glanced back nervously. A sneer spread across my face, and she quickly faced forward.

In the serving line I blindly waited as the servers filled up my tray. My mind was a blur of activity from psalms of forgiveness to the eerie look on Antonia's face as she drew her last breath.

"Bring your ass over here. Hurry up. Hurreeeeee up." Say was waving frantically from a table in a corner the moment I walked out of the serving line. Milan was seated next to him as usual, nudging him in the side with his elbow. I didn't even get to set my tray on the table or put my hind parts fully in the chair before he was going in, whispering questions left and right, his neck and wrist just a-flying and snapping with each and every word.

"Hi, ho. What the fuck? E'rebody saying you nixed Juarez ass—now I know my darling little boo-boo ain't no cold-blooded killa. What Juarez do, slip on a Ding Dong wrapper in the dark, fall, and bump her head or some shit? Why you ain't call nobody when it happened? Why you ain't tell the COs that shit? Um, why you ain't saying shit? What da hell went on up in that motherfucka last night, woman?"

Say gave me an exasperated wide-eyed stare, crossing his arms flamboyantly across his chest and popping his lips at me simultaneously.

"Bae, maybe it's because you ain't took a breath, pause, flash, or nothing long enough to even give the girl time to blink. She sitting over here looking like Bambi on the highway and you a damn eighteen wheeler right now." Milan's tone was calm and protective as he addressed Say in my defense.

"Bitch! A: how she looking like Bambi, that motherfucka was a boy; so B: you might want to compare her to the motherfucka who killed Bambi momma. We obviously got ourselves a gorilla, cough cough, I mean killa in our midst. Aeron leaves and this heffa wants to become a member of Murder Inc. Where dey do dat at?"

"Sayzano, Murder Inc.? Really? They ain't even relevant anymore, and who the hell anybody in Murder Inc. ever murder, fool? You need to shut up before I shut you up; you are talking out the side of your neck right now." Milan was starting to turn a bright shade of pink after this last statement.

As funny as their whisper argument was getting, I had to put a stop to it or I could see this getting completely out of hand. Leaning forward, I lowered my tone to barely above a whisper. "You two need to stop this right now." I did my best to keep my face blank, barely moving my lips as I spoke. "I did what I had to do and that's all y'all need to know. Okay?" I narrowed my eyes for emphasis, feeling like an angry mother hen, looking back and forth between the two of them until they nodded in understanding.

I was certain no one else had heard me, but anyone with even the slightest bit of common sense could look at Say and Milan and figure out what I'd probably just told them. They both sat there, slack-jawed, wide-eyed, and dead silent. The two of them were never quiet at the same time. You would have thought Antonia would just risen from the dead and sat down at the table with us.

"Stop this. I need both of you to act normal. Like none of this ever happened. It's a normal day and, Say, if you don't mind, my roots are something else. Can you redo my braids later?"

The smart reply that I was expecting from Say never came; he instead nodded slowly and stared down at his tray. Picking up my fork, I scooped up a heap of runny eggs and shoveled the bland-tasting mess into my mouth. Say and Milan followed suit. We spent the rest of the time eating in silence.

"I do have one question, Eva." It was Milan who spoke first as we were clearing our trays, his voice a barely audible whisper as he stood beside me. "What do you think Aeron will do when she gets word of all this? That's still her family. They all members of La Legal De Represalias. Them some stupid-powerful, filthy-rich, and extremely brutal people when they get crossed. If they don't like the news it's gonna get very bad, very fast," Milan stated as he glanced around nervously for eavesdroppers.

"A member of the La Di La what?" Sputtering, I turned to give Milan a good stare down, my expression showing my obvious confusion. Aeron had never mentioned whatever he was talking about, so this was all news to me.

He gave me a frustrated eye roll, slicing his hand through the air quickly and then through his hair in an agitated nervous motion, pulling it out of its neat ponytail. He fidgeted with getting it tied back behind his head as he explained.

"The Law of Retribution or Law of Talion." He paused, giving me an expectant look, but I still had no idea what he was stalking about. "The Lot. It's like a gang, some kind of underground organization. Why do you think Blakely let Juarez do whatever the hell she wanted to? You might wanna go unite with the sistas or some shit, because you are gonna need backup. If any of the Latina members in here find out and they think you seriously did something to her, they're gonna do something to you, sweetheart. Your little ripple might have started a damn tidal wave."

I didn't say anything. I honestly had no clue what to say. Before being here I knew next to nothing about gangs or gang affiliation. The thought never occurred to me about how Aeron would actually react to her sister's death, let alone the fact that either of them could have ties to an actual gang. I shrugged at Milan as if I didn't have a care in the world and ignored his look of exasperation and anger. At this point the only thing at the top of my prayer list was to make it out of prison and get my daughter. Second on my prayer list was my request for an absolutely spotless coroner's report.

Chapter 9

Demonology

After breakfast I skipped going out to the yard and instead decided to start doing some research. I walked into the rec room and signed in. The correctional officer behind the check-in desk never even looked up. She was too busy with the phone wedged between her ear and shoulder, lost in a conversation about some drug dealer who managed to get another officer to help him escape. His baby momma called asking where he was and the warden didn't want to give her a solid answer. I wanted to listen further but didn't want to catch her attention and get put out. The room was about the size of a small classroom. One wall was covered in shelves of encyclopedias and law manuals; the other was a random assortment of outdated magazines.

There were three raggedy prehistoric-looking Gateway computers side by side on a long table at the back of the room. Fortunately no one was using them. It was just too nice of a day for anyone to want to sit up in this dusty old closet surfing the Internet. Well, anyone except for me that is. With no idea where to start, out of habit I pulled up my Facebook account and logged in. I was thankful my password and everything still worked.

Depression hit me like a tidal wave as my profile picture stared back at me. That wasn't me, couldn't be. The girl in the picture had her hair pinned up with soft curls falling around her ears. There was a golden glow to her light brown skin from the camera flash, making her already large brown eyes look even larger. I looked at a me I didn't know anymore, a version of myself that was radiant and alive and in love with my fiancé and the Word of God.

My friends list used to be around 500 or so people. They were mostly members from the church, business clients, and associates. I didn't have very many friends outside of that. Rejection set in as I scrolled through the names of the fifty-two people still on my list.

Just look at how supportive your church home is now. All the tithing and time you spent caring and praying for those assholes when they were sick or needed a kind word. Where are they now, Church Girl?

The devil on my shoulder was being a real jerk today, giving me thoughts of doubt and self-loathing. Had it been another church member I probably would have done the same thing myself. Deleted them from my life, scared the dirty association might tarnish my name or leak into my livelihood.

My heart skipped in excitement as I passed over Brother Hall's image. He was always such a sweetheart, helping me with the kids during vacation Bible school and always offering to cover choir rehearsals when I had to work late. His profile was a collage of images from things he'd done recently around the church. There was one of him standing in the crowd, towering over everyone around him. His eyes were closed and his hands were in tight fists as he lifted them in praise. Gone was the nappy fro I remembered. His haircut looked good on him; it gave him a dignified, intelligently handsome appearance.

Seek and you will be shown, ask and you shall receive. Right?

It was a far cry, but what other choice did I have? I hit the message button and nervously constructed an e-mail that would hopefully get his attention and get him to give me a little help. I needed money in my commissary and I needed someone I could trust to help me with my legal proceedings and maybe even trying to get Jada.

> Brother Hall,
> I know you've heard the news by now. No. I didn't do any of it. I need help and don't know where else to turn. I can't tell you what it's been like for me in here and I can't bear to think of what my daughter might be going through without me. If you have a number I can call you at I'd appreciate it. It would be a collect call of course. Please don't reply to this and tell me you'll pray. I've prayed enough for both of us. Remember how we used to always say it's the real saints who'll get their knees dirty to pray with you instead of sitting in their comfortable home praying for you? Well, I need you down in the trenches with me more than I've ever needed anyone in my entire life.
> Eva

Using my sleeve I quickly brushed the tears from my eyes and hit send. I was about to close the page when a picture in the corner of the screen caught my eye. A chill shot through me as I stared at the "People You May Know" section. There was a dark, blurry image of a couple, like the picture had some kind of filter on it, but I'd recognize Dontay's grey eyes anywhere. The name beneath the picture was Ms.

LoveKush Bettathantheythink Bankhead. I squinted at the thumbnail-size picture. The figures were both shadowed out; he was standing behind her and their faces were blurred all except for his eyes. It appeared to have been done intentionally, like with some sort of photo editing program.

My hands were frozen in a claw-like position over the keyboard and mouse. I was afraid to click on the picture and enlarge it, paranoid that whoever this woman was would know I was secretly stalking her page. A thousand and one things ran through my mind all at once. *Did they take that picture before we got locked up? Was he cheating on me with this woman? If so how long had it been going on?* My finger was unmoving above the mouse; my heart thudded loudly in my ears drowning out everything around me. *Click that shit. Just do it.*

"Yooooo, you Church Girl, right?"

I physically jumped and probably even died for a half a second from fright as someone grabbed the back of my chair and swiveled me around. The room flew by in a quick blur. I could feel all the blood physically drain from my face in panic as I sat facing five Hispanic women I'd never seen before.

"They said cha ass was mute or some shit, but I don't believe dat. Nah, I think if chu know waz good, chu gonna talk to us."

The woman speaking was short, squat, and box shaped. A white bandana held her hair back from her round face, making her penciled-in black eyebrows and lip liner stand out starkly against her olive skin. I glanced around nervously looking for the guard who was at the desk, but of course she'd miraculously done the unthinkable and vanished.

"Okay. Wh . . . what would you like to discuss?" I sounded like a straight-up punk; my voice was small and shaky.

A smug smile spread across her face and she nodded to a tall, thin chick behind her. It happened so fast I didn't have a chance to blink, swallow, or even recite the Lord's Prayer. Someone grabbed me up from the chair and pinned my arms behind my back. A rough, callused hand slammed across my forehead, craning my head back, fully exposing my neck.

The one who had been speaking all this time walked up to me and held up a small blade. Cross-eyed, I tried to stare down my nose to focus on it, scared if I took my eyes off of it I'd feel it in my ribs or running across my throat. My neck muscles were constricting painfully from the awkward placement of my head. She came up to me as if she were going to give me a hug and placed her cheek right up against mine. Stale cigarettes and cheap body spray filled my nose as the tip of the blade barely touched the side of my throat. Her voice hissed into my ear like a snake that'd learned to speak broken English.

"Ssssoo, Church Girl, one quesssstion, one ansssss-wer. Chu kill Antonia?" she asked, pressing the shank hard into my neck, and I winced, certain it was drawing blood. She then turned her head, placing her ear almost directly on my lips, waiting for me to reply.

"She did it, Janisa, she know she did. Just slice her ass up like she deserve." The girl holding me provoked my interrogator in an angry whisper.

Bite it! Bite the bitch's ear off! Slam the bitch behind you into the desk so she lets go and grab the shank while the other one's squealing in pain. Stab anyone who stands between you and that door!

"No." My whispered response was directed more toward this inner demon I'd somehow manifested. It seemed to love bloodshed, reveled in revenge, made me think of the most ungodly ways to handle situations.

"Oh. No, she says." She turned to the other women and shrugged, they all started laughing. I didn't get the joke.

"According to her, I guess Antonia just died on her own. Wid no one in the cell wid her but dis bitch."

The girl holding my limbs hostage laughed, tightening her grip even more painfully. Hell, any tighter and I wouldn't have to worry about being shanked; my neck would probably snap.

"I didn't kill her." It was a pitiful attempt to save my life. I began to silently pray and ask God's forgiveness for everything I'd ever done. It was becoming obvious that they didn't care what I said.

You should have done what you had to do to keep your ass alive. Survival is all about fear and the strength of fear. Animals do it all the time. They camouflage themselves to look like something their predator will fear. Tell them you did it. Make these bitches fear your ass! Lie, make up a lie. Tell them you'd kill them all if you got the chance. You could do it, you've already done it!

I tried to shake the little voice that belonged to my inner demon out of my head. I guessed we all had it; some people just called it their conscience. Whatever it was, the only difference between me and these women was the fact that I refused to let my blood-thirsty inner demon control me—and they gave in to theirs every time.

The one with the blade turned back to me, her face contorted in anger at me speaking without being spoken to. She stormed over and punched me in the stomach with everything she had. The air whooshed from my lungs and the feeling of wanting to vomit and pass out at the same time took hold of my body. The girl behind me struggled to keep me on my feet as my body felt like collapsing in on itself from the pain. I'd never been hit before and definitely not that hard.

I was pulled roughly back up onto my feet and Janisa closed in for round two. A cold sweat was running down my neck and torso. I could feel the cotton fabric of my uniform sticking to my skin. Fighting back waves of nausea I tried to focus on Janisa as she closed the distance between us.

"I'll ask you one more time, Church Girl, did you—"

It happened so fast I had no idea how or why. Janisa fell away from me, a horrified scream frozen on her lips. She reminded me of the reaction my daughter had the first time she scraped her knee. There were a few moments where no sound came out, as tears slowly slid down her face. The sound caught up with her actions as if in slow motion as her scream pierced the air. It was all in a matter of seconds but everything seemed to be moving in slow motion. My captor released me in shock and I could hear her bump into the computer desk as she backed away from me.

The warm, rubbery portion of Janisa's ear flew from my mouth as I spat it toward the girl closest to her. She jumped back in terror and I smiled at her reaction, not realizing it made me look damn near insane. Janisa's blood was running down my chin and I could taste its metallic, coppery presence in my mouth, coating my teeth. *Lord, I'd better not get hepatitis or something from this.* Turning to the girl behind me, my intent was to gnaw my way through every last one of their asses and I lunged for her. I didn't expect her to react as quickly as she did. She kicked to fend off my attack, hitting me in the stomach.

"What the hell is going on in here?"

Crashing to the cold, hard tile floor never felt so good. I tried to catch my breath before glancing up to see who'd come into the room and saved my life. It was a white male officer; he didn't look familiar. The Latinas all quietly scurried out the door like a herd of panicked deer. Janisa ran past him, hiding her injury. The female CO who was on duty walked in past him with her head down. She shot me an angry glance out the corner of her eye before plopping back down at her post behind the check-in desk.

The white officer calmly walked over and helped me to my feet.

"You okay?" he asked while brushing imaginary dirt off my arm.

"I'm fine, thanks."

"Um, you're bleeding. We need to get you to the infirmary," he stated, his expression showing genuine concern.

"It's not my blood," I replied coldly and I began wiping the blood from my mouth on the front of my white shirt.

"Well, are you Evaline De . . . De . . ." He hesitated, trying to get my last name out.

I hated when people messed up my last name. They always did. You'd think I'd have gotten used to it by now. I interrupted him before he could butcher it any further.

"You say the first part like déjà in the phrase déjà vu, and just add 'ardin' to the end of that. Yes, I'm Evaline Desjardin; just call me Eva." I smiled weakly, my stomach still sending sparks of pain through my body if I inhaled too deeply.

"Well okay, Eva. I'm from the main office downstairs. Your probation has been approved and you are free to go, under certain restrictions of course. We need to get your clothes and belongings from processing so you can be on your way. I'll act like what I just saw never happened."

I stood there momentarily dazed, certain the Latinas had murdered me. My body was probably lying dead on the floor and I was floating above it. This had to be God's humorous way of ushering me up to heaven. Dumbfounded, I just stood there shaking from head to toe in disbelief, scared my legs would give out on me if I moved. I felt like laughing, crying, and hugging this angel who'd just saved my life in more ways than one.

"I thought I wouldn't be up for probation for another six months. How did it get approved? I didn't do anything or—"

He cut me off before I could continue, giving me a look that pretty much said to shut the hell up and go. "I don't do the fine details, ma'am. I just fetch and deliver." He nodded toward the door and I smiled my first genuine all-teeth-and-gums smile since being in prison.

The question still loomed out there. There was no way Brother Hall could have responded to my message that quickly or, maybe, he could have. God's works aren't made for our understanding; He only requires our cooperation.

Chapter 10

Deleted Delete Delet Dele
Del De D But Not Dead

I stared down into the bin that contained the only remnants of my life, feeling somewhat apprehensive about touching them let alone putting them on. The last time those clothes were on my body I was in a cold sweat, standing before a judge and a jury of my peers as they read my conviction and sentencing. Doom and gloom were the best words I could find to describe the grey and black pinstriped pant suit in front of me. Nothing good came from the last time I'd worn it and my stomach knotted at the thought of wearing it now.

My heart skipped a beat at the sight of my cell phone. Holding it in my hand made the realization of what was about to happen sink in. Joyful tears filled my eyes at the thought of being able to call who I wanted when I wanted to. Finally, I'd be able to sleep peacefully and have my baby girl back where she belonged.

A glimmer caught my eye and I felt instant unease at the sight of my engagement ring. I'd valued it so much that I'd checked it in out of fear of someone stealing it and now it was all but worthless to me. The four-karat princess-cut diamond twinkled at me, mocking me. It was a harsh reality check.

"You ready, Eva?"

Officer James, the man who saved me from Janisa and her hoard, appeared outside my cell door. My hands were ice-cold and clammy nubs as I tried to smooth my hair back into a wild, puffy ponytail. My ass needed a perm as soon as possible and some new clothes. The ones I had on were hanging loosely on my body, making it apparent that I'd lost a lot of weight.

I finally nodded, giving Officer James a polite smile. "Yes, sir, I'm as ready as I'll ever be."

He escorted me down the cell block and for the first time ever it was eerily silent. I could almost feel the hatred and envy like tiny pins in my skin from the eyes that followed me as I was led out. The only two people I felt bad about leaving, Say and Milan, were housed in a different unit. I made a mental note to send them letters and care packages for as long as they were in here.

Everything felt surreal as I stood in the small corridor at the main gate waiting for it to open. Fear crept up on me like a silent little monster. It scrambled up my ankle, and made goose bumps rise on my skin as it traveled up my body in anxious shivers until it had planted itself on my shoulder to whisper doubts in my ear.

What will you do now? Where will you go? You don't have anything or anyone now. . .

Grinding my teeth and stiffening my spine, I narrowed my eyes in determination.

I'll do whatever the hell I have to in order to find Jada and Dontay. Nothing can be worse than what I've already been through.

I stared into the rusted steel of the gate's bars visibly jumping when they opened with a loud clank. The short walk past the security point toward the doors that led outside seemed to take years. I wanted to break into a run and fling myself outside but I somehow managed to keep the wings that were dying to sprout from my feet under control.

The doors slowly opened automatically and I was hit with a humid gust of hot air as I stepped outside into a dreary rainy August afternoon. Raising my face toward the sky I welcomed the cool, misty rain, taking in deep breaths of fresh, free air. I wanted to erase the smell of prison from my memory as quickly as possible. The scent of bleach, metal, and misery clung to my skin and clothes like cigarette smoke in an old jacket. I visualized it seeping out of my pores with every breath I took.

"Eva?" Someone quietly spoke my name.

My eyes snapped open and standing right in front of me was Bishop Tisdale. He was head of my church and had been the closest thing I'd had to a father figure since my own refused to accept me.

"It's me," I confirmed, smiling as tears of gratitude spilled down my face. He looked exactly the same as I remembered as his face broke into a wide grin. His chubby cheeks looked a little fatter and his mustache was cut with razor-sharp precision. He had a graying goatee last time I'd seen him; it was gone now putting the deep dimple in his chin on prominent display. He pulled me into a tight hug and I couldn't help but notice how fat his belly had gotten.

Look like somebody been eating good; church folk couldn't send any money but they're obviously still contributing to that building fund. The only thing that fund is building is Bishop's relationship with the Cadillac dealership.

Shut up! Shut up!

I mentally struggled trying to get my negative, mean thoughts under control.

"Eva, I got a call from Brother Hall saying someone was either playing with him or your spirit had contacted him asking for help. The next day I call and they're saying to be here at two-thirty to pick you up." Bishop began walking toward a pristine black Cadillac XTS and I would have laughed if my mind weren't still reeling from what he'd said.

"Bishop, what do you mean by my spirit?" I asked, giving him a puzzled look across the roof of the car as he unlocked the door.

He gave me a nervous smile before answering, "Um, Eva, if you don't mind riding in the back. Only the missus sits in the passenger seat." He'd taken on the dignified tone that he used to address the congregation during services.

He's lying, he don't want you up front because he's probably scared to be too close to you.

Smiling sweetly I ignored my thoughts. "Sure, Bishop, the back seat is fine by me; just get me away from here as quickly as possible."

The air conditioning came out of the vents in a blast of cool new-car-smelling air and I resisted the urge to ask him to turn it off. It had to be close to eighty degrees out and he would probably combust in his full three-piece suit. I'd had enough recycled air to last me a lifetime; all I really wanted was to feel and breathe in fresh air.

"The reason I referred to your spirit is because we'd been told you'd passed on. That you hung yourself after the sentence." Bishop Tisdale's voice boomed over the gospel song playing on the radio. It was a live choir singing "Order My Steps."

I frowned; the old-school choir sound was not one of my favorites. It reminded me too much of being forced through service after service just about every other day when I lived with my parents. Bishop's shocking information combined with the choir music created an arrow that shot itself into my temple in the form of an instant headache.

Pressing my fingers to my temples I rubbed them slowly. "Bishop, who the fuck said . . . I'm sorry." Bishop frowned disapprovingly back at me through the rearview mirror. "Bishop, would you mind turning down the music? I can't think. I just need quiet. And, who told you that I'd killed myself? Why would someone say that?"

"Child, the Lord's music is the best thing for that headache. It's probably just spirits coming up out of you. Your parents told us that you'd passed on. We held a service and everything. They tried to get your daughter but she'd already been taken by Child Protective Services right around the same time that your house went up for auction. You can stay with me and Mirna until you get yourself together; we already prayed over it."

My body and mind felt as if they were both going to collapse from the weight of everything he'd said. Why in the world would my parents tell people something like that? Lord knows how many times I'd tried to call them collect and they wouldn't accept the charges after hearing me speak my name. My house, my baby, everything was taken away from me and I didn't do anything to deserve it.

Someone somewhere had decided to click on my life as if it were no different than a file in a directory and hit the delete button.

Chapter 11

Opportunity Quietly Knocks but Trouble Always Seems to Let Itself In

The bishop's house looked somewhat similar to a small three-story palace. It was surrounded by huge oak trees that towered above it, shading the yard. Two large pillars framed the entrance to the front door and the enormous window that sat high above it displayed a large shimmering chandelier. Stark white gravel crunched loudly under the Cadillac's tires as we pulled up the driveway and into a massive four-car garage. We parked in between a dark green Jaguar and a white Audi convertible.

I quietly followed the bishop toward the door that led into the house. I felt like a misplaced drifter going to someone else's home and having to use someone else's things. We entered through a pantry and into a beautiful oversized kitchen. A large yellow bowl stood out in stark contrast against the black marble counter-top. It was filled to the brim with Asian pears, apples, and oranges. As badly as I wanted one, I couldn't bring myself to ask. There was no way I'd go from being told when and where to do everything to being released and still having to ask permission for even the simplest things.

"Let me give you a quick tour. Mirna will be here in a little while to help with anything else you might need."

He led me through the kitchen toward the front of the house, pointing out the living room, dining room, and an extra bathroom. It was the briefest home tour I'd ever gotten.

He probably doesn't want you to know where the fine china or silverware is out of fear you'll rob them and run off in the middle of the night.

Tall, faceless African sculptures framed both sides of a door near the main stairwell. They were creepy black wood carvings that stood taller than me with elongated necks and long oval-shaped heads. One held a shield and spear; the other was apparently supposed to be a woman from the large cones protruding from the upper torso.

"Bought those when we opened a mission and school in Kenya. That's the Guardian and she's the Maiden."

His chest puffed out with pride as he spoke about his ugly statues and I was lost somewhere inside my head. There had to be some kind of way to piece my life back together. It wouldn't happen overnight but with determination and faith, I could turn my mess into a mosaic masterpiece. Bishop was staring at me expectantly; he must have asked me something but I hadn't heard a thing he'd said. Embarrassed to admit I wasn't paying attention I stared at him wide-eyed.

"Everything you need is down there; the basement is large enough for you to live comfortably. I'll let you explore, and send Mirna down when she gets in."

"Oh. Okay, thank you, Bishop. I appreciate everything you're doing."

He pulled me into a hug, patting me roughly on my back. "You live here now. Just call me Kev or Kevin. All that Bishop and Mr. nonsense won't fly in this house; makes me feel like I'm not at home."

"Okay Kevi . . . Kev." It felt awkward calling him by his first name but I'd try. "Is there a phone down there?" I asked as he let me go.

Bishop looked at me expectantly as if he were waiting for me to divulge why I wanted to use the phone, and I clammed up. I really needed to call my parents but trying to vocalize the who or why part of my need for a phone wasn't happening. This wasn't prison, he didn't need to have a say in who I talked to unless I tried to make a long-distance call.

"We are getting a line installed for you. It should be around Monday or Tuesday next week." He hesitated and began rubbing the corners of his mouth where his goatee used to be out of habit. "We think you should just lay low for a little while until we get a few things resolved. You don't understand the impact your conviction had on the community and the other members of the congregation. Then to tell everyone you were no longer with us and see devastation on everyone's faces all over again. Eva . . ."

"No, no. It's fine. Let's worry about what people will say. That's always been the way of the church right?" I snapped sarcastically.

I'd meant to keep the comment to myself but it came out and it was definitely too late to take it back. Bishop simply nodded his head as he opened the basement door. He was probably agreeing to his own silent argument about being crazy for taking me in. I walked past him and heard the door close quietly behind me.

What these people referred to as a basement would have passed for a loft or studio-style apartment. The room opened up to a large dark brown sectional that faced a wall with a flat-screen television. There was the faintest scent of apples and cinnamon and it actually made the space feel inviting. My steps were cushioned by the plush brown and tan speckled shag carpet as I walked past a wall lined with book shelves and curio cabinets. I quietly studied the painted faces of three naked mermaids lounging on a clock shaped like a coral reef. Their fins were varying shades of shiny blues and greens that stopped at their bared waists. All of the mermaids were posed in various positions but it was the one to the right that tugged at my core, making a knot form in my throat.

One mermaid had fiery red hair flaming around her serene seductive face; the other had bright hair the color of a wheat field and sapphire blue eyes. But, the one with the crown of hair blacker than coal billowing around her kept grabbing my attention. Her languid brown eyes were staring back at me as if she could see directly into my soul. She reminded me of Aeron, while simultaneously reminding me of Antonia.

"I'm sorry to put you down here with all of Kevin's unsightly trinkets," Mrs. Tisdale spoke from where she'd been standing on the stairwell, holding a small tray.

I whirled around, quickly wiping away a stray tear. She walked over, giving me a sincere smile.

"Your husband's trinkets are interesting to say the least. Not exactly what I'd ever imagine to find in a leader of the church's home," I replied, giggling at the eccentric artifact collection.

"We weren't always sanctified, baby." She chuckled. "Girl, we had lives and lived just like anybody else. That's why all that fool's foolishness is down here where we can still admire its beauty and value without being judged." Mrs. Tisdale's tone was soft and playful like we were old friends.

The woman barely spoke to me when I worked in the church, and it gave me the impression that she was just like the rest of the elders and their wives. I'd imagined she'd be stuffy and stuck-up, nothing like the sweet, charming person I was talking to. We were about the same build even though she had to be in her mid-forties; the woman definitely kept herself up. There wasn't a single wrinkle or crease in her light brown skin and her hazel eyes sparkled.

She set the tray on a small table in front of the couch. "I made you some soup and sandwiches. Figured your stomach might need to adjust to normal food so I kept it light. Forgive Kev, he's such a man. He wasn't thinking about anything but getting into his study to pour over his next sermon."

"Thank you, ma'am. Um, I don't know which one I want more: the food or a hot shower."

"Baby, eat the sandwich in the shower; it ain't gonna hurt the shower I know that for a fact. And call me Mirna." She laughed and walked toward another section of the basement.

I followed, feeling a little better in her warm presence. The bathroom was past the bedroom and was about the size of a small hotel room. It was decorated in green, white, and black, reminiscent of a comfy day spa. One complete wall was decorated with a large mural that looked like magnified raindrops dripping off of two bright green leaves. Fluffy white rugs were in various places on the floor that matched the equally fluffy-looking towels on a bamboo shelf in a corner. I balked at the steam and sauna options on the glass door to the shower.

"I wasn't sure what size you'd wear so we have a little of everything. There's a bathrobe on the top towel shelf, razors, soap, everything you need is in this cabinet." Mirna glided over to a small cabinet that looked like a fully stocked convenience store. There were so many

types of body washes and lotions I got excited just
thinking about which one I wanted to try first.

"Clothes are in the bedroom; we passed that on the
way in. You need anything let me know. I'll check on
you a little later."

She left and I stood momentarily confused as to how
a person could feel like a princess and a pauper at the
same damn time.

After what was probably the longest shower I'd ever
taken in my life I sat in front of the television, wrapped
in the enormous bathrobe. I'd picked a ginger-peach-
scented body wash and cream that smelled good
enough to eat out the bottle. The sandwiches were
gone in the blink of an eye. I ate the things so fast it's a
wonder I didn't choke. Even though the soup was cold I
still crushed it. There's nothing like homemade chicken
soup and I all but licked the bowl. Mirna was definitely
right about my stomach acting finicky. Not long after
eating my stomach turned into a huge painful cramp.

I wasn't used to Miracle Whip and real cheese. I took
a second shower, finally understanding why the food
in prison was so bland and uncomplicated. They didn't
have doors on those cells. The last thing they needed
was a cellblock full of shitty folk blowing up stalls with
only one toilet to share. I had to wash my hind parts
after that foolishness.

A smile spread across my face at the small cup of
peppermint tea Mirna had thoughtfully placed on the
tray. I had no desire to get up and go to the kitchen to
heat it up and sat lost in my thoughts sipping it cold.
The flavor reminded me of a Starlight Mint without
all the sugar. I didn't mind; my taste buds welcomed
something other than water or orange juice out the can.
The clock on the television receiver read five-thirty but

all the day's activities were catching up with me. Lights out was usually around seven but having real food and a real shower gave me a serious case of the itis.

My sleep should have been restful but it was far from it. I was plagued with replays of Antonia's last moments and she begged for her life repeatedly in my dream.

Dontay walked in and around our cell watching us, jeering Antonia on. He was wildly waving money around like we were nothing more than dogs to gamble on in a fight. Antonia finally slumped forward and Dontay shouted obscenities. His face morphed into Aeron and it was then her turn to chastise and curse me for what I'd done. She cried and yelled and I cried and apologized.

Seeing Aeron so hurt and upset made my heart fragment into hundreds of tiny pieces that fell to the floor. She picked them up one by one and one minute she was handing me back the pieces and then we were alone on the cot just as we were her last night there. She kissed me and I felt shame and excitement. I was confused at my reaction and angry at myself but I didn't want it to end. Her hands were all over me and I timidly began running my fingers along the small of her back.

She began whispering broken sentences in my ear, "I've missed you so much, Mami. I want you, let me make love to you."

Lying back in the bed her body slid gracefully on top of mine. Our clothes were gone and the simple contact of her bare skin against mine made me moan in delight. She nibbled softly on my shoulders before kissing her way down to my ribcage and I squirmed in anticipation. Her hair hung over her shoulder and slid along my body like a silky web of tiny fingers. It caressed my neck and nipples, softly cascaded across my stomach, leaving every inch of my skin that it touched in a raging pool of need. Aeron giggled at my reaction and made a game out teasing me with her hair. She rose back up, gently kissing my lips before teasing me all over again.

By the time she made her way down a second time, there was a raging river of need coursing between my legs. Her breath was hot against my skin and then Antonia was hovering over me. I could smell it before I saw it coming and new she was raising her hairy snatch up to my face. Shaking my head from side to side I tried to tell her no and she ignored me, slamming herself onto my face. Aeron called out to her in the distance and I thought, well now your sister can see what you've done and she can kill you. I won't be guilty anymore.

Aeron called out to me again and I tried to answer her but Antonia was laughing loudly. Each time I tried to open my mouth to call out to Aeron's hair would fill it until I couldn't breathe. It muffled my screams and cries for help.

My eyes flew open and I took a deep, panicked breath. I must have been holding my breath in my sleep—my lungs and my chest were tight from not getting any air. I shook my head trying to clear the dreadful images from my waking mind. My heart literally stopped cold in my chest as the bishop's face suddenly came into focus clear as day, scaring away all traces of sleepiness. I was completely awake and alert. The pressure I'd felt on my chest was from the weight of his body on mine.

Sweat dripped from his forehead into my eyes and I tried to scream and push him off but I couldn't move a single muscle. What kind of hellish nightmare had I awakened to?

He was moaning and moving against me but I couldn't feel him inside me. An alarm sounded in my head as I realized that I couldn't feel my legs, my toes, or any of my limbs.

God, help me please. What the hell did they do to me?

My voice was a panicked cry in my head but no matter how hard I tried I couldn't move, couldn't scream, and couldn't lash out. I controlled the only thing I had control of and squeezed my eyes tightly closed. It was like one of those dreams where you're half awake and half asleep. You can see and hear everything and things come out of corners or shadows but no matter how hard you try you can't move and you can't scream. It used to happen all the time when I was little and my auntie would say the witch was riding my back. My momma would say a spirit was trying to get to me and either way I'd be praying and sleeping with the light on for at least a month. Every ragged breath the bishop took had me trying to retreat into the darkest recesses of my own mind. Now, I had a bishop riding my back; the humiliation and helplessness I felt were overwhelming enough to smother me all on their own. Even though I couldn't feel it, a sudden desire to bleach and burn his touch from my skin was overwhelming me. Fury balled itself up inside my chest and sat there coiled around my heart like an explosive cobra.

You will kill this filthy, pretentious motherfucka for this shit! And they wonder why women go and cut off men's dicks—this is why. Slaughter his ass.

The devil on my left shoulder fed on the rage build-ing inside me and goaded me into retaliating; yet, even now, the Christian side of my mind tried to find rhyme or reason with what was happening.

Is this worth going back to prison, Eva?

Yes, it is!

You can't feel anything. Had you not had that bad dream you probably wouldn't have ever known this happened. Tell Mirna to watch him—he's bound to do it again and she can catch him. Let her witness everything with her own eyes.

Compared to this shit, that dream was as harmless as a cartoon. Like anyone would believe a word you said after what happened? Like Mirna would even believe you; he probably drugs her ass too. It would end up being a favor for her too.

I'd been holding my breath for most of the inner exchange in my head. I was hoping that I'd eventually pass out. It didn't work. Every time I got to the point where bright flashes of light sparked off behind my eyelids my brain would force my lungs to take in oxygen.

"Kevin James Tinsdale! What the hell?" Mirna's voice sliced into my silent nightmare. It was the most welcoming sound I'd ever heard as it interrupted the sound of Bishop's raging bull-like breathing thrashing in my ear.

"Woman. Why on earth are you yelling when you aren't sitting but two feet away from me?" Bishop questioned her through gritted teeth.

I didn't want to see him again, but I had to look. Peeking through my lashes as best as I could without them knowing I was drugged but awake I had a limited view. Bishop's head was turned to my left and I did my best to glance in the direction of Mirna's voice.

"Because the agreement was that I'd let you buy your plaything so you could act out all your ungodly anus play obsessions without destroying mine. In return I get the grand finale, and you were about to finale," she scolded him.

"The hell? I was not about to finale; you making me lose my focus and I'm going to have to start all over again to get him rock solid for you." The bishop sounded agitated.

Fuck no! Dontay only did that asshole thing twice and we never tried again. How dare this fool think he could just ram all up in my ass and . . .

Mirna, don't make this shit start all over or on my life I'll take you out as soon as I can move again.

Bishop's face lowered and I gagged at the sounds of slurping and sucking as he did whatever he was doing to places on my body that I didn't even want to know.

"No. There will be no starting over. It's momma's turn. You making Princess Pinky jealous." Mirna's voice was so close I already knew without peeking that she was lying beside me on the bed.

"That's why all that fool's foolishness is down here where we can still admire its beauty and value without being judged." Her words from our conversation swam around my head like a gold fish trapped in a plastic bag.

How many girls or women had they done this to? It couldn't have started with me. I used to have a youth choir at the local community center. Every few months one of my teenage girls would vanish without a trace. It would be the same each time, a runaway with no family in the area—no one to notice their absence. Except me.

"Whose pussy is this?" The bishop's voice drilled into my thoughts, interrupting any shocking conclusions I might have come to.

"This is Bishop's pussy." Mirna moaned her response and I wished for a mental shutdown valve or off button. The only good thing about him being on her was the fact that his heavy ass was up off of me. I went back to what got me through my first nights in prison and recited my psalms. The ending of every line was accented with a visualization of how I'd get the bishop and his wife back for what they'd done.

Somewhere between Psalm 91 and the image of the two of them tied up, staring at me, pleading for mercy, I fell asleep.

Chapter 12

If the Eyes Are the Windows to the Soul Your Windows Look Like They're in Need of Washing

Sun filtered through the high, narrow window in the bedroom. It blinded me, forcing the dull, slow ache in my head to increase until it was going at the rate of a jackhammer. My mouth was so parched that even when I tried to lick my lips to moisten them I got no relief. They felt cracked and dry, my tongue stuck to them and several places, stinging where the cracked skin split open. It was hazy but gradually the memories of the night before came back to me. Scared I'd try to move only to find myself permanently paralyzed, I sufficed with lying there motionless, assessing my body.

The cool sheets on the bed hung loosely around me. I could feel them pressed against my legs and arms, but nowhere else. Panic-stricken at the thought of being paralyzed I sprang into a sitting position, shocked at the green nightshirt and matching shorts that met my eyes when the blankets fell away. Quickly my eyes took survey of the room, searching for anything to prove that I hadn't dreamt the sordid events between the bishop and Mirna.

There was nothing out of place except the clothes on my body that I definitely couldn't remember putting on. It felt like I was waking up from a long night of drinking, and my one-night stand had decided to sneak out before I could even confirm whether I'd imagined him.

The sensation of pins and needles shooting through my toes made me put off trying to stand for a little while longer.

That big nigga probably fractured one of your damn spinal disks or some shit if that shit even happened.

My suspicions were confirmed as my brain finally registered the unforgettable ache in my rear end. Tears fell down my face and I cried every tear that I couldn't cry the night before due to whatever they'd drugged me with. Nausea hit me unexpectedly and I dry heaved until I thought I'd burst a blood vessel and my stomach cramped. There was nothing in there for it to expel.

Lying back on the bed, the most I could do was shakily curl myself into a tight ball. With my forehead pressed firmly against my knees, I tried to pray but couldn't find the words. I tried to recite something to calm myself down but for the life of me, I couldn't remember a single word of anything I'd ever read. What did they think they could do, offer me a place to stay only to use me every single night? I'd eventually have to leave to meet my parole officer and find work.

The food was drugged but nothing oral can paralyze a person like that. First they drug you to make you sleep. Then they inject you with something to make sure you can't move and don't wake up; we'll get their asses.

This isn't supposed to happen to people like me and not from people like them.

The sun had gone from the brightness of morning to the dull orange glow of the afternoon before I'd decided to move again. I showered and looked for my cell but couldn't find it from the day before.

Who's the thief now? They up there stealing ass and actual property.

Dressing myself in an oversized pair of blue sweats with a matching shirt I let my legs carry me toward the gate into hell outside of hell, far from prison hell.

To my surprise the doorknob surprisingly twisted and the door opened. I cautiously crept into the foyer, praying they'd forgotten to lock the door. The house was silent as I silently crept toward the front door. The welcoming aroma of what had to have been pot roast, biscuits, and sweet potato pie called me toward the kitchen. It tantalized my nose, making my stomach beg me to follow it like the sound of the ocean to a fisherman. As hungry as I was I couldn't bring myself to walk away from my only way of escaping.

The brass doorknob was ice cold in the palm of my hand. I turned the lock underneath the keyhole toward the word UNLOCK on the handle and twisted. My entire body was tighter than a rubber band. My nerves were taut and ready to snap at the slightest sound or commotion. My heart thudded like hummingbird's wings in my chest and nervous sweat began to bead on my upper lip. The door didn't budge and I quietly slipped the lock in the other direction, praying it would open, puzzled at the setback.

"Aw look who's awake. That door is a little tricky, baby; you want to go out for some fresh air you can step out onto the patio through the kitchen." Mirna's voice was sickening sweet as she spoke from behind me.

Turning slowly I composed myself, holding back the tears and nausea at having to deal with her. I was in no way psychologically prepared to face one half of the two-headed monster I'd unknowingly surrendered myself to.

Her usual smile was planted on her face.

Look at this fake-ass smile.

Her hands were busy drying a wine glass on the fold of her apron.

That's probably the glass she's going to use to drug your ass. Grab the vase off the table beside the wall and smack that corrupt bitch in the face.

"Hi, Mirna, I didn't hear you walk up. Yes, I've been feeling queasy all morning; some air is all I want right now," I responded, doing my best to conceal the venom in my voice with as much sugary sweetness as possible.

"Well come along. The bishop was in a mighty fine mood this morning. He's bringing home champagne after he leaves his office. We are going to officially celebrate your freedom, sweetheart."

Mirna turned and went into the kitchen, humming a song I couldn't quite make out. The socks on my feet made my footsteps soundless as I treaded across the white tile floor behind her. Gold veins glittered and glimmered in the lighting of the house and it came to my attention how decadent their tastes in decorating were. The living room I'd passed when I'd arrived was adorned with expensive-looking chairs with mahogany arms and legs.

Those are not Versace cushions on that chair. How the hell they even know what Versace is?

Golden Egyptian statues of cats and scarab beetles were placed in random settings along the way. From the expansive chandelier to the marble and the cars, all of the things they had were lavish and rich. Yet not a single cross, scripture, or biblical reference could be seen anywhere in their house. My stomach growled loudly as I entered the kitchen and potatoes, celery, and brown onion gravy filled my senses. I could almost taste the food in my mouth, see the biscuit soaking up the gravy.

"I know you've got to be hungry. Supper is ready if you want to sit down and eat with me. Kevin won't be home until later so I'll just keep his food warm."

As tempting as her offer sounded I was frightened that she'd drug me again.

The roast is still in the oven. If you stay the fuck with her and help her you can watch what she does. Might even see an opportunity to grab a knife and . . .

"Yes, that would be nice, thank you." I smiled politely and did my best to hide my discomfort as I lowered myself into one of the chairs at the table.

My eyes were on her like a barn owl hunting a mouse. I watched every move she made including where she got the silverware from and whether it mattered if I took the first bite. After she said grace I made a game out of organizing my food with my fork; she began to methodically cut into the roast on her plate. I made small talk, pretending to be fascinated with the scenery through the glass panels of the back door while I waited for her to chew and swallow.

Everything tasted like it had been made with ingredients straight from heaven's garden. My eyes closed in bliss and I savored every bite, amazed at how tender the roast was. I caught Mirna staring at me when I reopened them, but her expression was a little unreadable. She quickly resumed eating and I began to wonder whether I'd imagined the brief look in her eye that reminded me of . . .

"Where are my two favorite ladies?" Bishop's voice rumbled through the quiet house and my appetite was instantly gone. He appeared in the kitchen carrying a bottle of champagne and beaming a wide smile in our direction at the kitchen table.

"Champagne or cham-pleasure? Who says church folk can't drink? You just aren't supposed to drink to get drunk. Ha-ha," Bishop shouted out.

"I thought you were working late; we'd have waited for you before we started eating." Mirna's tone was somewhat disapproving.

It was hard to determine if she was upset because he came home early or because he didn't let her know he was coming home early. His back was turned to us as he got glasses and placed the bottle in the wine chiller on the counter setting the timer. My unease grew when I couldn't see the glasses or where he'd gotten them from.

Soup, tea, champagne. Whatever it is they probably hide it in a liquid for your ass to drink. That tea was bitter; soup was cold but the aftertaste was bitter. Don't drink a damn thing they give you. Switch your glasses around, dump it out, do whatever you have to do.

The timer dinged on the champagne chiller and I jumped when Bishop shot the cork out of the bottle with a resounding pop. He danced and blew a kiss in Mirna's direction, giving her a wink and a look that I instantly registered as sexual, promising, and absolutely dirty. The dread and trepidation that filled me at having to experience another night like last night made me sick to my stomach.

"If you would excuse me, I'm not feeling too good. Mirna, I think it's gonna take some time for my stomach to adjust to the food. I'm sorry."

Before either of them could reply I pushed away from the table and fled toward the basement, intent on getting as far away from them as possible. I spun in an exasperated circle as I noted every single window in the basement was nearly six feet up from the floor and nowhere near wide enough for me to fit through. I felt like a trapped lab rat and the thought made me run immediately into the bathroom to pretend like I was actually taking a shit. There were probably cameras all down here watching me even now.

I racked my brain trying to think of a way out. The front door was obviously not an option but they didn't use it anyway. And I was certain from what I could see at dinner there was no way to get off the fenced-in patio if the door was locked. So far I only knew of the bishop to come in through the garage into the kitchen. If I could get to that door and into the garage I could press the opener and just run. It now made sense why out of everything they provided the only thing I wasn't given were shoes.

Routine, get a routine and stick to it. They won't know what you know or what you plan if you do the same things and act the same. Take your shower and be mindful of something to use as a weapon. Those fucks didn't give you anything so tonight should be a quiet one. Find something, anything to get us the fuck out of here.

For the first time ever I nodded in agreement with that angry, malicious little voice. Starting the shower I contemplated any alternatives to escape without taking a life or causing anyone harm. They would have to deal with their sins when they answered to God. Or I could make sure they didn't have the chance to do this type of shit to anyone else and take care of them when the opportunity arrived. Get out of the house, get Dontay's thieving ass. I was slowly building a mental hit list.

Steam filled the bathroom and I undressed, preparing to get in the shower, when I noticed a bruise on my ribs. Facing the mirror over the sink I stared at what looked like a long oval on my side and four similar markings on my back. I stood there squinting at myself until it dawned on me. They were finger prints. Outraged I looked for something, anything to smash.

A small figurine beside the towel rack seemed like the perfect target and I stomped toward it.

The ground came flying up to smack me in the back of the head. I'd stepped on one of the rugs on the floor and it slid forward, catching me off-guard and off-balance. My eyes were closed tight as I waited for the pain to hit me. My head cracked against the floor so hard I was sure I'd fractured my damn skull. Waves of pain crashed from the back of my skull into the space behind my eyes and I groaned in agony.

I waited until the waves of pain slowed down into a steady constant pain that spanned across my entire head. My eyes opened and rolled as the ceiling spun above me. They focused and it was in that instant that I found the tiny camera sitting in the ceiling over the vanity no wider than an ink pen top. Its lens didn't fog up like the mirror and from my angle on the floor I could see how it refracted the light from the bulbs underneath it. I quickly looked away, and raised my hand to stare at my fingertips as if my eyes were still not focused.

"Eva. I brought you some tea for your stomach. Are you doing all right, baby?" Mirna's called out to me through the bathroom door.

I bet she did want to give me some more of that damn tea. She was obviously only checking on me because they were probably watching me.

"I'm okay, but thank you. I'm just going to take a shower and go to bed," I called out from the floor, the sound of my voice making me feel miserable.

"All right, baby. Do you want me to leave the tea for you?"

I struggled to sit up and responded, "No, thank you, Mirna. I don't really care for peppermint that much."

The clinking of the tray as she turned and left was reassuring. I climbed into the shower, sighing as the hot water washed over my skin. Glancing at the ceiling I couldn't make out any lenses or shapes that looked like one over the vanity and it didn't seem like it was aimed to see into the shower. Relaxing as I realized showers were the only chance that I'd get some privacy, I lathered myself up, reveling in the fragrance of the shower gel. The smell of the ginger and peach seemed to calm my headache down, but I only made it worst when the desperation of my situation hit me. I was being held captive and used as some kind of personal sex slave. It sounded like the plot to some kind of suspense, drama movie and yet I was actually living it. From what I could figure, everyone who knew me or of me thought I was either locked up or dead.

Everyone except Brother Hall and Aeron.

Chapter 13

Misogynistic Missionary

"Teach me how the hell to do it then, since you think you're an expert."

"This is the first crash-test dummy that I actually like, so pay close attention because this won't happen often." Two voices bantered back and forth somewhere nearby.

I tried opening my eyes and it felt as if my eyelids were attached to one hundred pound weights. They were so heavy that lifting them seemed to drain me of all my energy. There was no way this shit could possibly be happening again and I exhaled an indignant breath beyond furious at the fun the two of them were having at my expense. None of it made sense. I ate the same things Mirna ate—I didn't touch the champagne or drink anything and still my ass was stuck going through this bullshit again.

As their conversation registered in my head I realized why the fingerprints on my side and back were so odd looking. They weren't the bishop's; they were Mirna's.

"Flip her on her stomach; it's my turn to get this shit going."

The bishop's strained grunting and the sound of sheets sliding were the only indicators that I was being repositioned. Breathing now seemed harder, and even though I'd tried to suffocate myself the night before, the thought now had me in a panic.

"Baby, gimme that candle," the bishop's voice was directly beside my ear and I screamed, cried, and cursed him in my mind, praying for a chance to at least bite him.

Strawberry-scented wax filled the air and as it scorched my back all the way down to the crack of my ass. Searing pain ran along its path and scorching every single one of my nerves. The skin on my back was on fire and I began grinding my teeth together to block out the pain. I could feel everything and the familiar tingling in my toes was evidence that I'd be able to move if I wanted to.

It's time, it's time, it's time.

I waited until he pulled all the way out, leaving my ass feeling equally raw and just as sore as my back. The sound of the Bishop and Mirna kissing passionately beside me riled my temper. I knew I'd only have seconds. Edging my hand up under my hips I slid my fingers in between my legs as deep as I could from the angle I was lying in.

In one swift movement I pulled the wadded up toilet paper from inside myself where I'd hidden it. Yes, right up in the baby maker like a damn drug mule. My fingers quickly unraveled the paper that had turned into a semi-hardened shell. Turning my head in their direction I could see Mirna on top of the bishop. I dove at them, slicing wildly in every direction, a small razor in each hand. I was hell-bent on revenge and nothing was safe as I lashed out, shredding sheets and pillows.

One, two, three . . .

It was as if they were momentarily stunned at my sudden mobility. There was no fight or flight; the Bishop and Mirna were both stupefied. He was sput-

Ni'chelle Genovese

tering, his eyes bulging out of his head in shock, and I couldn't make out what he was saying over the sounds of my angry breaths and slashes. I'd somehow tapped into a deep and hateful place. It had me growling a low predatory sound with every slice. Controlling my hands was frustrating and I still couldn't fully sit up because the drugs were still wearing off.

Five, six, seven . . .

I counted in my head the number of times I slung the blades in their direction.

An angry red gash opened across Mirna's lower back and she wailed, rolling onto the floor in agony, momentarily escaping my reach. I leaned over, grabbing the candle from the side of the bed, smashing it against the fat pig's forehead. The glass shattered and piping hot wax covered Bishop's face and eyes. He squealed and flounced around on the bed before going into convulsions.

Pathetic muthafucka having a seizure or some shit?

Well, looks like we've already got one down, I answered my evil inner twin as I pulled myself down off the bed and stalked Mirna as she crawled pitifully toward the bedroom door.

When I'd taken my shower I had no real intention on doing what they'd made me do. I'd broken one of the razors, removing the twin blades and burying them in the center of a wad of toilet paper. In prison I'd seen Aeron do it with razors when she wanted to hide them in plain sight on the wall. She'd wet and then smooth the toilet paper out until it was almost see through, and it would harden like paper-mâché or plaster. I had no clue if it would even work with a ball of moist toilet paper but what the hell did I have to lose?

This was all supposed to go down in the kitchen when the bishop was at work. I was supposed to get Mirna first and then wait for him to come home and catch him off-guard. Thankfully the stuff they gave me wore off early for whatever reason. No one was ever going to humiliate me again and especially not under the guise of helping me. Antonia had to learn, these two needed to learn, and if my dearest, sweetest Dontay didn't give me the right answers he'd damn sure learn as well.

Mirna moaned from the force of my weight as I hoisted myself up and sat on her chest.

Dontay was out there somewhere and he was either thinking he'd pulled off the crime of the century or was sick to his stomach for having to do what he'd done. Aeron said money unmasks people and from what I'd seen of the bishop and his so-called godly wife maybe Dontay wasn't what I thought he was from the jump. Lost in my thoughts, I'd momentarily forgotten all about Mirna as she squirmed beneath me. Sneering down at her in disgust I thought about my life, the things I'd worked and longed for.

"The two of you could have easily helped me or sent me on my way. So tell me, Mirna, what turns good Christian folk into hostage-taking rapists? Is it the lust or the power?"

I waited for her answer and had to give her credit, for even now she glanced in her husband's direction for support. He'd stopped moving and was either dead or unconscious.

She stared up at me as her eyes did that shimmery dance that eyes do just before the tears start to fall. Under normal circumstances when a person cried I'd have felt bad, but her tears only made me impatient and irritated.

Her voice was a quiet, shaky whisper: "Kevin said that he bought you from a man. I don't know which man, I never asked. The man didn't want you anymore and Kevin bought you, that's all I know." Time stood still as the meaning behind her words settled into my being. Not only had Dontay played me for all of my money and my clients' money, but he'd also sold me? Like I was property? No, wait, like I was his property?

Fuck this, fuck her, Now is just as good a time as any to learn how the game is played. She is in the way, Bishop is in the way, they are all in the fucking way. At one point in time Antonia was on that list. You can either handle your business or get handled like business. Sounds like he's trying to handle you like business. I suggest you go handle him.

I couldn't have agreed with myself more.

Notes

Notes